PENGUI

THE AG

BY

D1434706

EDITH WHARTON (1862–1937). American novelist, noted
for her sharp depiction of New York society during the
late-nineteenth and early-twentieth centuries, she is best
remembered for classics such as *The Age of Innocence* and
The House of Mirth.

Edith Newbold Jones was born in 1862 in New York.
She was from a wealthy, distinguished family and was
educated by governesses and foreign travel. She 'came
out' into New York society at a very young age and in
1885 married a friend of her mothers, Edward Wharton, a
man several years older than herself. A close friend of
Henry James, she decided to follow literary pursuits and
began writing poems and stories for *Scribner's Magazine*.
Several volumes of short stories were published, but
success came with her first full-length novel *The Valley
of Decision* (1902), a reconstruction of eighteenth-century
Italy. *The House of Mirth* (1905), which chronicled the
failed life of social climber Lily Bart, established Edith
Wharton as a leading novelist of her time. In 1907 she
and her husband moved to France, and Europe was
thenceforth her permanent home. She wrote *Madame de
Treymes* and *The Fruit of the Tree*, a novel about the evils
of industrialism, in the same year, 1907. She returned to an
American setting with her atypical novelette *Ethan Frome*
(1911), a tragic story set in New England and poignantly
indicative of the forlorn state of her own marriage. After
her husband's nervous collapse, the Whartons separated
and then divorced in 1913. Edith Wharton settled in Paris
and around this time she wrote *The Reef* (1912) and *The
Custom of the Country* (1913), which portrays the break-
down of traditional New York culture. During the First
World War she was awarded the Cross of the Legion of
Honour for her relief work in Paris, and works such as
Fighting France, from Dunkerque to Belfort (1915), *The
Marne* (1918) and *A Son at the Front* (1923) strongly reflect her wartime experiences. Her masterpiece *The Age
of Innocence*, a novel again dealing with New York society

and manners, was published to wide acclaim in 1920 and won the Pulitzer Prize. Her later works include a series of four novelettes entitled *Old New York* (1924); three novels about parent–child relationships: *The Mother's Recompense* (1925), *Twilight Sleep* (1927) and *The Children* (1928); *Hudson River Bracketed* (1929) and its sequel *The Gods Arrive* (1932), stories contrasting the Middle West culture with New York society; and her autobiography *A Backward Glance* (1934). As well as many novels and short stories, she also wrote two volumes of poetry, several travel books and a critical work, *The Writing of Fiction* (1925). An unfinished novel, *The Buccaneers*, about a group of American girls attempting to enter English society, was published posthumously in 1938, one year after Edith Wharton's death.

Dealing with the conflict between social and individual fulfilment, *The Age of Innocence* is a brilliant, sharply ironic portrayal of the changing scene of fashionable American life in Old New York. In its mastery of form the novel reveals Henry James's influence on Edith Wharton's writing and is her most skilfully constructed work.

PENGUIN POPULAR CLASSICS

THE AGE OF INNOCENCE

EDITH WHARTON

PENGUIN BOOKS

PENGUIN BOOKS

Published by the Penguin Group
Penguin Books Ltd, 80 Strand, London WC2R ORL, England
Penguin Putnam Inc., 375 Hudson Street, New York, New York 10014, USA
Penguin Books Australia Ltd, Ringwood, Victoria, Australia
Penguin Books Canada Ltd, 10 Alcorn Avenue, Toronto, Ontario, Canada M4V 3B2
Penguin Books India (P) Ltd, 11 Community Centre, Panchsheel Park, New Delhi — 110 017, India
Penguin Books (NZ) Ltd, Cnr Rosedale and Airborne Roads, Albany, Auckland, New Zealand
Penguin Books (South Africa) (Pty) Ltd, 24 Sturdee Avenue, Rosebank 2196 South Africa

Penguin Books Ltd, Registered Offices: 80 Strand, London WC2R ORL, England

www.penguin.com

First published 1920
Published in Penguin Popular Classics 1996
11

Printed in England by Cox & Wyman Ltd, Reading, Berkshire

BOOK I

I.

ON a January evening of the early seventies, Christine
Nilsson was singing in Faust at the Academy of
Music in New York.

Though there was already talk of the erection, in
remote metropolitan distances "above the Forties," of a
new Opera House which should compete in costliness
and splendour with those of the great European capitals,
the world of fashion was still content to reassemble
every winter in the shabby red and gold boxes of the
sociable old Academy. Conservatives cherished it for
being small and inconvenient, and thus keeping out the
"new people" whom New York was beginning to dread
and yet be drawn to; and the sentimental clung to it for
its historic associations, and the musical for its excellent
acoustics, always so problematic a quality in halls built
for the hearing of music.

It was Madame Nilsson's first appearance that winter,
and what the daily press had already learned to describe
as "an exceptionally brilliant audience" had gathered to
hear her, transported through the slippery, snowy streets
in private broughams, in the spacious family landau, or
in the humbler but more convenient "Brown *coupé*." To
come to the Opera in a Brown *coupé* was almost as honourable a way of arriving as in one's own carriage; and
departure by the same means had the immense advantage
of enabling one (with a playful allusion to democratic
principles) to scramble into the first Brown conveyance
in the line, instead of waiting till the cold-and-gin con-

[1]

gested nose of one's own coachman gleamed under the portico of the Academy. It was one of the great livery-stableman's most masterly intuitions to have discovered that Americans want to get away from amusement even more quickly than they want to get to it.

When Newland Archer opened the door at the back of the club box the curtain had just gone up on the garden scene. There was no reason why the young man should not have come earlier, for he had dined at seven, alone with his mother and sister, and had lingered afterward over a cigar in the Gothic library with glazed black-walnut bookcases and finial-topped chairs which was the only room in the house where Mrs. Archer allowed smoking. But, in the first place, New York was a metropolis, and perfectly aware that in metropolises it was "not the thing" to arrive early at the opera; and what was or was not "the thing" played a part as impor-tant in Newland Archer's New York as the inscrutable totem terrors that had ruled the destinies of his fore-fathers thousands of years ago.

The second reason for his delay was a personal one. He had dawdled over his cigar because he was at heart a dilettante, and thinking over a pleasure to come often gave him a subtler satisfaction than its realisation. This was especially the case when the pleasure was a delicate one, as his pleasures mostly were; and on this occasion the moment he looked forward to was so rare and exquisite in quality that—well, if he had timed his arrival in accord with the prima donna's stage-manager he could not have entered the Academy at a more significant moment than just as she was singing: "He loves me—he loves me not—*he loves me!*" and sprinkling the fall-ing daisy petals with notes as clear as dew.

She sang, of course, "*M'ama!*" and not "he loves me,"

[2]

since an unalterable and unquestioned law of the musical
world required that the German text of French operas
sung by Swedish artists should be translated into Italian
for the clearer understanding of English-speaking audiences. This seemed as natural to Newland Archer as
all the other conventions on which his life was moulded:
such as the duty of using two silver-backed brushes with
his monogram in blue enamel to part his hair, and of
never appearing in society without a flower (preferably
a gardenia) in his buttonhole.

"*M'ama . . . non m'ama . . .*" the prima donna sang,
and "*M'ama!*", with a final burst of love triumphant, as
she pressed the dishevelled daisy to her lips and lifted
her large eyes to the sophisticated countenance of the
little brown Faust-Capoul, who was vainly trying, in a
tight purple velvet doublet and plumed cap, to look as
pure and true as his artless victim.

Newland Archer, leaning against the wall at the back
of the club box, turned his eyes from the stage and
scanned the opposite side of the house. Directly facing
him was the box of old Mrs. Manson Mingott, whose
monstrous obesity had long since made it impossible for
her to attend the Opera, but who was always represented
on fashionable nights by some of the younger members
of the family. On this occasion, the front of the box
was filled by her daughter-in-law, Mrs. Lovell Mingott,
and her daughter, Mrs. Welland; and slightly withdrawn
behind these brocaded matrons sat a young girl in white
with eyes ecstatically fixed on the stage-lovers. As
Madame Nilsson's "*M'ama!*" thrilled out above the silent
house (the boxes always stopped talking during the Daisy
Song) a warm pink mounted to the girl's cheek, mantled
her brow to the roots of her fair braids, and suffused the
young slope of her breast to the line where it met a

modest tulle tucker fastened with a single gardenia. She dropped her eyes to the immense bouquet of lilies-of-the-valley on her knee, and Newland Archer saw her white-gloved finger-tips touch the flowers softly. He drew a breath of satisfied vanity and his eyes returned to the stage.

No expense had been spared on the setting, which was acknowledged to be very beautiful even by people who shared his acquaintance with the Opera houses of Paris and Vienna. The foreground, to the footlights, was covered with emerald green cloth. In the middle distance symmetrical mounds of woolly green moss bounded by croquet hoops formed the base of shrubs shaped like orange-trees but studded with large pink and red roses. Gigantic pansies, considerably larger than the roses, and closely resembling the floral pen-wipers made by female parishioners for fashionable clergymen, sprang from the moss beneath the rose-trees; and here and there a daisy grafted on a rose-branch flowered with a luxuriance prophetic of Mr. Luther Burbank's far-off prodigies.

In the centre of this enchanted garden Madame Nilsson, in white cashmere slashed with pale blue satin, a reticule dangling from a blue girdle, and large yellow braids carefully disposed on each side of her muslin chemisette, listened with downcast eyes to M. Capoul's impassioned wooing, and affected a guileless incomprehension of his designs whenever, by word or glance, he persuasively indicated the ground floor window of the neat brick villa projecting obliquely from the right wing.

"The darling!" thought Newland Archer, his glance flitting back to the young girl with the lilies-of-the-valley. "She doesn't even guess what it's all about." And he contemplated her absorbed young face with a thrill of possessorship in which pride in his own masculine initiation was mingled with a tender reverence for her abysmal purity. "We'll read Faust together . . . by the Italian lakes . . ." he thought, somewhat hazily confusing the scene of his projected honey-moon with the masterpieces of literature which it would be his manly privilege to reveal to his bride. It was only that afternoon that May Welland had let him guess that she "cared" (New York's consecrated phrase of maiden avowal), and already his imagination, leaping ahead of the engagement ring, the betrothal kiss and the march from Lohengrin, pictured her at his side in some scene of old European witchery.

He did not in the least wish the future Mrs. Newland Archer to be ⏑ simpleton. He meant her (thanks to his enlightening companionship) to develop a social tact and readiness of wit enabling her to hold her own with the most popular married women of the "younger set," in which it was the recognised custom to attract masculine homage while playfully discouraging it. If he had probed to the bottom of his vanity (as he sometimes nearly did) he would have found there the wish that his wife should be as worldly-wise and as eager to please as the married lady whose charms had held his fancy through two mildly agitated years; without, of course, any hint of the frailty which had so nearly marred that unhappy being's life, and had disarranged his own plans for a whole winter.

How this miracle of fire and ice was to be created, and to sustain itself in a harsh world, he had never taken the time to think out; but he was content to hold his view without analysing it, since he knew it was that of all the carefully-brushed, white-waistcoated, buttonhole-flowered gentlemen who succeeded each other in the club box, exchanged friendly greetings with him, and turned their opera-glasses critically on the circle of ladies who were the product of the system. In matters intellectual and artistic Newland Archer felt himself distinctly the superior of these chosen specimens of old New York gentility; he had probably read more, thought more, and even seen a good deal more of the world, than any other man of the number. Singly they betrayed their inferiority; but grouped together they represented "New York," and the habit of masculine solidarity made him accept their doctrine on all the issues called moral. He instinctively felt that in this respect it would be trouble-some—and also rather bad form—to strike out for himself.

"Well—upon my soul!" exclaimed Lawrence Lefferts, turning his opera-glass abruptly away from the stage. Lawrence Lefferts was, on the whole, the foremost authority on "form" in New York. He had probably devoted more time than any one else to the study of this intricate and fascinating question; but study alone could not account for his complete and easy competence. One had only to look at him, from the slant of his bald forehead and the curve of his beautiful fair moustache to the long patent-leather feet at the other end of his lean and elegant person, to feel that the knowledge of "form" must be congenital in any one who knew how to wear such good clothes so carelessly and carry such height with so much lounging grace. As a young admirer had once said of him: "If anybody can tell a fellow just when to wear a black tie with evening clothes and when not to, it's Larry Lefferts." And on the question of pumps versus patent-leather "Oxfords" his authority had never been disputed.

"My God!" he said; and silently handed his glass to old Sillerton Jackson.

Newland Archer, following Lefferts's glance, saw with surprise that his exclamation had been occasioned by the entry of a new figure into old Mrs. Mingott's box. It was that of a slim young woman, a little less tall than May Welland, with brown hair growing in close curls about her temples and held in place by a narrow band of diamonds. The suggestion of this headdress, which gave her what was then called a "Josephine look," was carried out in the cut of the dark blue velvet gown rather theatrically caught up under her bosom by a girdle with a large old-fashioned clasp. The wearer of this unusual dress, who seemed quite unconscious of the attention it was attracting, stood a moment in the centre of the box, discussing with Mrs. Welland the propriety of taking the latter's place in the front right-hand corner; then she yielded with a slight smile, and seated herself in line with Mrs. Welland's sister-in-law, Mrs. Lovell Mingott, who was installed in the opposite corner.

Mr. Sillerton Jackson had returned the opera-glass to Lawrence Lefferts. The whole of the club turned instinctively, waiting to hear what the old man had to say; for old Mr. Jackson was as great an authority on "family" as Lawrence Lefferts was on "form." He knew all the ramifications of New York's cousinships; and could not only elucidate such complicated questions as that of the connection between the Mingotts (through the Thorleys) with the Dallases of South Carolina, and that of the relationship of the elder branch of Philadelphia Thorleys to the Albany Chiverses (on no account to be confused with the Manson Chiverses of University Place), but could also enumerate the leading characteristics of each family: as, for instance, the fabulous stinginess of the younger lines of Leffertses (the Long Island ones); or the fatal tendency of the Rushworths to make foolish matches; or the insanity recurring in every second generation of the Albany Chiverses, with whom their New York cousins had always refused to intermarry—with the disastrous exception of poor Medora Manson, who, as everybody knew . . . but then her mother was a Rushworth.

In addition to this forest of family trees, Mr. Sillerton Jackson carried between his narrow hollow temples, and under his soft thatch of silver hair, a register of most of the scandals and mysteries that had smouldered under the unruffled surface of New York society within the last fifty years. So far indeed did his information extend, and so acutely retentive was his memory, that he was supposed to be the only man who could have told you who Julius Beaufort, the banker, really was, and what had become of handsome Bob Spicer, old Mrs. Manson Mingott's father, who had disappeared so mysteriously (with a large sum of trust money) a month after his marriage, on the very day that a beautiful Spanish dancer who had been delighting thronged audiences in the old Opera-house on the Battery had taken ship for Cuba. But these mysteries, and many others, were closely locked in Mr. Jackson's breast; for not only did his keen sense of honour forbid his repeating anything privately imparted, but he was fully aware that his reputation for discretion increased his opportunities of finding out what he wanted to know.

The club box, therefore, waited in visible suspense while Mr. Sillerton Jackson handed back Lawrence Lefferts's opera-glass. For a moment he silently scrutinised the attentive group out of his filmy blue eyes overhung by old veined lids; then he gave his moustache a thoughtful twist, and said simply: "I didn't think the Mingotts would have tried it on."

II

NEWLAND ARCHER, during this brief episode, had been thrown into a strange state of embarrassment.

It was annoying that the box which was thus attracting the undivided attention of masculine New York should be that in which his betrothed was seated between her mother and aunt; and for a moment he could not identify the lady in the Empire dress, nor imagine why her presence created such excitement among the initiated. Then light dawned on him, and with it came a momentary rush of indignation. No, indeed; no one would have thought the Mingotts would have tried it on!

But they had; they undoubtedly had; for the low-toned comments behind him left no doubt in Archer's mind that the young woman was May Welland's cousin, the cousin always referred to in the family as "poor Ellen Olenska." Archer knew that she had suddenly arrived from Europe a day or two previously; he had even heard from Miss Welland (not disapprovingly) that she had been to see poor Ellen, who was staying with old Mrs. Mingott. Archer entirely approved of family solidarity, and one of the qualities he most admired in the Mingotts was their resolute championship of the few black sheep that their blameless stock had produced. There was nothing mean or ungenerous in the young man's heart, and he was glad that his future wife should not be restrained by false prudery from being kind (in private) to her unhappy cousin; but to receive Countess Olenska in the family circle was a different thing from producing her in public, at the Opera of all places, and in the very box with the young girl whose engagement to him, Newland Archer, was to be announced within a few weeks. No, he felt as old Sillerton Jackson felt; he did not think the Mingotts would have tried it on!

He knew, of course, that whatever man dared (within Fifth Avenue's limits) that old Mrs. Manson Mingott, the Matriarch of the line, would dare. He had always admired the high and mighty old lady, who, in spite of having been only Catherine Spicer of Staten Island, with a father mysteriously discredited, and neither money nor position enough to make people forget it, had allied herself with the head of the wealthy Mingott line, married her two daughters to "foreigners" (an Italian marquis and an English banker), and put the crowning touch to her audacities by building a large house of pale cream-coloured stone (when brown sandstone seemed as much the only wear as a frock-coat in the afternoon) in an inaccessible wilderness near the Central Park.

Old Mrs. Mingott's foreign daughters had become a legend. They never came back to see their mother, and the latter being, like many persons of active mind and dominating will, sedentary and corpulent in her habit, had philosophically remained at home. But the cream-coloured house (supposed to be modelled on the private hotels of the Parisian aristocracy) was there as a visible proof of her moral courage; and she throned in it, among pre-Revolutionary furniture and souvenirs of the Tuileries of Louis Napoleon (where she had shone in her middle age), as placidly as if there were nothing peculiar in living above Thirty-fourth Street, or in having French windows that opened like doors instead of sashes that pushed up.

Every one (including Mr. Sillerton Jackson) was agreed that old Catherine had never had beauty—a gift which, in the eyes of New York, justified every success, and excused a certain number of failings. Unkind people said that, like her Imperial namesake, she had won her way to success by strength of will and hardness of heart, and a kind of haughty effrontery that was somehow justified by the extreme decency and dignity of her private life. Mr. Manson Mingott had died when she was only twenty-eight, and had "tied up" the money with an additional caution born of the general distrust of the Spicers; but his bold young widow went her way fearlessly, mingled freely in foreign society, married her daughters in heaven knew what corrupt and fashionable circles, hobnobbed with Dukes and Ambassadors, associated familiarly with Papists, entertained Opera singers, and was the intimate friend of Mme. Taglioni; and all the while (as Sillerton Jackson was the first to proclaim) there had never been a breath on her reputation; the only respect, he always added, in which she differed from the earlier Catherine.

Mrs. Manson Mingott had long since succeeded in untying her husband's fortune, and had lived in affluence for half a century; but memories of her early straits had made her excessively thrifty, and though, when she bought a dress or a piece of furniture, she took care that it should be of the best, she could not bring herself to spend much on the transient pleasures of the table. Therefore, for totally different reasons, her food was as poor as Mrs. Archer's, and her wines did nothing to redeem it. Her relatives considered that the penury of her table discredited the Mingott name, which had always been associated with good living; but people continued to come to her in spite of the "made dishes" and flat champagne, and in reply to the remonstrances of her son Lovell (who tried to retrieve the family credit by having the best *chef* in New York) she used to say laughingly: "What's the use of two good cooks in one family, now that I've married the girls and can't eat sauces?"

Newland Archer, as he mused on these things, had once more turned his eyes toward the Mingott box. He saw that Mrs. Welland and her sister-in-law were facing their semi-circle of critics with the Mingottian *aplomb* which old Catherine had inculcated in all her tribe, and that only May Welland betrayed, by a heightened colour (perhaps due to the knowledge that he was watching her) a sense of the gravity of the situation. As for the cause of the commotion, she sat gracefully in her corner of the box, her eyes fixed on the stage, and revealing, as she leaned forward, a little more shoulder and bosom than New York was accustomed to seeing, at least in ladies who had reasons for wishing to pass unnoticed.

Few things seemed to Newland Archer more awful than an offence against "Taste," that far-off divinity of whom "Form" was the mere visible representative and vicegerent. Madame Olenska's pale and serious face appealed to his fancy as suited to the occasion and to her unhappy situation; but the way her dress (which had no tucker) sloped away from her thin shoulders shocked and troubled him. He hated to think of May Welland's being exposed to the influence of a young woman so careless of the dictates of Taste.

"After all," he heard one of the younger men begin behind him (everybody talked through the Mephistopheles-and-Martha scenes), "after all, just *what* happened?"

"Well—she left him; nobody attempts to deny that."

"He's an awful brute, isn't he?" continued the young enquirer, a candid Thorley, who was evidently preparing to enter the lists as the lady's champion.

"The very worst; I knew him at Nice," said Lawrence Lefferts with authority. "A half-paralysed white sneering fellow—rather handsome head, but eyes with a lot of lashes. Well, I'll tell you the sort: when he wasn't with women he was collecting china. Paying any price for both, I understand."

There was a general laugh, and the young champion said: "Well, then——?"

"Well, then; she bolted with his secretary."

"Oh, I see." The champion's face fell.

"It didn't last long, though: I heard of her a few months later living alone in Venice. I believe Lovell Mingott went out to get her. He said she was desperately unhappy. That's all right—but this parading her at the Opera's another thing."

"Perhaps," young Thorley hazarded, "she's too unhappy to be left at home."

This was greeted with an irreverent laugh, and the youth blushed deeply, and tried to look as if he had meant to insinuate what knowing people called a *"double entendre."*

"Well—it's queer to have brought Miss Welland, anyhow," some one said in a low tone, with a side-glance at Archer.

"Oh, that's part of the campaign: Granny's orders, no doubt," Lefferts laughed. "When the old lady does a thing she does it thoroughly."

The act was ending, and there was a general stir in the box. Suddenly Newland Archer felt himself impelled to decisive action. The desire to be the first man to enter Mrs. Welland's box, to proclaim to the waiting world his engagement to May Welland, and to see her through whatever difficulties her cousin's anomalous situation might involve her in; this impulse had abruptly overruled all scruples and hesitations, and sent him hurrying through the red corridors to the farther side of the house.

As he entered the box his eyes met Miss Welland's, and he saw that she had instantly understood his motive, though the family dignity which both considered so high a virtue would not permit her to tell him so. The persons of their world lived in an atmosphere of faint implications and pale delicacies, and the fact that he and she understood each other without a word seemed to the young man to bring them nearer than any explanation would have done. Her eyes said: "You see why Mamma brought me," and his answered: "I would not for the world have had you stay away."

"You know my niece Countess Olenska?" Mrs. Welland enquired as she shook hands with her future son-in-law. Archer bowed without extending his hand, as was the custom on being introduced to a lady; and Ellen Olenska bent her head slightly, keeping her own pale-gloved hands clasped on her huge fan of eagle feathers. Having greeted Mrs. Lovell Mingott, a large blonde lady in creaking satin, he sat down beside his betrothed, and said in a low tone: "I hope you've told Madame Olenska that we're engaged? I want everybody to know—I want you to let me announce it this evening at the ball."

Miss Welland's face grew rosy as the dawn, and she looked at him with radiant eyes. "If you can persuade Mamma," she said; "but why should we change what is already settled?" He made no answer but that which his eyes returned, and she added, still more confidently smiling: "Tell my cousin yourself: I give you leave. She says she used to play with you when you were children."

She made way for him by pushing back her chair, and promptly, and a little ostentatiously, with the desire that the whole house should see what he was doing, Archer seated himself at the Countess Olenska's side.

"We *did* use to play together, didn't we?" she asked, turning her grave eyes to his. "You were a horrid boy, and kissed me once behind a door; but it was your cousin Vandie Newland, who never looked at me, that I was in love with." Her glance swept the horse-shoe curve of boxes. "Ah, how this brings it all back to me—I see everybody here in knickerbockers and pantalettes," she said, with her trailing slightly foreign accent, her eyes returning to his face.

Agreeable as their expression was, the young man was shocked that they should reflect so unseemly a picture of the august tribunal before which, at that very moment, her case was being tried. Nothing could be in worse taste than misplaced flippancy; and he answered somewhat stiffly: "Yes, you have been away a very long time."

"Oh, centuries and centuries; so long," she said, "that I'm sure I'm dead and buried, and this dear old place is heaven;" which, for reasons he could not define, struck Newland Archer as an even more disrespectful way of describing New York society.

III

IT invariably happened in the same way.

Mrs. Julius Beaufort, on the night of her annual ball, never failed to appear at the Opera; indeed, she always gave her ball on an Opera night in order to emphasise her complete superiority to household cares, and her possession of a staff of servants competent to organise every detail of the entertainment in her absence.

The Beauforts' house was one of the few in New York that possessed a ball-room (it antedated even Mrs. Manson Mingott's and the Headly Chiverses); and at a time when it was beginning to be thought "provincial" to put a "crash" over the drawing-room floor and move the furniture upstairs, the possession of a ballroom that was used for no other purpose, and left for three-hundred-and-sixty-four days of the year to shuttered darkness, with its gilt chairs stacked in a corner and its chandelier in a bag; this undoubted superiority was felt to compensate for whatever was regrettable in the Beaufort past.

Mrs. Archer, who was fond of coining her social philosophy into axioms, had once said: "We all have our pet common people—" and though the phrase was a daring one, its truth was secretly admitted in many an exclusive bosom. But the Beauforts were not exactly common; some people said they were even worse. Mrs. Beaufort belonged indeed to one of America's most honoured families; she had been the lovely Regina Dallas

THE AGE OF INNOCENCE

(of the South Carolina branch), a penniless beauty introduced to New York society by her cousin, the imprudent Medora Manson, who was always doing the wrong thing from the right motive. When one was related to the Mansons and the Rushworths one had a *"droit de cité"* (as Mr. Sillerton Jackson, who had frequented the Tuileries, called it) in New York society; but did one not forfeit it in marrying Julius Beaufort?

The question was: who *was* Beaufort? He passed for an Englishman, was agreeable, handsome, ill-tempered, hospitable and witty. He had come to America with letters of recommendation from old Mrs. Manson Mingott's English son-in-law, the banker, and had speedily made himself an important position in the world of affairs; but his habits were dissipated, his tongue was bitter, his antecedents were mysterious; and when Medora Manson announced her cousin's engagement to him it was felt to be one more act of folly in poor Medora's long record of imprudences.

But folly is as often justified of her children as wisdom, and two years after young Mrs. Beaufort's marriage it was admitted that she had the most distinguished house in New York. No one knew exactly how the miracle was accomplished. She was indolent, passive, the caustic even called her dull; but dressed like an idol, hung with pearls, growing younger and blonder and more beautiful each year, she throned in Mr. Beaufort's heavy brown-stone palace, and drew all the world there without lifting her jewelled little finger. The knowing people said it was Beaufort himself who trained the servants, taught the *chef* new dishes, told the gardeners what hot-house flowers to grow for the dinner-table and the drawing-rooms, selected the guests, brewed the after-dinner punch and dictated the little notes his wife wrote to her friends. If he did, these domestic activities were privately performed, and he presented to the world the appearance of a careless and hospitable millionaire strolling into his own drawing-room with the detachment of an invited guest, and saying: "My wife's gloxinias are a marvel, aren't they? I believe she gets them out from Kew."

Mr. Beaufort's secret, people were agreed, was the way he carried things off. It was all very well to whisper that he had been "helped" to leave England by the international banking-house in which he had been employed; he carried off that rumour as easily as the rest—though New York's business conscience was no less sensitive than its moral standard—he carried everything before him, and all New York into his drawing-rooms, and for over twenty years now people had said they were "going to the Beauforts' " with the same tone of security as if they had said they were going to Mrs. Manson Mingott's, and with the added satisfaction of knowing they would get hot canvas-back ducks and vintage wines, instead of tepid Veuve Clicquot without a year and warmed-up croquettes from Philadelphia.

Mrs. Beaufort, then, had as usual appeared in her box just before the Jewel Song; and when, again as usual, she rose at the end of the third act, drew her opera cloak about her lovely shoulders, and disappeared, New York knew that meant that half an hour later the ball would begin.

The Beaufort house was one that New Yorkers were proud to show to foreigners, especially on the night of the annual ball. The Beauforts had been among the first people in New York to own their own red velvet carpet and have it rolled down the steps by their own footmen, under their own awning, instead of hiring it with the supper and the ball-room chairs. They had also inaugurated the custom of letting the ladies take their cloaks off in the hall, instead of shuffling up to the hostess's bedroom and recurling their hair with the aid of the gas-burner; Beaufort was understood to have said that he supposed all his wife's friends had maids who saw to it that they were properly *coiffées* when they left home.

Then the house had been boldly planned with a ball-room, so that, instead of squeezing through a narrow passage to get to it (as at the Chiverses') one marched solemnly down a vista of enfiladed drawing-rooms (the sea-green, the crimson and the *bouton d'or*), seeing from afar the many-candled lustres reflected in the polished parquetry, and beyond that the depths of a conservatory where camellias and tree-ferns arched their costly foliage over seats of black and gold bamboo.

Newland Archer, as became a young man of his position, strolled in somewhat late. He had left his overcoat with the silk-stockinged footmen (the stockings were one of Beaufort's few fatuities), had dawdled a while in the library hung with Spanish leather and furnished with Buhl and malachite, where a few men were chatting and putting on their dancing-gloves, and had finally joined the line of guests whom Mrs. Beaufort was receiving on the threshold of the crimson drawing-room.

Archer was distinctly nervous. He had not gone back to his club after the Opera (as the young bloods usually did), but, the night being fine, had walked for some distance up Fifth Avenue before turning back in the direction of the Beauforts' house. He was definitely afraid that the Mingotts might be going too far; that, in fact, they might have Granny Mingott's orders to bring the Countess Olenska to the ball.

From the tone of the club box he had perceived how grave a mistake that would be; and, though he was more than ever determined to "see the thing through," he felt less chivalrously eager to champion his betrothed's cousin than before their brief talk at the Opera.

Wandering on to the *bouton d'or* drawing-room (where Beaufort had had the audacity to hang "Love Victorious," the much-discussed nude of Bouguereau) Archer found Mrs. Welland and her daughter standing near the ball-room door. Couples were already gliding over the floor beyond: the light of the wax candles fell on revolving tulle skirts, on girlish heads wreathed with modest blossoms, on the dashing aigrettes and ornaments of the young married women's *coiffures,* and on the glitter of highly glazed shirt-fronts and fresh glacé gloves.

Miss Welland, evidently about to join the dancers, hung on the threshold, her lilies-of-the-valley in her hand (she carried no other bouquet), her face a little pale, her eyes burning with a candid excitement. A group of young men and girls were gathered about her, and there was much hand-clasping, laughing and pleasantry) on which Mrs. Welland, standing slightly apart, shed the beam of a qualified approval. It was evident that Miss Welland was in the act of announcing her engagement, while her mother affected the air of parental reluctance considered suitable to the occasion.

Archer paused a moment. It was at his express wish that the announcement had been made, and yet it was not thus that he would have wished to have his happiness known. To proclaim it in the heat and noise of a crowded ball-room was to rob it of the fine bloom of privacy which should belong to things nearest the heart. His joy was so deep that this blurring of the surface left its essence untouched; but he would have liked to keep the surface pure too. It was something of a satisfaction to find that May Welland shared this feeling. Her eyes fled to his beseechingly, and their look said: "Remember, we're doing this because it's right."

No appeal could have found a more immediate response in Archer's breast; but he wished that the necessity of their action had been represented by some ideal reason, and not simply by poor Ellen Olenska. The group about Miss Welland made way for him with significant smiles, and after taking his share of the felicitations he drew his betrothed into the middle of the ballroom floor and put his arm about her waist.

"Now we shan't have to talk," he said, smiling into her candid eyes, as they floated away on the soft waves of the Blue Danube.

She made no answer. Her lips trembled into a smile, but the eyes remained distant and serious, as if bent on some ineffable vision. "Dear," Archer whispered, pressing her to him: it was borne in on him that the first hours of being engaged, even if spent in a ball-room, had in them something grave and sacramental. What a new life it was going to be, with this whiteness, radiance, goodness at one's side!

The dance over, the two, as became an affianced couple, wandered into the conservatory; and sitting behind a tall screen of tree-ferns and camellias Newland pressed her gloved hand to his lips.

"You see I did as you asked me to," she said.

"Yes: I couldn't wait," he answered smiling. After a moment he added: "Only I wish it hadn't had to be at a ball."

"Yes, I know." She met his glance comprehendingly. "But after all—even here we're alone together, aren't we?"

"Oh, dearest—always!" Archer cried.

Evidently she was always going to understand; she was always going to say the right thing. The discovery made the cup of his bliss overflow, and he went on gaily: "The worst of it is that I want to kiss you and I can't." As he spoke he took a swift glance about the conservatory, assured himself of their momentary privacy, and catching her to him laid a fugitive pressure on her lips. To counteract the audacity of this proceeding he led her to a bamboo sofa in a less secluded part of the conservatory, and sitting down beside her broke a lily-of-the-valley from her bouquet. She sat silent, and the world lay like a sunlit valley at their feet.

"Did you tell my cousin Ellen?" she asked presently, as if she spoke through a dream.

He roused himself, and remembered that he had not done so. Some invincible repugnance to speak of such things to the strange foreign woman had checked the words on this lips.

"No—I hadn't the chance after all," he said, fibbing hastily.

"Ah." She looked disappointed, but gently resolved on gaining her point. "You must, then, for I didn't either; and I shouldn't like her to think—"

"Of course not. But aren't you, after all, the person to do it?"

She pondered on this. "If I'd done it at the right time, yes: but now that there's been a delay I think you must explain that I'd asked you to tell her at the Opera, before our speaking about it to everybody here. Otherwise she might think I had forgotten her. You see, she's one of the family, and she's been away so long that she's rather—sensitive."

Archer looked at her glowingly. "Dear and great angel! Of course I'll tell her." He glanced a trifle apprehensively toward the crowded ball-room. "But I haven't seen her yet. Has she come?"

"No; at the last minute she decided not to."

"At the last minute?" he echoed, betraying his surprise that she should ever have considered the alternative possible.

"Yes. She's awfully fond of dancing," the young girl answered simply. "But suddenly she made up her mind that her dress wasn't smart enough for a ball, though we thought it so lovely; and so my aunt had to take her home."

"Oh, well—" said Archer with happy indifference. Nothing about his betrothed pleased him more than her resolute determination to carry to its utmost limit that ritual of ignoring the "unpleasant" in which they had both been brought up.

"She knows as well as I do," he reflected, "the real reason of her cousin's staying away; but I shall never let her see by the least sign that I am conscious of there being a shadow of a shade on poor Ellen Olenska's reputation."

IV.

IN the course of the next day the first of the usual betrothal visits were exchanged. The New York ritual
was precise and inflexible in such matters; and in conformity with it Newland Archer first went with his
mother and sister to call on Mrs. Welland, after which
he and Mrs. Welland and May drove out to old Mrs.
Manson Mingott's to receive that venerable ancestress's
blessing.

A visit to Mrs. Manson Mingott was always an amusing episode to the young man. The house in itself
was already an historic document, though not, of course,
as venerable as certain other old family houses in University Place and lower Fifth Avenue. Those were of
the purest 1830, with a grim harmony of cabbage-rose-
garlanded carpets, rosewood consoles, round-arched fire-
places with black marble mantels, and immense glazed
book-cases of mahogany; whereas old Mrs. Mingott, who
had built her house later, had bodily cast out the massive
furniture of her prime, and mingled with the Mingott
heirlooms the frivolous upholstery of the Second Empire. It was her habit to sit in a window of her sitting-
room on the ground floor, as if watching calmly for
life and fashion to flow northward to her solitary doors.
She seemed in no hurry to have them come, for her patience was equalled by her confidence. She was sure
that presently the hoardings, the quarries, the one-story

saloons, the wooden green-houses in ragged gardens, and the rocks from which goats surveyed the scene, would vanish before the advance of residences as stately as her own—perhaps (for she was an impartial woman) even statelier; and that the cobblestones over which the old clattering omnibuses bumped would be replaced by smooth asphalt, such as people reported having seen in Paris. Meanwhile, as every one she cared to see came to *her* (and she could fill her rooms as easily as the Beauforts, and without adding a single item to the *menu* of her suppers), she did not suffer from her geographic isolation.

The immense accretion of flesh which had descended on her in middle life like a flood of lava on a doomed city had changed her from a plump active little woman with a neatly-turned foot and ankle into something as vast and august as a natural phenomenon. She had accepted this submergence as philosophically as all her other trials, and now, in extreme old age, was rewarded by presenting to her mirror an almost unwrinkled expanse of firm pink and white flesh, in the centre of which the traces of a small face survived as if awaiting excavation. A flight of smooth double chins led down to the dizzy depths of a still-snowy bosom veiled in snowy muslins that were held in place by a miniature portrait of the late Mr. Mingott; and around and below, wave after wave of black silk surged away over the edges of a capacious armchair, with two tiny white hands poised like gulls on the surface of the billows.

The burden of Mrs. Manson Mingott's flesh had long since made it impossible for her to go up and down stairs, and with characteristic independence she had made her reception rooms upstairs and established herself (in flagrant violation of all the New York proprieties)

[25]

on the ground floor of her house; so that, as you sat in her sitting-room window with her, you caught (through a door that was always open, and a looped-back yellow damask portière) the unexpected vista of a bedroom with a huge low bed upholstered like a sofa, and a toilet-table with frivolous lace flounces and a gilt-framed mirror.

Her visitors were startled and fascinated by the foreignness of this arrangement, which recalled scenes in French fiction, and architectural incentives to immorality such as the simple American had never dreamed of. That was how women with lovers lived in the wicked old societies, in apartments with all the rooms on one floor, and all the indecent propinquities that their novels described. It amused Newland Archer (who had secretly situated the love-scenes of "Monsieur de Camors" in Mrs. Mingott's bedroom) to picture her blameless life led in the stage-setting of adultery; but he said to himself, with considerable admiration, that if a lover had been what she wanted, the intrepid woman would have had him too.

To the general relief the Countess Olenska was not present in her great-aunt's drawing-room during the visit of the betrothed couple. Mrs. Mingott said she had gone out; which, on a day of such glaring sunlight, and at the "shopping hour," seemed in itself an indelicate thing for a compromised woman to do. But at any rate it spared them the embarrassment of her presence, and the faint shadow that her unhappy past might seem to shed on their radiant future. The visit went off successfully, as was to have been expected. Old Mrs. Mingott was delighted with the engagement, which, being long foreseen by watchful relatives, had been carefully passed upon in family council; and the engagement ring, a large thick sapphire set in invisible claws, met with her unqualified admiration.

"It's the new setting: of course it shows the stone beautifully, but it looks a little bare to old-fashioned eyes," Mrs. Welland had explained, with a conciliatory sideglance at her future son-in-law.

"Old-fashioned eyes? I hope you don't mean mine, my dear? I like all the novelties," said the ancestress, lifting the stone to her small bright orbs, which no glasses had ever disfigured. "Very handsome," she added, returning the jewel; "very liberal. In my time a cameo set in pearls was thought sufficient. But it's the hand that sets off the ring, isn't it, my dear Mr. Archer?" and she waved one of her tiny hands, with small pointed nails and rolls of aged fat encircling the wrist like ivory bracelets. "Mine was modelled in Rome by the great Ferrigiani. You should have May's done: no doubt he'll have it done, my child. Her hand is large—it's these modern sports that spread the joints—but the skin is white.—And when's the wedding to be?" she broke off, fixing her eyes on Archer's face.

"Oh—" Mrs. Welland murmured, while the young man, smiling at his betrothed, replied: "As soon as ever it can, if only you'll back me up, Mrs. Mingott."

"We must give them time to get to know each other a little better, aunt Catherine," Mrs. Welland interposed, with the proper affectation of reluctance; to which the ancestress rejoined: "Know each other? Fiddlesticks! Everybody in New York has always known everybody. Let the young man have his way, my dear; don't wait till the bubble's off the wine. Marry them before Lent; I may catch pneumonia any winter now, and I want to give the wedding-breakfast."

These successive statements were received with the

proper expressions of amusement, incredulity and gratitude; and the visit was breaking up in a vein of mild pleasantry when the door opened to admit the Countess Olenska, who entered in bonnet and mantle followed by the unexpected figure of Julius Beaufort.

There was a cousinly murmur of pleasure between the ladies, and Mrs. Mingott held out Ferrigiani's model to the banker. "Ha! Beaufort, this is a rare favour!" (She had an odd foreign way of addressing men by their surnames.)

"Thanks. I wish it might happen oftener," said the visitor in his easy arrogant way. "I'm generally so tied down; but I met the Countess Ellen in Madison Square, and she was good enough to let me walk home with her."

"Ah—I hope the house will be gayer, now that Ellen's here!" cried Mrs. Mingott with a glorious effrontery. "Sit down—sit down, Beaufort: push up the yellow armchair; now I've got you I want a good gossip. I hear your ball was magnificent; and I understand you invited Mrs. Lemuel Struthers? Well—I've a curiosity to see the woman myself."

She had forgotten her relatives, who were drifting out into the hall under Ellen Olenska's guidance. Old Mrs. Mingott had always professed a great admiration for Julius Beaufort, and there was a kind of kinship in their cool domineering way and their short-cuts through the conventions. Now she was eagerly curious to know what had decided the Beauforts to invite (for the first time) Mrs. Lemuel Struthers, the widow of Struthers's Shoe-polish, who had returned the previous year from a long initiatory sojourn in Europe to lay siege to the tight little citadel of New York. "Of course if you and Regina invite her the thing is settled. Well, we need new blood and new money—and I hear she's still very good-looking," the carnivorous old lady declared.

In the hall, while Mrs. Welland and May drew on their furs, Archer saw that the Countess Olenska was looking at him with a faintly questioning smile.

"Of course you know already—about May and me," he said, answering her look with a shy laugh. "She scolded me for not giving you the news last night at the Opera: I had her orders to tell you that we were engaged —but I couldn't, in that crowd."

The smile passed from Countess Olenska's eyes to her lips: she looked younger, more like the bold brown Ellen Mingott of his boyhood. "Of course I know; yes. And I'm so glad. But one doesn't tell such things first in a crowd." The ladies were on the threshold and she held out her hand.

"Good-bye; come and see me some day," she said, still looking at Archer.

In the carriage, on the way down Fifth Avenue, they talked pointedly of Mrs. Mingott, of her age, her spirit, and all her wonderful attributes. No one alluded to Ellen Olenska; but Archer knew that Mrs. Welland was thinking: "It's a mistake for Ellen to be seen, the very day after her arrival, parading up Fifth Avenue at the crowded hour with Julius Beaufort—" and the young man himself mentally added: "And she ought to know that a man who's just engaged doesn't spend his time calling on married women. But I daresay in the set she's lived in they do—they never do anything else." And, in spite of the cosmopolitan views on which he prided himself, he thanked heaven that he was a New Yorker, and about to ally himself with one of his own kind.

V

THE next evening old Mr. Sillerton Jackson came to dine with the Archers.

Mrs. Archer was a shy woman and shrank from society; but she liked to be well-informed as to its doings. Her old friend Mr. Sillerton Jackson applied to the investigation of his friends' affairs the patience of a collector and the science of a naturalist; and his sister, Miss Sophy Jackson, who lived with him, and was entertained by all the people who could not secure her much-sought-after brother, brought home bits of minor gossip that filled out usefully the gaps in his picture.

Therefore, whenever anything happened that Mrs. Archer wanted to know about, she asked Mr. Jackson to dine; and as she honoured few people with her invitations, and as she and her daughter Janey were an excellent audience, Mr. Jackson usually came himself instead of sending his sister. If he could have dictated all the conditions, he would have chosen the evening when Newland was out; not because the young man was uncongenial to him (the two got on capitally at their club) but because the old anecdotist sometimes felt, on Newland's part, a tendency to weigh his evidence that the ladies of the family never showed.

Mr. Jackson, if perfection had been attainable on earth, would also have asked that Mrs. Archer's food should be a little better. But then New York, as far back as the

y

[30]

THE AGE OF INNOCENCE

mind of man could travel, had been divided into the two
great fundamental groups of the Mingotts and Mansons
and all their clan, who cared about eating and clothes
and money, and the Archer-Newland-van-der-Luyden
tribe, who were devoted to travel, horticulture and the best
fiction, and looked down on the grosser forms of pleasure.

You couldn't have everything, after all. If you dined
with the Lovell Mingotts you got canvas-back and terrapin and vintage wines; at Adeline Archer's you could
talk about Alpine scenery and "The Marble Faun"; and
luckily the Archer Madeira had gone round the Cape.
Therefore when a friendly summons came from Mrs.
Archer, Mr. Jackson, who was a true eclectic, would
usually say to his sister: "I've been a little gouty since
my last dinner at the Lovell Mingotts'—it will do me good
to diet at Adeline's."

Mrs. Archer, who had long been a widow, lived with
her son and daughter in West Twenty-eighth Street. An
upper floor was dedicated to Newland, and the two
women squeezed themselves into narrower quarters below. In an unclouded harmony of tastes and interests
they cultivated ferns in Wardian cases, made macramé
lace and wool embroidery on linen, collected American
revolutionary glazed ware, subscribed to "Good Words,"
and read Ouida's novels for the sake of the Italian atmosphere. (They preferred those about peasant life,
because of the descriptions of scenery and the pleasanter
sentiments, though in general they liked novels about
people in society, whose motives and habits were more
comprehensible, spoke severely of Dickens, who "had
never drawn a gentleman," and considered Thackeray
less at home in the great world than Bulwer—who,
however, was beginning to be thought old-fashioned.)

Mrs. and Miss Archer were both great lovers of

scenery. It was what they principally sought and admired on their occasional travels abroad; considering architecture and painting as subjects for men, and chiefly for learned persons who read Ruskin. Mrs. Archer had been born a Newland, and mother and daughter, who were as like as sisters, were both, as people said, "true Newlands"; tall, pale, and slightly round-shouldered, with long noses, sweet smiles and a kind of drooping distinction like that in certain faded Reynolds portraits. Their physical resemblance would have been complete if an elderly *embonpoint* had not stretched Mrs. Archer's black brocade, while Miss Archer's brown and purple poplins hung, as the years went on, more and more slackly on her virgin frame.

Mentally, the likeness between them, as Newland was aware, was less complete than their identical mannerisms often made it appear. The long habit of living together in mutually dependent intimacy had given them the same vocabulary, and the same habit of beginning their phrases "Mother thinks" or "Janey thinks," according as one or the other wished to advance an opinion of her own; but in reality, while Mrs. Archer's serene unimaginativeness rested easily in the accepted and familiar, Janey was subject to starts and aberrations of fancy welling up from springs of suppressed romance.

Mother and daughter adored each other and revered their son and brother; and Archer loved them with a tenderness made compunctious and uncritical by the sense of their exaggerated admiration, and by his secret satisfaction in it. After all, he thought it a good thing for a man to have his authority respected in his own house, even if his sense of humour sometimes made him question the force of his mandate.

On this occasion the young man was very sure that Mr.

Jackson would rather have had him dine out; but he had his own reasons for not doing so.

Of course old Jackson wanted to talk about Ellen Olenska, and of course Mrs. Archer and Janey wanted to hear what he had to tell. All three would be slightly embarrassed by Newland's presence, now that his prospective relation to the Mingott clan had been made known; and the young man waited with an amused curiosity to see how they would turn the difficulty.

They began, obliquely, by talking about Mrs. Lemuel Struthers.

"It's a pity the Beauforts asked her," Mrs. Archer said gently. "But then Regina always does what he tells her; and *Beaufort*—"

"Certain *nuances* escape Beaufort," said Mr. Jackson, cautiously inspecting the broiled shad, and wondering for the thousandth time why Mrs. Archer's cook always burnt the roe to a cinder. (Newland, who had long shared his wonder, could always detect it in the older man's expression of melancholy disapproval.)

"Oh, necessarily; Beaufort is a vulgar man," said Mrs. Archer. "My grandfather Newland always used to say to my mother: 'Whatever you do, don't let that fellow Beaufort be introduced to the girls.' But at least he's had the advantage of associating with gentlemen; in England too, they say. It's all very mysterious—" She glanced at Janey and paused. She and Janey knew every fold of the Beaufort mystery, but in public Mrs. Archer continued to assume that the subject was not one for the unmarried.

"But this Mrs. Struthers," Mrs. Archer continued; "what did you say *she* was, Sillerton?"

"Out of a mine: or rather out of the saloon at the head of the pit. Then with Living Wax-Works, touring

New England. After the police broke *that* up, they say
she lived—" Mr. Jackson in his turn glanced at Janey,
whose eyes began to bulge from under her prominent
lids. There were still hiatuses for her in Mrs. Struthers's
past.

"Then," Mr. Jackson continued (and Archer saw he
was wondering why no one had told the butler never to
slice cucumbers with a steel knife), "then Lemuel Struthers came along. They say his advertiser used the girl's
head for the shoe-polish posters; her hair's intensely
black, you know—the Egyptian style. Anyhow, he—
eventually—married her." There were volumes of in-
nuendo in the way the "eventually" was spaced, and each
syllable given its due stress.

"Oh, well—at the pass we've come to nowadays, it
doesn't matter," said Mrs. Archer indifferently. The
ladies were not really interested in Mrs. Struthers just
then; the subject of Ellen Olenska was too fresh and too
absorbing to them. Indeed, Mrs. Struthers's name had
been introduced by Mrs. Archer only that she might
presently be able to say: "And Newland's new cousin—
Countess Olenska? Was *she* at the ball too?"

There was a faint touch of sarcasm in the reference to
her son, and Archer knew it and had expected it. Even
Mrs. Archer, who was seldom unduly pleased with human
events, had been altogether glad of her son's engagement.
("Especially after that silly business with Mrs. Rushworth," as she had remarked to Janey, alluding to what
had once seemed to Newland a tragedy of which his soul
would always bear the scar.) There was no better
match in New York than May Welland, look at the question from whatever point you chose. Of course such a
marriage was only what Newland was entitled to; but
young men are so foolish and incalculable—and some

women so ensnaring and unscrupulous—that it was nothing short of a miracle to see one's only son safe past the Siren Isle and in the haven of a blameless domesticity.

All this Mrs. Archer felt, and her son knew she felt; but he knew also that she had been perturbed by the premature announcement of his engagement, or rather by its cause; and it was for that reason—because on the whole he was a tender and indulgent master—that he had stayed at home that evening. "It's not that I don't approve of the Mingotts' *esprit de corps;* but why Newland's engagement should be mixed up with that Olenska woman's comings and goings I don't see," Mrs. Archer grumbled to Janey, the only witness of her slight lapses from perfect sweetness.

She had behaved beautifully—and in beautiful behaviour she was unsurpassed—during the call on Mrs. Welland; but Newland knew (and his betrothed doubtless guessed) that all through the visit she and Janey were nervously on the watch for Madame Olenska's possible intrusion; and when they left the house together she had permitted herself to say to her son: "I'm thankful that Augusta Welland received us alone."

These indications of inward disturbance moved Archer the more that he too felt that the Mingotts had gone a little too far. But, as it was against all the rules of their code that the mother and son should ever allude to what was uppermost in their thoughts, he simply replied: "Oh, well, there's always a phase of family parties to be gone through when one gets engaged, and the sooner it's over the better." At which his mother merely pursed her lips under the lace veil that hung down from her grey velvet bonnet trimmed with frosted grapes.

Her revenge, he felt—her lawful revenge—would be to "draw" Mr. Jackson that evening on the Countess

Olenska; and, having publicly done his duty as a future member of the Mingott clan, the young man had no objection to hearing the lady discussed in private—except that the subject was already beginning to bore him.

Mr. Jackson had helped himself to a slice of the tepid *filet* which the mournful butler had handed him with a look as sceptical as his own, and had rejected the mushroom sauce after a scarcely perceptible sniff. He looked baffled and hungry, and Archer reflected that he would probably finish his meal on Ellen Olenska.

Mr. Jackson leaned back in his chair, and glanced up at the candlelit Archers, Newlands and van der Luydens' hanging in dark frames on the dark walls.

"Ah, how your grandfather Archer loved a good dinner, my dear Newland!" he said, his eyes on the portrait of a plump full-chested young man in a stock and a blue coat, with a view of a white-columned country-house behind him. "Well—well—well . . . I wonder what he would have said to all these foreign marriages!"

Mrs. Archer ignored the allusion to the ancestral *cuisine* and Mr. Jackson continued with deliberation: "No, she was *not* at the ball."

"Ah—" Mrs. Archer murmured, in a tone that implied: "She had that decency."

"Perhaps the Beauforts don't know her," Janey suggested, with her artless malice.

Mr. Jackson gave a faint sip, as if he had been tasting invisible Madeira. "Mrs. Beaufort may not—but Beaufort certainly does, for she was seen walking up Fifth Avenue this afternoon with him by the whole of New York."

"Mercy—" moaned Mrs. Archer, evidently perceiving the uselessness of trying to ascribe the actions of foreigners to a sense of delicacy.

[36]

"I wonder if she wears a round hat or a bonnet in the afternoon," Janey speculated. "At the Opera I know she had on dark blue velvet, perfectly plain and flat—like a night-gown."

"Janey!" said her mother; and Miss Archer blushed and tried to look audacious.

"It was, at any rate, in better taste not to go to the ball," Mrs. Archer continued.

A spirit of perversity moved her son to rejoin: "I don't think it was a question of taste with her. May said she meant to go, and then decided that the dress in question wasn't smart enough."

Mrs. Archer smiled at this confirmation of her inference. "Poor Ellen," she simply remarked; adding compassionately: "We must always bear in mind what an eccentric bringing-up Medora Manson gave her. What can you expect of a girl who was allowed to wear black satin at her coming-out ball?"

"Ah—don't I remember her in it!" said Mr. Jackson; adding: "Poor girl!" in the tone of one who, while enjoying the memory, had fully understood at the time what the sight portended.

"It's odd," Janey remarked, "that she should have kept such an ugly name as Ellen. I should have changed it to Elaine." She glanced about the table to see the effect of this.

Her brother laughed. "Why Elaine?"

"I don't know; it sounds more—more Polish," said Janey, blushing.

"It sounds more conspicuous; and that can hardly be what she wishes," said Mrs. Archer distantly.

"Why not?" broke in her son, growing suddenly argumentative. "Why shouldn't she be conspicuous if she chooses? Why should she slink about as if it were she who had disgraced herself? She's 'poor Ellen' certainly, because she had the bad luck to make a wretched marriage; but I don't see that that's a reason for hiding her head as if she were the culprit."

"That, I suppose," said Mr. Jackson, speculatively, "is the line the Mingotts mean to take."

The young man reddened. "I didn't have to wait for their cue, if that's what you mean, sir. Madame Olenska has had an unhappy life: that doesn't make her an outcast."

"There are rumours," began Mr. Jackson, glancing at Janey.

"Oh, I know: the secretary," the young man took him up. "Nonsense, mother; Janey's grown-up. They say, don't they," he went on, "that the secretary helped her to get away from her brute of a husband, who kept her practically a prisoner? Well, what if he did? I hope there isn't a man among us who wouldn't have done the same in such a case."

Mr. Jackson glanced over his shoulder to say to the sad butler: "Perhaps . . . that sauce . . . just a little, after all—"; then, having helped himself, he remarked: "I'm told she's looking for a house. She means to live here."

"I hear she means to get a divorce," said Janey boldly.

"I hope she will!" Archer exclaimed.

The word had fallen like a bombshell in the pure and tranquil atmosphere of the Archer dining-room. Mrs. Archer raised her delicate eye-brows in the particular curve that signified: "The butler—" and the young man, himself mindful of the bad taste of discussing such intimate matters in public, hastily branched off into an account of his visit to old Mrs. Mingott.

After dinner, according to immemorial custom, Mrs.

Archer and Janey trailed their long silk draperies up to the drawing-room, where, while the gentlemen smoked below stairs, they sat beside a Carcel lamp with an engraved globe, facing each other across a rosewood work-table with a green silk bag under it, and stitched at the two ends of a tapestry band of field-flowers destined to adorn an "occasional" chair in the drawing-room of young Mrs. Newland Archer.

While this rite was in progress in the drawing-room, Archer settled Mr. Jackson in an armchair near the fire in the Gothic library and handed him a cigar. Mr. Jackson sank into the armchair with satisfaction, lit his cigar with perfect confidence (it was Newland who bought them), and stretching his thin old ankles to the coals, said: "You say the secretary merely helped her to get away, my dear fellow? Well, he was still helping her a year later, then; for somebody met 'em living at Lausanne together."

Newland reddened. "Living together? Well, why not? Who had the right to make her life over if she hadn't? I'm sick of the hypocrisy that would bury alive a woman of her age if her husband prefers to live with harlots."

He stopped and turned away angrily to light his cigar. "Women ought to be free—as free as we are," he declared, making a discovery of which he was too irritated to measure the terrific consequences.

Mr. Sillerton Jackson stretched his ankles nearer the coals and emitted a sardonic whistle.

"Well," he said after a pause, "apparently Count Olenski takes your view; for I never heard of his having lifted a finger to get his wife back."

VI.

THAT evening, after Mr. Jackson had taken himself away, and the ladies had retired to their chintz-curtained bedroom, Newland Archer mounted thoughtfully to his own study. A vigilant hand had, as usual, kept the fire alive and the lamp trimmed; and the room, with its rows and rows of books, its bronze and steel statuettes of "The Fencers" on the mantelpiece and its many photographs of famous pictures, looked singularly home-like and welcoming.

As he dropped into his armchair near the fire his eyes rested on a large photograph of May Welland, which the young girl had given him in the first days of their romance, and which had now displaced all the other portraits on the table. With a new sense of awe he looked at the frank forehead, serious eyes and gay innocent mouth of the young creature whose soul's custodian he was to be. That terrifying product of the social system he belonged to and believed in, the young girl who knew nothing and expected everything, looked back at him like a stranger through May Welland's familiar features; and once more it was borne in on him that marriage was not the safe anchorage he had been taught to think, but an uncharted voyage on seas.

The case of the Countess Olenska had stirred up old settled convictions and set them drifting dangerously through his mind. His own exclamation: "Women should be free—as free as we are," struck to the root of

THE AGE OF INNOCENCE

a problem that it was agreed in his world to regard as non-existent. "Nice" women, however wronged, would never claim the kind of freedom he meant, and generous-minded men like himself were therefore—in the heat of argument—the more chivalrously ready to concede it to them. Such verbal generosities were in fact only a humbugging disguise of the inexorable conventions that tied things together and bound people down to the old pattern. But here he was pledged to defend, on the part of his betrothed's cousin, conduct that, on his own wife's part, would justify him in calling down on her all the thunders of Church and State. Of course the dilemma was purely hypothetical; since he wasn't a blackguard Polish nobleman, it was absurd to speculate what his wife's rights would be if he *were*. But Newland Archer was too imaginative not to feel that, in his case and May's, the tie might gall for reasons far less gross and palpable. What could he and she really know of each other, since it was his duty, as a "decent" fellow, to conceal his past from her, and hers, as a marriageable girl, to have no past to conceal? What if, for some one of the subtler reasons that would tell with both of them, they should tire of each other, misunderstand or irritate each other? He reviewed his friends' marriages—the supposedly happy ones—and saw none that answered, even remotely, to the passionate and tender comradeship which he pictured as his permanent relation with May Welland. He perceived that such a picture presupposed, on her part, the experience, the versatility, the freedom of judgment, which she had been carefully trained not to possess; and with a shiver of foreboding he saw his marriage becoming what most of the other marriages about him were: a dull association of material and social interests held together by ignorance on the one side and hypocrisy on the other.

Lawrence Lefferts occurred to him as the husband who had most completely realised this enviable ideal. As became the high-priest of form, he had formed a wife so completely to his own convenience that, in the most conspicuous moments of his frequent love-affairs with other men's wives, she went about in smiling unconsciousness, saying that "Lawrence was so frightfully strict"; and had been known to blush indignantly, and avert her gaze, when some one alluded in her presence to the fact that Julius Beaufort (as became a "foreigner" of doubtful origin) had what was known in New York as "another establishment."

Archer tried to console himself with the thought that he was not quite such an ass as Larry Lefferts, nor May such a simpleton as poor Gertrude; but the difference was after all one of intelligence and not of standards. In reality they all lived in a kind of hieroglyphic world, where the real thing was never said or done or even thought, but only represented by a set of arbitrary signs; as when Mrs. Welland, who knew exactly why Archer had pressed her to announce her daughter's engagement at the Beaufort ball (and had indeed expected him to do no less), yet felt obliged to simulate reluctance, and the air of having had her hand forced, quite as, in the books on Primitive Man that people of advanced culture were beginning to read, the savage bride is dragged with shrieks from her parents' tent.

The result, of course, was that the young girl who was the centre of this elaborate system of mystification remained the more inscrutable for her very frankness and assurance. She was frank, poor darling, because she had nothing to conceal, assured because she knew of nothing to be on her guard against; and with no better preparation than this, she was to be plunged overnight into what people evasively called "the facts of life."

The young man was sincerely but placidly in love. He delighted in the radiant good looks of his betrothed, in her health, her horsemanship, her grace and quickness at games, and the shy interest in books and ideas that she was beginning to develop under his guidance. (She had advanced far enough to join him in ridiculing the Idyls of the King, but not to feel the beauty of Ulysses and the Lotus Eaters.) She was straightforward, loyal and brave; she had a sense of humour (chiefly proved by her laughing at *his* jokes); and he suspected, in the depths of her innocently-gazing soul, a glow of feeling that it would be a joy to waken. But when he had gone the brief round of her he returned discouraged by the thought that all this frankness and innocence were only an artificial product. Untrained human nature was not frank and innocent; it was full of the twists and defences of an instinctive guile. And he felt himself oppressed by this creation of factitious purity, so cunningly manufactured by a conspiracy of mothers and aunts and grandmothers and long-dead ancestresses, because it was supposed to be what he wanted, what he had a right to, in order that he might exercise his lordly pleasure in smashing it like an image made of snow.

There was a certain triteness in these reflections: they were those habitual to young men on the approach of their wedding day. But they were generally accompanied by a sense of compunction and self-abasement of which Newland Archer felt no trace. He could not deplore (as Thackeray's heroes so often exasperated him by doing) that he had not a blank page to offer his bride in exchange for the unblemished one she was to give to him. He could not get away from the fact that if he had been brought up as she had they would have been no more fit to find their way about than the Babes in the Wood; nor could he, for all his anxious cogitations, see any honest reason (any, that is, unconnected with his own momentary pleasure, and the passion of masculine vanity) why his bride should not have been allowed the same freedom of experience as himself.

Such questions, at such an hour, were bound to drift through his mind; but he was conscious that their uncomfortable persistence and precision were due to the inopportune arrival of the Countess Olenska. Here he was, at the very moment of his betrothal—a moment for pure thoughts and cloudless hopes—pitchforked into the coil of scandal which raised all the special problems he would have preferred to let lie. "Hang Ellen Olenska!" he grumbled, as he covered his fire and began to undress. He could not really see why her fate should have the least bearing on his; yet he dimly felt that he had only just begun to measure the risks of the championship which his engagement had forced upon him.

A few days later the bolt fell.

The Lovell Mingotts had sent out cards for what was known as "a formal dinner" (that is, three extra footmen, two dishes for each course, and a Roman punch in the middle), and had headed their invitations with the words "To meet the Countess Olenska," in accordance with the hospitable American fashion, which treats strangers as if they were royalties, or at least as their ambassadors.

The guests had been selected with a boldness and discrimination in which the initiated recognised the firm hand of Catherine the Great. Associated with such immemorial standbys as the Selfridge Merrys, who were

THE AGE OF INNOCENCE

asked everywhere because they always had been, the
Beauforts, on whom there was a claim of relationship,
and Mr. Sillerton Jackson and his sister Sophy (who
went wherever her brother told her to), were some of
the most fashionable and yet most irreproachable of the
dominant "young married" set; the Lawrence Leffertses,
Mrs. Lefferts Rushworth (the lovely widow), the Harry
Thorleys, the Reggie Chiverses and young Morris
Dagonet and his wife (who was a van der Luyden).
The company indeed was perfectly assorted, since all the
members belonged to the little inner group of people
who, during the long New York season, disported themselves together daily and nightly with apparently undi-
minished zest.

Forty-eight hours later the unbelievable had happened;
every one had refused the Mingotts' invitation except the
Beauforts and old Mr. Jackson and his sister. The intended slight was emphasised by the fact that even the
Reggie Chiverses, who were of the Mingott clan, were
among those inflicting it; and by the uniform wording of
the notes, in all of which the writers "regretted that they
were unable to accept," without the mitigating plea of a
"previous engagement" that ordinary courtesy prescribed.

New York society was, in those days, far too small,
and too scant in its resources, for every one in it (including livery-stable-keepers, butlers and cooks) not to know
exactly on which evenings people were free; and it was
thus possible for the recipients of Mrs. Lovell Mingott's
invitations to make cruelly clear their determination not
to meet the Countess Olenska.

The blow was unexpected; but the Mingotts, as their
way was, met it gallantly. Mrs. Lovell Mingott confided the case to Mrs. Welland, who confided it to Newland Archer; who, aflame at the outrage, appealed pas-

sionately and authoritatively to his mother; who, after a painful period of inward resistance and outward temporising, succumbed to his instances (as she always did), and immediately embracing his cause with an energy redoubled by her previous hesitations, put on her grey velvet bonnet and said: "I'll go and see Louisa van der Luyden."

The New York of Newland Archer's day was a small and slippery pyramid, in which, as yet, hardly a fissure had been made or a foothold gained. At its base was a firm foundation of what Mrs. Archer called "plain people"; an honourable but obscure majority of respectable families who (as in the case of the Spicers or the Leffertses or the Jacksons) had been raised above their level by marriage with one of the ruling clans. People, Mrs. Archer always said, were not as particular as they used to be; and with old Catherine Spicer ruling one end of Fifth Avenue, and Julius Beaufort the other, you couldn't expect the old traditions to last much longer.

Firmly narrowing upward from this wealthy but inconspicuous substratum was the compact and dominant group which the Mingotts, Newlands, Chiverses and Mansons so actively represented. Most people imagined them to be the very apex of the pyramid; but they themselves (at least those of Mrs. Archer's generation) were aware that, in the eyes of the professional genealogist, only a still smaller number of families could lay claim to that eminence.

"Don't tell me," Mrs. Archer would say to her children, "all this modern newspaper rubbish about a New York aristocracy. If there is one, neither the Mingotts nor the Mansons belong to it; no, nor the Newlands or the Chiverses either. Our grandfathers and great-grandfathers were just respectable English or Dutch merchants, who

THE AGE OF INNOCENCE

came to the colonies to make their fortune, and stayed here because they did so well. One of your great-grandfathers signed the Declaration, and another was a general on Washington's staff, and received General Burgoyne's sword after the battle of Saratoga. These are things to be proud of, but they have nothing to do with rank or class. New York has always been a commercial community, and there are not more than three families in it who can claim an aristocratic origin in the real sense of the word."

Mrs. Archer and her son and daughter, like every one else in New York, knew who these privileged beings were: the Dagonets of Washington Square, who came of an old English county family allied with the Pitts and Foxes; the Lannings, who had intermarried with the descendants of Count de Grasse, and the van der Luydens, direct descendants of the first Dutch governor of Manhattan, and related by pre-revolutionary marriages to several members of the French and British aristocracy.

The Lannings survived only in the person of two very old but lively Miss Lannings, who lived cheerfully and reminiscently among family portraits and Chippendale; the Dagonets were a considerable clan, allied to the best names in Baltimore and Philadelphia; but the van der Luydens, who stood above all of them, had faded into a kind of super-terrestrial twilight, from which only two figures impressively emerged; those of Mr. and Mrs. Henry van der Luyden.

Mrs. Henry van der Luyden had been Louisa Dagonet, and her mother had been the granddaughter of Colonel du Lac, of an old Channel Island family, who had fought under Cornwallis and had settled in Maryland, after the war, with his bride, Lady Angelica Trevenna, fifth daughter of the Earl of St. Austrey. The tie between the

[47]

Dagonets, the du Lacs of Maryland, and their aristocratic Cornish kinsfolk, the Trevennas, had always remained close and cordial. Mr. and Mrs. van der Luyden
had more than once paid long visits to the present head
of the house of Trevenna, the Duke of St. Austrey, at
his country-seat in Cornwall and at St. Austrey in Glou-
cestershire; and his Grace had frequently announced his
intention of some day returning their visit (without the
Duchess, who feared the Atlantic).

Mr. and Mrs. van der Luyden divided their time between Trevenna, their place in Maryland, and Skuytercliff, the great estate on the Hudson which had been one
of the colonial grants of the Dutch government to the
famous first Governor, and of which Mr. van der Luyden was still "Patroon." Their large solemn house in
Madison Avenue was seldom opened, and when they
came to town they received in it only their most intimate
friends.

"I wish you would go with me, Newland," his mother
said, suddenly pausing at the door of the Brown *coupé*.
"Louisa is fond of you; and of course it's on account of
dear May that I'm taking this step—and also because, if
we don't all stand together, there'll be no such thing as
Society left."

VII

MRS. HENRY VAN DER LUYDEN listened in silence to her cousin Mrs. Archer's narrative.

It was all very well to tell yourself in advance that Mrs. van der Luyden was always silent, and that, though noncommittal by nature and training, she was very kind to the people she really liked. Even personal experience of these facts was not always a protection from the chill that descended on one in the high-ceilinged white-walled Madison Avenue drawing-room, with the pale brocaded armchairs so obviously uncovered for the occasion, and the gauze still veiling the ormolu mantel ornaments and the beautiful old carved frame of Gainsborough's "Lady Angelica du Lac."

Mrs. van der Luyden's portrait by Huntington (in black velvet and Venetian point) faced that of her lovely ancestress. It was generally considered "as fine as a Cabanel," and, though twenty years had elapsed since its execution, was still "a perfect likeness." Indeed the Mrs. van der Luyden who sat beneath it listening to Mrs. Archer might have been the twin-sister of the fair and still youngish woman drooping against a gilt armchair before a green rep curtain. Mrs. van der Luyden still wore black velvet and Venetian point when she went into society—or rather (since she never dined out) when she threw open her own doors to receive it. Her fair hair, which had faded without turning grey, was still parted in flat overlapping points on her forehead, and the straight nose that divided her pale blue eyes was only a little more pinched about the nostrils than when the portrait had been painted. She always, indeed, struck Newland Archer as having been rather gruesomely preserved in the airless atmosphere of a perfectly irreproachable existence, as bodies caught in glaciers keep for years a rosy life-in-death.

Like all his family, he esteemed and admired Mrs. van der Luyden; but he found her gentle bending sweetness less approachable than the grimness of some of his mother's old aunts, fierce spinsters who said "No" on principle before they knew what they were going to be asked.

Mrs. van der Luyden's attitude said neither yes nor no, but always appeared to incline to clemency till her thin lips, wavering into the shadow of a smile, made the almost invariable reply: "I shall first have to talk this over with my husband."

She and Mr. van der Luyden were so exactly alike that Archer often wondered how, after forty years of the closest conjugality, two such merged identities ever separated themselves enough for anything as controversial as a talking-over. But as neither had ever reached a decision without prefacing it by this mysterious conclave, Mrs. Archer and her son, having set forth their case, waited resignedly for the familiar phrase.

Mrs. van der Luyden, however, who had seldom surprised any one, now surprised them by reaching her long hand toward the bell-rope.

"I think," she said, "I should like Henry to hear what you have told me."

A footman appeared, to whom she gravely added: "If Mr. van der Luyden has finished reading the newspaper, please ask him to be kind enough to come."

She said "reading the newspaper" in the tone in which a Minister's wife might have said: "Presiding at a Cabinet meeting"—not from any arrogance of mind, but because the habit of a life-time, and the attitude of her friends and relations, had led her to consider Mr. van der Luyden's least gesture as having an almost sacerdotal importance.

Her promptness of action showed that she considered the case as pressing as Mrs. Archer; but, lest she should be thought to have committed herself in advance, she added, with the sweetest look: "Henry always enjoys seeing you, dear Adeline; and he will wish to congratulate Newland."

The double doors had solemnly reopened and between them appeared Mr. Henry van der Luyden, tall, spare and frock-coated, with faded fair hair, a straight nose like his wife's and the same look of frozen gentleness in eyes that were merely pale grey instead of pale blue.

Mr. van der Luyden greeted Mrs. Archer with cousinly affability, proffered to Newland low-voiced congratulations couched in the same language as his wife's, and seated himself in one of the brocade armchairs with the simplicity of a reigning sovereign.

"I had just finished reading the Times," he said, laying his long finger-tips together. "In town my mornings are so much occupied that I find it more convenient to read the newspapers after luncheon."

"Ah, there's a great deal to be said for that plan—indeed I think my uncle Egmont used to say he found it less agitating not to read the morning papers till after dinner," said Mrs. Archer responsively.

"Yes: my good father abhorred hurry. But now we live in a constant rush," said Mr. van der Luyden in measured tones, looking with pleasant deliberation about the large shrouded room which to Archer was so complete an image of its owners.

"But I hope you *had* finished your reading, Henry?" his wife interposed.

"Quite—quite," he reassured her.

"Then I should like Adeline to tell you—"

"Oh, it's really Newland's story," said his mother smiling; and proceeded to rehearse once more the monstrous tale of the affront inflicted on Mrs. Lovell Mingott.

"Of course," she ended, "Augusta Welland and Mary Mingott both felt that, especially in view of Newland's engagement, you and Henry *ought to know.*"

"Ah—" said Mr. van der Luyden, drawing a deep breath.

There was a silence during which the tick of the monumental ormolu clock on the white marble mantelpiece grew as loud as the boom of a minute-gun. Archer contemplated with awe the two slender faded figures, seated side by side in a kind of viceregal rigidity, mouth-pieces of some remote ancestral authority which fate compelled them to wield, when they would so much rather have lived in simplicity and seclusion, digging invisible weeds out of the perfect lawns of Skuytercliff, and playing Patience together in the evenings.

Mr. van der Luyden was the first to speak.

"You really think this is due to some—some intentional interference of Lawrence Lefferts's?" he enquired, turning to Archer.

"I'm certain of it, sir. Larry has been going it rather harder than usual lately—if cousin Louisa won't mind my mentioning it—having rather a stiff affair with the postmaster's wife in their village, or some one of that sort; and whenever poor Gertrude Lefferts begins to suspect anything, and he's afraid of trouble, he gets up a fuss of this kind, to show how awfully moral he is, and talks at the top of his voice about the impertinence of inviting his wife to meet people he doesn't wish her to know. He's simply using Madame Olenska as a lightning-rod; I've seen him try the same thing often before."

"*The Leffertses!*—" said Mrs. van der Luyden.

"*The Leffertses!*—" echoed Mrs. Archer. "What would uncle Egmont have said of Lawrence Lefferts's pronouncing on anybody's social position? It shows what Society has come to."

"We'll hope it has not quite come to that," said Mr. van der Luyden firmly.

"Ah, if only you and Louisa went out more!" sighed Mrs. Archer.

But instantly she became aware of her mistake. The van der Luydens were morbidly sensitive to any criticism of their secluded existence. They were the arbiters of fashion, the Court of last Appeal, and they knew it, and bowed to their fate. But being shy and retiring persons, with no natural inclination for their part, they lived as much as possible in the sylvan solitude of Skuytercliff, and when they came to town, declined all invitations on the plea of Mrs. van der Luyden's health.

Newland Archer came to his mother's rescue. "Everybody in New York knows what you and cousin Louisa represent. That's why Mrs. Mingott felt she ought not to allow this slight on Countess Olenska to pass without consulting you."

Mrs. van der Luyden glanced at her husband, who glanced back at her.

"It is the principle that I dislike," said Mr. van der Luyden. "As long as a member of a well-known family is backed up by that family it should be considered—final."

"It seems so to me," said his wife, as if she were producing a new thought.

"I had no idea," Mr. van der Luyden continued, "that things had come to such a pass." He paused, and looked at his wife again. "It occurs to me, my dear, that the Countess Olenska is already a sort of relation—through Medora Manson's first husband. At any rate, she will be when Newland marries." He turned toward the young man. "Have you read this morning's Times, Newland?"

"Why, yes, sir," said Archer, who usually tossed off half a dozen papers with his morning coffee.

Husband and wife looked at each other again. Their pale eyes clung together in prolonged and serious consultation; then a faint smile fluttered over Mrs. van der Luyden's face. She had evidently guessed and approved.

Mr. van der Luyden turned to Mrs. Archer. "If Louisa's health allowed her to dine out—I wish you would say to Mrs. Lovell Mingott—she and I would have been happy to—er—fill the places of the Lawrence Leffertses at her dinner." He paused to let the irony of this sink in. "As you know, this is impossible." Mrs. Archer sounded a sympathetic assent. "But Newland tells me he has read this morning's Times; therefore he has probably seen that Louisa's relative, the Duke of St. Austrey, arrives next week on the Russia. He is coming to enter his new sloop, the Guinevere, in next summer's International Cup Race; and also to have a little canvasback shooting at Trevenna." Mr. van der Luyden paused again, and continued with increasing benevolence: "Before taking him down to Maryland we are inviting a few friends to meet him here—only a little dinner—with a reception afterward. I am sure Louisa will be as glad as I am if

Countess Olenska will let us include her among our guests." He got up, bent his long body with a stiff friendliness toward his cousin, and added: "I think I have Louisa's authority for saying that she will herself leave the invitation to dine when she drives out presently: with our cards—of course with our cards."

Mrs. Archer, who knew this to be a hint that the seventeen-hand chestnuts which were never kept waiting were at the door, rose with a hurried murmur of thanks. Mrs. van der Luyden beamed on her with the smile of Esther interceding with Ahasuerus; but her husband raised a protesting hand.

"There is nothing to thank me for, dear Adeline; nothing whatever. This kind of thing must not happen in New York; it shall not, as long as I can help it," he pronounced with sovereign gentleness as he steered his cousins to the door.

Two hours later, every one knew that the great C-spring barouche in which Mrs. van der Luyden took the air at all seasons had been seen at old Mrs. Mingott's door, where a large square envelope was handed in; and that evening at the Opera Mr. Sillerton Jackson was able to state that the envelope contained a card inviting the Countess Olenska to the dinner which the van der Luydens were giving the following week for their cousin, the Duke of St. Austrey.

Some of the younger men in the club box exchanged a smile at this announcement, and glanced sideways at Lawrence Lefferts, who sat carelessly in the front of the box, pulling his long fair moustache, and who remarked with authority, as the soprano paused: "No one but Patti ought to attempt the Sonnambula."

VIII

I T was generally agreed in New York that the Countess
Olenska had "lost her looks."

She had appeared there first, in Newland Archer's
boyhood, as a brilliantly pretty little girl of nine or ten,
of whom people said that she "ought to be painted." Her
parents had been continental wanderers, and after a
roaming babyhood she had lost them both, and been taken
in charge by her aunt, Medora Manson, also a wanderer,
who was herself returning to New York to "settle down."

Poor Medora, repeatedly widowed, was always coming
home to settle down (each time in a less expensive house),
and bringing with her a new husband or an adopted child;
but after a few months she invariably parted from her
husband or quarrelled with her ward, and, having got rid
of her house at a loss, set out again on her wanderings.
As her mother had been a Rushworth, and her last unhappy marriage had linked her to one of the crazy
Chiverses, New York looked indulgently on her eccentricities; but when she returned with her little orphaned
niece, whose parents had been popular in spite of their
regrettable taste for travel, people thought it a pity that
the pretty child should be in such hands.

Every one was disposed to be kind to little Ellen
Mingott, though her dusky red cheeks and tight curls
gave her an air of gaiety that seemed unsuitable in a child
who should still have been in black for her parents. It
was one of the misguided Medora's many peculiarities to

flout the unalterable rules that regulated American mourning, and when she stepped from the steamer her family were scandalised to see that the crape veil she wore for her own brother was seven inches shorter than those of her sisters-in-law, while little Ellen was in crimson merino and amber beads, like a gipsy foundling.

But New York had so long resigned itself to Medora that only a few old ladies shook their heads over Ellen's gaudy clothes, while her other relations fell under the charm of her high colour and high spirits. She was a fearless and familiar little thing, who asked disconcerting questions, made precocious comments, and possessed outlandish arts, such as dancing a Spanish shawl dance and singing Neapolitan love-songs to a guitar. Under the direction of her aunt (whose real name was Mrs. Thorley Chivers, but who, having received a Papal title, had resumed her first husband's patronymic, and called herself the Marchioness Manson, because in Italy she could turn it into Manzoni) the little girl received an expensive but incoherent education, which included "drawing from the model," a thing never dreamed of before, and playing the piano in quintets with professional musicians.

Of course no good could come of this; and when, a few years later, poor Chivers finally died in a madhouse, his widow (draped in strange weeds) again pulled up stakes and departed with Ellen, who had grown into a tall bony girl with conspicuous eyes. For some time no more was heard of them; then news came of Ellen's marriage to an immensely rich Polish nobleman of legendary fame, whom she had met at a ball at the Tuileries, and who was said to have princely establishments in Paris, Nice and Florence, a yacht at Cowes, and many square miles of shooting in Transylvania. She disappeared in a kind of sulphurous apotheosis, and when a few years later Medora again came back to New York, subdued, impoverished, mourning a third husband, and in quest of a still smaller house, people wondered that her rich niece had not been able to do something for her. Then came the news that Ellen's own marriage had ended in disaster, and that she was herself returning home to seek rest and oblivion among her kinsfolk.

These things passed through Newland Archer's mind a week later as he watched the Countess Olenska enter the van der Luyden drawing-room on the evening of the momentous dinner. The occasion was a solemn one, and he wondered a little nervously how she would carry it off. She came rather late, one hand still ungloved, and fastening a bracelet about her wrist; yet she entered without any appearance of haste or embarrassment the drawing-room in which New York's most chosen company was somewhat awfully assembled.

In the middle of the room she paused, looking about her with a grave mouth and smiling eyes; and in that instant Newland Archer rejected the general verdict on her looks. It was true that her early radiance was gone. The red cheeks had paled; she was thin, worn, a little older-looking than her age, which must have been nearly thirty. But there was about her the mysterious authority of beauty, a sureness in the carriage of the head, the movement of the eyes, which, without being in the least theatrical, struck his as highly trained and full of a conscious power. At the same time she was simpler in manner than most of the ladies present, and many people (as he heard afterward from Janey) were disappointed that her appearance was not more "stylish"—for stylishness was what New York most valued. It was, perhaps, Archer reflected, because her early vivacity had disappeared; because she was so quiet—quiet in her movements, her voice, and the tones of her low-pitched voice. New York had expected something a good deal more reasonant in a young woman with such a history.

The dinner was a somewhat formidable business. Dining with the van der Luydens was at best no light matter, and dining there with a Duke who was their cousin was almost a religious solemnity. It pleased Archer to think that only an old New Yorker could perceive the shade of difference (to New York) between being merely a Duke and being the van der Luydens' Duke. New York took stray noblemen calmly, and even (except in the Struthers set) with a certain distrustful *hauteur;* but when they presented such credentials as these they were received with an old-fashioned cordiality that they would have been greatly mistaken in ascribing solely to their standing in Debrett. It was for just such distinctions that the young man cherished his old New York even while he smiled at it.

The van der Luydens had done their best to emphasise the importance of the occasion. The du Lac Sèvres and the Trevenna George II plate were out; so was the van der Luyden "Lowestoft" (East India Company) and the Dagonet Crown Derby. Mrs. van der Luyden looked more than ever like a Cabanel, and Mrs. Archer, in her grandmother's seed-pearls and emeralds, reminded her son of an Isabey miniature. All the ladies had on their handsomest jewels, but it was characteristic of the house and the occasion that these were mostly in rather heavy old-fashioned settings; and old Miss Lanning, who had been persuaded to come, actually wore her mother's cameos and a Spanish blonde shawl.

The Countess Olenska was the only young woman at the dinner; yet, as Archer scanned the smooth plump elderly faces between their diamond necklaces and towering ostrich feathers, they struck him as curiously immature compared with hers. It frightened him to think what must have gone to the making of her eyes.

The Duke of St. Austrey, who sat at his hostess's right, was naturally the chief figure of the evening. But if the Countess Olenska was less conspicuous than had been hoped, the Duke was almost invisible. Being a well-bred man he had not (like another recent ducal visitor) come to the dinner in a shooting-jacket; but his evening clothes were so shabby and baggy, and he wore them with such an air of their being homespun, that (with his stooping way of sitting, and the vast beard spreading over his shirt-front) he hardly gave the appearance of being in dinner attire. He was short, round-shouldered, sunburnt, with a thick nose, small eyes and a sociable smile; but he seldom spoke, and when he did it was in such low tones that, despite the frequent silences of expectation about the table, his remarks were lost to all but his neighbours.

When the men joined the ladies after dinner the Duke went straight up to the Countess Olenska, and they sat down in a corner and plunged into animated talk. Neither seemed aware that the Duke should first have paid his respects to Mrs. Lovell Mingott and Mrs. Headly Chivers, and the Countess have conversed with that amiable hypochondriac, Mr. Urban Dagonet of Washington Square, who, in order to have the pleasure of meeting her, had broken through his fixed rule of not dining out between January and April. The two chatted together for nearly twenty minutes; then the Countess rose and, walking alone across the wide drawing-room, sat down at Newland Archer's side.

It was not the custom in New York drawing-rooms for a lady to get up and walk away from one gentleman in order to seek the company of another. Etiquette required that she should wait, immovable as an idol, while the men who wished to converse with her succeeded each other at her side. But the Countess was apparently unaware of having broken any rule; she sat at perfect ease in a corner of the sofa beside Archer, and looked at him with the kindest eyes.

"I want you to talk to me about May," she said.

Instead of answering her he asked: "You knew the Duke before?"

"Oh, yes—we used to see him every winter at Nice. He's very fond of gambling—he used to come to the house a great deal." She said it in the simplest manner, as if she had said: "He's fond of wild-flowers"; and after a moment she added candidly: "I think he's the dullest man I ever met."

This pleased her companion so much that he forgot the slight shock her previous remark had caused him. It was undeniably exciting to meet a lady who found the van der Luydens' Duke dull, and dared to utter the opinion. He longed to question her, to hear more about the life of which her careless words had given him so illuminating a glimpse; but he feared to touch on distressing memories, and before he could think of anything to say she had strayed back to her original subject.

"May is a darling; I've seen no young girl in New York so handsome and so intelligent. Are you very much in love with her?"

Newland Archer reddened and laughed. "As much as a man can be."

She continued to consider him thoughtfully, as if not to miss any shade of meaning in what he said, "Do you think, then, there is a limit?"

"To being in love? If there is, I haven't found it!"

She glowed with sympathy. "Ah—it's really and truly a romance?"

"The most romantic of romances!"

"How delightful! And you found it all out for yourselves—it was not in the least arranged for you?"

Archer looked at her incredulously. "Have you forgotten," he asked with a smile, "that in our country we don't allow our marriages to be arranged for us?"

A dusky blush rose to her cheek, and he instantly regretted his words.

"Yes," she answered, "I'd forgotten. You must forgive me if I sometimes make these mistakes. I don't always remember that everything here is good that was—that was bad where I've come from." She looked down at her Viennese fan of eagle feathers, and he saw that her lips trembled.

"I'm so sorry," he said impulsively; "but you *are* among friends here, you know."

"Yes—I know. Wherever I go I have that feeling. That's why I came home. I want to forget everything else, to become a complete American again, like the Mingotts and Wellands, and you and your delightful mother, and all the other good people here tonight. Ah, here's May arriving, and you will want to hurry away to her," she added, but without moving; and her eyes turned back from the door to rest on the young man's face.

The drawing-rooms were beginning to fill up with after-dinner guests, and following Madame Olenska's glance Archer saw May Welland entering with her mother. In her dress of white and silver, with a wreath of silver blossoms in her hair, the tall girl looked like a Diana just alight from the chase.

"Oh," said Archer, "I have so many rivals; you see

[62]

she's already surrounded. There's the Duke being introduced."

"Then stay with me a little longer," Madame Olenska said in a low tone, just touching his knee with her plumed fan. It was the lightest touch, but it thrilled him like a caress.

"Yes, let me stay," he answered in the same tone, hardly knowing what he said; but just then Mr. van der Luyden came up, followed by old Mr. Urban Dagonet. The Countess greeted them with her grave smile, and Archer, feeling his host's admonitory glance on him, rose and surrendered his seat.

Madame Olenska held out her hand as if to bid him good-bye.

"Tomorrow, then, after five—I shall expect you," she said; and then turned back to make room for Mr. Dagonet.

"Tomorrow—" Archer heard himself repeating, though there had been no engagement, and during their talk she had given him no hint that she wished to see him again.

As he moved away he saw Lawrence Lefferts, tall and resplendent, leading his wife up to be introduced; and heard Gertrude Lefferts say, as she beamed on the Countess with her large unperceiving smile: "But I think we used to go to dancing-school together when we were children—." Behind her, waiting their turn to name themselves to the Countess, Archer noticed a number of the recalcitrant couples who had declined to meet her at Mrs. Lovell Mingott's. As Mrs. Archer remarked: "When the van der Luydens chose, they knew how to give a lesson." The wonder was that they chose so seldom.

The young man felt a touch on his arm and saw Mrs. van der Luyden looking down on him from the pure eminence of black velvet and the family diamonds. "It was good of you, dear Newland, to devote yourself so unselfishly to Madame Olenska. I told your cousin Henry he must really come to the rescue."

He was aware of smiling at her vaguely, and she added, as if condescending to his natural shyness: "I've never seen May looking lovelier. The Duke thinks her the handsomest girl in the room."

IX

THE Countess Olenska had said "after five"; and at
half after the hour Newland Archer rang the bell
of the peeling stucco house with a giant wistaria throt-
tling its feeble cast-iron balcony, which she had hired,
far down West Twenty-third Street, from the vagabond
Medora.

It was certainly a strange quarter to have settled in.
Small dress-makers, bird-stuffers and "people who
wrote" were her nearest neighbours; and further down
the dishevelled street Archer recognised a dilapidated
wooden house, at the end of a paved path, in which a
writer and journalist called Winsett, whom he used to
come across now and then, had mentioned that he lived.
Winsett did not invite people to his house; but he had
once pointed it out to Archer in the course of a nocturnal
stroll, and the latter had asked himself, with a little
shiver, if the humanities were so meanly housed in other
capitals.

Madame Olenska's own dwelling was redeemed from
the same appearance only by a little more paint about
the window-frames; and as Archer mustered its modest
front he said to himself that the Polish Count must have
robbed her of her fortune as well as of her illusions.

The young man had spent an unsatisfactory day. He
had lunched with the Wellands, hoping afterward to
carry off May for a walk in the Park. He wanted to

[65]

have her to himself, to tell her how enchanting she had looked the night before, and how proud he was of her, and to press her to hasten their marriage. But Mrs. Welland had firmly reminded him that the round of family visits was not half over, and, when he hinted at advancing the date of the wedding, had raised reproachful eye-brows and sighed out: "Twelve dozen of everything—hand-embroidered—"

Packed in the family landau they rolled from one tribal doorstep to another, and Archer, when the afternoon's round was over, parted from his betrothed with the feeling that he had been shown off like a wild animal cunningly trapped. He supposed that his readings in anthropology caused him to take such a coarse view of what was after all a simple and natural demonstration of family feeling; but when he remembered that the Wellands did not expect the wedding to take place till the following autumn, and pictured what his life would be till then, a dampness fell upon his spirits.

"Tomorrow," Mrs. Welland called after him, "we'll do the Chiverses and the Dallases"; and he perceived that she was going through their two families alphabetically, and that they were only in the first quarter of the alphabet.

He had meant to tell May of the Countess Olenska's request—her command, rather—that he should call on her that afternoon; but in the brief moments when they were alone he had had more pressing things to say. Besides, it struck him as a little absurd to allude to the matter. He knew that May most particularly wanted him to be kind to her cousin; was it not that wish which had hastened the announcement of their engagement? It gave him an odd sensation to reflect that, but for the Countess's arrival, he might have been, if not still a free man,

at least a man less irrevocably pledged. But May had
willed it so, and he felt himself somehow relieved of
further responsibility—and therefore at liberty, if he
chose, to call on her cousin without telling her.

As he stood on Madame Olenska's threshold curiosity
was his uppermost feeling. He was puzzled by the tone
in which she had summoned him; he concluded that she
was less simple than she seemed.

The door was opened by a swarthy foreign-looking
maid, with a prominent bosom under a gay neckerchief,
whom he vaguely fancied to be Sicilian. She welcomed
him with all her white teeth, and answering his enquiries
by a head-shake of incomprehension led him through the
narrow hall into a low firelit drawing-room. The room
was empty, and she left him, for an appreciable time, to
wonder whether she had gone to find her mistress, or
whether she had not understood what he was there for,
and thought it might be to wind the clocks—of which he
perceived that the only visible specimen had stopped.
He knew that the southern races communicated with each
other in the language of pantomime, and was mortified to
find her shrugs and smiles so unintelligible. At length
she returned with a lamp; and Archer, having meanwhile
put together a phrase out of Dante and Petrarch, evoked
the answer: *"La signora è fuori; ma verrà subito";* which
he took to mean: "She's out—but you'll soon see."

What he saw, meanwhile, with the help of the lamp,
was the faded shadowy charm of a room unlike any
room he had known. He knew that the Countess Olenska
had brought some of her possessions with her—bits of
wreckage, she called them—and these, he supposed, were
represented by some small slender tables of dark wood,
a delicate little Greek bronze on the chimney-piece, and a

stretch of red damask nailed on the discoloured wall-paper behind a couple of Italian-looking pictures in old frames.

Newland Archer prided himself on his knowledge of Italian art. His boyhood had been saturated with Ruskin, and he had read all the latest books: John Addington Symonds, Vernon Lee's "Euphorion," the essays of P. G. Hamerton, and a wonderful new volume called "The Renaissance" by Walter Pater. He talked easily of Botticelli, and spoke of Fra Angelico with a faint condescension. But these pictures bewildered him, for they were like nothing that he was accustomed to look at (and therefore able to see) when he travelled in Italy; and perhaps, also, his powers of observation were impaired by the oddness of finding himself in this strange empty house, where apparently no one expected him. He was sorry that he had not told May Welland of Countess Olenska's request, and a little disturbed by the thought that his betrothed might come in to see her cousin. What would she think if she found him sitting there with the air of intimacy implied by waiting alone in the dusk at a lady's fireside?

But since he had come he meant to wait; and he sank into a chair and stretched his feet to the logs.

It was odd to have summoned him in that way, and then forgotten him; but Archer felt more curious than mortified. The atmosphere of the room was so different from any he had ever breathed that self-consciousness vanished in the sense of adventure. He had been before in drawing-rooms hung with red damask, with pictures "of the Italian school"; what struck him was the way in which Medora Manson's shabby hired house, with its blighted background of pampas grass and Rogers statuettes, had, by a turn of the hand, and the skilful use of a few properties, been transformed into something intimate, "foreign," subtly suggestive of old romantic scenes and sentiments. He tried to analyse the trick, to find a clue to it in the way the chairs and tables were grouped, in the fact that only two Jacqueminot roses (of which nobody ever bought less than a dozen) had been placed in the slender vase at his elbow, and in the vague pervading perfume that was not what one put on handkerchiefs, but rather like the scent of some far-off bazaar, a smell made up of Turkish coffee and ambergris and dried roses.

His mind wandered away to the question of what May's drawing-room would look like. He knew that Mr. Welland, who was behaving "very handsomely," already had his eye on a newly built house in East Thirty-ninth Street. The neighbourhood was thought remote, and the house was built in a ghastly greenish-yellow stone that the younger architects were beginning to employ as a protest against the brownstone of which the uniform hue coated New York like a cold chocolate sauce; but the plumbing was perfect. Archer would have liked to travel, to put off the housing question; but, though the Wellands approved of an extended European honeymoon (perhaps even a winter in Egypt), they were firm as to the need of a house for the returning couple. The young man felt that his fate was sealed: for the rest of his life he would go up every evening between the cast-iron railings of that greenish-yellow doorstep, and pass through a Pompeian vestibule into a hall with a wainscoting of varnished yellow wood. But beyond that his imagination could not travel. He knew the drawing-room above had a bay window, but he could not fancy how May would deal with it. She submitted cheerfully to the purple satin and yellow tuftings of the Welland drawing-room, to its sham Buhl tables and gilt vitrines full of modern

Saxe. He saw no reason to suppose that she would want anything different in her own house; and his only comfort was to reflect that she would probably let him arrange his library as he pleased—which would be, of course, with "sincere" Eastlake furniture, and the plain new book-cases without glass doors.

The round-bosomed maid came in, drew the curtains, pushed back a log, and said consolingly: *"Verrà—verrà."* When she had gone Archer stood up and began to wander about. Should he wait any longer? His position was becoming rather foolish. Perhaps he had misunderstood Madame Olenska—perhaps she had not invited him after all.

Down the cobblestones of the quiet street came the ring of a stepper's hoofs; they stopped before the house, and he caught the opening of a carriage door. Parting the curtains he looked out into the early dusk. A street-lamp faced him, and in its light he saw Julius Beaufort's compact English brougham, drawn by a big roan, and the banker descending from it, and helping out Madame Olenska.

Beaufort stood, hat in hand, saying something which his companion seemed to negative; then they shook hands, and he jumped into his carriage while she mounted the steps.

When she entered the room she showed no surprise at seeing Archer there; surprise seemed the emotion that she was least addicted to.

"How do you like my funny house?" she asked. "To me it's like heaven."

As she spoke she untied her little velvet bonnet and tossing it away with her long cloak stood looking at him with meditative eyes.

"You've arranged it delightfully," he rejoined, alive to

the flatness of the words, but imprisoned in the conventional by his consuming desire to be simple and striking.

"Oh, it's a poor little place. My relations despise it. But at any rate it's less gloomy than the van der Luydens'."

The words gave him an electric shock, for few were the rebellious spirits who would have dared to call the stately home of the van der Luydens gloomy. Those privileged to enter it shivered there, and spoke of it as "handsome." But suddenly he was glad that she had given voice to the general shiver.

"It's delicious—what you've done here," he repeated.

"I like the little house," she admitted; "but I suppose what I like is the blessedness of its being here, in my own country and my own town; and then, of being alone in it." She spoke so low that he hardly heard the last phrase; but in his awkwardness he took it up.

"You like so much to be alone?"

"Yes; as long as my friends keep me from feeling lonely." She sat down near the fire, said: "Nastasia will bring the tea presently," and signed to him to return to his armchair, adding: "I see you've already chosen your corner."

Leaning back, she folded her arms under her head, and looked at the fire under drooping lids.

"This is the hour I like best—don't you?"

A proper sense of his dignity caused him to answer: "I was afraid you'd forgotten the hour. Beaufort must have been very engrossing."

She looked amused. "Why—have you waited long? Mr. Beaufort took me to see a number of houses—since it seems I'm not to be allowed to stay in this one." She appeared to dismiss both Beaufort and himself from her mind, and went on: "I've never been in a city where

there seems to be such a feeling against living in *des
quartiers excentriques*. What does it matter where one
lives? I'm told this street is respectable."

"It's not fashionable."

"Fashionable! Do you all think so much of that?
Why not make one's own fashions? But I suppose I've
lived too independently; at any rate, I want to do what
you all do—I want to feel cared for and safe."

He was touched, as he had been the evening before
when she spoke of her need of guidançe.

"That's what your friends want you to feel. New
York's an awfully safe place," he added with a flash of
sarcasm.

"Yes, isn't it? One feels that," she cried, missing the
mockery. "Being here is like—like—being taken on a
holiday when one has been a good little girl and done all
one's lessons."

The analogy was well meant, but did not altogether
please him. He did not mind being flippant about New
York, but disliked to hear any one else take the same
tone. He wondered if she did not begin to see what a
powerful engine it was, and how nearly it had crushed
her. The Lovell Mingotts' dinner, patched up *in extremis*
out of all sorts of social odds and ends, ought to have
taught her the narrowness of her escape; but either she
had been all along unaware of having skirted disaster,
or else she had lost sight of it in the triumph of the
van der Luyden evening. Archer inclined to the former
theory; he fancied that her New York was still completely undifferentiated, and the conjecture nettled him.

"Last night," he said, "New York laid itself out for
you. The van der Luydens do nothing by halves."

"No: how kind they are! It was such a nice party.
Every one seems to have such an esteem for them."

The terms were hardly adequate; she might have spoken in that way of a tea-party at the dear old Miss Lannings'.

"The van der Luydens," said Archer, feeling himself pompous as he spoke, "are the most powerful influence in New York society. Unfortunately—owing to her health—they receive very seldom."

She unclasped her hands from behind her head, and looked at him meditatively.

"Isn't that perhaps the reason?"

"The reason—?"

"For their great influence; that they make themselves so rare."

He coloured a little, stared at her—and suddenly felt the penetration of the remark. At a stroke she had pricked the van der Luydens and they collapsed. He laughed, and sacrificed them.

Nastasia brought the tea, with handleless Japanese cups and little covered dishes, placing the tray on a low table.

"But you'll explain these things to me—you'll tell me all I ought to know," Madame Olenska continued, leaning forward to hand him his cup.

"It's you who are telling me; opening my eyes to things I'd looked at so long that I'd ceased to see them."

She detached a small gold cigarette-case from one of her bracelets, held it out to him, and took a cigarette herself. On the chimney were long spills for lighting them.

"Ah, then we can both help each other. But I want help so much more. You must tell me just what to do."

It was on the tip of his tongue to reply: "Don't be seen driving about the streets with Beaufort—" but he was being too deeply drawn into the atmosphere of the

room, which was her atmosphere, and to give advice of
that sort would have been like telling some one who was
bargaining for attar-of-roses in Samarkand that one
should always be provided with arctics for a New York
winter. New York seemed much farther off than Samarkand, and if they were indeed to help each other she was
rendering what might prove the first of their mutual
services by making him look at his native city objectively.
Viewed thus, as through the wrong end of a telescope,
it looked disconcertingly small and distant; but then from
Samarkand it would.

A flame darted from the logs and she bent over the
fire, stretching her thin hands so close to it that a faint
halo shone about the oval nails. The light touched to
russet the rings of dark hair escaping from her braids,
and made her pale face paler.

"There are plenty of people to tell you what to do,"
Archer rejoined, obscurely envious of them.

"Oh—all my aunts? And my dear old Granny?" She
considered the idea impartially. "They're all a little
vexed with me for setting up for myself—poor Granny
especially. She wanted to keep me with her; but I had
to be free—" He was impressed by this light way of
speaking of the formidable Catherine, and moved by the
thought of what must have given Madame Olenska this
thirst for even the loneliest kind of freedom. But the
idea of Beaufort gnawed him.

"I think I understand how you feel," he said. "Still,
your family can advise you; explain differences; show
you the way."

She lifted her thin black eyebrows. "Is New York
such a labyrinth? I thought it so straight up and down—
like Fifth Avenue. And with all the cross streets numbered!" She seemed to guess his faint disapproval of

this, and added, with the rare smile that enchanted her whole face: "If you knew how I like it for just *that*— the straight-up-and-downness, and the big honest labels on everything!"

He saw his chance. "Everything may be labelled—but everybody is not."

"Perhaps. I may simplify too much—but you'll warn me if I do." She turned from the fire to look at him. "There are only two people here who make me feel as if they understood what I mean and could explain things to me: you and Mr. Beaufort."

Archer winced at the joining of the names, and then, with a quick readjustment, understood, sympathised and pitied. So close to the powers of evil she must have lived that she still breathed more freely in their air. But since she felt that he understood her also, his business would be to make her see Beaufort as he really was, with all he represented—and abhor it.

He answered gently: "I understand. But just at first don't let go of your old friends' hands: I mean the older women, your Granny Mingott, Mrs. Welland, Mrs. van der Luyden. They like and admire you—they want to help you."

She shook her head and sighed. "Oh, I know—I know! But on condition that they don't hear anything unpleasant. Aunt Welland put it in those very words when I tried. . . . Does no one want to know the truth here, Mr. Archer? The real loneliness is living among all these kind people who only ask one to pretend!" She lifted her hands to her face, and he saw her thin shoulders shaken by a sob.

"Madame Olenska!—Oh, don't, Ellen," he cried, starting up and bending over her. He drew down one of her hands, clasping and chafing it like a child's while he murmured reassuring words; but in a moment she freed herself, and looked up at him with wet lashes.

"Does no one cry here, either? I suppose there's no need to, in heaven," she said, straightening her loosened braids with a laugh, and bending over the tea-kettle. It was burnt into his consciousness that he had called her "Ellen"—called her so twice; and that she had not noticed it. Far down the inverted telescope he saw the faint white figure of May Welland—in New York.

Suddenly Nastasia put her head in to say something in her rich Italian.

Madame Olenska, again with a hand at her hair, uttered an exclamation of assent—a flashing *"Già—già"* —and the Duke of St. Austrey entered, piloting a tremendous black-wigged and red-plumed lady in overflowing furs.

"My dear Countess, I've brought an old friend of mine to see you—Mrs. Struthers. She wasn't asked to the party last night, and she wants to know you."

The Duke beamed on the group, and Madame Olenska advanced with a murmur of welcome toward the queer couple. She seemed to have no idea how oddly matched they were, nor what a liberty the Duke had taken in bringing his companion—and to do him justice, as Archer perceived, the Duke seemed as unaware of it himself.

"Of course I want to know you, my dear," cried Mrs. Struthers in a round rolling voice that matched her bold feathers and her brazen wig. "I want to know everybody who's young and interesting and charming. And the Duke tells me you like music—didn't you, Duke? You're a pianist yourself, I believe? Well, do you want to hear Joachim play tomorrow evening at my house? You know I've something going on every Sunday evening —it's the day when New York doesn't know what to do with itself, and so I say to it: 'Come and be amused.' And the Duke thought you'd be tempted by Joachim. You'll find a number of your friends."

Madame Olenska's face grew brilliant with pleasure. "How kind! How good of the Duke to think of me!" She pushed a chair up to the tea-table and Mrs. Struthers sank into it delectably. "Of course I shall be too happy to come."

"That's all right, my dear. And bring your young gentleman with you." Mrs. Struthers extended a hail-fellow hand to Archer. "I can't put a name to you— but I'm sure I've met you—I've met everybody, here, or in Paris or London. Aren't you in diplomacy? All the diplomatists come to me. You like music too? Duke, you must be sure to bring him."

The Duke said "Rather" from the depths of his beard, and Archer withdrew with a stiffly circular bow that made him feel as full of spine as a self-conscious school-boy among careless and unnoticing elders.

He was not sorry for the *dénouement* of his visit: he only wished it had come sooner, and spared him a certain waste of emotion. As he went out into the wintry night, New York again became vast and imminent, and May Welland the loveliest woman in it. He turned into his florist's to send her the daily box of lilies-of-the-valley which, to his confusion, he found he had forgotten that morning.

As he wrote a word on his card and waited for an envelope he glanced about the embowered shop, and his eye lit on a cluster of yellow roses. He had never seen any as sun-golden before, and his first impulse was to send them to May instead of the lilies. But they did not look like her—there was something too rich, too strong, in their fiery beauty. In a sudden revulsion of mood, and almost without knowing what he did, he signed to the florist to lay the roses in another long box, and slipped his card into a second envelope, on which he wrote the name of the Countess Olenska; then, just as he was turning away, he drew the card out again, and left the empty envelope on the box.

"They'll go at once?" he enquired, pointing to the roses. The florist assured him that they would.

X

THE next day he persuaded May to escape for a
walk in the Park after luncheon. As was the custom in old-fashioned Episcopalian New York, she usually
accompanied her parents to church on Sunday after-
noons; but Mrs. Welland condoned her truancy, having
that very morning won her over to the necessity of a
long engagement, with time to prepare a hand-embroidered trousseau containing the proper number of dozens.

The day was delectable. The bare vaulting of trees
along the Mall was ceiled with lapis lazuli, and arched
above snow that shone like splintered crystals. It was
the weather to call out May's radiance, and she burned
like a young maple in the frost. Archer was proud of
the glances turned on her, and the simple joy of possessorship cleared away his underlying perplexities.

"It's so delicious—waking every morning to smell
lilies-of-the-valley in one's room!" she said.

"Yesterday they came late. I hadn't time in the
morning—"

"But your remembering each day to send them makes
me love them so much more than if you'd given a standing order, and they came every morning on the minute,
like one's music-teacher—as I know Gertrude Lefferts's
did, for instance, when she and Lawrence were engaged."

"Ah—they would!" laughed Archer, amused at her
keenness. He looked sideways at her fruit-like cheek
and felt rich and secure enough to add: "When I sent

your lilies yesterday afternoon I saw some rather gorgeous yellow roses and packed them off to Madame Olenska. Was that right?"

"How dear of you! Anything of that kind delights her. It's odd she didn't mention it: she lunched with us today, and spoke of Mr. Beaufort's having sent her wonderful orchids, and cousin Henry van der Luyden a whole hamper of carnations from Skuytercliff. She seems so surprised to receive flowers. Don't people send them in Europe? She thinks it such a pretty custom."

"Oh, well, no wonder mine were overshadowed by Beaufort's," said Archer irritably. Then he remembered that he had not put a card with the roses, and was vexed at having spoken of them. He wanted to say: "I called on your cousin yesterday," but hesitated. If Madame Olenska had not spoken of his visit it might seem awkward that he should. Yet not to do so gave the affair an air of mystery that he disliked. To shake off the question he began to talk of their own plans, their future, and Mrs. Welland's insistence on a long engagement.

"If you call it long! Isabel Chivers and Reggie were engaged for two years: Grace and Thorley for nearly a year and a half. Why aren't we very well off as we are?"

It was the traditional maidenly interrogation, and he felt ashamed of himself for finding it singularly childish. No doubt she simply echoed what was said for her; but she was nearing her twenty-second birthday, and he wondered at what age "nice" women began to speak for themselves.

"Never, if we won't let them, I suppose," he mused, and recalled his mad outburst to Mr. Sillerton Jackson: "Women ought to be as free as we are—"

It would presently be his task to take the bandage from

this young woman's eyes, and bid her look forth on the world. But how many generations of the women who had gone to her making had descended bandaged to the family vault? He shivered a little, remembering some of the new ideas in his scientific books, and the much-cited instance of the Kentucky cave-fish, which had ceased to develop eyes because they had no use for them. What if, when he had bidden May Welland to open hers, they could only look out blankly at blankness?

"We might be much better off. We might be altogether together—we might travel."

Her face lit up. "That would be lovely," she owned: she would love to travel. But her mother would not understand their wanting to do things so differently.

"As if the mere 'differently' didn't account for it!" the wooer insisted.

"Newland! You're so original!" she exulted.

His heart sank, for he saw that he was saying all the things that young men in the same situation were expected to say, and that she was making the answers that instinct and tradition taught her to make—even to the point of calling him original.

"Original! We're all as like each other as those dolls cut out of the same folded paper. We're like patterns stencilled on a wall. Can't you and I strike out for ourselves, May?"

He had stopped and faced her in the excitement of their discussion, and her eyes rested on him with a bright unclouded admiration.

"Mercy—shall we elope?" she laughed.

"If you would—"

"You *do* love me, Newland! I'm so happy."

"But then—why not be happier?"

"We can't behave like people in novels, though, can we?"

"Why not—why not—why not?"

She looked a little bored by his insistence. She knew very well that they couldn't, but it was troublesome to have to produce a reason. "I'm not clever enough to argue with you. But that kind of thing is rather—vulgar, isn't it?" she suggested, relieved to have hit on a word that would assuredly extinguish the whole subject.

"Are you so much afraid, then, of being vulgar?"

She was evidently staggered by this. "Of course I should hate it—so would you," she rejoined, a trifle irritably.

He stood silent, beating his stick nervously against his boot-top; and feeling that she had indeed found the right way of closing the discussion, she went on light-heartedly: "Oh, did I tell you that I showed Ellen my ring? She thinks it the most beautiful setting she ever saw. There's nothing like it in the rue de la Paix, she said. I do love you, Newland, for being so artistic!"

The next afternoon, as Archer, before dinner, sat smoking sullenly in his study, Janey wandered in on him. He had failed to stop at his club on the way up from the office where he exercised the profession of the law in the leisurely manner common to well-to-do New Yorkers of his class. He was out of spirits and slightly out of temper, and a haunting horror of doing the same thing every day at the same hour besieged his brain.

"Sameness—sameness!" he muttered, the word running through his head like a persecuting tune as he saw the familiar tall-hatted figures lounging behind the plate-glass; and because he usually dropped in at the club at that hour he had gone home instead. He knew not only what they were likely to be talking about, but the part each one would take in the discussion. The Duke of course would be their principal theme; though the appearance in Fifth Avenue of a golden-haired lady in a small canary-coloured brougham with a pair of black cobs (for which Beaufort was generally thought responsible) would also doubtless be thoroughly gone into. Such "women" (as they were called) were few in New York, those driving their own carriages still fewer, and the appearance of Miss Fanny Ring in Fifth Avenue at the fashionable hour had profoundly agitated society. Only the day before, her carriage had passed Mrs. Lovell Mingott's, and the latter had instantly rung the little bell at her elbow and ordered the coachman to drive her home. "What if it had happened to Mrs. van der Luyden?" people asked each other with a shudder. Archer could hear Lawrence Lefferts, at that very hour, holding forth on the disintegration of society.

He raised his head irritably when his sister Janey entered, and then quickly bent over his book (Swinburne's "Chastelard"—just out) as if he had not seen her. She glanced at the writing-table heaped with books, opened a volume of the "Contes Drôlatiques," made a wry face over the archaic French, and sighed: "What learned things you read!"

"Well—?" he asked, as she hovered Cassandra-like before him.

"Mother's very angry."

"Angry? With whom? About what?"

"Miss Sophy Jackson has just been here. She brought word that her brother would come in after dinner: she couldn't say very much, because he forbade her to: he wishes to give all the details himself. He's with cousin Louisa van der Luyden now."

"For heaven's sake, my dear girl, try a fresh start. It would take an omniscient Deity to know what you're talking about."

"It's not a time to be profane, Newland. . . . Mother feels badly enough about your not going to church . . ."

With a groan he plunged back into his book.

"Newland! Do listen. Your friend Madame Olenska was at Mrs. Lemuel Struthers's party last night: she went there with the Duke and Mr. Beaufort."

At the last clause of this announcement a senseless anger swelled the young man's breast. To smother it he laughed. "Well, what of it? I knew she meant to."

Janey paled and her eyes began to project. "You knew she meant to—and you didn't try to stop her? To warn her?"

"Stop her? Warn her?" He laughed again. "I'm not engaged to be married to the Countess Olenska!" The words had a fantastic sound in his own ears.

"You're marrying into her family."

"Oh, family—family!" he jeered.

"Newland—don't you care about Family?"

"Not a brass farthing."

"Nor about what cousin Louisa van der Luyden will think?"

"Not the half of one—if she thinks such old maid's rubbish."

"Mother is not an old maid," said his virgin sister with pinched lips.

He felt like shouting back: "Yes, she is, and so are the van der Luydens, and so we all are, when it comes to being so much as brushed by the wing-tip of Reality." But he saw her long gentle face puckering into tears, and felt ashamed of the useless pain he was inflicting.

"Hang Countess Olenska! Don't be a goose, Janey—I'm not her keeper."

"No; but you *did* ask the Wellands to announce your engagement sooner so that we might all back her up; and if it hadn't been for that cousin Louisa would never have invited her to the dinner for the Duke."

"Well—what harm was there in inviting her? She was the best-looking woman in the room; she made the dinner a little less funereal than the usual van der Luyden banquet."

"You know cousin Henry asked her to please you: he persuaded cousin Louisa. And now they're so upset that they're going back to Skuytercliff tomorrow. I think, Newland, you'd better come down. You don't seem to understand how mother feels."

In the drawing-room Newland found his mother. She raised a troubled brow from her needlework to ask: "Has Janey told you?"

"Yes." He tried to keep his tone as measured as her own. "But I can't take it very seriously."

"Not the fact of having offended cousin Louisa and cousin Henry?"

"The fact that they can be offended by such a trifle as Countess Olenska's going to the house of a woman they consider common."

"*Consider—!*"

"Well, who is; but who has good music, and amuses people on Sunday evenings, when the whole of New York is dying of inanition."

"Good music? All I know is, there was a woman who got up on a table and sang the things they sing at the places you go to in Paris. There was smoking and champagne."

"Well—that kind of thing happens in other places, and the world still goes on."

"I don't suppose, dear, you're really defending the French Sunday?"

"I've heard you often enough, mother, grumble at the English Sunday when we've been in London."

"New York is neither Paris nor London."

"Oh, no, it's not!" her son groaned.

"You mean, I suppose, that society here is not as brilliant? You're right, I daresay; but we belong here, and people should respect our ways when they come among us. Ellen Olenska especially: she came back to get away from the kind of life people lead in brilliant societies."

Newland made no answer, and after a moment his mother ventured: "I was going to put on my bonnet and ask you to take me to see cousin Louisa for a moment before dinner." He frowned, and she continued: "I thought you might explain to her what you've just said: that society abroad is different . . . that people are not as particular, and that Madame Olenska may not have realised how we feel about such things. It would be, you know, dear," she added with an innocent adroitness, "in Madame Olenska's interest if you did."

"Dearest mother, I really don't see how we're concerned in the matter. The Duke took Madame Olenska to Mrs. Struthers's—in fact he brought Mrs. Struthers to call on her. I was there when they came. If the van der Luydens want to quarrel with anybody, the real culprit is under their own roof."

"Quarrel? Newland, did you ever know of cousin Henry's quarrelling? Besides, the Duke's his guest; and a stranger too. Strangers don't discriminate: how should they? Countess Olenska is a New Yorker, and should have respected the feelings of New York."

"Well, then, if they must have a victim, you have my leave to throw Madame Olenska to them," cried her son, exasperated. "I don't see myself—or you either—offering ourselves up to expiate her crimes."

"Oh, of course you see only the Mingott side," his mother answered, in the sensitive tone that was her nearest approach to anger.

The sad butler drew back the drawing-room portières and announced: "Mr. Henry van der Luyden."

Mrs. Archer dropped her needle and pushed her chair back with an agitated hand.

"Another lamp," she cried to the retreating servant, while Janey bent over to straighten her mother's cap.

Mr. van der Luyden's figure loomed on the threshold, and Newland Archer went forward to greet his cousin.

"We were just talking about you, sir," he said.

Mr. van der Luyden seemed overwhelmed by the announcement. He drew off his glove to shake hands with the ladies, and smoothed his tall hat shyly, while Janey pushed an arm-chair forward, and Archer continued: "And the Countess Olenska."

Mrs. Archer paled.

"Ah—a charming woman. I have just been to see her," said Mr. van der Luyden, complacency restored to his brow. He sank into the chair, laid his hat and gloves on the floor beside him in the old-fashioned way, and went on: "She has a real gift for arranging flowers. I had sent her a few carnations from Skuytercliff, and I was astonished. Instead of massing them in big bunches as our head-gardener does, she had scattered them about loosely, here and there . . . I can't say how. The Duke had told me: he said: 'Go and see how cleverly she's arranged her drawing-room.' And she has. I should really like to take Louisa to see her, if the neighbourhood were not so—unpleasant."

A dead silence greeted this unusual flow of words from Mr. van der Luyden. Mrs. Archer drew her embroidery out of the basket into which she had nervously tumbled it, and Newland, leaning against the chimney-place and twisting a humming-bird-feather screen in his hand, saw Janey's gaping countenance lit up by the coming of the second lamp.

"The fact is," Mr. van der Luyden continued, stroking his long grey leg with a bloodless hand weighed down by the Patroon's great signet-ring, "the fact is, I dropped in to thank her for the very pretty note she wrote me about my flowers; and also—but this is between ourselves, of course—to give her a friendly warning about allowing the Duke to carry her off to parties with him. I don't know if you've heard—"

Mrs. Archer produced an indulgent smile. "Has the Duke been carrying her off to parties?"

"You know what these English grandees are. They're all alike. Louisa and I are very fond of our cousin—but it's hopeless to expect people who are accustomed to the European courts to trouble themselves about our little republican distinctions. The Duke goes where he's amused." Mr. van der Luyden paused, but no one spoke. "Yes—it seems he took her with him last night to Mrs. Lemuel Struthers's. Sillerton Jackson has just been to us with the foolish story, and Louisa was rather troubled. So I thought the shortest way was to go straight to Countess Olenska and explain—by the merest hint, you know—how we feel in New York about certain things. I felt I might, without indelicacy, because the evening she dined with us she rather suggested . . . rather let me see that she would be grateful for guidance. And she *was*."

Mr. van der Luyden looked about the room with what would have been self-satisfaction on features less purged of the vulgar passions. On his face it became a mild benevolence which Mrs. Archer's countenance dutifully reflected.

"How kind you both are, dear Henry—always! Newland will particularly appreciate what you have done because of dear May and his new relations."

She shot an admonitory glance at her son, who said: "Immensely, sir. But I was sure you'd like Madame Olenska."

Mr. van der Luyden looked at him with extreme gentleness. "I never ask to my house, my dear Newland," he said, "any one whom I do not like. And so I have just told Sillerton Jackson." With a glance at the clock he rose and added: "But Louisa will be waiting. We are dining early, to take the Duke to the Opera."

After the portières had solemnly closed behind their visitor a silence fell upon the Archer family.

"Gracious—how romantic!" at last broke explosively from Janey. No one knew exactly what inspired her elliptic comments, and her relations had long since given up trying to interpret them.

Mrs. Archer shook her head with a sigh. "Provided it all turns out for the best," she said, in the tone of one who knows how surely it will not. "Newland, you must stay and see Sillerton Jackson when he comes this evening: I really shan't know what to say to him."

"Poor mother! But he won't come—" her son laughed, stooping to kiss away her frown.

XI

SOME two weeks later, Newland Archer, sitting in abstracted idleness in his private compartment of the office of Letterblair, Lamson and Low, attorneys at law, was summoned by the head of the firm.

Old Mr. Letterblair, the accredited legal adviser of three generations of New York gentility, throned behind his mahogany desk in evident perplexity. As he stroked his close-clipped white whiskers and ran his hand through the rumpled grey locks above his jutting brows, his disrespectful junior partner thought how much he looked like the Family Physician annoyed with a patient whose symptoms refuse to be classified.

"My dear sir—" he always addressed Archer as "sir" —"I have sent for you to go into a little matter; a matter which, for the moment, I prefer not to mention either to Mr. Skipworth or Mr. Redwood." The gentlemen he spoke of were the other senior partners of the firm; for, as was always the case with legal associations of old standing in New York, all the partners named on the office letter-head were long since dead; and Mr. Letterblair, for example, was, professionally speaking, his own grandson.

He leaned back in his chair with a furrowed brow. "For family reasons—" he continued.

Archer looked up.

"The Mingott family," said Mr. Letterblair with an explanatory smile and bow. "Mrs. Manson Mingott sent for me yesterday. Her grand-daughter the Countess Olenska wishes to sue her husband for divorce. Certain papers have been placed in my hands." He paused and drummed on his desk. "In view of your prospective alliance with the family I should like to consult you— to consider the case with you—before taking any farther steps."

Archer felt the blood in his temples. He had seen the Countess Olenska only once since his visit to her, and then at the Opera, in the Mingott box. During this interval she had become a less vivid and importunate image, receding from his foreground as May Welland resumed her rightful place in it. He had not heard her divorce spoken of since Janey's first random allusion to it, and had dismissed the tale as unfounded gossip. Theoretically, the idea of divorce was almost as distasteful to him as to his mother; and he was annoyed that Mr. Letterblair (no doubt prompted by old Catherine Mingott) should be so evidently planning to draw him into the affair. After all, there were plenty of Mingott men for such jobs, and as yet he was not even a Mingott by marriage.

He waited for the senior partner to continue. Mr. Letterblair unlocked a drawer and drew out a packet. "If you will run your eye over these papers—"

Archer frowned. "I beg your pardon, sir; but just because of the prospective relationship, I should prefer your consulting Mr. Low or Mr. Lamson."

Mr. Letterblair looked surprised and slightly offended. It was unusual for a junior to reject such an opening.

He bowed. "I respect your scruple, sir; but in this case I believe true delicacy requires you to do as I ask. Indeed, the suggestion is not mine but Mrs. Manson

Mingott's and her son's. I have seen Lovell Mingott; and also Mr. Welland. They all named you."

Archer felt his temper rising. He had been somewhat languidly drifting with events for the last fortnight, and letting May's fair looks and radiant nature obliterate the rather importunate pressure of the Mingott claims. But this behest of old Mrs. Mingott's roused him to a sense of what the clan thought they had the right to exact from a prospective son-in-law; and he chafed at the rôle.

"Her uncles ought to deal with this," he said.

"They have. The matter has been gone into by the family. They are opposed to the Countess's idea; but she is firm, and insists on a legal opinion."

The young man was silent: he had not opened the packet in his hand.

"Does she want to marry again?"

"I believe it is suggested; but she denies it."

"Then—"

"Will you oblige me, Mr. Archer, by first looking through these papers? Afterward, when we have talked the case over, I will give you my opinion."

Archer withdrew reluctantly with the unwelcome documents. Since their last meeting he had half-unconsciously collaborated with events in ridding himself of the burden of Madame Olenska. His hour alone with her by the firelight had drawn them into a momentary intimacy on which the Duke of St. Austrey's intrusion with Mrs. Lemuel Struthers, and the Countess's joyous greeting of them, had rather providentially broken. Two days later Archer had assisted at the comedy of her reinstatement in the van der Luydens' favour, and had said to himself, with a touch of tartness, that a lady who knew how to thank all-powerful elderly gentlemen to such good purpose for a bunch of flowers did not need either the private consolations or the public championship of a young man of his small compass. To look at the matter in this light simplified his own case and surprisingly furbished up all the dim domestic virtues. He could not picture May Welland, in whatever conceivable emergency, hawking about her private difficulties and lavishing her confidences on strange men; and she had never seemed to him finer or fairer than in the week that followed. He had even yielded to her wish for a long engagement, since she had found the one disarming answer to his plea for haste.

"You know, when it comes to the point, your parents have always let you have your way ever since you were a little girl," he argued; and she had answered, with her clearest look: "Yes; and that that's what makes it so hard to refuse the very last thing they'll ever ask of me as a little girl."

That was the old New York note; that was the kind of answer he would like always to be sure of his wife's making. If one had habitually breathed the New York air there were times when anything less crystalline seemed stifling.

The papers he had retired to read did not tell him much in fact; but they plunged him into an atmosphere in which he choked and spluttered. They consisted mainly of an exchange of letters between Count Olenski's solicitors and a French legal firm to whom the Countess had applied for the settlement of her financial situation. There was also a short letter from the Count to his wife: after reading it, Newland Archer rose, jammed the papers back into their envelope, and reëntered Mr. Letterblair's office.

"Here are the letters, sir. If you wish I'll see Madame Olenska," he said in a constrained voice.

"Thank you—thank you, Mr. Archer. Come and dine with me tonight if you're free, and we'll go into the matter afterward: in case you wish to call on our client tomorrow."

Newland Archer walked straight home again that afternoon. It was a winter evening of transparent clearness, with an innocent young moon above the house-tops; and he wanted to fill his soul's lungs with the pure radiance, and not exchange a word with any one till he and Mr. Letterblair were closeted together after dinner. It was impossible to decide otherwise than he had done: he must see Madame Olenska himself rather than let her secrets be bared to other eyes. A great wave of compassion had swept away his indifference and impatience: she stood before him as an exposed and pitiful figure, to be saved at all costs from farther wounding herself in her mad plunges against fate.

He remembered what she had told him of Mrs. Welland's request to be spared whatever was "unpleasant" in her history, and winced at the thought that it was perhaps this attitude of mind which kept the New York air so pure. "Are we only Pharisees after all?" he wondered, puzzled by the effort to reconcile his instinctive disgust at human vileness with his equally instinctive pity for human frailty.

For the first time he perceived how elementary his own principles had always been. He passed for a young man who had not been afraid of risks, and he knew that his secret love-affair with poor silly Mrs. Thorley Rushworth had not been too secret to invest him with a becoming air of adventure. But Mrs. Rushworth was "that kind of woman"; foolish, vain, clandestine by nature, and far more attracted by the secrecy and peril of the affair than by such charms and qualities as he possessed. When the fact dawned on him it nearly broke his heart, but now it seemed the redeeming feature of the case. The affair, in short, had been of the kind that most of the young men of his age had been through, and emerged from with calm consciences and an undisturbed belief in the abysmal distinction between the women one loved and respected and those one enjoyed—and pitied. In this view they were sedulously abetted by their mothers, aunts and other elderly female relatives, who all shared Mrs. Archer's belief that when "such things happened" it was undoubtedly foolish of the man, but somehow always criminal of the woman. All the elderly ladies whom Archer knew regarded any woman who loved imprudently as necessarily unscrupulous and designing, and mere simple-minded man as powerless in her clutches. The only thing to do was to persuade him, as early as possible, to marry a nice girl, and then trust to her to look after him.

In the complicated old European communities, Archer began to guess, love-problems might be less simple and less easily classified. Rich and idle and ornamental societies must produce many more such situations; and there might even be one in which a woman naturally sensitive and aloof would yet, from the force of circumstances, from sheer defencelessness and loneliness, be drawn into a tie inexcusable by conventional standards.

On reaching home he wrote a line to the Countess Olenska, asking at what hour of the next day she could receive him, and despatched it by a messenger-boy, who returned presently with a word to the effect that she was going to Skuytercliff the next morning to stay over Sunday with the van der Luydens, but that he would find her alone that evening after dinner. The note was written on a rather untidy half-sheet, without date or address, but her hand was firm and free. He was amused at the idea of her week-ending in the stately solitude of Skuytercliff, but immediately afterward felt that there, of all places, she would most feel the chill of minds rigorously averted from the "unpleasant."

He was at Mr. Letterblair's punctually at seven, glad of the pretext for excusing himself soon after dinner. He had formed his own opinion from the papers entrusted to him, and did not especially want to go into the matter with his senior partner. Mr. Letterblair was a widower, and they dined alone, copiously and slowly, in a dark shabby room hung with yellowing prints of "The Death of Chatham" and "The Coronation of Napoleon." On the sideboard, between fluted Sheraton knifecases, stood a decanter of Haut Brion, and another of the old Lanning port (the gift of a client), which the wastrel Tom Lanning had sold off a year or two before his mysterious and discreditable death in San Francisco— an incident less publicly humiliating to the family than the sale of the cellar.

After a velvety oyster soup came shad and cucumbers, then a young broiled turkey with corn fritters, followed by a canvas-back with currant jelly and a celery mayonnaise. Mr. Letterblair, who lunched on a sandwich and tea, dined deliberately and deeply, and insisted on his guest's doing the same. Finally, when the closing rites had been accomplished, the cloth was removed, cigars were lit, and Mr. Letterblair, leaning back in his chair and pushing the port westward, said, spreading his back agreeably to the coal fire behind him: "The whole family are against a divorce. And I think rightly."

Archer instantly felt himself on the other side of the argument. "But why, sir? If there ever was a case—"

"Well—what's the use? *She's* here—he's there; the Atlantic's between them. She'll never get back a dollar more of her money than what he's voluntarily returned to her: their damned heathen marriage settlements take precious good care of that. As things go over there, Olenski's acted generously: he might have turned her out without a penny."

The young man knew this and was silent.

"I understand, though," Mr. Letterblair continued, "that she attaches no importance to the money. Therefore, as the family say, why not let well enough alone?"

Archer had gone to the house an hour earlier in full agreement with Mr. Letterblair's view; but put into words by this selfish, well-fed and supremely indifferent old man it suddenly became the Pharisaic voice of a society wholly absorbed in barricading itself against the unpleasant.

"I think that's for her to decide."

"H'm—have you considered the consequences if she decides for divorce?"

"You mean the threat in her husband's letter? What weight would that carry? It's no more than the vague charge of an angry blackguard."

"Yes; but it might make some unpleasant talk if he really defends the suit."

"Unpleasant—!" said Archer explosively.

Mr. Letterblair looked at him from under enquiring eyebrows, and the young man, aware of the uselessness of trying to explain what was in his mind, bowed acquiescently while his senior continued: "Divorce is always unpleasant."

"You agree with me?" Mr. Letterblair resumed, after a waiting silence.

"Naturally," said Archer.

"Well, then, I may count on you; the Mingotts may count on you; to use your influence against the idea?"

Archer hesitated. "I can't pledge myself till I've seen the Countess Olenska," he said at length.

"Mr. Archer, I don't understand you. Do you want to marry into a family with a scandalous divorce-suit hanging over it?"

"I don't think that has anything to do with the case."

Mr. Letterblair put down his glass of port and fixed on his young partner a cautious and apprehensive gaze.

Archer understood that he ran the risk of having his mandate withdrawn, and for some obscure reason he disliked the prospect. Now that the job had been thrust on him he did not propose to relinquish it; and, to guard against the possibility, he saw that he must reassure the unimaginative old man who was the legal conscience of the Mingotts.

"You may be sure, sir, that I shan't commit myself till I've reported to you; what I meant was that I'd rather not give an opinion till I've heard what Madame Olenska has to say."

Mr. Letterblair nodded approvingly at an excess of caution worthy of the best New York tradition, and the young man, glancing at his watch, pleaded an engagement and took leave.

XII

OLD-FASHIONED New York dined at seven, and the habit of after-dinner calls, though derided in Archer's set, still generally prevailed. As the young man strolled up Fifth Avenue from Waverley Place, the long thoroughfare was deserted but for a group of carriages standing before the Reggie Chiverses' (where there was a dinner for the Duke), and the occasional figure of an elderly gentleman in heavy overcoat and muffler ascending a brownstone doorstep and disappearing into a gas-lit hall. Thus, as Archer crossed Washington Square, he remarked that old Mr. du Lac was calling on his cousins the Dagonets, and turning down the corner of West Tenth Street he saw Mr. Skipworth, of his own firm, obviously bound on a visit to the Miss Lannings. A little farther up Fifth Avenue, Beaufort appeared on his doorstep, darkly projected against a blaze of light, descended to his private brougham, and rolled away to a mysterious and probably unmentionable destination. It was not an Opera night, and no one was giving a party, so that Beaufort's outing was undoubtedly of a clandestine nature. Archer connected it in his mind with a little house beyond Lexington Avenue in which beribboned window curtains and flower-boxes had recently appeared, and before whose newly painted door the canary-coloured brougham of Miss Fanny Ring was frequently seen to wait.

Beyond the small and slippery pyramid which composed Mrs. Archer's world lay the almost unmapped quarter inhabited by artists, musicians and "people who wrote." These scattered fragments of humanity had never shown any desire to be amalgamated with the social structure. In spite of odd ways they were said to be, for the most part, quite respectable; but they preferred to keep to themselves. Medora Manson, in her prosperous days, had inaugurated a "literary salon"; but it had soon died out owing to the reluctance of the literary to frequent it.

Others had made the same attempt, and there was a household of Blenkers—an intense and voluble mother, and three blowsy daughters who imitated her—where one met Edwin Booth and Patti and William Winter, and the new Shakespearian actor George Rignold, and some of the magazine editors and musical and literary critics.

Mrs. Archer and her group felt a certain timidity concerning these persons. They were odd, they were uncertain, they had things one didn't know about in the background of their lives and minds. Literature and art were deeply respected in the Archer set, and Mrs. Archer was always at pains to tell her children how much more agreeable and cultivated society had been when it included such figures as Washington Irving, Fitz-Greene Halleck and the poet of "The Culprit Fay." The most celebrated authors of that generation had been "gentlemen"; perhaps the unknown persons who succeeded them had gentlemanly sentiments, but their origin, their appearance, their hair, their intimacy with the stage and the Opera, made any old New York criterion inapplicable to them.

"When I was a girl," Mrs. Archer used to say, "we knew everybody between the Battery and Canal Street; and only the people one knew had carriages. It was perfectly easy to place any one then; now one can't tell, and I prefer not to try."

Only old Catherine Mingott, with her absence of moral prejudices and almost *parvenu* indifference to the subtler distinctions, might have bridged the abyss; but she had never opened a book or looked at a picture, and cared for music only because it reminded her of gala nights at the *Italiens*, in the days of her triumph at the Tuileries. Possibly Beaufort, who was her match in daring, would have succeeded in bringing about a fusion; but his grand house and silk-stockinged footmen were an obstacle to informal sociability. Moreover, he was as illiterate as old Mrs. Mingott, and considered "fellows who wrote" as the mere paid purveyors of rich men's pleasures; and no one rich enough to influence his opinion had ever questioned it.

Newland Archer had been aware of these things ever since he could remember, and had accepted them as part of the structure of his universe. He knew that there were societies where painters and poets and novelists and men of science, and even great actors, were as sought after as Dukes; he had often pictured to himself what it would have been to live in the intimacy of drawing-rooms dominated by the talk of Mérimée (whose "Lettres à une Inconnue" was one of his inseparables), of Thackeray, Browning or William Morris. But such things were inconceivable in New York, and unsettling to think of. Archer knew most of the "fellows who wrote," the musicians and the painters: he met them at the Century, or at the little musical and theatrical clubs that were beginning to come into existence. He enjoyed them there, and was bored with them at the Blenkers', where they were mingled with fervid and dowdy women who passed them about like captured curiosities; and even

after his most exciting talks with Ned Winsett he always
came away with the feeling that if his world was small,
so was theirs, and that the only way to enlarge either was
to reach a stage of manners where they would naturally
merge.

He was reminded of this by trying to picture the society
in which the Countess Olenska had lived and suffered,
and also—perhaps—tasted mysterious joys. He remembered with what amusement she had told him that her
grandmother Mingott and the Wellands objected to her
living in a "Bohemian" quarter given over to "people
who wrote." It was not the peril but the poverty that
her family disliked; but that shade escaped her, and she
supposed they considered literature compromising.

She herself had no fears of it, and the books scattered about her drawing-room (a part of the house in
which books were usually supposed to be "out of place"),
though chiefly works of fiction, had whetted Archer's
interest with such new names as those of Paul Bourget,
Huysmans, and the Goncourt brothers. Ruminating on
these things as he approached her door, he was once more
conscious of the curious way in which she reversed his
values, and of the need of thinking himself into conditions incredibly different from any that he knew if he
were to be of use in her present difficulty.

Nastasia opened the door, smiling mysteriously. On
the bench in the hall lay a sable-lined overcoat, a folded
opera hat of dull silk with a gold J. B. on the lining,
and a white silk muffler: there was no mistaking the fact
that these costly articles were the property of Julius
Beaufort.

Archer was angry: so angry that he came near scrib-
bling a word on his card and going away; then he

remembered that in writing to Madame Olenska he had been kept by excess of discretion from saying that he wished to see her privately. He had therefore no one but himself to blame if she had opened her doors to other visitors; and he entered the drawing-room with the dogged determination to make Beaufort feel himself in the way, and to outstay him.

The banker stood leaning against the mantelshelf, which was draped with an old embroidery held in place by brass candelabra containing church candles of yellowish wax. He had thrust his chest out, supporting his shoulders against the mantel and resting his weight on one large patent-leather foot. As Archer entered he was smiling and looking down on his hostess, who sat on a sofa placed at right angles to the chimney. A table banked with flowers formed a screen behind it, and against the orchids and azaleas which the young man recognised as tributes from the Beaufort hot-houses, Madame Olenska sat half-reclined, her head propped on a hand and her wide sleeve leaving the arm bare to the elbow.

It was usual for ladies who received in the evenings to wear what were called "simple dinner dresses": a close-fitting armour of whale-boned silk, slightly open in the neck, with lace ruffles filling in the crack, and tight sleeves with a flounce uncovering just enough wrist to show an Etruscan gold bracelet or a velvet band. But Madame Olenska, heedless of tradition, was attired in a long robe of red velvet bordered about the chin and down the front with glossy black fur. Archer remembered, on his last visit to Paris, seeing a portrait by the new painter, Carolus Duran, whose pictures were the sensation of the Salon, in which the lady wore one of these bold sheath-like robes with her chin nestling in fur. There was something perverse and provocative in the notion of fur worn in the evening in a heated drawing-room, and in the combination of a muffled throat and bare arms; but the effect was undeniably pleasing.

"Lord love us—three whole days at Skuytercliff!" Beaufort was saying in his loud sneering voice as Archer entered. "You'd better take all your furs, and a hot-water-bottle."

"Why? Is the house so cold?" she asked, holding out her left hand to Archer in a way mysteriously suggesting that she expected him to kiss it.

"No; but the missus is," said Beaufort, nodding carelessly to the young man.

"But I thought her so kind. She came herself to invite me. Granny says I must certainly go."

"Granny would, of course. And *I* say it's a shame you're going to miss the little oyster supper I'd planned for you at Delmonico's next Sunday, with Campanini and Scalchi and a lot of jolly people."

She looked doubtfully from the banker to Archer.

"Ah—that does tempt me! Except the other evening at Mrs. Struthers's I've not met a single artist since I've been here."

"What kind of artists? I know one or two painters, very good fellows, that I could bring to see you if you'd allow me," said Archer boldly.

"Painters? Are there painters in New York?" asked Beaufort, in a tone implying that there could be none since he did not buy their pictures; and Madame Olenska said to Archer, with her grave smile: "That would be charming. But I was really thinking of dramatic artists, singers, actors, musicians. My husband's house was always full of them."

She said the words "my husband" as if no sinister associations were connected with them, and in a tone that seemed almost to sigh over the lost delights of her married life. Archer looked at her perplexedly, wondering if it were lightness or dissimulation that enabled her to touch so easily on the past at the very moment when she was risking her reputation in order to break with it.

"I do think," she went on, addressing both men, "that the *imprévu* adds to one's enjoyment. It's perhaps a mistake to see the same people every day."

"It's confoundedly dull, anyhow; New York is dying of dulness," Beaufort grumbled. "And when I try to liven it up for you, you go back on me. Come—think better of it! Sunday is your last chance, for Campanini leaves next week for Baltimore and Philadelphia; and I've a private room, and a Steinway, and they'll sing all night for me."

"How delicious! May I think it over, and write to you tomorrow morning?"

She spoke amiably, yet with the least hint of dismissal in her voice. Beaufort evidently felt it, and being unused to dismissals, stood staring at her with an obstinate line between his eyes.

"Why not now?"

"It's too serious a question to decide at this late hour."

"Do you call it late?"

She returned his glance coolly. "Yes; because I have still to talk business with Mr. Archer for a little while."

"Ah," Beaufort snapped. There was no appeal from her tone, and with a slight shrug he recovered his composure, took her hand, which he kissed with a practised air, and calling out from the threshold: "I say, Newland, if you can persuade the Countess to stop in town of course you're included in the supper," left the room with his heavy important step.

For a moment Archer fancied that Mr. Letterblair must have told her of his coming; but the irrelevance of her next remark made him change his mind.

"You know painters, then? You live in their *milieu?*" she asked, her eyes full of interest.

"Oh, not exactly. I don't know that the arts have a *milieu* here, any of them; they're more like a very thinly settled outskirt."

"But you care for such things?"

"Immensely. When I'm in Paris or London I never miss an exhibition. I try to keep up."

She looked down at the tip of the little satin boot that peeped from her long draperies.

"I used to care immensely too: my life was full of such things. But now I want to try not to."

"You want to try not to?"

"Yes: I want to cast off all my old life, to become just like everybody else here."

Archer reddened. "You'll never be like everybody else," he said.

She raised her straight eyebrows a little. "Ah, don't say that. If you knew how I hate to be different!"

Her face had grown as sombre as a tragic mask. She leaned forward, clasping her knee in her thin hands, and looking away from him into remote dark distances.

"I want to get away from it all," she insisted.

He waited a moment and cleared his throat. "I know. Mr. Letterblair has told me."

"Ah?"

"That's the reason I've come. He asked me to—you see I'm in the firm."

She looked slightly surprised, and then her eyes

[106]

brightened. "You mean you can manage it for me? I can talk to you instead of Mr. Letterblair? Oh, that will be so much easier!"

Her tone touched him, and his confidence grew with his self-satisfaction. He perceived that she had spoken of business to Beaufort simply to get rid of him; and to have routed Beaufort was something of a triumph.

"I am here to talk about it," he repeated.

She sat silent, her head still propped by the arm that rested on the back of the sofa. Her face looked pale and extinguished, as if dimmed by the rich red of her dress. She struck Archer, of a sudden, as a pathetic and even pitiful figure.

"Now we're coming to hard facts," he thought, conscious in himself of the same instinctive recoil that he had so often criticised in his mother and her contemporaries. How little practice he had had in dealing with unusual situations! Their very vocabulary was unfamiliar to him, and seemed to belong to fiction and the stage. In face of what was coming he felt as awkward and embarrassed as a boy.

After a pause Madame Olenska broke out with unexpected vehemence: "I want to be free; I want to wipe out all the past."

"I understand that."

Her face warmed. "Then you'll help me?"

"First—" he hesitated—"perhaps I ought to know a little more."

She seemed surprised. "You know about my husband—my life with him?"

He made a sign of assent.

"Well—then—what more is there? In this country are such things tolerated? I'm a Protestant—our church does not forbid divorce in such cases."

"Certainly not."

They were both silent again, and Archer felt the spectre of Count Olenski's letter grimacing hideously between them. The letter filled only half a page, and was just what he had described it to be in speaking of it to Mr. Letterblair: the vague charge of an angry blackguard. But how much truth was behind it? Only Count Olenski's wife could tell.

"I've looked through the papers you gave to Mr. Letterblair," he said at length.

"Well—can there be anything more abominable?"

"No."

She changed her position slightly, screening her eyes with her lifted hand.

"Of course you know," Archer continued, "that if your husband chooses to fight the case—as he threatens to—"

"Yes—?"

"He can say things—things that might be unpl—might be disagreeable to you: say them publicly, so that they would get about, and harm you even if—"

"If—?"

"I mean: no matter how unfounded they were."

She paused for a long interval; so long that, not wishing to keep his eyes on her shaded face, he had time to imprint on his mind the exact shape of her other hand, the one on her knee, and every detail of the three rings on her fourth and fifth fingers; among which, he noticed, a wedding ring did not appear.

"What harm could such accusations, even if he made them publicly, do me here?"

It was on his lips to exclaim: "My poor child—far more harm than anywhere else!" Instead, he answered, in a voice that sounded in his ears like Mr. Letterblair's: "New York society is a very small world compared with the one you've lived in. And it's ruled, in spite of appearances, by a few people with—well, rather old-fashioned ideas."

She said nothing, and he continued: "Our ideas about marriage and divorce are particularly old-fashioned. Our legislation favours divorce — our social customs don't."

"Never?"

"Well—not if the woman, however injured, however irreproachable, has appearances in the least degree against her, has exposed herself by any unconventional action to—to offensive insinuations—"

She drooped her head a little lower, and he waited again, intensely hoping for a flash of indignation, or at least a brief cry of denial. None came.

A little travelling clock ticked purringly at her elbow, and a log broke in two and sent up a shower of sparks. The whole hushed and brooding room seemed to be waiting silently with Archer.

"Yes," she murmured at length, "that's what my family tell me."

He winced a little. "It's not unnatural—"

"*Our* family," she corrected herself; and Archer coloured. "For you'll be my cousin soon," she continued gently.

"I hope so."

"And you take their view?"

He stood up at this, wandered across the room, stared with void eyes at one of the pictures against the old red damask, and came back irresolutely to her side. How could he say: "Yes, if what your husband hints is true, or if you've no way of disproving it?"

"Sincerely—" she interjected, as he was about to speak.

He looked down into the fire. "Sincerely, then—what should you gain that would compensate for the possibility —the certainty—of a lot of beastly talk?"

"But my freedom—is that nothing?"

It flashed across him at that instant that the charge in the letter was true, and that she hoped to marry the partner of her guilt. How was he to tell her that, if she really cherished such a plan, the laws of the State were inexorably opposed to it? The mere suspicion that the thought was in her mind made him feel harshly and impatiently toward her. "But aren't you as free as air as it is?" he returned. "Who can touch you? Mr. Letterblair tells me the financial question has been settled—"

"Oh, yes," she said indifferently.

"Well, then: is it worth while to risk what may be infinitely disagreeable and painful? Think of the newspapers—their vileness! It's all stupid and narrow and unjust—but one can't make over society."

"No," she acquiesced; and her tone was so faint and desolate that he felt a sudden remorse for his own hard thoughts.

"The individual, in such cases, is nearly always sacrificed to what is supposed to be the collective interest: people cling to any convention that keeps the family together—protects the children, if there are any," he rambled on, pouring out all the stock phrases that rose to his lips in his intense desire to cover over the ugly reality which her silence seemed to have laid bare. Since she would not or could not say the one word that would have cleared the air, his wish was not to let her feel that he was trying to probe into her secret. Better keep on the surface, in the prudent old New York way, than risk uncovering a wound he could not heal.

"It's my business, you know," he went on, "to help you to see these things as the people who are fondest of you see them. The Mingotts, the Wellands, the van der Luydens, all your friends and relations: if I didn't show you honestly how they judge such questions, it wouldn't be fair of me, would it?" He spoke insistently, almost pleading with her in his eagerness to cover up that yawning silence.

She said slowly: "No; it wouldn't be fair."

The fire had crumbled down to greyness, and one of the lamps made a gurgling appeal for attention. Madame Olenska rose, wound it up and returned to the fire, but without resuming her seat.

Her remaining on her feet seemed to signify that there was nothing more for either of them to say, and Archer stood up also.

"Very well; I will do what you wish," she said abruptly. The blood rushed to his forehead; and, taken aback by the suddenness of her surrender, he caught her two hands awkwardly in his.

"I—I do want to help you," he said.

"You do help me. Good night, my cousin."

He bent and laid his lips on her hands, which were cold and lifeless. She drew them away, and he turned to the door, found his coat and hat under the faint gas-light of the hall, and plunged out into the winter night bursting with the belated eloquence of the inarticulate.

XIII

IT WAS a crowded night at Wallack's theatre.

The play was "The Shaughraun," with Dion Boucicault in the title rôle and Harry Montague and Ada Dyas as the lovers. The popularity of the admirable English company was at its height, and the Shaughraun always packed the house. In the galleries the enthusiasm was unreserved; in the stalls and boxes, people smiled a little at the hackneyed sentiments and clap-trap situations, and enjoyed the play as much as the galleries did.

There was one episode, in particular, that held the house from floor to ceiling. It was that in which Harry Montague, after a sad, almost monosyllabic scene of parting with Miss Dyas, bade her good-bye, and turned to go. The actress, who was standing near the mantel-piece and looking down into the fire, wore a gray cashmere dress without fashionable loopings or trimmings, moulded to her tall figure and flowing in long lines about her feet. Around her neck was a narrow black velvet ribbon with the ends falling down her back.

When her wooer turned from her she rested her arms against the mantel-shelf and bowed her face in her hands. On the threshold he paused to look at her; then he stole back, lifted one of the ends of velvet ribbon, kissed it, and left the room without her hearing him or changing her attitude. And on this silent parting the curtain fell.

It was always for the sake of that particular scene

that Newland Archer went to see "The Shaughraun."
He thought the adieux of Montague and Ada Dyas as
fine as anything he had ever seen Croisette and Bressant
do in Paris, or Madge Robertson and Kendall in London;
in its reticence, its dumb sorrow, it moved him more
than the most famous histrionic outpourings.

On the evening in question the little scene acquired an
added poignancy by reminding him—he could not have
said why—of his leave-taking from Madame Olenska
after their confidential talk a week or ten days earlier.

It would have been as difficult to discover any resemblance between the two situations as between the appearance of the persons concerned. Newland Archer could
not pretend to anything approaching the young English
actor's romantic good looks, and Miss Dyas was a tall
red-haired woman of monumental build whose pale and
pleasantly ugly face was utterly unlike Ellen Olenska's
vivid countenance. Nor were Archer and Madame
Olenska two lovers parting in heart-broken silence; they
were client and lawyer separating after a talk which had
given the lawyer the worst possible impression of the
client's case. Wherein, then, lay the resemblance that
made the young man's heart beat with a kind of restro-
spective excitement? It seemed to be in Madame Olenska's mysterious faculty of suggesting tragic and moving possibilities outside the daily run of experience.
She had hardly ever said a word to him to produce
this impression, but it was a part of her, either a projection of her mysterious and outlandish background or
of something inherently dramatic, passionate and unusual in herself. Archer had always been inclined to
think that chance and circumstance played a small part
in shaping people's lots compared with their innate tendency to have things happen to them. This tendency he

had felt from the first in Madame Olenska. The quiet, almost passive young woman struck him as exactly the kind of person to whom things were bound to happen, no matter how much she shrank from them and went out of her way to avoid them. The exciting fact was her having lived in an atmosphere so thick with drama that her own tendency to provoke it had apparently passed unperceived. It was precisely the odd absence of surprise in her that gave him the sense of her having been plucked out of a very maelstrom: the things she took for granted gave the measure of those she had rebelled against.

Archer had left her with the conviction that Count Olenski's accusation was not unfounded. The mysterious person who figured in his wife's past as "the secretary" had probably not been unrewarded for his share in her escape. The conditions from which she had fled were intolerable, past speaking of, past believing: she was young, she was frightened, she was desperate—what more natural than that she should be grateful to her rescuer? The pity was that her gratitude put her, in the law's eyes and the world's, on a par with her abominable husband. Archer had made her understand this, as he was bound to do; he had also made her understand that simple-hearted kindly New York, on whose larger charity she had apparently counted, was precisely the place where she could least hope for indulgence.

To have to make this fact plain to her—and to witness her resigned acceptance of it—had been intolerably painful to him. He felt himself drawn to her by obscure feelings of jealousy and pity, as if her dumbly-confessed error had put her at his mercy, humbling yet endearing her. He was glad it was to him she had revealed her secret, rather than to the cold scrutiny of Mr. Letterblair, or the embarrassed gaze of her family. He immediately took it upon himself to assure them both that she had given up her idea of seeking a divorce, basing her decision on the fact that she had understood the uselessness of the proceeding; and with infinite relief they had all turned their eyes from the "unpleasantness" she had spared them.

"I was sure Newland would manage it," Mrs. Welland had said proudly of her future son-in-law; and old Mrs. Mingott, who had summoned him for a confidential interview, had congratulated him on his cleverness, and added impatiently: "Silly goose! I told her myself what nonsense it was. Wanting to pass herself off as Ellen Mingott and an old maid, when she has the luck to be a married woman and a Countess!"

These incidents had made the memory of his last talk with Madame Olenska so vivid to the young man that as the curtain fell on the parting of the two actors his eyes filled with tears, and he stood up to leave the theatre.

In doing so, he turned to the side of the house behind him, and saw the lady of whom he was thinking seated in a box with the Beauforts, Lawrence Lefferts and one or two other men. He had not spoken with her alone since their evening together, and had tried to avoid being with her in company; but now their eyes met, and as Mrs. Beaufort recognised him at the same time, and made her languid little gesture of invitation, it was impossible not to go into the box.

Beaufort and Lefferts made way for him, and after a few words with Mrs. Beaufort, who always preferred to look beautiful and not have to talk, Archer seated himself behind Madame Olenska. There was no one else in the box but Mr. Sillerton Jackson, who was telling Mrs. Beaufort in a confidential undertone about Mrs. Lemuel Struthers's last Sunday reception (where some people reported that there had been dancing). Under cover of this circumstantial narrative, to which Mrs. Beaufort listened with her perfect smile, and her head at just the right angle to be seen in profile from the stalls, Madame Olenska turned and spoke in a low voice.

"Do you think," she asked, glancing toward the stage, "he will send her a bunch of yellow roses tomorrow morning?"

Archer reddened, and his heart gave a leap of surprise. He had called only twice on Madame Olenska, and each time he had sent her a box of yellow roses, and each time without a card. She had never before made any allusion to the flowers, and he supposed she had never thought of him as the sender. Now her sudden recognition of the gift, and her associating it with the tender leave-taking on the stage, filled him with an agitated pleasure.

"I was thinking of that too—I was going to leave the theatre in order to take the picture away with me," he said.

To his surprise her colour rose, reluctantly and duskily. She looked down at the mother-of-pearl opera-glass in her smoothly gloved hands, and said, after a pause: "What do you do while May is away?"

"I stick to my work," he answered, faintly annoyed by the question.

In obedience to a long-established habit, the Wellands had left the previous week for St. Augustine, where, out of regard for the supposed susceptibility of Mr. Welland's bronchial tubes, they always spent the latter part of the winter. Mr. Welland was a mild and silent man, with no opinions but with many habits. With these habits none might interfere; and one of them demanded that his wife and daughter should always go with him on his annual journey to the south. To preserve an unbroken domesticity was essential to his peace of mind; he would not have known where his hair-brushes were, or how to provide stamps for his letters, if Mrs. Welland had not been there to tell him.

As all the members of the family adored each other, and as Mr. Welland was the central object of their idolatry, it never occurred to his wife and May to let him go to St. Augustine alone; and his sons, who were both in the law, and could not leave New York during the winter, always joined him for Easter and travelled back with him.

It was impossible for Archer to discuss the necessity of May's accompanying her father. The reputation of the Mingotts' family physician was largely based on the attack of pneumonia which Mr. Welland had never had; and his insistence on St. Augustine was therefore inflexible. Originally, it had been intended that May's engagement should not be announced till her return from Florida, and the fact that it had been made known sooner could not be expected to alter Mr. Welland's plans. Archer would have liked to join the travellers and have a few weeks of sunshine and boating with his betrothed; but he too was bound by custom and conventions. Little arduous as his professional duties were, he would have been convicted of frivolity by the whole Mingott clan if he had suggested asking for a holiday in mid-winter; and he accepted May's departure with the resignation which he perceived would have to be one of the principal constituents of married life.

He was conscious that Madame Olenska was looking

at him under lowered lids. "I have done what you
wished—what you advised," she said abruptly.

"Ah—I'm glad," he returned, embarrassed by her
broaching the subject at such a moment.

"I understand—that you were right," she went on a
little breathlessly; "but sometimes life is difficult . . .
perplexing . . ."

"I know."

"And I wanted to tell you that I *do* feel you were
right; and that I'm grateful to you," she ended, lifting
her opera-glass quickly to her eyes as the door of the
box opened and Beaufort's resonant voice broke in on
them.

Archer stood up, and left the box and the theatre.

Only the day before he had received a letter from
May Welland in which, with characteristic candour, she
had asked him to "be kind to Ellen" in their absence.
"She likes you and admires you so much—and you know,
though she doesn't show it, she's still very lonely and
unhappy. I don't think Granny understands her, or
uncle Lovell Mingott either; they really think she's
much worldlier and fonder of society than she is. And
I can quite see that New York must seem dull to her,
though the family won't admit it. I think she's been
used to lots of things we haven't got; wonderful music,
and picture shows, and celebrities—artists and authors
and all the clever people you admire. Granny can't
understand her wanting anything but lots of dinners and
clothes—but I can see that you're almost the only person
in New York who can talk to her about what she really
cares for."

His wise May—how he had loved her for that letter!
But he had not meant to act on it; he was too busy, to
begin with, and he did not care, as an engaged man, to

play too conspicuously the part of Madame Olenska's champion. He had an idea that she knew how to take care of herself a good deal better than the ingenuous May imagined. She had Beaufort at her feet, Mr. van der Luyden hovering above her like a protecting deity, and any number of candidates (Lawrence Lefferts among them) waiting their opportunity in the middle distance. Yet he never saw her, or exchanged a word with her, without feeling that, after all, May's ingenuousness almost amounted to a gift of divination. Ellen Olenska was lonely and she was unhappy.

XIV

AS HE came out into the lobby Archer ran across his friend Ned Winsett, the only one among what Janey called his "clever people" with whom he cared to probe into things a little deeper than the average level of club and chop-house banter.

He had caught sight, across the house, of Winsett's shabby round-shouldered back, and had once noticed his eyes turned toward the Beaufort box. The two men shook hands, and Winsett proposed a bock at a little German restaurant around the corner. Archer, who was not in the mood for the kind of talk they were likely to get there, declined on the plea that he had work to do at home; and Winsett said: "Oh, well so have I for that matter, and I'll be the Industrious Apprentice too."

They strolled along together, and presently Winsett said: "Look here, what I'm really after is the name of the dark lady in that swell box of yours—with the Beauforts, wasn't she? The one your friend Lefferts seems so smitten by."

Archer, he could not have said why, was slightly annoyed. What the devil did Ned Winsett want with Ellen Olenska's name? And above all, why did he couple it with Lefferts's? It was unlike Winsett to manifest such curiosity; but after all, Archer remembered, he was a journalist.

"It's not for an interview, I hope?" he laughed.

"Well—not for the press; just for myself," Winsett

rejoined. "The fact is she's a neighbour of mine—queer quarter for such a beauty to settle in—and she's been awfully kind to my little boy, who fell down her area chasing his kitten, and gave himself a nasty cut. She rushed in bareheaded, carrying him in her arms, with his knee all beautifully bandaged, and was so sympathetic and beautiful that my wife was too dazzled to ask her name."

A pleasant glow dilated Archer's heart. There was nothing extraordinary in the tale : any woman would have done as much for a neighbour's child. But it was just like Ellen, he felt, to have rushed in bareheaded, carrying the boy in her arms, and to have dazzled poor Mrs. Winsett into forgetting to ask who she was.

"That is the Countess Olenska—a granddaughter of old Mrs. Mingott's."

"Whew—a Countess !" whistled Ned Winsett. "Well, I didn't know Countesses were so neighbourly. Mingotts ain't."

"They would be, if you'd let them."

"Ah, well—" It was their old interminable argument as to the obstinate unwillingness of the "clever people" to frequent the fashionable, and both men knew there that was no use in prolonging it.

"I wonder," Winsett broke off, "how a Countess happens to live in our slum?"

"Because she doesn't care a hang about where she lives—or about any of our little social sign-posts," said Archer, with a secret pride in his own picture of her.

"H'm—been in bigger places, I suppose," the other commented. "Well, here's my corner. So long."

He slouched off across Broadway, and Archer stood looking after him and musing on his last words.

Ned Winsett had those flashes of penetration; they

were the most interesting thing about him, and always made Archer wonder why they had allowed him to accept failure so stolidly at an age when most men are still struggling.

Archer had known that Winsett had a wife and child, but he had never seen them. The two men always met at the Century, or at some haunt of journalists and theatrical people, such as the restaurant where Winsett had proposed to go for a bock. He had given Archer to understand that his wife was an invalid; which might be true of the poor lady, or might merely mean that she was lacking in social gifts or in evening clothes, or in both. Winsett himself had a savage abhorrence of social observances: Archer, who dressed in the evening because he thought it cleaner and more comfortable to do so, and who had never stopped to consider that cleanliness and comfort are two of the costliest items in a modest budget, regarded Winsett's attitude as part of the boring "Bohemian" pose that always made fashionable people, who changed their clothes without talking about it, and were not forever harping on the number of servants one kept, seem to much simpler and less self-conscious than the others. Nevertheless, he was always stimulated by Winsett, and whenever he caught sight of the journalist's lean bearded face and melancholy eyes he would rout him out of his corner and carry him off for a long talk.

Winsett was not a journalist by choice. He was a pure man of letters, untimely born in a world that had no need of letters; but after publishing one volume of brief and exquisite literary appreciations, of which one hundred and twenty copies were sold, thirty given away, and the balance eventually destroyed by the publishers (as per contract) to make room for more marketable material, he had abandoned his real calling, and taken a sub-editorial job on a women's weekly, where fashion-plates and paper patterns alternated with New England love-stories and advertisements of temperance drinks.

On the subject of "Hearth-fires" (as the paper was called) he was inexhaustibly entertaining; but beneath his fun lurked the sterile bitterness of the still young man who has tried and given up. His conversation always made Archer take the measure of his own life, and feel how little it contained; but Winsett's, after all, contained still less, and though their common fund of intellectual interests and curiosities made their talks exhilarating, their exchange of views usually remained within the limits of a pensive dilettantism.

"The fact is, life isn't much a fit for either of us," Winsett had once said. "I'm down and out; nothing to be done about it. I've got only one ware to produce, and there's no market for it here, and won't be in my time. But you're free and you're well-off. Why don't *you* get into touch? There's only one way to do it: to go into politics."

Archer threw his head back and laughed. There one saw at a flash the unbridgeable difference between men like Winsett and the others—Archer's kind. Every one in polite circles knew that, in America, "a gentleman couldn't go into politics." But, since he could hardly put it in that way to Winsett, he answered evasively: "Look at the career of the honest man in American politics! They don't want us."

"Who's 'they'? Why don't you all get together and be 'they' yourselves?"

Archer's laugh lingered on his lips in a slightly condescending smile. It was useless to prolong the discussion: everybody knew the melancholy fate of the few gentlemen who had risked their clean linen in municipal or state politics in New York. The day was past when that sort of thing was possible: the country was in possession of the bosses and the emigrant, and decent people had to fall back on sport or culture.

"Culture! Yes—if we had it! But there are just a few little local patches, dying out here and there for lack of—well, hoeing and cross-fertilising: the last remnants of the old European tradition that your forebears brought with them. But you're in a pitiful little minority: you've got no centre, no competition, no audience. You're like the pictures on the walls of a deserted house: 'The Portrait of a Gentleman.' You'll never amount to anything, any of you, till you roll up your sleeves and get right down into the muck. That, or emigrate . . . God! If I could emigrate . . ."

Archer mentally shrugged his shoulders and turned the conversation back to books, where Winsett, if uncertain, was always interesting. Emigrate! As if a gentleman could abandon his own country! One could no more do that than one could roll up one's sleeves and go down into the muck. A gentleman simply stayed at home and abstained. But you couldn't make a man like Winsett see that; and that was why the New York of literary clubs and exotic restaurants, though a first shake made it seem more of a kaleidoscope, turned out, in the end, to be a smaller box, with a more monotonous pattern, than the assembled atoms of Fifth Avenue.

The next morning Archer scoured the town in vain for more yellow roses. In consequence of this search he arrived late at the office, perceived that his doing so made no difference whatever to any one, and was filled with sudden exasperation at the elaborate futility of his life. Why should he not be, at that moment, on the sands of St. Augustine with May Welland? No one was deceived by his pretense of professional activity. In old-fashioned legal firms like that of which Mr. Letterblair was the head, and which were mainly engaged in the management of large estates and "conservative" investments, there were always two or three young men, fairly well-off, and without professional ambition, who, for a certain number of hours of each day, sat at their desk accomplishing trivial tasks, or simply reading the newspapers. Though it was supposed to be proper for them to have an occupation, the crude fact of money-making was still regarded as derogatory, and the law, being a profession, was accounted a more gentlemanly pursuit than business. But none of these young men had much hope of really advancing in his profession, or any earnest desire to do so; and over many of them the green mould of the perfunctory was already perceptibly spreading.

It made Archer shiver to think that it might be spreading over him too. He had, to be sure, other tastes and interests; he spent his vacations in European travel, cultivated the "clever people" May spoke of, and generally tried to "keep up," as he had somewhat wistfully put it to Madame Olenska. But once he was married, what would become of this narrow margin of life in which his real experiences were lived? He had seen enough of other young men who had dreamed his dream, though perhaps less ardently, and who had gradually sunk into the placid and luxurious routine of their elders.

From the office he sent a note by messenger to Madame Olenska, asking if he might call that afternoon, and begging her to let him find a reply at his club; but at the club he found nothing, nor did he receive any

letter the following day. This unexpected silence mortified him beyond reason, and though the next morning he
saw a glorious cluster of yellow roses behind a florist's
window-pane, he left it there. It was only on the third
morning that he received a line by post from the Countess
Olenska. To his surprise it was dated from Skuytercliff,
whither the van der Luydens had promptly retreated
after putting the Duke on board his steamer.

"I ran away," the writer began abruptly (without the
usual preliminaries), "the day after I saw you at the
play, and these kind friends have taken me in. I wanted
to be quiet, and think things over. You were right in
telling me how kind they were; I feel myself so safe
here. I wish that you were with us." She ended with a
conventional "Yours sincerely," and without any allusion to the date of her return.

The tone of the note surprised the young man. What
was Madame Olenska running away from, and why did
she feel the need to be safe? His first thought was of
some dark menace from abroad; then he reflected that
he did not know her epistolary style, and that it might
run to picturesque exaggeration. Women always exaggerated; and moreover she was not wholly at her ease in
English, which she often spoke as if she were translating
from the French. "Je me suis évadée—" put in that way,
the opening sentence immediately suggested that she
might merely have wanted to escape from a boring round
of engagements; which was very likely true, for he
judged her to be capricious, and easily wearied of the
pleasure of the moment.

It amused him to think of the van der Luydens' having
carried her off to Skuytercliff on a second visit, and this
time for an indefinite period. The doors of Skuytercliff
were rarely and grudgingly opened to visitors, and a

chilly week-end was the most ever offered to the few thus privileged. But Archer had seen, on his last visit to Paris, the delicious play of Labiche, "Le Voyage de M. Perrichon," and he remembered M. Perrichon's dogged and undiscouraged attachment to the young man whom he had pulled out of the glacier. The van der Luydens had rescued Madame Olenska from a doom almost as icy; and though there were many other reasons for being attracted to her, Archer knew that beneath them all lay the gentle and obstinate determination to go on rescuing her.

He felt a distinct disappointment on learning that she was away; and almost immediately remembered that, only the day before, he had refused an invitation to spend the following Sunday with the Reggie Chiverses at their house on the Hudson, a few miles below Skuytercliff.

He had had his fill long ago of the noisy friendly parties at Highbank, with coasting, ice-boating, sleighing, long tramps in the snow, and a general flavour of mild flirting and milder practical jokes. He had just received a box of new books from his London bookseller, and had preferred the prospect of a quiet Sunday at home with his spoils. But he now went into the club writing-room, wrote a hurried telegram, and told the servant to send it immediately. He knew that Mrs. Reggie didn't object to her visitors' suddenly changing their minds, and that there was always a room to spare in her elastic house.

XV

NEWLAND ARCHER arrived at the Chiverses' on
Friday evening, and on Saturday went conscien-
tiously through all the rites appertaining to a week-end
at Highbank.

In the morning he had a spin in the ice-boat with his
hostess and a few of the hardier guests; in the afternoon he "went over the farm" with Reggie, and listened,
in the elaborately appointed stables, to long and impres-
sive disquisitions on the horse; after tea he talked in a
corner of the firelit hall with a young lady who had
professed herself broken-hearted when his engagement
was announced, but was now eager to tell him of her
own matrimonial hopes; and finally, about midnight, he
assisted in putting a gold-fish in one visitor's bed, dressed
up a burglar in the bath-room of a nervous aunt, and
saw in the small hours by joining in a pillow-fight that
ranged from the nurseries to the basement. But on
Sunday after luncheon he borrowed a cutter, and drove
over to Skuytercliff.

People had always been told that the house at Skuytercliff was an Italian villa. Those who had never been
to Italy believed it; so did some who had. The house
had been built by Mr. van der Luyden in his youth, on
his return from the "grand tour," and in anticipation
of his approaching marriage with Miss Louisa Dagonet.
It was a large square wooden structure, with tongued
and grooved walls painted pale green and white, a Corin-

thian portico, and fluted pilasters between the windows. From the high ground on which it stood a series of terraces bordered by balustrades and urns descended in the steel-engraving style to a small irregular lake with an asphalt edge overhung by rare weeping conifers. To the right and left, the famous weedless lawns studded with "specimen" trees (each of a different variety) rolled away to long ranges of grass crested with elaborate cast-iron ornaments; and below, in a hollow, lay the four-roomed stone house which the first Patroon had built on the land granted him in 1612.

Against the uniform sheet of snow and the greyish winter sky the Italian villa loomed up rather grimly; even in summer it kept its distance, and the boldest coleus bed had never ventured nearer than thirty feet from its awful front. Now, as Archer rang the bell, the long tinkle seemed to echo through a mausoleum; and the surprise of the butler who at length responded to the call was as great as though he had been summoned from his final sleep.

Happily Archer was of the family, and therefore, irregular though his arrival was, entitled to be informed that the Countess Olenska was out, having driven to afternoon service with Mrs. van der Luyden exactly three quarters of an hour earlier.

"Mr. van der Luyden," the butler continued, "is in, sir; but my impression is that he is either finishing his nap or else reading yesterday's Evening Post. I heard him say, sir, on his return from church this morning, that he intended to look through the Evening Post after luncheon; if you like, sir, I might go to the library door and listen—"

But Archer, thanking him, said that he would go and

[129]

meet the ladies; and the butler, obviously relieved, closed the door on him majestically.

A groom took the cutter to the stables, and Archer struck through the park to the high-road. The village of Skuytercliff was only a mile and a half away, but he knew that Mrs. van der Luyden never walked, and that he must keep to the road to meet the carriage. Presently, however, coming down a foot-path that crossed the highway, he caught sight of a slight figure in a red cloak, with a big dog running ahead. He hurried forward, and Madame Olenska stopped short with a smile of welcome.

"Ah, you've come!" she said, and drew her hand from her muff.

The red cloak made her look gay and vivid, like the Ellen Mingott of old days; and he laughed as he took her hand, and answered: "I came to see what you were running away from."

Her face clouded over, but she answered: "Ah, well—you will see, presently."

The answer puzzled him. "Why—do you mean that you've been overtaken?"

She shrugged her shoulders, with a little movement like Nastasia's, and rejoined in a lighter tone: "Shall we walk on? I'm so cold after the sermon. And what does it matter, now you're here to protect me?"

The blood rose to his temples and he caught a fold of her cloak. "Ellen—what is it? You must tell me."

"Oh, presently—let's run a race first: my feet are freezing to the ground," she cried; and gathering up the cloak she fled away across the snow, the dog leaping about her with challenging barks. For a moment Archer stood watching, his gaze delighted by the flash of the red meteor against the snow; then he started after her,

[130]

and they met, panting and laughing, at a wicket that led into the park.

She looked up at him and smiled. "I knew you'd come!"

"That shows you wanted me to," he returned, with a disproportionate joy in their nonsense. The white glitter of the trees filled the air with its own mysterious brightness, and as they walked on over the snow the ground seemed to sing under their feet.

"Where did you come from?" Madame Olenska asked.

He told her, and added: "It was because I got your note."

After a pause she said, with a just perceptible chill in her voice: "May asked you to take care of me."

"I didn't need any asking."

"You mean—I'm so evidently helpless and defenceless? What a poor thing you must all think me! But women here seem not—seem never to feel the need: any more than the blessed in heaven."

He lowered his voice to ask: "What sort of a need?"

"Ah, don't ask me! I don't speak your language," she retorted petulantly.

The answer smote him like a blow, and he stood still in the path, looking down at her.

"What did I come for, if I don't speak yours?"

"Oh, my friend—!" She laid her hand lightly on his arm, and he pleaded earnestly: "Ellen—why won't you tell me what's happened?"

She shrugged again. "Does anything ever happen in heaven?"

He was silent, and they walked on a few yards without exchanging a word. Finally she said: "I will tell you—but where, where, where? One can't be alone for a minute in that great seminary of a house, with all the doors wide open, and always a servant bringing tea, or a log for the fire, or the newspaper! Is there no-where in an American house where one may be by one's self? You're so shy, and yet you're so public. I always feel as if I were in the convent again—or on the stage, before a dreadfully polite audience that never applauds."

"Ah, you don't like us!" Archer exclaimed.

They were walking past the house of the old Patroon, with its squat walls and small square windows com-pactly grouped about a central chimney. The shutters stood wide, and through one of the newly-washed win-dows Archer caught the light of a fire.

"Why—the house is open!" he said.

She stood still. "No; only for today, at least. I wanted to see it, and Mr. van der Luyden had the fire lit and the windows opened, so that we might stop there on the way back from church this morning." She ran up the steps and tried the door. "It's still unlocked—what luck! Come in and we can have a quiet talk. Mrs. van der Luyden has driven over to see her old aunts at Rhinebeck and we shan't be missed at the house for another hour."

He followed her into the narrow passage. His spirits, which had dropped at her last words, rose with an irrational leap. The homely little house stood there, its panels and brasses shining in the firelight, as if magically created to receive them. A big bed of embers still gleamed in the kitchen chimney, under an iron pot hung from an ancient crane. Rush-bottomed arm-chairs faced each other across the tiled hearth, and rows of Delft plates stood on shelves against the walls. Archer stooped over and threw a log upon the embers.

Madame Olenska, dropping her cloak, sat down in one

of the chairs. Archer leaned against the chimney and looked at her.

"You're laughing now; but when you wrote me you were unhappy," he said.

"Yes." She paused. "But I can't feel unhappy when you're here."

"I sha'n't be here long," he rejoined, his lips stiffening with the effort to say just so much and no more.

"No; I know. But I'm improvident: I live in the moment when I'm happy."

The words stole through him like a temptation, and to close his senses to it he moved away from the hearth and stood gazing out at the black tree-boles against the snow. But it was as if she too had shifted her place, and he still saw her, between himself and the trees, drooping over the fire with her indolent smile. Archer's heart was beating insubordinately. What if it were from him that she had been running away, and if she had waited to tell him so till they were here alone together in this secret room.

"Ellen, if I'm really a help to you—if you really wanted me to come—tell me what's wrong, tell me what it is you're running away from," he insisted.

He spoke without shifting his position, without even turning to look at her: if the thing was to happen, it was to happen in this way, with the whole width of the room between them, and his eyes still fixed on the outer snow.

For a long moment she was silent; and in that moment Archer imagined her, almost heard her, stealing up behind him to throw her light arms about his neck. While he waited, soul and body throbbing with the miracle to come, his eyes mechanically received the image of a heavily-coated man with his fur collar turned up who was advancing along the path to the house. The man was Julius Beaufort.

"Ah—!" Archer cried, bursting into a laugh.

Madame Olenska had sprung up and moved to his side, slipping her hand into his; but after a glance through the window her face paled and she shrank back.

"So that was it?" Archer said derisively.

"I didn't know he was here," Madame Olenska murmured. Her hand still clung to Archer's; but he drew away from her, and walking out into the passage threw open the door of the house.

"Hallo, Beaufort—this way! Madame Olenska was expecting you," he said.

During his journey back to New York the next morning, Archer relived with a fatiguing vividness his last moments at Skuytercliff.

Beaufort, though clearly annoyed at finding him with Madame Olenska, had, as usual, carried off the situation high-handedly. His way of ignoring people whose presence inconvenienced him actually gave them, if they were sensitive to it, a feeling of invisibility, of non-existence. Archer, as the three strolled back through the park, was aware of this odd sense of disembodiment; and humbling as it was to his vanity it gave him the ghostly advantage of observing unobserved.

Beaufort had entered the little house with his usual easy assurance; but he could not smile away the vertical line between his eyes. It was fairly clear that Madame Olenska had not known that he was coming, though her words to Archer had hinted at the possibility; at any rate, she had evidently not told him where she was going when she left New York, and her unexplained departure had exasperated him. The ostensible reason of his ap-

THE AGE OF INNOCENCE

pearance was the discovery, the very night before, of a
"perfect little house," not in the market, which was really
just the thing for her, but would be snapped up instantly
if she didn't take it; and he was loud in mock-reproaches
for the dance she had led him in running away just as
he had found it.

"If only this new dodge for talking along a wire had
been a little bit nearer perfection I might have told you
all this from town, and been toasting my toes before the
club fire at this minute, instead of tramping after you
through the snow," he grumbled, disguising a real irritation under the pretence of it; and at this opening Madame
Olenska twisted the talk away to the fantastic possibility
that they might one day actually converse with each other
from street to street, or even—incredible dream!—from
one town to another. This struck from all three allusions
to Edgar Poe and Jules Verne, and such platitudes as
naturally rise to the lips of the most intelligent when they
are talking against time, and dealing with a new invention in which it would seem ingenuous to believe too
soon; and the question of the telephone carried them
safely back to the big house.

Mrs. van der Luyden had not yet returned; and Archer
took his leave and walked off to fetch the cutter, while
Beaufort followed the Countess Olenska indoors. It
was probable that, little as the van der Luydens encouraged unannounced visits, he could count on being asked
to dine, and sent back to the station to catch the nine
o'clock train; but more than that he would certainly not
get, for it would be inconceivable to his hosts that a
gentleman travelling without luggage should wish to
spend the night, and distasteful to them to propose it
to a person with whom they were on terms of such
limited cordiality as Beaufort.

Beaufort knew all this, and must have foreseen it; and his taking the long journey for so small a reward gave the measure of his impatience. He was undeniably in pursuit of the Countess Olenska; and Beaufort had only one object in view in his pursuit of pretty women. His dull and childless home had long since palled on him; and in addition to more permanent consolations he was always in quest of amorous adventures in his own set. This was the man from whom Madame Olenska was avowedly flying: the question was whether she had fled because his importunities displeased her, or because she did not wholly trust herself to resist them; unless, indeed, all her talk of flight had been a blind, and her departure no more than a manœuvre.

Archer did not really believe this. Little as he had actually seen of Madame Olenska, he was beginning to think that he could read her face, and if not her face, her voice; and both had betrayed annoyance, and even dismay, at Beaufort's sudden appearance. But, after all, if this were the case, was it not worse than if she had left New York for the express purpose of meeting him? If she had done that, she ceased to be an object of interest, she threw in her lot with the vulgarest of dissemblers: a woman engaged in a love affair with Beaufort "classed" herself irretrievably.

No, it was worse a thousand times if, judging Beaufort, and probably despising him, she was yet drawn to him by all that gave him an advantage over the other men about her: his habit of two continents and two societies, his familiar association with artists and actors and people generally in the world's eye, and his careless contempt for local prejudices. Beaufort was vulgar, he was uneducated, he was purse-proud; but the circumstances of his life, and a certain native shrewdness, made

[136]

him better worth talking to than many men, morally and socially his betters, whose horizon was bounded by the Battery and the Central Park. How should any one coming from a wider world not feel the difference and be attracted by it?

Madame Olenska, in a burst of irritation, had said to Archer that he and she did not talk the same language; and the young man knew that in some respects this was true. But Beaufort understood every turn of her dialect, and spoke it fluently: his view of life, his tone, his attitude, were merely a coarser reflection of those revealed in Count Olenski's letter. This might seem to be to his disadvantage with Count Olenski's wife; but Archer was too intelligent to think that a young woman like Ellen Olenska would necessarily recoil from everything that reminded her of her past. She might believe herself wholly in revolt against it; but what had charmed her in it would still charm her, even though it were against her will.

Thus, with a painful impartiality, did the young man make out the case for Beaufort, and for Beaufort's victim. A longing to enlighten her was strong in him; and there were moments when he imagined that all she asked was to be enlightened.

That evening he unpacked his books from London. The box was full of things he had been waiting for impatiently; a new volume of Herbert Spencer, another collection of Guy de Maupassant's incomparable tales, and a novel called "Middlemarch," as to which there had lately been interesting things said in the reviews. He had declined three dinner invitations in favour of this feast; but though he turned the pages with the sensuous joy of the book-lover, he did not know what he was reading, and one book after another dropped from his hand. Suddenly, among them, he lit on a small volume of verse which he had ordered because the name had attracted him: "The House of Life." He took it up, and found himself plunged in an atmosphere unlike any he had ever breathed in books; so warm, so rich, and yet so ineffably tender, that it gave new and haunting beauty to the most elementary of human passions. All through the night he pursued through those enchanted pages the vision of a woman who had the face of Ellen Olenska; but when he woke the next morning, and looked out at the brownstone houses across the street, and thought of his desk in Mr. Letterblair's office, and the family pew in Grace Church, his hour in the park of Skuytercliff became as far outside the pale of probability as the visions of the night.

"Mercy, how pale you look, Newland!" Janey commented over the coffee-cups at breakfast; and his mother added: "Newland, dear, I've noticed lately that you've been coughing; I do hope you're not letting yourself be overworked?" For it was the conviction of both ladies that, under the iron despotism of his senior partners, the young man's life was spent in the most exhausting professional labours—and he had never thought it necessary to undeceive them.

The next two or three days dragged by heavily. The taste of the usual was like cinders in his mouth, and there were moments when he felt as if he were being buried alive under his future. He heard nothing of the Countess Olenska, or of the perfect little house, and though he met Beaufort at the club they merely nodded at each other across the whist-tables. It was not till the fourth evening that he found a note awaiting him on his return home. "Come late tomorrow: I must explain to you. Ellen." These were the only words it contained.

[138]

The young man, who was dining out, thrust the note into his pocket, smiling a little at the Frenchness of the "to you." After dinner he went to a play; and it was not until his return home, after midnight, that he drew Madame Olenska's missive out again and re-read it slowly a number of times. There were several ways of answering it, and he gave considerable thought to each one during the watches of an agitated night. That on which, when morning came, he finally decided was to pitch some clothes into a portmanteau and jump on board a boat that was leaving that very afternoon for St. Augustine.

XVI

WHEN Archer walked down the sandy main street of St. Augustine to the house which had been pointed out to him as Mr. Welland's, and saw May Welland standing under a magnolia with the sun in her hair, he wondered why he had waited so long to come.

Here was truth, here was reality, here was the life that belonged to him; and he,, who fancied himself so scornful of arbitrary restraints, had been afraid to break away from his desk because of what people might think of his stealing a holiday!

Her first exclamation was: "Newland—has anything happened?" and it occurred to him that it would have been more "feminine" if she had instantly read in his eyes why he had come. But when he answered: "Yes— I found I had to see you," her happy blushes took the chill from her surprise, and he saw how easily he would be forgiven, and how soon even Mr. Letterblair's mild disapproval would be smiled away by a tolerant family.

Early as it was, the main street was no place for any but formal greetings, and Archer longed to be alone with May, and to pour out all his tenderness and his impatience. It still lacked an hour to the late Welland breakfast-time, and instead of asking him to come in she proposed that they should walk out to an old orange-garden beyond the town. She had just been for a row on the river, and the sun that netted the little waves with gold seemed to have caught her in its meshes. Across the warm brown of her cheek her blown hair glittered like silver wire; and her eyes too looked lighter, almost pale in their youthful limpidity. As she walked beside Archer with her long swinging gait her face wore the vacant serenity of a young marble athlete.

To Archer's strained nerves the vision was as soothing as the sight of the blue sky and the lazy river. They sat down on a bench under the orange-trees and he put his arm about her and kissed her. It was like drinking at a cold spring with the sun on it; but his pressure may have been more vehement than he had intended, for the blood rose to her face and she drew back as if he had startled her.

"What is it?" he asked, smiling; and she looked at him with surprise, and answered: "Nothing."

A slight embarrassment fell on them, and her hand slipped out of his. It was the only time that he had kissed her on the lips except for their fugitive embrace in the Beaufort conservatory, and he saw that she was disturbed, and shaken out of her cool boyish composure.

"Tell me what you do all day," he said, crossing his arms under his tilted-back head, and pushing his hat forward to screen the sun-dazzle. To let her talk about familiar and simple things was the easiest way of carrying on his own independent train of thought; and he sat listening to her simple chronicle of swimming, sailing and riding, varied by an occasional dance at the primitive inn when a man-of-war came in. A few pleasant people from Philadelphia and Baltimore were picknicking at the inn, and the Selfridge Merrys had come down for three weeks because Kate Merry had had bronchitis. They were planning to lay out a lawn tennis court on the sands; but no one but Kate and May had racquets, and most of the people had not even heard of the game.

All this kept her very busy, and she had not had time to do more than look at the little vellum book that Archer had sent her the week before (the "Sonnets from the Portuguese") ; but she was learning by heart "How they brought the Good News from Ghent to Aix," because it was one of the first things he had ever read to her; and it amused her to be able to tell him that Kate Merry had never even heard of a poet called Robert Browning.

Presently she started up, exclaiming that they would be late for breakfast; and they hurried back to the tumble-down house with its paintless porch and unpruned hedge of plumbago and pink geraniums where the Wellands were installed for the winter. Mr. Welland's sensitive domesticity shrank from the discomforts of the slovenly southern hotel, and at immense expense, and in face of almost insuperable difficulties, Mrs. Welland was obliged, year after year, to improvise an establishment partly made up of discontented New York servants and partly drawn from the local African supply.

"The doctors want my husband to feel that he is in his own home; otherwise he would be so wretched that the climate would not do him any good," she explained, winter after winter, to the sympathising Philadelphians and Baltimoreans; and Mr. Welland, beaming across a breakfast table miraculously supplied with the most varied delicacies, was presently saying to Archer: "You see, my dear fellow, we camp—we literally camp. I tell my wife and May that I want to teach them how to rough it."

Mr. and Mrs. Welland had been as much surprised as their daughter by the young man's sudden arrival; but it had occurred to him to explain that he had felt himself on the verge of a nasty cold, and this seemed to Mr. Welland an all-sufficient reason for abandoning any duty.

"You can't be too careful, especially toward spring,"

he said, heaping his plate with straw-coloured griddle-cakes and drowning them in golden syrup. If I'd only been as prudent at your age May would have been dancing at the Assemblies now, instead of spending her winters in a wilderness with an old invalid."

"Oh, but I love it here, Papa; you know I do. If only Newland could stay I should like it a thousand times better than New York."

"Newland must stay till he has quite thrown off his cold," said Mrs. Welland indulgently; and the young man laughed, and said he supposed there was such a thing as one's profession.

He managed, however, after an exchange of telegrams with the firm, to make his cold last a week; and it shed an ironic light on the situation to know that Mr. Letterblair's indulgence was partly due to the satisfactory way in which his brilliant young junior partner had settled the troublesome matter of the Olenski divorce. Mr. Letterblair had let Mrs. Welland know that Mr. Archer had "rendered an invaluable service" to the whole family, and that old Mrs. Manson Mingott had been particularly pleased; and one day when May had gone for a drive with her father in the only vehicle the place produced Mrs. Welland took occasion to touch on a topic which she always avoided in her daughter's presence.

"I'm afraid Ellen's ideas are not at all like ours. She was barely eighteen when Medora Manson took her back to Europe—you remember the excitement when she appeared in black at her coming-out ball? Another of Medora's fads—really this time it was almost prophetic! That must have been at least twelve years ago; and since then Ellen has never been to America. No wonder she is completely Europeanised."

"But European society is not given to divorce: Coun-

THE AGE OF INNOCENCE

tess Olenska thought she would be conforming to American ideas in asking for her freedom." It was the first time that the young man had pronounced her name since he had left Skuytercliff, and he felt the colour rise to his cheek.

Mrs. Welland smiled compassionately. "That is just like the extraordinary things that foreigners invent about us. They think we dine at two o'clock and countenance divorce! That is why it seems to me so foolish to entertain them when they come to New York. They accept our hospitality, and then they go home and repeat the same stupid stories."

Archer made no comment on this, and Mrs. Welland continued: "But we do most thoroughly appreciate your persuading Ellen to give up the idea. Her grandmother and her uncle Lovell could do nothing with her; both of them have written that her changing her mind was entirely due to your influence—in fact she said so to her grandmother. She has an unbounded admiration for you. Poor Ellen—she was always a wayward child. I wonder what her fate will be?"

"What we've all contrived to make it," he felt like answering. "If you'd all of you rather she should be Beaufort's mistress than some decent fellow's wife you've certainly gone the right way about it."

He wondered what Mrs. Welland would have said if he had uttered the words instead of merely thinking them. He could picture the sudden decomposure of her firm placid features, to which a lifelong mastery over trifles had given an air of factitious authority. Traces still lingered on them of a fresh beauty like her daughter's; and he asked himself if May's face was doomed to thicken into the same middle-aged image of invincible innocence.

Ah, no, he did not want May to have that kind of innocence, the innocence that seals the mind against imagination and the heart against experience!

"I verily believe," Mrs. Welland continued, "that if the horrible business had come out in the newspapers it would have been my husband's death-blow. I don't know any of the details; I only ask not to, as I told poor Ellen when she tried to talk to me about it. Having an invalid to care for, I have to keep my mind bright and happy. But Mr. Welland was terribly upset; he had a slight temperature every morning while we were waiting to hear what had been decided. It was the horror of his girl's learning that such things were possible—but of course, dear Newland, you felt that too. We all knew that you were thinking of May."

"I'm always thinking of May," the young man rejoined, rising to cut short the conversation.

He had meant to seize the opportunity of his private talk with Mrs. Welland to urge her to advance the date of his marriage. But he could think of no arguments that would move her, and with a sense of relief he saw Mr. Welland and May driving up to the door.

His only hope was to plead again with May, and on the day before his departure he walked with her to the ruinous garden of the Spanish Mission. The background lent itself to allusions to European scenes; and May, who was looking her loveliest under a wide-brimmed hat that cast a shadow of mystery over her too-clear eyes, kindled into eagerness as he spoke of Granada and the Alhambra.

"We might be seeing it all this spring—even the Easter ceremonies at Seville," he urged, exaggerating his demands in the hope of a larger concession.

"Easter in Seville? And it will be Lent next week!" she laughed.

"Why shouldn't we be married in Lent?" he rejoined; but she looked so shocked that he saw his mistake.

"Of course I didn't mean that, dearest; but soon after Easter—so that we could sail at the end of April. I know I could arrange it at the office."

She smiled dreamily upon the possibility; but he perceived that to dream of it sufficed her. It was like hearing him read aloud out of his poetry books the beautiful things that could not possibly happen in real life.

"Oh, do go on, Newland; I do love your descriptions."

"But why should they be only descriptions? Why shouldn't we make them real?"

"We shall, dearest, of course; next year." Her voice lingered over it.

"Don't you want them to be real sooner? Can't I persuade you to break away now?"

She bowed her head, vanishing from him under her conniving hat-brim.

"Why should we dream away another year? Look at me, dear! Don't you understand how I want you for my wife?"

For a moment she remained motionless; then she raised on him eyes of such despairing clearness that he half-released her waist from his hold. But suddenly her look changed and deepened inscrutably. "I'm not sure if I *do* understand," she said. "Is it—is it because you're not certain of continuing to care for me?"

Archer sprang up from his seat. "My God—perhaps —I don't know," he broke out angrily.

May Welland rose also; as they faced each other she seemed to grow in womanly stature and dignity. Both were silent for a moment, as if dismayed by the unforeseen trend of their words: then she said in a low voice: "If that is it—is there some one else?"

"Some one else—between you and me?" He echoed her words slowly, as though they were only half-intelligible and he wanted time to repeat the question to himself. She seemed to catch the uncertainty of his voice, for she went on in a deepening tone: "Let us talk frankly, Newland. Sometimes I've felt a difference in you; especially since our engagement has been announced."

"Dear—what madness!" he recovered himself to exclaim.

She met his protest with a faint smile. "If it is, it won't hurt us to talk about it." She paused, and added, lifting her head with one of her noble movements: "Or even if it's true: why shouldn't we speak of it? You might so easily have made a mistake."

He lowered his head, staring at the black leaf-pattern on the sunny path at their feet. "Mistakes are always easy to make; but if I had made one of the kind you suggest, is it likely that I should be imploring you to hasten our marriage?"

She looked downward too, disturbing the pattern with the point of her sunshade while she struggled for expression. "Yes," she said at length. "You might want—once for all—to settle the question: it's one way."

Her quiet lucidity startled him, but did not mislead him into thinking her insensible. Under her hat-brim he saw the pallor of her profile, and a slight tremor of the nostril above her resolutely steadied lips.

"Well—?" he questioned, sitting down on the bench, and looking up at her with a frown that he tried to make playful.

She dropped back into her seat and went on: "You mustn't think that a girl knows as little as her parents imagine. One hears and one notices—one has one's feelings and ideas. And of course, long before you told me that you cared for me, I'd known that there was some one else you were interested in; every one was talking about it two years ago at Newport. And once I saw you sitting together on the verandah at a dance—and when she came back into the house her face was sad, and I felt sorry for her; I remembered it afterward, when we were engaged."

Her voice had sunk almost to a whisper, and she sat clasping and unclasping her hands about the handle of her sunshade. The young man laid his upon them with a gentle pressure; his heart dilated with an inexpressible relief.

"My dear child—was *that* it? If you only knew the truth!"

She raised her head quickly. "Then there is a truth I don't know?"

He kept his hand over hers. "I meant, the truth about the old story you speak of."

"But that's what I want to know, Newland—what I ought to know. I couldn't have my happiness made out of a wrong—an unfairness—to somebody else. And I want to believe that it would be the same with you. What sort of a life could we build on such foundations?"

Her face had taken on a look of such tragic courage that he felt like bowing himself down at her feet. "I've wanted to say this for a long time," she went on. "I've wanted to tell you that, when two people really love each other, I understand that there may be situations which make it right that they should—should go against public opinion. And if you feel yourself in any way pledged . . . pledged to the person we've spoken of . . . and if there is any way . . . any way in which you can fulfill your pledge . . . even by her getting a divorce . . . Newland, don't give her up because of me!"

His surprise at discovering that her fears had fastened upon an episode so remote and so completely of the past as his love affair with Mrs. Thorley Rushworth gave way to wonder at the generosity of her view. There was something superhuman in an attitude so recklessly unorthodox, and if other problems had not pressed on him he would have been lost in wonder at the prodigy of the Wellands' daughter urging him to marry his former mistress. But he was still dizzy with the glimpse of the precipice they had skirted, and full of a new awe at the mystery of young-girlhood.

For a moment he could not speak; then he said: "There is no pledge—no obligation whatever—of the kind you think. Such cases don't always—present themselves quite as simply as . . . But that's no matter . . . I love your generosity, because I feel as you do about those things . . . I feel that each case must be judged individually, on its own merits . . . irrespective of stupid conventionalities . . . I mean, each woman's right to her liberty—" He pulled himself up, startled by the turn his thoughts had taken, and went on, looking at her with a smile: "Since you understand so many things, dearest, can't you go a little farther, and understand the uselessness of our submitting to another form of the same foolish conventionalities? If there's no one and nothing between us, isn't that an argument for marrying quickly, rather than for more delay?"

She flushed with joy and lifted her face to his; as he bent to it he saw that her eyes were full of happy tears. But in another moment she seemed to have descended from her womanly eminence to helpless and timorous girlhood; and he understood that her courage and initiative were all for others, and that she had none for herself. It was evident that the effort of speaking had been much greater than her studied composure betrayed, and that at his first word of reassurance she had dropped back into the usual, as a too-adventurous child takes refuge in its mother's arms.

Archer had no heart to go on pleading with her; he was too much disappointed at the vanishing of the new being who had cast that one deep look at him from her transparent eyes. May seemed to be aware of his disappointment, but without knowing how to alleviate it; and they stood up and walked silently home.

XVII

"YOUR cousin the Countess called on mother while you were away," Janey Archer announced to her brother on the evening of his return.

The young man, who was dining alone with his mother and sister, glanced up in surprise and saw Mrs. Archer's gaze demurely bent on her plate. Mrs. Archer did not regard her seclusion from the world as a reason for being forgotten by it; and Newland guessed that she was slightly annoyed that he should be suprised by Madame Olenska's visit.

"She had on a black velvet polonaise with jet buttons, and a tiny green monkey muff; I never saw her so stylishly dressed," Janey continued. "She came alone, early on Sunday afternoon; luckily the fire was lit in the drawing-room. She had one of those new card-cases. She said she wanted to know us because you'd been so good to her."

Newland laughed. "Madame Olenska always takes that tone about her friends. She's very happy at being among her own people again."

"Yes, so she told us," said Mrs. Archer. "I must say she seems thankful to be here."

"I hope you liked her, mother."

Mrs. Archer drew her lips together. "She certainly lays herself out to please, even when she is calling on an old lady."

"Mother doesn't think her simple," Janey interjected, her eyes screwed upon her brother's face.

"It's just my old-fashioned feeling; dear May is my ideal," said Mrs. Archer.

"Ah," said her son, "they're not alike."

Archer had left St. Augustine charged with many messages for old Mrs. Mingott; and a day or two after his return to town he called on her.

The old lady received him with unusual warmth; she was grateful to him for persuading the Countess Olenska to give up the idea of a divorce; and when he told her that he had deserted the office without leave, and rushed down to St. Augustine simply because he wanted to see May, she gave an adipose chuckle and patted his knee with her puff-ball hand.

"Ah, ah—so you kicked over the traces, did you? And I suppose Augusta and Welland pulled long faces, and behaved as if the end of the world had come? But little May—she knew better, I'll be bound?"

"I hoped she did; but after all she wouldn't agree to what I'd gone down to ask for."

"Wouldn't she indeed? And what was that?"

"I wanted to get her to promise that we should be married in April. What's the use of our wasting another year?"

Mrs. Manson Mingott screwed up her little mouth into a grimace of mimic prudery and twinkled at him through malicious lids. " 'Ask Mamma,' I suppose—the usual story. Ah, these Mingotts—all alike! Born in a rut, and you can't root 'em out of it. When I built this house you'd have thought I was moving to California! Nobody ever *had* built above Fortieth Street—no, says I, nor above the Battery either, before Christopher Columbus discovered America. No, no; not one of them wants to be different; they're as scared of it as the small-pox. Ah, my dear Mr. Archer, I thank my stars I'm nothing but a vulgar Spicer; but there's not one of my own children that takes after me but my little Ellen." She broke off, still twinkling at him, and asked, with the casual irrelevance of old age: "Now, why in the world didn't you marry my little Ellen?"

Archer laughed. "For one thing, she wasn't there to be married."

"No—to be sure; more's the pity. And now it's too late; her life is finished." She spoke with the cold-blooded complacency of the aged throwing earth into the grave of young hopes. The young man's heart grew chill, and he said hurriedly: "Can't I persuade you to use your influence with the Wellands, Mrs. Mingott? I wasn't made for long engagements."

Old Catherine beamed on him approvingly. "No; I can see that. You've got a quick eye. When you were a little boy I've no doubt you liked to be helped first." She threw back her head with a laugh that made her chins ripple like little waves. "Ah, here's my Ellen now!" she exclaimed, as the portières parted behind her.

Madame Olenska came forward with a smile. Her face looked vivid and happy, and she held out her hand gaily to Archer while she stooped to her grandmother's kiss.

"I was just saying to him, my dear: 'Now, why didn't you marry my little Ellen?'"

Madame Olenska looked at Archer, still smiling. "And what did he answer?"

"Oh, my darling, I leave you to find that out! He's been down to Florida to see his sweetheart."

"Yes, I know." She still looked at him. "I went to see your mother, to ask where you'd gone. I sent a note that you never answered, and I was afraid you were ill."

He muttered something about leaving unexpectedly, in a great hurry, and having intended to write to her from St. Augustine.

"And of course once you were there you never thought of me again!" She continued to beam on him with a gaiety that might have been a studied assumption of indifference.

"If she still needs me, she's determined not to let me see it," he thought, stung by her manner. He wanted to thank her for having been to see his mother, but under the ancestress's malicious eye he felt himself tongue-tied and constrained.

"Look at him—in such hot haste to get married that he took French leave and rushed down to implore the silly girl on his knees! That's something like a lover— that's the way handsome Bob Spicer carried off my poor mother; and then got tired of her before I was weaned —though they only had to wait eight months for me! But there—you're not a Spicer, young man; luckily for you and for May. It's only my poor Ellen that has kept any of their wicked blood; the rest of them are all model Mingotts," cried the old lady scornfully.

Archer was aware that Madame Olenska, who had seated herself at her grandmother's side, was still thoughtfully scrutinising him. The gaiety had faded from her eyes, and she said with great gentleness: "Surely, Granny, we can persuade them between us to do as he wishes."

Archer rose to go, and as his hand met Madame Olenska's he felt that she was waiting for him to make some allusion to her unanswered letter.

[154]

"When can I see you?" he asked, as she walked with him to the door of the room.

"Whenever you like; but it must be soon if you want to see the little house again. I am moving next week."

A pang shot through him at the memory of his lamplit hours in the low-studded drawing-room. Few as they had been, they were thick with memories.

"Tomorrow evening?"

She nodded. "Tomorrow; yes; but early. I'm going out."

The next day was a Sunday, and if she were "going out" on a Sunday evening it could, of course, be only to Mrs. Lemuel Struthers's. He felt a slight movement of annoyance, not so much at her going there (for he rather liked her going where she pleased in spite of the van der Luydens), but because it was the kind of house at which she was sure to meet Beaufort, where she must have known beforehand that she would meet him—and where she was probably going for that purpose.

"Very well; tomorrow evening," he repeated, inwardly resolved that he would not go early, and that by reaching her door late he would either prevent her from going to Mrs. Struthers's, or else arrive after she had started—which, all things considered, would no doubt be the simplest solution.

It was only half-past eight, after all, when he rang the bell under the wistaria; not as late as he had intended by half an hour—but a singular restlessness had driven him to her door. He reflected, however, that Mrs. Struthers's Sunday evenings were not like a ball, and that her guests, as if to minimise their delinquency, usually went early.

The one thing he had not counted on, in entering Madame Olenska's hall, was to find hats and overcoats there. Why had she bidden him to come early if she was having people to dine? On a closer inspection of the garments besides which Nastasia was laying his own, his resentment gave way to curiosity. The overcoats were in fact the very strangest he had ever seen under a polite roof; and it took but a glance to assure himself that neither of them belonged to Julius Beaufort. One was a shaggy yellow ulster of "reach-me-down" cut, the other a very old and rusty cloak with a cape—something like what the French called a "Macfarlane." This garment, which appeared to be made for a person of prodigious size, had evidently seen long and hard wear, and its greenish-black folds gave out a moist sawdusty smell suggestive of prolonged sessions against bar-room walls. On it lay a ragged grey scarf and an odd felt hat of semiclerical shape.

Archer raised his eyebrows enquiringly at Nastasia, who raised hers in return with a fatalistic "Già!" as she threw open the drawing-room door.

The young man saw at once that his hostess was not in the room; then, with surprise, he discovered another lady standing by the fire. This lady, who was long, lean and loosely put together, was clad in raiment intricately looped and fringed, with plaids and stripes and bands of plain colour disposed in a design to which the clue seemed missing. Her hair, which had tried to turn white and only succeeded in fading, was surmounted by a Spanish comb and black lace scarf, and silk mittens, visibly darned, covered her rheumatic hands.

Beside her, in a cloud of cigar-smoke, stood the owners of the two overcoats, both in morning clothes that they had evidently not taken off since morning. In one of the two, Archer, to his surprise, recognised Ned Winsett; the other and older, who was unknown to him, and

THE AGE OF INNOCENCE

whose gigantic frame declared him to be the wearer of the "Macfarlane," had a feebly leonine head with crumpled grey hair, and moved his arms with large pawing gestures, as though he were distributing lay blessings to a kneeling multitude.

These three persons stood together on the hearth-rug, their eyes fixed on an extraordinarily large bouquet of crimson roses, with a knot of purple pansies at their base, that lay on the sofa where Madame Olenska usually sat.

"What they must have cost at this season—though of course it's the sentiment one cares about!" the lady was saying in a sighing staccato as Archer came in.

The three turned with surprise at his appearance, and the lady, advancing, held out her hand.

"Dear Mr. Archer—almost my cousin Newland!" she said. "I am the Marchioness Manson."

Archer bowed, and she continued: "My Ellen has taken me in for a few days. I came from Cuba, where I have been spending the winter with Spanish friends—such delightful distinguished people: the highest nobility of old Castile—how I wish you could know them! But I was called away by our dear great friend here, Dr. Carver. You don't know Dr. Agathon Carver, founder of the Valley of Love Community?"

Dr. Carver inclined his leonine head, and the Marchioness continued: "Ah, New York—New York—how little the life of the spirit has reached it! But I see you do know Mr. Winsett."

"Oh, yes—I reached him some time ago; but not by that route," Winsett said with his dry smile.

The Marchioness shook her head reprovingly. "How do you know, Mr. Winsett? The spirit bloweth where it listeth."

[157]

"List—oh, list!" interjected Dr. Carver in a stentorian murmur.

"But do sit down, Mr. Archer. We four have been having a delightful little dinner together, and my child has gone up to dress. She expects you; she will be down in a moment. We were just admiring these marvellous flowers, which will surprise her when she reappears."

Winsett remained on his feet. "I'm afraid I must be off. Please tell Madame Olenska that we shall all feel lost when she abandons our street. This house has been an oasis."

"Ah, but she won't abandon *you*. Poetry and art are the breath of life to her. It *is* poetry you write, Mr. Winsett?"

"Well, no; but I sometimes read it," said Winsett, including the group in a general nod and slipping out of the room.

"A caustic spirit—*un peu sauvage*. But so witty; Dr. Carver, you *do* think him witty?"

"I never think of wit," said Dr. Carver severely.

"Ah—ah—you never think of wit! How merciless he is to us weak mortals, Mr. Archer! But he lives only in the life of the spirit; and tonight he is mentally preparing the lecture he is to deliver presently at Mrs. Blenker's. Dr. Carver, would there be time, before you start for the Blenkers' to explain to Mr. Archer your illuminating discovery of the Direct Contact? But no; I see it is nearly nine o'clock, and we have no right to detain you while so many are waiting for your message."

Dr. Carver looked slightly disappointed at this conclusion, but, having compared his ponderous gold timepiece with Madame Olenska's little travelling-clock, he reluctantly gathered up his mighty limbs for departure.

"I shall see you later, dear friend?" he suggested to

the Marchioness, who replied with a smile: "As soon as Ellen's carriage comes I will join you; I do hope the lecture won't have begun."

Dr. Carver looked thoughtfully at Archer. "Perhaps, if this young gentleman is interested in my experiences, Mrs. Blenker might allow you to bring him with you?"

"Oh, dear friend, if it were possible—I am sure she would be too happy. But I fear my Ellen counts on Mr. Archer herself."

"That," said Dr. Carver, "is unfortunate—but here is my card." He handed it to Archer, who read on it, in Gothic characters:

```
Agathon Carver
The Valley of Love
Kittasquattamy, N. Y.
```

Dr. Carver bowed himself out, and Mrs. Manson, with a sigh that might have been either of regret or relief, again waved Archer to a seat.

"Ellen will be down in a moment; and before she comes, I am so glad of this quiet moment with you."

Archer murmured his pleasure at their meeting, and the Marchioness continued, in her low sighing accents: "I know everything, dear Mr. Archer—my child has told me all you have done for her. Your wise advice: your courageous firmness—thank heaven it was not too late!"

The young man listened with considerable embarrassment. Was there any one, he wondered, to whom Madame Olenska had not proclaimed his intervention in her private affairs?

THE AGE OF INNOCENCE

"Madame Olenska exaggerates; I simply gave her a legal opinion, as she asked me to."

"Ah, but in doing it—in doing it you were the unconscious instrument of—of—what word have we moderns for Providence, Mr. Archer?" cried the lady, tilting her head on one side and drooping her lids mysteriously. "Little did you know that at that very moment I was being appealed to: being approached, in fact—from the other side of the Atlantic!"

She glanced over her shoulder, as though fearful of being overheard, and then, drawing her chair nearer, and raising a tiny ivory fan to her lips, breathed behind it: "By the Count himself—my poor, mad, foolish Olenski; who asks only to take her back on her own terms."

"Good God!" Archer exclaimed, springing up.

"You are horrified? Yes, of course; I understand. I don't defend poor Stanislas, though he has always called me his best friend. He does not defend himself—he casts himself at her feet: in my person." She tapped her emaciated bosom. "I have his letter here."

"A letter?— Has Madame Olenska seen it?" Archer stammered, his brain whirling with the shock of the announcement.

The Marchioness Manson shook her head softly. "Time—time; I must have time. I know my Ellen—haughty, intractable; shall I say, just a shade unforgiving?"

"But, good heavens, to forgive is one thing; to go back into that hell—"

"Ah, yes," the Marchioness acquiesced. "So she describes it—my sensitive child! But on the material side, Mr. Archer, if one may stoop to consider such things; do you know what she is giving up? Those roses there on the sofa—acres like them, under glass and in the

open, in his matchless terraced gardens at Nice! Jewels
—historic pearls: the Sobieski emeralds—sables—but she
cares nothing for all these! Art and beauty, those she
does care for, she lives for, as I always have; and those
also surrounded her. Pictures, priceless furniture, music,
brilliant conversation—ah, that, my dear young man, if
you'll excuse me, is what you've no conception of here!
And she had it all; and the homage of the greatest. She
tells me she is not thought handsome in New York—good
heavens! Her portrait has been painted nine times; the
greatest artists in Europe have begged for the privilege.
Are these things nothing? And the remorse of an ador-
ing husband?"

As the Marchioness Manson rose to her climax her
face assumed an expression of ecstatic retrospection
which would have moved Archer's mirth had he not
been numb with amazement.

He would have laughed if any one had foretold to him
that his first sight of poor Medora Manson would have
'been in the guise of a messenger of Satan; but he was
in no mood for laughing now, and she seemed to him to
come straight out of the hell from which Ellen Olenska
had just escaped.

"She knows nothing yet—of all this?" he asked
abruptly.

Mrs. Manson laid a purple finger on her lips. "Nothing directly—but does she suspect? Who can tell? The
truth is, Mr. Archer, I have been waiting to see you.
From the moment I heard of the firm stand you had
taken, and of your influence over her, I hoped it might
be possible to count on your support—to convince
you . . ."

"That she ought to go back? I would rather see her
dead!" cried the young man violently.

[161]

"Ah," the Marchioness murmured, without visible resentment. For a while she sat in her arm-chair, opening and shutting the absurd ivory fan between her mittened fingers; but suddenly she lifted her head and listened.

"Here she comes," she said in a rapid whisper; and then, pointing to the bouquet on the sofa: "Am I to understand that you prefer *that*, Mr. Archer? After all, marriage is marriage . . . and my niece is still a wife. . . ."

XVIII

"WHAT are you two plotting together, aunt Medora?" Madame Olenska cried as she came into the room.

She was dressed as if for a ball. Everything about her shimmered and glimmered softly, as if her dress had been woven out of candle-beams; and she carried her head high, like a pretty woman challenging a roomful of rivals.

"We were saying, my dear, that here was something beautiful to surprise you with," Mrs. Manson rejoined, rising to her feet and pointing archly to the flowers.

Madame Olenska stopped short and looked at the bouquet. Her colour did not change, but a sort of white radiance of anger ran over her like summer lightning. "Ah," she exclaimed, in a shrill voice that the young man had never heard, "who is ridiculous enough to send me a bouquet? Why a bouquet? And why tonight of all nights? I am not going to a ball; I am not a girl engaged to be married. But some people are always ridiculous."

She turned back to the door, opened it, and called out: "Nastasia!"

The ubiquitous handmaiden promptly appeared, and Archer heard Madame Olenska say, in an Italian that she seemed to pronounce with intentional deliberateness in order that he might follow it: "Here—throw this into the dust-bin!" and then, as Nastasia stared protestingly: "But no—it's not the fault of the poor flowers. Tell the boy to carry them to the house three doors away, the house of Mr. Winsett, the dark gentleman who dined here. His wife is ill—they may give her pleasure . . . The boy is out, you say? Then, my dear one, run yourself; here, put my cloak over you and fly. I want the thing out of the house immediately! And, as you live, don't say they come from me!"

She flung her velvet opera cloak over the maid's shoulders and turned back into the drawing-room, shutting the door sharply. Her bosom was rising high under its lace, and for a moment Archer thought she was about to cry; but she burst into a laugh instead, and looking from the Marchioness to Archer, asked abruptly: "And you two—have you made friends!"

"It's for Mr. Archer to say, darling; he has waited patiently while you were dressing."

"Yes—I gave you time enough: my hair wouldn't go," Madame Olenska said, raising her hand to the heaped-up curls of her *chignon*. "But that reminds me: I see Dr. Carver is gone, and you'll be late at the Blenkers'. Mr. Archer, will you put my aunt in the carriage?"

She followed the Marchioness into the hall, saw her fitted into a miscellaneous heap of overshoes, shawls and tippets, and called from the doorstep: "Mind, the carriage is to be back for me at ten!" Then she returned to the drawing-room, where Archer, on re-entering it, found her standing by the mantelpiece, examining herself in the mirror. It was not usual, in New York society, for a lady to address her parlour-maid as "my dear one," and send her out on an errand wrapped in her own opera-cloak; and Archer, through all his deeper feelings, tested the pleasurable excitement of being in a world where action followed on emotion with such Olympian speed.

Madame Olenska did not move when he came up behind her, and for a second their eyes met in the mirror; then she turned, threw herself into her sofa-corner, and sighed out: "There's time for a cigarette."

He handed her the box and lit a spill for her; and as the flame flashed up into her face she glanced at him with laughing eyes and said: "What do you think of me in a temper?"

Archer paused a moment; then he answered with sudden resolution: "It makes me understand what your aunt has been saying about you."

"I knew she'd been talking about me. Well?"

"She said you were used to all kinds of things—splendours and amusements and excitements—that we could never hope to give you here."

Madame Olenska smiled faintly into the circle of smoke about her lips.

"Medora is incorrigibly romantic. It has made up to her for so many things!"

Archer hesitated again, and again took his risk. "Is your aunt's romanticism always consistent with accuracy?"

"You mean: does she speak the truth?" Her niece considered. "Well, I'll tell you: in almost everything she says, there's something true and something untrue. But why do you ask? What has she been telling you?"

He looked away into the fire, and then back at her shining presence. His heart tightened with the thought that this was their last evening by that fireside, and that in a moment the carriage would come to carry her away.

"She says—she pretends that Count Olenski has asked her to persuade you to go back to him."

Madame Olenska made no answer. She sat motionless, holding her cigarette in her half-lifted hand. The expression of her face had not changed; and Archer remembered that he had before noticed her apparent incapacity for surprise.

"You knew, then?" he broke out.

She was silent for so long that the ash dropped from her cigarette. She brushed it to the floor. "She has hinted about a letter: poor darling! Medora's hints—"

"Is it at your husband's request that she has arrived here suddenly?"

Madame Olenska seemed to consider this question also. "There again: one can't tell. She told me she had had a 'spiritual summons,' whatever that is, from Dr. Carver. I'm afraid she's going to marry Dr. Carver . . . poor Medora, there's always some one she wants to marry. But perhaps the people in Cuba just got tired of her! I think she was with them as a sort of paid companion. Really, I don't know why she came."

"But you do believe she has a letter from your husband?"

Again Madame Olenska brooded silently; then she said: "After all, it was to be expected."

The young man rose and went to lean against the fireplace. A sudden restlessness possessed him, and he was tongue-tied by the sense that their minutes were numbered, and that at any moment he might hear the wheels of the returning carriage.

"You know that your aunt believes you will go back?"

Madame Olenska raised her head quickly. A deep blush rose to her face and spread over her neck and shoulders. She blushed seldom and painfully, as if it hurt her like a burn.

"Many cruel things have been believed of me," she said.

"Oh, Ellen—forgive me; I'm a fool and a brute!"

She smiled a little. "You are horribly nervous; you

have your own troubles. I know you think the Wellands are unreasonable about your marriage, and of course I agree with you. In Europe people don't understand our long American engagements, I suppose they are not as calm as we are." She pronounced the "we" with a faint emphasis that gave it an ironic sound.

Archer felt the irony but did not dare to take it up. After all, she had perhaps purposely deflected the conversation from her own affairs, and after the pain his last words had evidently caused her he felt that all he could do was to follow her lead. But the sense of the waning hour made him desperate: he could not bear the thought that a barrier of words should drop between them again.

"Yes," he said abruptly; "I went south to ask May to marry me after Easter. There's no reason why we shouldn't be married then."

"And May adores you—and yet you couldn't convince her? I thought her too intelligent to be the slave of such absurd superstitions."

"She *is* too intelligent—she's not their slave."

Madame Olenska looked at him. "Well, then—I don't understand."

Archer reddened, and hurried on with a rush. "We had a frank talk—almost the first. She thinks my impatience a bad sign."

"Merciful heavens—a bad sign?"

"She thinks it means that I can't trust myself to go on caring for her. She thinks, in short, I want to marry her at once to get away from some one that I—care for more."

Madame Olenska examined this curiously. "But if she thinks that—why isn't she in a hurry too?"

"Because she's not like that: she's so much nobler.

[167]

She insists all the more on the long engagement, to give me time—"

"Time to give her up for the other woman?"

"If I want to."

Madame Olenska leaned toward the fire and gazed into it with fixed eyes. Down the quiet street Archer heard the approaching trot of her horses.

"That *is* noble," she said, with a slight break in her voice.

"Yes. But it's ridiculous."

"Ridiculous? Because you don't care for any one else?"

"Because I don't mean to marry any one else."

"Ah." There was another long interval. At length she looked up at him and asked: "This other woman—does she love you?"

"Oh, there's no other woman; I mean, the person that May was thinking of is—was never—"

"Then, why, after all, are you in such haste?"

"There's your carriage," said Archer.

She half-rose and looked about her with absent eyes. Her fan and gloves lay on the sofa beside her and she picked them up mechanically.

"Yes; I suppose I must be going."

"You're going to Mrs. Struthers's?"

"Yes." She smiled and added: "I must go where I am invited, or I should be too lonely. Why not come with me?"

Archer felt that at any cost he must keep her beside him, must make her give him the rest of her evening. Ignoring her question, he continued to lean against the chimney-piece, his eyes fixed on the hand in which she held her gloves and fan, as if watching to see if he had the power to make her drop them.

"May guessed the truth," he said. "There is another woman—but not the one she thinks."

Ellen Olenska made no answer, and did not move. After a moment he sat down beside her, and, taking her hand, softly unclasped it, so that the gloves and fan fell on the sofa between them.

She started up, and freeing herself from him moved away to the other side of the hearth. "Ah, don't make love to me! Too many people have done that," she said, frowning.

Archer, changing colour, stood up also: it was the bitterest rebuke she could have given him. "I have never made love to you," he said, "and I never shall. But you are the woman I would have married if it had been possible for either of us."

"Possible for either of us?" She looked at him with unfeigned astonishment. "And you say that—when it's you who've made it impossible?"

He stared at her, groping in a blackness through which a single arrow of light tore its blinding way.

"*I've* made it impossible——?"

"You, you, *you!*" she cried, her lip trembling like a child's on the verge of tears. "Isn't it you who made me give up divorcing—give it up because you showed me how selfish and wicked it was, how one must sacrifice one's self to preserve the dignity of marriage . . . and to spare one's family the publicity, the scandal? And because my family was going to be your family—for May's sake and for yours—I did what you told me, what you proved to me that I ought to do. Ah," she broke out with a sudden laugh, "I've made no secret of having done it for you!"

She sank down on the sofa again, crouching among the festive ripples of her dress like a stricken masquerader; and the young man stood by the fireplace and continued to gaze at her without moving.

"Good God," he groaned. "When I thought—"

"You thought?"

"Ah, don't ask me what I thought!"

Still looking at her, he saw the same burning flush creep up her neck to her face. She sat upright, facing him with a rigid dignity.

"I do ask you."

"Well, then: there were things in that letter you asked me to read—"

"My husband's letter?"

"Yes."

"I had nothing to fear from that letter: absolutely nothing! All I feared was to bring notoriety, scandal, on the family—on you and May."

"Good God," he groaned again, bowing his face in his hands.

The silence that followed lay on them with the weight of things final and irrevocable. It seemed to Archer to be crushing him down like his own grave-stone; in all the wide future he saw nothing that would ever lift that load from his heart. He did not move from his place, or raise his head from his hands; his hidden eye-balls went on staring into utter darkness.

"At least I loved you—" he brought out.

On the other side of the hearth, from the sofa-corner where he supposed that she still crouched, he heard a faint stifled crying like a child's. He started up and came to her side.

"Ellen! What madness! Why are you crying? Nothing's done that can't be undone. I'm still free, and you're going to be." He had her in his arms, her face like a wet flower at his lips, and all their vain terrors shrivelling up like ghosts at sunrise. The one thing that astonished him now was that he should have stood for five minutes arguing with her across the width of the room, when just touching her made everything so simple.

She gave him back all his kiss, but after a moment he felt her stiffening in his arms, and she put him aside and stood up.

"Ah, my poor Newland—I suppose this had to be. But it doesn't in the least alter things," she said, looking down at him in her turn from the hearth.

"It alters the whole of life for me."

"No, no—it mustn't, it can't. You're engaged to May Welland; and I'm married."

He stood up too, flushed and resolute. "Nonsense! It's too late for that sort of thing. We've no right to lie to other people or to ourselves. We won't talk of your marriage; but do you see me marrying May after this?"

She stood silent, resting her thin elbows on the mantelpiece, her profile reflected in the glass behind her. One of the locks of her *chignon* had become loosened and hung on her neck; she looked haggard and almost old.

"I don't see you," she said at length, "putting that question to May. Do you?"

He gave a reckless shrug. "It's too late to do anything else."

"You say that because it's the easiest thing to say at this moment—not because it's true. In reality it's too late to do anything but what we'd both decided on."

"Ah, I don't understand you!"

She forced a pitiful smile that pinched her face instead of smoothing it. "You don't understand because you haven't yet guessed how you've changed things for me: oh, from the first—long before I knew all you'd done."

"All I'd done?"

"Yes. I was perfectly unconscious at first that people here were shy of me—that they thought I was a dreadful sort of person. It seems they had even refused to meet me at dinner. I found that out afterward; and how you'd made your mother go with you to the van der Luydens'; and how you'd insisted on announcing your engagement at the Beaufort ball, so that I might have two families to stand by me instead of one—"

At that he broke into a laugh.

"Just imagine," she said, "how stupid and unobservant I was! I knew nothing of all this till Granny blurted it out one day. New York simply meant peace and freedom to me: it was coming home. And I was so happy at being among my own people that every one I met seemed kind and good, and glad to see me. But from the very beginning," she continued, "I felt there was no one as kind as you; no one who gave me reasons that I understood for doing what at first seemed so hard and —unnecessary. The very good people didn't convince me; I felt they'd never been tempted. But you knew; you understood; you had felt the world outside tugging at one with all its golden hands—and yet you hated the things it asks of one; you hated happiness bought by disloyalty and cruelty and indifference. That was what I'd never known before—and it's better than anything I've known."

She spoke in a low even voice, without tears or visible agitation; and each word, as it dropped from her, fell into his breast like burning lead. He sat bowed over, his head between his hands, staring at the hearth-rug, and at the tip of the satin shoe that showed under her dress. Suddenly he knelt down and kissed the shoe.

She bent over him, laying her hands on his shoulders,

and looking at him with eyes so deep that he remained motionless under her gaze.

"Ah, don't let us undo what you've done!" she cried. "I can't go back now to that other way of thinking. I can't love you unless I give you up."

His arms were yearning up to her; but she drew away, and they remained facing each other, divided by the distance that her words had created. Then, abruptly, his anger overflowed.

"And Beaufort? Is he to replace me?"

As the words sprang out he was prepared for an answering flare of anger; and he would have welcomed it as fuel for his own. But Madame Olenska only grew a shade paler, and stood with her arms hanging down before her, and her head slightly bent, as her way was when she pondered a question.

"He's waiting for you now at Mrs. Struthers's; why don't you go to him?" Archer sneered.

She turned to ring the bell. "I shall not go out this evening; tell the carriage to go and fetch the Signora Marchesa," she said when the maid came.

After the door had closed again Archer continued to look at her with bitter eyes. "Why this sacrifice? Since you tell me that you're lonely I've no right to keep you from your friends."

She smiled a little under her wet lashes. "I shan't be lonely now. I *was* lonely; I *was* afraid. But the emptiness and the darkness are gone; when I turn back into myself now I'm like a child going at night into a room where there's always a light."

Her tone and her look still enveloped her in a soft inaccessibility, and Archer groaned out again: "I don't understand you!"

"Yet you understand May!"

[173]

He reddened under the retort, but kept his eyes on her. "May is ready to give me up."

"What! Three days after you've entreated her on your knees to hasten your marriage?"

"She's refused; that gives me the right—"

"Ah, you've taught me what an ugly word that is," she said.

He turned away with a sense of utter weariness. He felt as though he had been struggling for hours up the face of a steep precipice, and now, just as he had fought his way to the top, his hold had given way and he was pitching down headlong into darkness.

If he could have got her in his arms again he might have swept away her arguments; but she still held him at a distance by something inscrutably aloof in her look and attitude, and by his own awed sense of her sincerity. At length he began to plead again.

"If we do this now it will be worse afterward—worse for every one—"

"No—no—no!" she almost screamed, as if he frightened her.

At that moment the bell sent a long twinkle through the house. They had heard no carriage stopping at the door, and they stood motionless, looking at each other with startled eyes.

Outside, Nastasia's step crossed the hall, the outer door opened, and a moment later she came in carrying a telegram which she handed to the Countess Olenska.

"The lady was very happy at the flowers," Nastasia said, smoothing her apron. "She thought it was her *signor marito* who had sent them, and she cried a little and said it was a folly."

Her mistress smiled and took the yellow envelope. She tore it open and carried it to the lamp; then, when the door had closed again, she handed the telegram to Archer.

It was dated from St. Augustine, and addressed to the Countess Olenska. In it he read: "Granny's telegram successful. Papa and Mamma agree marriage after Easter. Am telegraphing Newland. Am too happy for words and love you dearly. Your grateful May."

Half an hour later, when Archer unlocked his own front-door, he found a similar envelope on the hall-table on top of his pile of notes and letters. The message inside the envelope was also from May Welland, and ran as follows: "Parents consent wedding Tuesday after Easter at twelve Grace Church eight bridesmaids please see Rector so happy love May."

Archer crumpled up the yellow sheet in his fist as if the gesture could annihilate the news it contained. Then he pulled out a small pocket-diary and turned over the pages with trembling fingers; but he did not find what he wanted, and cramming the telegram into his pocket he mounted the stairs.

A light was shining through the door of the little hall-room which served Janey as a dressing-room and boudoir, and her brother rapped impatiently on the panel. The door opened, and his sister stood before him in her immemorial purple flannel dressing-gown, with her hair "on pins." Her face looked pale and apprehensive.

"Newland! I hope there's no bad news in that telegram? I waited on purpose, in case—" (No item of his correspondence was safe from Janey.)

He took no notice of her question. "Look here—what day is Easter this year?"

She looked shocked at such unchristian ignorance.

"Easter? Newland! Why, of course, the first week in April. Why?"

"The first week?" He turned again to the pages of his diary, calculating rapidly under his breath. "The first week, did you say?" He threw back his head with a long laugh.

"For mercy's sake what's the matter?"

"Nothing's the matter, except that I'm going to be married in a month."

Janey fell upon his neck and pressed him to her purple flannel breast. "Oh Newland, how wonderful! I'm so glad! But, dearest, why do you keep on laughing? Do hush, or you'll wake Mamma."

END OF BOOK I

BOOK II

XIX

THE day was fresh, with a lively spring wind full of dust. All the old ladies in both families had got out their faded sables and yellowing ermines, and the smell of camphor from the front pews almost smothered the faint spring scent of the lilies banking the altar.

Newland Archer, at a signal from the sexton, had come out of the vestry and placed himself with his best man on the chancel step of Grace Church.

The signal meant that the brougham bearing the bride and her father was in sight; but there was sure to be a considerable interval of adjustment and consultation in the lobby, where the bridesmaids were already hovering like a cluster of Easter blossoms. During this unavoidable lapse of time the bridegroom, in proof of his eagerness was expected to expose himself alone to the gaze of the assembled company; and Archer had gone through this formality as resignedly as through all the others which made of a nineteenth century New York wedding a rite that seemed to belong to the dawn of history. Everything was equally easy—or equally painful, as one chose to put it—in the path he was committed to tread, and he had obeyed the flurried injunctions of his best man as piously as other bridegrooms had obeyed his own, in the days when he had guided them through the same labyrinth.

So far he was reasonably sure of having fulfilled all

his obligations. The bridesmaids' eight bouquets of white lilac and lilies-of-the-valley had been sent in due time, as well as the gold and sapphire sleeve-links of the eight ushers and the best man's cat's-eye scarf-pin; Archer had sat up half the night trying to vary the wording of his thanks for the last batch of presents from men friends and ex-lady-loves; the fees for the Bishop and the Rector were safely in the pocket of his best man; his own luggage was already at Mrs. Manson Mingott's, where the wedding-breakfast was to take place, and so were the travelling clothes into which he was to change; and a private compartment had been engaged in the train that was to carry the young couple to their unknown destination—concealment of the spot in which the bridal night was to be spent being one of the most sacred taboos of the prehistoric ritual.

"Got the ring all right?" whispered young van der Luyden Newland, who was inexperienced in the duties of a best man, and awed by the weight of his responsibility.

Archer made the gesture which he had seen so many bridegrooms make: with his ungloved right hand he felt in the pocket of his dark grey waistcoat, and assured himself that the little gold circlet (engraved inside: *Newland to May, April* ——, 187—) was in its place; then, resuming his former attitude, his tall hat and pearl-grey gloves with black stitchings grasped in his left hand, he stood looking at the door of the church.

Overhead, Handel's March swelled pompously through the imitation stone vaulting, carrying on its waves the faded drift of the many weddings at which, with cheerful indifference, he had stood on the same chancel step watching other brides float up the nave toward other bridegrooms.

"How like a first night at the Opera!" he thought, recognising all the same faces in the same boxes (no, pews), and wondering if, when the Last Trump sounded, Mrs. Selfridge Merry would be there with the same towering ostrich feathers in her bonnet, and Mrs. Beaufort with the same diamond earrings and the same smile —and whether suitable proscenium seats were already prepared for them in another world.

After that there was still time to review, one by one, the familiar countenances in the first rows; the women's sharp with curiosity and excitement, the men's sulky with the obligation of having to put on their frock-coats before luncheon, and fight for food at the wedding-breakfast.

"Too bad the breakfast is at old Catherine's," the bridegroom could fancy Reggie Chivers saying. "But I'm told that Lovell Mingott insisted on its being cooked by his own *chef*, so it ought to be good if one can only get at it." And he could imagine Sillerton Jackson adding with authority: "My dear fellow, haven't you heard? It's to be served at small tables, in the new English fashion."

Archer's eyes lingered a moment on the left-hand pew, where his mother, who had entered the church on Mr. Henry van der Luyden's arm, sat weeping softly under her Chantilly veil, her hands in her grandmother's ermine muff.

"Poor Janey!" he thought, looking at his sister, "even by screwing her head around she can see only the people in the few front pews; and they're mostly dowdy New-lands and Dagonets."

On the hither side of the white ribbon dividing off the seats reserved for the families he saw Beaufort, tall and red-faced, scrutinising the women with his arro-

gant stare. Beside him sat his wife, all silvery chinchilla
and violets; and on the far side of the ribbon, Lawrence
Lefferts's sleekly brushed head seemed to mount guard
over the invisible deity of "Good Form" who presided
at the ceremony.

Archer wondered how many flaws Lefferts's keen eyes
would discover in the ritual of his divinity; then he suddenly recalled that he too had once thought such questions important. The things that had filled his days
seemed now like a nursery parody of life, or like the
wrangles of mediæval schoolmen over metaphysical terms
that nobody had ever understood. A stormy discussion
as to whether the wedding presents should be "shown"
had darkened the last hours before the wedding; and it
seemed inconceivable to Archer that grown-up people
should work themselves into a state of agitation over
such trifles, and that the matter should have been decided
(in the negative) by Mrs. Welland's saying, with indignant tears: "I should as soon turn the reporters loose in
my house." Yet there was a time when Archer had
had definite and rather aggressive opinions on all such
problems, and when everything concerning the manners
and customs of his little tribe had seemed to him fraught
with world-wide significance.

"And all the while, I suppose," he thought, "real people were living somewhere, and real things happening
to them . . ."

"There they come!" breathed the best man excitedly;
but the bridegroom knew better.

The cautious opening of the door of the church meant
only that Mr. Brown the livery-stable keeper (gowned in
black in his intermittent character of sexton) was taking
a preliminary survey of the scene before marshalling
his forces. The door was softly shut again; then after

another interval it swung majestically open, and a murmur ran through the church: "The family!"

Mrs. Welland came first, on the arm of her eldest son. Her large pink face was appropriately solemn, and her plum-coloured satin with pale blue side-panels, and blue ostrich plumes in a small satin bonnet, met with general approval; but before she had settled herself with a stately rustle in the pew opposite Mrs. Archer's the spectators were craning their necks to see who was coming after her. Wild rumours had been abroad the day before to the effect that Mrs. Manson Mingott, in spite of her physical disabilities, had resolved on being present at the ceremony; and the idea was so much in keeping with her sporting character that bets ran high at the clubs as to her being able to walk up the nave and squeeze into a seat. It was known that she had insisted on sending her own carpenter to look into the possibility of taking down the end panel of the front pew, and to measure the space between the seat and the front; but the result had been discouraging, and for one anxious day her family had watched her dallying with the plan of being wheeled up the nave in her enormous Bath chair and sitting enthroned in it at the foot of the chancel.

The idea of this monstrous exposure of her person was so painful to her relations that they could have covered with gold the ingenious person who suddenly discovered that the chair was too wide to pass between the iron uprights of the awning which extended from the church door to the curbstone. The idea of doing away with this awning, and revealing the bride to the mob of dressmakers and newspaper reporters who stood outside fighting to get near the joints of the canvas, exceeded even old Catherine's courage, though for a moment she had weighed the possibility. "Why, they might take a photograph of my child *and put it in the papers!*" Mrs. Welland exclaimed when her mother-in-law's last plan was hinted to her; and from this unthinkable indecency the clan recoiled with a collective shudder. The ancestress had had to give in; but her concession was bought only by the promise that the wedding-breakfast should take place under her roof, though (as the Washington Square connection said) with the Wellands' house in easy reach it was hard to have to make a special price with Brown to drive one to the other end of nowhere.

Though all these transactions had been widely reported by the Jacksons a sporting minority still clung to the belief that old Catherine would appear in church, and there was a distinct lowering of the temperature when she was found to have been replaced by her daughter-in-law. Mrs. Lovell Mingott had the high colour and glassy stare induced in ladies of her age and habit by the effort of getting into a new dress; but once the disappointment occasioned by her mother-in-law's non-appearance had subsided, it was agreed that her black Chantilly over lilac satin, with a bonnet of Parma violets, formed the happiest contrast to Mrs. Welland's blue and plum-colour. Far different was the impression produced by the gaunt and mincing lady who followed on Mr. Mingott's arm, in a wild dishevelment of stripes and fringes and floating scarves; and as this last apparition glided into view Archer's heart contracted and stopped beating.

He had taken it for granted that the Marchioness Manson was still in Washington, where she had gone some four weeks previously with her niece, Madame Olenska. It was generally understood that their abrupt departure was due to Madame Olenska's desire to remove her aunt from the baleful eloquence of Dr. Agathon Carver, who had nearly succeeded in enlisting her as a recruit for the Valley of Love; and in the circumstances no one had expected either of the ladies to return for the wedding. For a moment Archer stood with his eyes fixed on Medora's fantastic figure, straining to see who came behind her; but the little procession was at an end, for all the lesser members of the family had taken their seats, and the eight tall ushers, gathering themselves together like birds or insects preparing for some migratory manoeuvre, were already slipping through the side doors into the lobby.

"Newland—I say: *she's here!*" the best man whispered.

Archer roused himself with a start.

A long time had apparently passed since his heart had stopped beating, for the white and rosy procession was in fact half way up the nave, the Bishop, the Rector and two white-winged assistants were hovering about the flower-banked altar, and the first chords of the Spohr symphony were strewing their flower-like notes before the bride.

Archer opened his eyes (but could they really have been shut, as he imagined?), and felt his heart beginning to resume its usual task. The music, the scent of the lilies on the altar, the vision of the cloud of tulle and orange-blossoms floating nearer and nearer, the sight of Mrs. Archer's face suddenly convulsed with happy sobs, the low benedictory murmur of the Rector's voice, the ordered evolutions of the eight pink bridesmaids and the eight black ushers: all these sights, sounds and sensations, so familiar in themselves, so unutterably strange and meaningless in his new relation to them, were confusedly mingled in his brain.

"My God," he thought, *"have* I got the ring?"—and

once more he went through the bridegroom's convulsive gesture.

Then, in a moment, May was beside him, such radiance streaming from her that it sent a faint warmth through his numbness, and he straightened himself and smiled into her eyes.

"Dearly beloved, we are gathered together here," the Rector began . . .

The ring was on her hand, the Bishop's benediction had been given, the bridesmaids were a-poise to resume their place in the procession, and the organ was showing preliminary symptoms of breaking out into the Mendelssohn March, without which no newly-wedded couple had ever emerged upon New York.

"Your arm—*I say, give her your arm!*" young Newland nervously hissed; and once more Archer became aware of having been adrift far off in the unknown. What was it that had sent him there, he wondered? Perhaps the glimpse, among the anonymous spectators in the transept, of a dark coil of hair under a hat which, a moment later, revealed itself as belonging to an unknown lady with a long nose, so laughably unlike the person whose image she had evoked that he asked himself if he were becoming subject to hallucinations.

And now he and his wife were pacing slowly down the nave, carried forward on the light Mendelssohn ripples, the spring day beckoning to them through widely opened doors, and Mrs. Welland's chestnuts, with big white favours on their frontlets, curvetting and showing off at the far end of the canvas tunnel.

The footman, who had a still bigger white favour on his lapel, wrapped May's white cloak about her, and Archer jumped into the brougham at her side. She

turned to him with a triumphant smile and their hands
clasped under her veil.

"Darling!" Archer said—and suddenly the same black
abyss yawned before him and he felt himself sinking
into it, deeper and deeper, while his voice rambled on
smoothly and cheerfully: "Yes, of course I thought I'd
lost the ring; no wedding would be complete if the poor
devil of a bridegroom didn't go through that. But you
did keep me waiting, you know! I had time to think of
every horror that might possibly happen."

She surprised him by turning, in full Fifth Avenue,
and flinging her arms about his neck. "But none ever *can*
happen now, can it, Newland, as long as we two are
together?"

Every detail of the day had been so carefully thought
out that the young couple, after the wedding-breakfast,
had ample time to put on their travelling-clothes, descend
the wide Mingott stairs between laughing bridesmaids
and weeping parents, and get into the brougham under
the traditional shower of rice and satin slippers; and
there was still half an hour left in which to drive to the
station, buy the last weeklies at the bookstall with the air
of seasoned travellers, and settle themselves in the reserved compartment in which May's maid had already
placed her dove-coloured travelling cloak and glaringly
new dressing-bag from London.

The old du Lac aunts at Rhinebeck had put their house
at the disposal of the bridal couple, with a readiness
inspired by the prospect of spending a week in New York
with Mrs. Archer; and Archer, glad to escape the usual
"bridal suite" in a Philadelphia or Baltimore hotel, had
accepted with an equal alacrity.

May was enchanted at the idea of going to the country,

and childishly amused at the vain efforts of the eight bridesmaids to discover where their mysterious retreat was situated. It was thought "very English" to have a country-house lent to one, and the fact gave a last touch of distinction to what was generally conceded to be the most brilliant wedding of the year; but where the house was no one was permitted to know, except the parents of bride and groom, who, when taxed with the knowledge, pursed their lips and said mysteriously: "Ah, they didn't tell us—" which was manifestly true, since there was no need to.

Once they were settled in their compartment, and the train, shaking off the endless wooden suburbs, had pushed out into the pale landscape of spring, talk became easier than Archer had expected. May was still, in look and tone, the simple girl of yesterday, eager to compare notes with him as to the incidents of the wedding, and discussing them as impartially as a bridesmaid talking it all over with an usher. At first Archer had fancied that this detachment was the disguise of an inward tremor; but her clear eyes revealed only the most tranquil unawareness. She was alone for the first time with her husband; but her husband was only the charming comrade of yesterday. There was no one whom she liked as much, no one whom she trusted as completely, and the culminating "lark" of the whole delightful adventure of engagement and marriage was to be off with him alone on a journey, like a grown-up person, like a "married woman," in fact.

It was wonderful that—as he had learned in the Mission garden at St. Augustine—such depths of feeling could co-exist with such absence of imagination. But he remembered how, even then, she had surprised him by dropping back to inexpressive girlishness as soon as

[188]

her conscience had been eased of its burden; and he saw that she would probably go through life dealing to the best of her ability with each experience as it came, but never anticipating any by so much as a stolen glance.

Perhaps that faculty of unawareness was what gave her eyes their transparency, and her face the look of representing a type rather than a person; as if she might have been chosen to pose for a Civic Virtue or a Greek goddess. The blood that ran so close to her fair skin might have been a preserving fluid rather than a ravaging element; yet her look of indestructible youthfulness made her seem neither hard nor dull, but only primitive and pure. In the thick of this meditation Archer suddenly felt himself looking at her with the startled gaze of a stranger, and plunged into a reminiscence of the wedding-breakfast and of Granny Mingott's immense and triumphant pervasion of it.

May settled down to frank enjoyment of the subject. "I was surprised, though—weren't you?—that aunt Medora came after all. Ellen wrote that they were neither of them well enough to take the journey; I do wish it had been she who had recovered! Did you see the exquisite old lace she sent me?"

He had known that the moment must come sooner or later, but he had somewhat imagined that by force of willing he might hold it at bay.

"Yes—I—no: yes, it was beautiful," he said, looking at her blindly, and wondering if, whenever he heard those two syllables, all his carefully built-up world would tumble about him like a house of cards.

"Aren't you tired? It will be good to have some tea when we arrive—I'm sure the aunts have got everything beautifully ready," he rattled on, taking her hand in his; and her mind rushed away instantly to the magnificent tea and coffee service of Baltimore silver which the Beauforts had sent, and which "went" so perfectly with uncle Lovell Mingott's trays and side-dishes.

In the spring twilight the train stopped at the Rhinebeck station, and they walked along the platform to the waiting carriage.

"Ah, how awfully kind of the van der Luydens—they've sent their man over from Skuytercliff to meet us," Archer exclaimed, as a sedate person out of livery approached them and relieved the maid of her bags.

"I'm extremely sorry, sir," said this emissary, "that a little accident has occurred at the Miss du Lacs': a leak in the water-tank. It happened yesterday, and Mr. van der Luyden, who heard of it this morning, sent a house-maid up by the early train to get the Patroon's house ready. It will be quite comfortable, I think you'll find, sir; and the Miss du Lacs have sent their cook over, so that it will be exactly the same as if you'd been at Rhinebeck."

Archer stared at the speaker so blankly that he repeated in still more apologetic accents: "It'll be exactly the same, sir, I do assure you—" and May's eager voice broke out, covering the embarrassed silence: "The same as Rhinebeck? The Patroon's house? But it will be a hundred thousand times better—won't it, Newland? It's too dear and kind of Mr. van der Luyden to have thought of it."

And as they drove off, with the maid beside the coachman, and their shining bridal bags on the seat before them, she went on excitedly: "Only fancy, I've never been inside it—have you? The van der Luydens show it to so few people. But they opened it for Ellen, it seems, and she told me what a darling little place it was:

she says it's the only house she's seen in America that she could imagine being perfectly happy in."

"Well—that's what we're going to be, isn't it?" cried her husband gaily; and she answered with her boyish smile: "Ah, it's just our luck beginning—the wonderful luck we're always going to have together!"

XX

"OF COURSE we must dine with Mrs. Carfry, dearest," Archer said; and his wife looked at him with an anxious frown across the monumental Britannia ware of their lodging house breakfast-table.

In all the rainy desert of autumnal London there were only two people whom the Newland Archers knew; and these two they had sedulously avoided, in conformity with the old New York tradition that it was not "dignified" to force one's self on the notice of one's acquaintances in foreign countries.

Mrs. Archer and Janey, in the course of their visits to Europe, had so unflinchingly lived up to this principle, and met the friendly advances of their fellow-travellers with an air of such impenetrable reserve, that they had almost achieved the record of never having exchanged a word with a "foreigner" other than those employed in hotels and railway-stations. Their own compatriots—save those previously known or properly accredited—they treated with an even more pronounced disdain; so that, unless they ran across a Chivers, a Dagonet or a Mingott, their months abroad were spent in an unbroken *tête-à-tête*. But the utmost precautions are sometimes unavailing; and one night at Botzen one of the two English ladies in the room across the passage (whose names, dress and social situation were already intimately known to Janey) had knocked on the door and asked if Mrs. Archer had a bottle of liniment. The other lady—

the intruder's sister, Mrs. Carfry—had been seized with a sudden attack of bronchitis; and Mrs. Archer, who never travelled without a complete family pharmacy, was fortunately able to produce the required remedy.

Mrs. Carfry was very ill, and as she and her sister Miss Harle were travelling alone they were profoundly grateful to the Archer ladies, who supplied them with ingenious comforts and whose efficient maid helped to nurse the invalid back to health.

When the Archers left Botzen they had no idea of ever seeing Mrs. Carfry and Miss Harle again. Nothing, to Mrs. Archer's mind, would have been more "undignified" than to force one's self on the notice of a "foreigner" to whom one had happened to render an accidental service. But Mrs. Carfry and her sister, to whom this point of view was unknown, and who would have found it utterly incomprehensible, felt themselves linked by an eternal gratitude to the "delightful Americans" who had been so kind at Botzen. With touching fidelity they seized every chance of meeting Mrs. Archer and Janey in the course of their continental travels, and displayed a supernatural acuteness in finding out when they were to pass through London on their way to or from the States. The intimacy became indissoluble, and Mrs. Archer and Janey, whenever they alighted at Brown's Hotel, found themselves awaited by two affectionate friends who, like themselves, cultivated ferns in Wardian cases, made macramé lace, read the memoirs of the Baroness Bunsen and had views about the occupants of the leading London pulpits. As Mrs. Archer said, it made "another thing of London" to know Mrs. Carfry and Miss Harle; and by the time that Newland became engaged the tie between the families was so firmly established that it was thought "only right" to send a wedding invitation to the two English ladies, who sent, in return, a pretty bouquet of pressed Alpine flowers under glass. And on the dock, when Newland and his wife sailed for England, Mrs. Archer's last word had been: "You must take May to see Mrs. Carfry."

Newland and his wife had had no idea of obeying this injunction; but Mrs. Carfry, with her usual acuteness, had run them down and sent them an invitation to dine; and it was over this invitation that May Archer was wrinkling her brows across the tea and muffins.

"It's all very well for you, Newland; you *know* them. But I shall feel so shy among a lot of people I've never met. And what shall I wear?"

Newland leaned back in his chair and smiled at her. She looked handsomer and more Diana-like than ever. The moist English air seemed to have deepened the bloom of her cheeks and softened the slight hardness of her virginal features; or else it was simply the inner glow of happiness, shining through like a light under ice.

"Wear, dearest? I thought a trunkful of things had come from Paris last week."

"Yes, of course. I meant to say that I shan't know *which* to wear." She pouted a little. "I've never dined out in London; and I don't want to be ridiculous."

He tried to enter into her perplexity. "But don't Englishwomen dress just like everybody else in the evening?"

"Newland! How can you ask such funny questions? When they go to the theatre in old ball-dresses and bare heads."

"Well, perhaps they wear new ball-dresses at home; but at any rate Mrs. Carfry and Miss Harle won't. They'll wear caps like my mother's—and shawls; very soft shawls."

"Yes; but how will the other women be dressed?"

"Not as well as you, dear," he rejoined, wondering what had suddenly developed in her Janey's morbid interest in clothes.

She pushed back her chair with a sigh. "That's dear of you, Newland; but it doesn't help me much."

He had an inspiration. "Why not wear your wedding-dress? That can't be wrong, can it?"

"Oh, dearest! If I only had it here! But it's gone to Paris to be made over for next winter, and Worth hasn't sent it back."

"Oh, well—" said Archer, getting up. "Look here—the fog's lifting. If we made a dash for the National Gallery we might manage to catch a glimpse of the pictures."

The Newland Archers were on their way home, after a three months' wedding-tour which May, in writing to her girl friends, vaguely summarised as "blissful."

They had not gone to the Italian Lakes: on reflection, Archer had not been able to picture his wife in that particular setting. Her own inclination (after a month with the Paris dressmakers) was for mountaineering in July and swimming in August. This plan they punctually fulfilled, spending July at Interlaken and Grindelwald, and August at a little place called Etretat, on the Normandy coast, which some one had recommended as quaint and quiet. Once or twice, in the mountains, Archer had pointed southward and said: "There's Italy"; and May, her feet in a gentian-bed, had smiled cheerfully, and replied: "It would be lovely to go there next winter, if only you didn't have to be in New York."

But in reality travelling interested her even less than he had expected. She regarded it (once her clothes were ordered) as merely an enlarged opportunity for walking, riding, swimming, and trying her hand at the fascinating new game of lawn tennis; and when they finally got back to London (where they were to spend a fortnight while he ordered *his* clothes) she no longer concealed the eagerness with which she looked forward to sailing.

In London nothing interested her but the theatres and the shops; and she found the theatres less exciting than the Paris *cafés chantants* where, under the blossoming horse-chestnuts of the Champs Élysées, she had had the novel experience of looking down from the restaurant terrace on an audience of "cocottes," and having her husband interpret to her as much of the songs as he thought suitable for bridal ears.

Archer had reverted to all his old inherited ideas about marriage. It was less trouble to conform with the tradition and treat May exactly as all his friends treated their wives than to try to put into practice the theories with which his untrammelled bachelorhood had dallied. There was no use in trying to emancipate a wife who had not the dimmest notion that she was not free; and he had long since discovered that May's only use of the liberty she supposed herself to possess would be to lay it on the altar of her wifely adoration. Her innate dignity would always keep her from making the gift abjectly; and a day might even come (as it once had) when she would find strength to take it altogether back if she thought she were doing it for his own good. But with a conception of marriage so uncomplicated and incurious as hers such a crisis could be brought about only by something visibly outrageous in his own conduct; and the fineness of her feeling for him made that unthinkable. Whatever happened, he knew, she would always be loyal, gallant and unresentful; and that pledged him to the practice of the same virtues.

All this tended to draw him back into his old habits of mind. If her simplicity had been the simplicity of pettiness he would have chafed and rebelled; but since the lines of her character, though so few, were on the same fine mould as her face, she became the tutelary divinity of all his old traditions and reverences.

Such qualities were scarcely of the kind to enliven foreign travel, though they made her so easy and pleasant a companion; but he saw at once how they would fall into place in their proper setting. He had no fear of being oppressed by them, for his artistic and intellectual life would go on, as it always had, outside the domestic circle; and within it there would be nothing small and stifling—coming back to his wife would never be like entering a stuffy room after a tramp in the open. And when they had children the vacant corners in both their lives would be filled.

All these things went through his mind during their long slow drive from Mayfair to South Kensington, where Mrs. Carfry and her sister lived. Archer too would have preferred to escape their friends' hospitality: in conformity with the family tradition he had always travelled as a sight-seer and looker-on, affecting a haughty unconsciousness of the presence of his fellow-beings. Once only, just after Harvard, he had spent a few gay weeks at Florence with a band of queer Europeanised Americans, dancing all night with titled ladies in palaces, and gambling half the day with the rakes and dandies of the fashionable club; but it had all seemed to him, though the greatest fun in the world, as unreal as a carnival. These queer cosmopolitan women, deep in complicated love-affairs which they appeared to feel the need of retailing to every one they met, and the magnificent young officers and elderly dyed wits who were the subjects or the recipients of their confidences, were too different from the people Archer had grown up among, too much like expensive and rather malodorous hot-house exotics, to detain his imagination long. To introduce his wife into such a society was out of the question; and in the course of his travels no other had shown any marked eagerness for his company.

Not long after their arrival in London he had run across the Duke of St. Austrey, and the Duke, instantly and cordially recognising him, had said: "Look me up, won't you?"—but no proper-spirited American would have considered that a suggestion to be acted on, and the meeting was without a sequel. They had even managed to avoid May's English aunt, the banker's wife, who was still in Yorkshire; in fact, they had purposely postponed going to London till the autumn in order that their arrival during the season might not appear pushing and snobbish to these unknown relatives.

"Probably there'll be nobody at Mrs. Carfry's—London's a desert at this season, and you've made yourself much too beautiful," Archer said to May, who sat at his side in the hansom so spotlessly splendid in her sky-blue cloak edged with swansdown that it seemed wicked to expose her to the London grime.

"I don't want them to think that we dress like savages," she replied, with a scorn that Pocahontas might have resented; and he was struck again by the religious reverence of even the most unworldly American women for the social advantages of dress.

"It's their armour," he thought, "their defence against the unknown, and their defiance of it." And he understood for the first time the earnestness with which May, who was incapable of tying a ribbon in her hair to charm him, had gone through the solemn rite of selecting and ordering her extensive wardrobe.

He had been right in expecting the party at Mrs. Carfry's to be a small one. Besides their hostess and her sister, they found, in the long chilly drawing-room, only another shawled lady, a genial Vicar who was her husband, a silent lad whom Mrs. Carfry named as her nephew, and a small dark gentleman with lively eyes whom she introduced as his tutor, pronouncing a French name as she did so.

Into this dimly-lit and dim-featured group May Archer floated like a swan with the sunset on her: she seemed larger, fairer, more voluminously rustling than her husband had ever seen her; and he perceived that the rosiness and rustlingness were the tokens of an extreme and infantile shyness.

"What on earth will they expect me to talk about?" her helpless eyes implored him, at the very moment that her dazzling apparition was calling forth the same anxiety in their own bosoms. But beauty, even when distrustful of itself, awakens confidence in the manly heart; and the Vicar and the French-named tutor were soon manifesting to May their desire to put her at her ease.

In spite of their best efforts, however, the dinner was a languishing affair. Archer noticed that his wife's way of showing herself at her ease with foreigners was to become more uncompromisingly local in her references, so that, though her loveliness was an encouragement to admiration, her conversation was a chill to repartee. The Vicar soon abandoned the struggle; but the tutor, who spoke the most fluent and accomplished English, gallantly continued to pour it out to her until the ladies, to the manifest relief of all concerned, went up to the drawing-room.

The Vicar, after a glass of port, was obliged to hurry away to a meeting, and the shy nephew, who appeared to be an invalid, was packed off to bed. But Archer and the tutor continued to sit over their wine, and suddenly Archer found himself talking as he had not done since his last symposium with Ned Winsett. The Carfry nephew, it turned out, had been threatened with consumption, and had had to leave Harrow for Switzerland, where he had spent two years in the milder air of Lake Leman. Being a bookish youth, he had been entrusted to M. Rivière, who had brought him back to England, and was to remain with him till he went up to Oxford the following spring; and M. Rivière added with simplicity that he should then have to look out for another job.

It seemed impossible, Archer thought, that he should be long without one, so varied were his interests and so many his gifts. He was a man of about thirty, with a thin ugly face (May would certainly have called him common-looking) to which the play of his ideas gave an intense expressiveness; but there was nothing frivolous or cheap in his animation.

His father, who had died young, had filled a small diplomatic post, and it had been intended that the son should follow the same career; but an insatiable taste for letters had thrown the young man into journalism, then into authorship (apparently unsuccessful), and at length—after other experiments and vicissitudes which he spared his listener—into tutoring English youths in Switzerland. Before that, however, he had lived much in Paris, frequented the Goncourt *grenier*, been advised by Maupassant not to attempt to write (even that seemed to Archer a dazzling honour!), and had often talked with

Mérimée in his mother's house. He had obviously always been desperately poor and anxious (having a mother and an unmarried sister to provide for), and it was apparent that his literary ambitions had failed. His situation, in fact, seemed, materially speaking, no more brilliant than Ned Winsett's; but he had lived in a world in which, as he said, no one who loved ideas need hunger mentally. As it was precisely of that love that poor Winsett was starving to death, Archer looked with a sort of vicarious envy at this eager impecunious young man who had fared so richly in his poverty.

"You see, Monsieur, it's worth everything, isn't it, to keep one's intellectual liberty, not to enslave one's powers of appreciation, one's critical independence? It was because of that that I abandoned journalism, and took to so much duller work: tutoring and private secretary-ship. There is a good deal of drudgery, of course; but one preserves one's moral freedom, what we call in French one's *quant à soi*. And when one hears good talk one can join in it without compromising any opinions but one's own; or one can listen, and answer it inwardly. Ah, good conversation—there's nothing like it, is there? The air of ideas is the only air worth breathing. And so I have never regretted giving up either diplomacy or journalism—two different forms of the same self-abdication." He fixed his vivid eyes on Archer as he lit another cigarette. "*Voyez-vous*, Monsieur, to be able to look life in the face: that's worth living in a garret for, isn't it? But, after all, one must earn enough to pay for the garret; and I confess that to grow old as a private tutor—or a 'private' anything—is almost as chilling to the imagination as a second secretaryship at Bucharest. Sometimes I feel I must make a plunge: an immense plunge. Do you suppose, for instance, there

[201]

would be any opening for me in America—in New York?"

Archer looked at him with startled eyes. New York, for a young man who had frequented the Goncourts and Flaubert, and who thought the life of ideas the only one worth living! He continued to stare at M. Rivière perplexedly, wondering how to tell him that his very superiorities and advantages would be the surest hindrance to success.

"New York—New York—but must it be especially New York?" he stammered, utterly unable to imagine what lucrative opening his native city could offer to a young man to whom good conversation appeared to be the only necessity.

A sudden flush rose under M. Rivière's sallow skin. "I—I thought it your metropolis: is not the intellectual life more active there?" he rejoined; then, as if fearing to give his hearer the impression of having asked a favour, he went on hastily: "One throws out random suggestions—more to one's self than to others. In reality, I see no immediate prospect—" and rising from his seat he added, without a trace of constraint: "But Mrs. Carfry will think that I ought to be taking you upstairs."

During the homeward drive Archer pondered deeply on this episode. His hour with R. Rivière had put new air into his lungs, and his first impulse had been to invite him to dine the next day; but he was beginning to understand why married men did not always immediately yield to their first impulses.

"That young tutor is an interesting fellow: we had some awfully good talk after dinner about books and things," he threw out tentatively in the hansom.

May roused herself from one of the dreamy silences

into which he had read so many meanings before six months of marriage had given him the key to them.

"The little Frenchman? Wasn't he dreadfully common?" she questioned coldly; and he guessed that she nursed a secret disappointment at having been invited out in London to meet a clergyman and a French tutor. The disappointment was not occasioned by the sentiment ordinarily defined as snobbishness, but by old New York's sense of what was due to it when it risked its dignity in foreign lands. If May's parents had entertained the Carfrys in Fifth Avenue they would have offered them something more substantial than a parson and a schoolmaster.

But Archer was on edge, and took her up.

"Common—common *where?*" he queried; and she returned with unusual readiness: "Why, I should say anywhere but in his school-room. Those people are always awkward in society. But then," she added disarmingly, "I suppose I shouldn't have known if he was clever."

Archer disliked her use of the word "clever" almost as much as her use of the word "common"; but he was beginning to fear his tendency to dwell on the things he disliked in her. After all, her point of view had always been the same. It was that of all the people he had grown up among, and he had always regarded it as necessary but negligible. Until a few months ago he had never known a "nice" woman who looked at life differently; and if a man married it must necessarily be among the nice.

"Ah—then I won't ask him to dine!" he concluded with a laugh; and May echoed, bewildered: "Goodness—ask the Carfrys' tutor?"

"Well, not on the same day with the Carfrys, if you

prefer I shouldn't. But I did rather want another talk with him. He's looking for a job in New York."

Her surprise increased with her indifference: he almost fancied that she suspected him of being tainted with "foreignness."

"A job in New York? What sort of a job? People don't have French tutors: what does he want to do?"

"Chiefly to enjoy good conversation, I understand," her husband retorted perversely; and she broke into an appreciative laugh. "Oh, Archer, how funny! Isn't that *French?*"

On the whole, he was glad to have the matter settled for him by her refusing to take seriously his wish to invite M. Rivière. Another after-dinner talk would have made it difficult to avoid the question of New York; and the more Archer considered it the less he was able to fit M. Rivière into any conceivable picture of New York as he knew it.

He perceived with a flash of chilling insight that in future many problems would be thus negatively solved for him; but as he paid the hansom and followed his wife's long train into the house he took refuge in the comforting platitude that the first six months were always the most difficult in marriage. "After that I suppose we shall have pretty nearly finished rubbing off each other's angles," he reflected; but the worst of it was that May's pressure was already bearing on the very angles whose sharpness he most wanted to keep.

XXI

THE small bright lawn stretched away smoothly to
the big bright sea.

The turf was neatly hemmed with an edge of scarlet
geranium and coleus, and cast-iron vases painted in
chocolate colour, standing at intervals along the winding
path that led to the sea, looped their garlands of petunia
and ivy geranium above the neatly raked gravel.

Half way between the edge of the cliff and the square
wooden house (which was also chocolate-coloured, but
with the tin roof of the verandah striped in yellow and
brown to represent an awning) two large targets had
been placed against a background of shrubbery. On the
other side of the lawn, facing the targets, was pitched a
real tent, with benches and garden-seats about it. A
number of ladies in summer dresses and gentlemen in
grey frock-coats and tall hats stood on the lawn or sat
upon the benches; and every now and then a slender
girl in starched muslin would step from the tent, bow
in hand, and speed her shaft at one of the targets, while
the spectators interrupted their talk to watch the result.

Newland Archer, standing on the verandah of the
house, looked curiously down upon this scene. On each
side of the shiny painted steps was a large blue china
flower-pot on a bright yellow china stand. A spiky
green plant filled each pot, and below the verandah ran
a wide border of blue hydrangeas edged with more red
geraniums. Behind him, the French windows of the

drawing-rooms through which he had passed gave glimpses, between swaying lace curtains, of glassy parquet floors islanded with chintz *poufs,* dwarf arm-chairs, and velvet tables covered with trifles in silver.

The Newport Archery Club always held its August meeting at the Beauforts'. The sport, which had hitherto known no rival but croquet, was beginning to be discarded in favour of lawn-tennis; but the latter game was still considered too rough and inelegant for social occasions, and as an opportunity to show off pretty dresses and graceful attitudes the bow and arrow held their own.

Archer looked down with wonder at the familiar spectacle. It surprised him that life should be going on in the old way when his own reactions to it had so completely changed. It was Newport that had first brought home to him the extent of the change. In New York, during the previous winter, after he and May had settled down in the new greenish-yellow house with the bow-window and the Pompeian vestibule, he had dropped back with relief into the old routine of the office, and the renewal of this daily activity had served as a link with his former self. Then there had been the pleasurable excitement of choosing a showy grey stepper for May's brougham (the Wellands had given the carriage), and the abiding occupation and interest of arranging his new library, which, in spite of family doubts and disapprovals, had been carried out as he had dreamed, with a dark embossed paper, Eastlake bookcases and "sincere" arm-chairs and tables. At the Century he had found Winsett again, and at the Knickerbocker the fashionable young men of his own set; and what with the hours dedicated to the law and those given to dining out or entertaining friends at home, with an occasional evening at the Opera or the play, the life he was living had still seemed a fairly real and inevitable sort of business.

But Newport represented the escape from duty into an atmosphere of unmitigated holiday-making. Archer had tried to persuade May to spend the summer on a remote island off the coast of Maine (called, appropriately enough, Mount Desert), where a few hardy Bostonians and Philadelphians were camping in "native" cottages, and whence came reports of enchanting scenery and a wild, almost trapper-like existence amid woods and waters.

But the Wellands always went to Newport, where they owned one of the square boxes on the cliffs, and their son-in-law could adduce no good reason why he and May should not join them there. As Mrs. Welland rather tartly pointed out, it was hardly worth while for May to have worn herself out trying on summer clothes in Paris if she was not to be allowed to wear them; and this argument was of a kind to which Archer had as yet found no answer.

May herself could not understand his obscure reluctance to fall in with so reasonable and pleasant a way of spending the summer. She reminded him that he had always liked Newport in his bachelor days, and as this was indisputable he could only profess that he was sure he was going to like it better than ever now that they were to be there together. But as he stood on the Beaufort verandah and looked out on the brightly peopled lawn it came home to him with a shiver that he was not going to like it at all.

It was not May's fault, poor dear. If, now and then, during their travels, they had fallen slightly out of step, harmony had been restored by their return to the conditions she was used to. He had always foreseen that she would not disappoint him; and he had been right. He had married (as most young men did) because he had met a perfectly charming girl at the moment when a series of rather aimless sentimental adventures were ending in premature disgust; and she had represented peace, stability, comradeship, and the steadying sense of an unescapable duty.

He could not say that he had been mistaken in his choice, for she had fulfilled all that he had expected. It was undoubtedly gratifying to be the husband of one of the handsomest and most popular young married women in New York, especially when she was also one of the sweetest-tempered and most reasonable of wives; and Archer had never been insensible to such advantages. As for the momentary madness which had fallen upon him on the eve of his marriage, he had trained himself to regard it as the last of his discarded experiments. The idea that he could ever, in his senses, have dreamed of marrying the Countess Olenska had become almost unthinkable, and she remained in his memory simply as the most plaintive and poignant of a line of ghosts.

But all these abstractions and eliminations made of his mind a rather empty and echoing place, and he supposed that was one of the reasons why the busy animated people on the Beaufort lawn shocked him as if they had been children playing in a grave-yard.

He heard a murmur of skirts beside him, and the Marchioness Manson fluttered out of the drawing-room window. As usual, she was extraordinarily festooned and bedizened, with a limp Leghorn hat anchored to her head by many windings of faded gauze, and a little

black velvet parasol on a carved ivory handle absurdly
balanced over her much larger hat-brim.

"My dear Newland, I had no idea that you and May
had arrived! You yourself came only yesterday, you
say? Ah, business—business—professional duties . . . I
understand. Many husbands, I know, find it impossible
to join their wives here except for the week-end." She
cocked her head on one side and languished at him
through screwed-up eyes. "But marriage is one long
sacrifice, as I used often to remind my Ellen—"

Archer's heart stopped with the queer jerk which it
had given once before, and which seemed suddenly to
slam a door between himself and the outer world; but
this break of continuity must have been of the briefest,
for he presently heard Medora answering a question
he had apparently found voice to put.

"No, I am not staying here, but with the Blenkers,
in their delicious solitude at Portsmouth. Beaufort was
kind enough to send his famous trotters for me this
morning, so that I might have at least a glimpse of one
of Regina's garden-parties; but this evening I go back to
rural life. The Blenkers, dear original beings, have
hired a primitive old farm-house at Portsmouth where
they gather about them representative people . . ." She
drooped slightly beneath her protecting brim, and added
with a faint blush: "This week Dr. Agathon Carver is
holding a series of Inner Thought meetings there. A
contrast indeed to this gay scene of worldly pleasure—
but then I have always lived on contrasts! To me the
only death is monotony. I always say to Ellen: Beware
of monotony; it's the mother of all the deadly sins. But
my poor child is going through a phase of exaltation,
of abhorrence of the world. You know, I suppose, that
she has declined all invitations to stay at Newport, even

with her grandmother Mingott? I could hardly persuade her to come with me to the Blenkers', if you will
believe it! The life she leads is morbid, unnatural. Ah,
if she had only listened to me when it was still possible
. . . When the door was still open . . . But shall we
go down and watch this absorbing match? I hear your
May is one of the competitors."

Strolling toward them from the tent Beaufort advanced over the lawn, tall, heavy, too tightly buttoned
into a London frock-coat, with one of his own orchids
in its buttonhole. Archer, who had not seen him for two
or three months, was struck by the change in his
appearance. In the hot summer light his floridness
seemed heavy and bloated, and but for his erect square-
shouldered walk he would have looked like an over-fed
and over-dressed old man.

There were all sorts of rumours afloat about Beaufort.
In the spring he had gone off on a long cruise to the
West Indies in his new steam-yacht, and it was reported
that, at various points where he had touched, a lady
resembling Miss Fanny Ring had been seen in his company. The steam-yacht, built in the Clyde, and fitted
with tiled bath-rooms and other unheard-of luxuries, was
said to have cost him half a million; and the pearl necklace which he had presented to his wife on his return
was as magnificent as such expiatory offerings are apt
to be. Beaufort's fortune was substantial enough to
stand the strain; and yet the disquieting rumours persisted, not only in Fifth Avenue but in Wall Street.
Some people said he had speculated unfortunately in
railways, others that he was being bled by one of the
most insatiable members of her profession; and to every
report of threatened insolvency Beaufort replied by a
fresh extravagance: the building of a new row of orchid-

houses, the purchase of a new string of race-horses, or the addition of a new Meissonnier or Cabanel to his picture-gallery.

He advanced toward the Marchioness and Newland with his usual half-sneering smile. "Hullo, Medora! Did the trotters do their business? Forty minutes, eh? . . . Well, that's not so bad, considering your nerves had to be spared." He shook hands with Archer, and then, turning back with them, placed himself on Mrs. Manson's other side, and said, in a low voice, a few words which their companion did not catch.

The Marchioness replied by one of her queer foreign jerks, and a *"Que voulez-vous?"* which deepened Beaufort's frown; but he produced a good semblance of a congratulatory smile as he glanced at Archer to say: "You know May's going to carry off the first prize."

"Ah, then it remains in the family," Medora rippled; and at that moment they reached the tent and Mrs. Beaufort met them in a girlish cloud of mauve muslin and floating veils.

May Welland was just coming out of the tent. In her white dress, with a pale green ribbon about the waist and a wreath of ivy on her hat, she had the same Diana-like aloofness as when she had entered the Beaufort ball-room on the night of her engagement. In the interval not a thought seemed to have passed behind her eyes or a feeling through her heart; and though her husband knew that she had the capacity for both he marvelled afresh at the way in which experience dropped away from her.

She had her bow and arrow in her hand, and placing herself on the chalk-mark traced on the turf she lifted the bow to her shoulder and took aim. The attitude was so full of a classic grace that a murmur of appreciation followed her appearance, and Archer felt the glow of proprietorship that so often cheated him into momentary well-being. Her rivals—Mrs. Reggie Chivers, the Merry girls, and divers rosy Thorleys, Dagonets and Mingotts, stood behind her in a lovely anxious group, brown heads and golden bent above the scores, and pale muslins and flower-wreathed hats mingled in a tender rainbow. All were young and pretty, and bathed in summer bloom; but not one had the nymph-like ease of his wife, when, with tense muscles and happy frown, she bent her soul upon some feat of strength.

"Gad," Archer heard Lawrence Lefferts say, "not one of the lot holds the bow as she does;" and Beaufort retorted: "Yes; but that's the only kind of target she'll ever hit."

Archer felt irrationally angry. His host's contemptuous tribute to May's "niceness" was just what a husband should have wished to hear said of his wife. The fact that a coarse-minded man found her lacking in attraction was simply another proof of her quality; yet the words sent a faint shiver through his heart. What if "niceness" carried to that supreme degree were only a negation, the curtain dropped before an emptiness? As he looked at May, returning flushed and calm from her final bull's-eye, he had the feeling that he had never yet lifted that curtain.

She took the congratulations of her rivals and of the rest of the company with the simplicity that was her crowning grace. No one could ever be jealous of her triumphs because she managed to give the feeling that she would have been just as serene if she had missed them. But when her eyes met her husband's her face glowed with the pleasure she saw in his.

Mrs. Welland's basket-work poney-carriage was waiting for them, and they drove off among the dispersing carriages, May handling the reins and Archer sitting at her side.

The afternoon sunlight still lingered upon the bright lawns and shrubberies, and up and down Bellevue Avenue rolled a double line of victorias, dog-carts, landaus and "vis-à-vis," carrying well-dressed ladies and gentlemen away from the Beaufort garden-party, or homeward from their daily afternoon turn along the Ocean Drive.

"Shall we go to see Granny?" May suddenly proposed. "I should like to tell her myself that I've won the prize. There's lots of time before dinner."

Archer acquiesced, and she turned the ponies down Narragansett Avenue, crossed Spring Street and drove out toward the rocky moorland beyond. In this un-fashionable region Catherine the Great, always indifferent to precedent and thrifty of purse, had built herself in her youth a many-peaked and cross-beamed *cottage-orné* on a bit of cheap land overlooking the bay. Here, in a thicket of stunted oaks, her verandahs spread themselves above the island-dotted waters. A winding drive led up between iron stags and blue glass balls embedded in mounds of geraniums to a front door of highly-varnished walnut under a striped verandah-roof; and behind it ran a narrow hall with a black and yellow star-patterned parquet floor, upon which opened four small square rooms with heavy flock-papers under ceilings on which an Italian house-painter had lavished all the divinities of Olympus. One of these rooms had been turned into a bedroom by Mrs. Mingott when the burden of flesh descended on her, and in the adjoining one she spent her days, enthroned in a large arm-chair between the open door and window, and perpetually waving a palm-leaf fan which the prodigious projection of her bosom kept so far from the rest of her person that the air it set in motion stirred only the fringe of the anti-macassars on the chair-arms.

Since she had been the means of hastening his marriage old Catherine had shown to Archer the cordiality which a service rendered excites toward the person served. She was persuaded that irrepressible passion was the cause of his impatience; and being an ardent admirer of impulsiveness (when it did not lead to the spending of money) she always received him with a genial twinkle of complicity and a play of allusion to which May seemed fortunately impervious.

She examined and appraised with much interest the diamond-tipped arrow which had been pinned on May's bosom at the conclusion of the match, remarking that in her day a filigree brooch would have been thought enough, but that there was no denying that Beaufort did things handsomely.

"Quite an heirloom, in fact, my dear," the old lady chuckled. "You must leave it in fee to your eldest girl." She pinched May's white arm and watched the colour flood her face. "Well, well, what have I said to make you shake out the red flag? Ain't there going to be any daughters—only boys, eh? Good gracious, look at her blushing again all over her blushes! What—can't I say that either? Mercy me—when my children beg me to have all those gods and goddesses painted out overhead I always say I'm too thankful to have somebody about me that *nothing* can shock!"

Archer burst into a laugh, and May echoed it, crimson to the eyes.

"Well, now tell me all about the party, please, my dears, for I shall never get a straight word about it out of that silly Medora," the ancestress continued; and, as May exclaimed: "Cousin Medora? But I thought she was going back to Portsmouth?" she answered placidly: "So she is—but she's got to come here first to pick up Ellen. Ah—you didn't know Ellen had come to spend the day with me? Such fol-de-rol, her not coming for the summer; but I gave up arguing with young people about fifty years ago. Ellen—*Ellen!*" she cried in her shrill old voice, trying to bend forward far enough to catch a glimpse of the lawn beyond the verandah.

There was no answer, and Mrs. Mingott rapped impatiently with her stick on the shiny floor. A mulatto maid-servant in a bright turban, replying to the summons, informed her mistress that she had seen "Miss Ellen" going down the path to the shore; and Mrs. Mingott turned to Archer.

"Run down and fetch her, like a good grandson; this pretty lady will describe the party to me," she said; and Archer stood up as if in a dream.

He had heard the Countess Olenska's name pronounced often enough during the year and a half since they had last met, and was even familiar with the main incidents of her life in the interval. He knew that she had spent the previous summer at Newport, where she appeared to have gone a great deal into society, but that in the autumn she had suddenly sub-let the "perfect house" which Beaufort had been at such pains to find for her, and decided to establish herself in Washington. There, during the winter, he had heard of her (as one always heard of pretty women in Washington) as shining in the "brilliant diplomatic society" that was supposed to make up for the social short-comings of the Administration. He had listened to these accounts, and to various contradictory reports on her appearance, her conversation, her point of view and her choice of friends, with the detachment with which one listens to reminiscences of some one long since dead; not till Medora suddenly spoke her name at the archery match had Ellen Olenska become a living presence to him again. The Marchioness's foolish lisp had called up a vision of the little fire-lit drawing-room and the sound of the carriage-wheels returning down the deserted street. He thought of a story he had read, of some peasant children in Tuscany lighting a bunch of straw in a wayside cavern, and revealing old silent images in their painted tomb . . .

The way to the shore descended from the bank on which the house was perched to a walk above the water planted with weeping willows. Through their veil Archer caught the glint of the Lime Rock, with its white-washed turret and the tiny house in which the heroic light-house keeper, Ida Lewis, was living her last venerable years. Beyond it lay the flat reaches and ugly government chimneys of Goat Island, the bay spreading northward in a shimmer of gold to Prudence Island with its low growth of oaks, and the shores of Conanicut faint in the sunset haze.

From the willow walk projected a slight wooden pier ending in a sort of pagoda-like summer-house; and in the pagoda a lady stood, leaning against the rail, her back to the shore. Archer stopped at the sight as if he had waked from sleep. That vision of the past was a dream, and the reality was what awaited him in the house on the bank overhead: was Mrs. Welland's pony-carriage circling around and around the oval at the door, was May sitting under the shameless Olympians and glowing with secret hopes, was the Welland villa at the far end of Bellevue Avenue, and Mr. Welland, already dressed for dinner, and pacing the drawing-room floor, watch in hand, with dyspeptic impatience—for it was one of the houses in which one always knew exactly what is happening at a given hour.

"What am I? A son-in-law—" Archer thought.

The figure at the end of the pier had not moved. For a long moment the young man stood half way down the bank, gazing at the bay furrowed with the coming and going of sail-boats, yacht-launches, fishing-craft and the trailing black coal-barges hauled by noisy tugs. The lady in the summer-house seemed to be held by the same sight. Beyond the grey bastions of Fort Adams a long-drawn sunset was splintering up into a thousand fires, and the radiance caught the sail of a cat-boat as it beat out through the channel between the Lime Rock and the shore. Archer, as he watched, remembered the scene in the Shaughraun, and Montague lifting Ada Dyas's ribbon to his lips without her knowing that he was in the room.

"She doesn't know—she hasn't guessed. Shouldn't I know if she came up behind me, I wonder?" he mused; and suddenly he said to himself: "If she doesn't turn before that sail crosses the Lime Rock light I'll go back."

The boat was gliding out on the receding tide. It slid before the Lime Rock, blotted out Ida Lewis's little house, and passed across the turret in which the light was hung. Archer waited till a wide space of water sparkled between the last reef of the island and the stern of the boat; but still the figure in the summer-house did not move.

He turned and walked up the hill.

"I'm sorry you didn't find Ellen—I should have liked to see her again," May said as they drove home through the dusk. "But perhaps she wouldn't have cared—she seems so changed."

"Changed?" echoed her husband in a colourless voice, his eyes fixed on the ponies' twitching ears.

"So indifferent to her friends, I mean; giving up New York and her house, and spending her time with such queer people. Fancy how hideously uncomfortable she must be at the Blenkers'! She says she does it to keep cousin Medora out of mischief: to prevent her marrying dreadful people. But I sometimes think we've always bored her."

Archer made no answer, and she continued, with a tinge of hardness that he had never before noticed in her frank fresh voice: "After all, I wonder if she wouldn't be happier with her husband."

He burst into a laugh. *"Sancta simplicitas!"* he exclaimed; and as she turned a puzzled frown on him he added: "I don't think I ever heard you say a cruel thing before."

"Cruel?"

"Well—watching the contortions of the damned is supposed to be a favourite sport of the angels; but I believe even they don't think people happier in hell."

"It's a pity she ever married abroad then," said May, in the placid tone with which her mother met Mr. Welland's vagaries; and Archer felt himself gently relegated to the category of unreasonable husbands.

They drove down Bellevue Avenue and turned in between the chamfered wooden gate-posts surmounted by cast-iron lamps which marked the approach to the Welland villa. Lights were already shining through its windows, and Archer, as the carriage stopped, caught a glimpse of his father-in-law, exactly as he had pictured him, pacing the drawing-room, watch in hand and wearing the pained expression that he had long since found to be much more efficacious than anger.

The young man, as he followed his wife into the hall, was conscious of a curious reversal of mood. There was something about the luxury of the Welland house and the density of the Welland atmosphere, so charged with minute observances and exactions, that always stole into his system like a narcotic. The heavy carpets, the watchful servants, the perpetually reminding tick of disciplined clocks, the perpetually renewed stack of cards and invitations on the hall table, the whole chain of tyrannical trifles binding one hour to the next, and each member of the household to all the others, made any less systematised and affluent existence seem unreal and precarious. But now it was the Welland house, and the life he was expected to lead in it, that had become unreal and irrelevant, and the brief scene on the shore, when he had stood irresolute, half-way down the bank, was as close to him as the blood in his veins.

All night he lay awake in the big chintz bedroom at May's side, watching the moonlight slant along the carpet, and thinking of Ellen Olenska driving home across the gleaming beaches behind Beaufort's trotters.

XXII

A PARTY for the Blenkers—the Blenkers?"
Mr. Welland laid down his knife and fork and
looked anxiously and incredulously across the luncheon-
table at his wife, who, adjusting her gold eye-glasses,
read aloud, in the tone of high comedy: "Professor and
Mrs. Emerson Sillerton request the pleasure of Mr. and
Mrs. Welland's company at the meeting of the Wednesday Afternoon Club on August 25th at 3 o'clock punctually. To meet Mrs. and the Misses Blenker.
"Red Gables, Catherine Street.   R. S. V. P."

"Good gracious—" Mr. Welland gasped, as if a second
reading had been necessary to bring the monstrous ab-
surdity of the thing home to him.

"Poor Amy Sillerton—you never can tell what her
husband will do next," Mrs. Welland sighed. "I suppose
he's just discovered the Blenkers."

Professor Emerson Sillerton was a thorn in the side
of Newport society; and a thorn that could not be
plucked out, for it grew on a venerable and venerated
family tree. He was, as people said, a man who had had
"every advantage." His father was Sillerton Jackson's
uncle, his mother a Pennilow of Boston; on each side
there was wealth and position, and mutual suitability.
Nothing—as Mrs. Welland had often remarked—nothing
on earth obliged Emerson Sillerton to be an archæologist,
or indeed a Professor of any sort, or to live in Newport
in winter, or do any of the other revolutionary things
[220]

that he did. But at least, if he was going to break with tradition and flout society in the face, he need not have married poor Amy Dagonet, who had a right to expect "something different," and money enough to keep her own carriage.

No one in the Mingott set could understand why Amy Sillerton had submitted so tamely to the eccentricities of a husband who filled the house with long-haired men and short-haired women, and, when he travelled, took her to explore tombs in Yucatan instead of going to Paris or Italy. But there they were, set in their ways, and apparently unaware that they were different from other people; and when they gave one of their dreary annual garden-parties every family on the Cliffs, because of the Sillerton-Pennilow-Dagonet connection, had to draw lots and send an unwilling representative.

"It's a wonder," Mrs. Welland remarked, "that they didn't choose the Cup Race day! Do you remember, two years ago, their giving a party for a black man on the day of Julia Mingott's *thé dansant?* Luckily this time there's nothing else going on that I know of—for of course some of us will have to go."

Mr. Welland sighed nervously. " 'Some of us,' my dear—more than one? Three o'clock is such a very awkward hour. I have to be here at half-past three to take my drops: it's really no use trying to follow Bencomb's new treatment if I don't do it systematically; and if I join you later, of course I shall miss my drive." At the thought he laid down his knife and fork again, and a flush of anxiety rose to his finely-wrinkled cheek.

"There's no reason why you should go at all, my dear," his wife answered with a cheerfulness that had become automatic. "I have some cards to leave at the other end of Bellevue Avenue, and I'll drop in at about half-past three and stay long enough to make poor Amy feel that she hasn't been slighted." She glanced hesitatingly at her daughter. "And if Newland's afternoon is provided for perhaps May can drive you out with the ponies, and try their new russet harness."

It was a principle in the Welland family that people's days and hours should be what Mrs. Welland called "provided for." The melancholy possibility of having to "kill time" (especially for those who did not care for whist or solitaire) was a vision that haunted her as the spectre of the unemployed haunts the philanthropist. Another of her principles was that parents should never (at least visibly) interfere with the plans of their married children; and the difficulty of adjusting this respect for May's independence with the exigency of Mr. Welland's claims could be overcome only by the exercise of an ingenuity which left not a second of Mrs. Welland's own time unprovided for.

"Of course I'll drive with Papa—I'm sure Newland will find something to do," May said, in a tone that gently reminded her husband of his lack of response. It was a cause of constant distress to Mrs. Welland that her son-in-law showed so little foresight in planning his days. Often already, during the fortnight that he had passed under her roof, when she enquired how he meant to spend his afternoon, he had answered paradoxically: "Oh, I think for a change I'll just save it instead of spending it—" and once, when she and May had had to go on a long-postponed round of afternoon calls, he had confessed to having lain all the afternoon under a rock on the beach below the house.

"Newland never seems to look ahead," Mrs. Welland once ventured to complain to her daughter; and May answered serenely: "No; but you see it doesn't matter, because when there's nothing particular to do he reads a book."

"Ah, yes—like his father!" Mrs. Welland agreed, as if allowing for an inherited oddity; and after that the question of Newland's unemployment was tacitly dropped.

Nevertheless, as the day for the Sillerton reception approached, May began to show a natural solicitude for his welfare, and to suggest a tennis match at the Chiverses', or a sail on Julius Beaufort's cutter, as a means of atoning for her temporary desertion. "I shall be back by six, you know, dear: Papa never drives later than that—" and she was not reassured till Archer said that he thought of hiring a run-about and driving up the island to a stud-farm to look at a second horse for her brougham. They had been looking for this horse for some time, and the suggestion was so acceptable that May glanced at her mother as if to say: "You see he knows how to plan out his time as well as anv of us."

The idea of the stud-farm and the brougham horse had germinated in Archer's mind on the very day when the Emerson Sillerton invitation had first been mentioned; but he had kept it to himself as if there were something clandestine in the plan, and discovery might prevent its execution. He had, however, taken the precaution to engage in advance a run-about with a pair of old livery-stable trotters that could still do their eighteen miles on level roads; and at two o'clock, hastily deserting the luncheon-table, he sprang into the light carriage and drove off.

The day was perfect. A breeze from the north drove little puffs of white cloud across an ultramarine sky, with a bright sea running under it. Bellevue Avenue was empty at that hour, and after dropping the stable-lad at

the corner of Mill Street Archer turned down the Old
Beach Road and drove across Eastman's Beach.

He had the feeling of unexplained excitement with
which, on half-holidays at school, he used to start off into
the unknown. Taking his pair at an easy gait, he counted
on reaching the stud-farm, which was not far beyond
Paradise Rocks, before three o'clock; so that, after looking over the horse (and trying him if he seemed promis-
ing) he would still have four golden hours to dispose of.

As soon as he heard of the Sillerton's party he had
said to himself that the Marchioness Manson would certainly come to Newport with the Blenkers, and that
Madame Olenska might again take the opportunity of
spending the day with her grandmother. At any rate,
the Blenker habitation would probably be deserted, and
he would be able, without indiscretion, to satisfy a vague
curiosity concerning it. He was not sure that he wanted
to see the Countess Olenska again; but ever since he had
looked at her from the path above the bay he had wanted,
irrationally and indescribably, to see the place she was
living in, and to follow the movements of her imagined
figure as he had watched the real one in the summer-
house. The longing was with him day and night, an incessant undefinable craving, like the sudden whim of a
sick man for food or drink once tasted and long since forgotten. He could not see beyond the craving, or picture
what it might lead to, for he was not conscious of any
wish to speak to Madame Olenska or to hear her voice.
He simply felt that if he could carry away the vision of
the spot of earth she walked on, and the way the sky and
sea enclosed it, the rest of the world might seem less
empty.

When he reached the stud-farm a glance showed him
that the horse was not what he wanted; nevertheless he

took a turn behind it in order to prove to himself that he was not in a hurry. But at three o'clock he shook out the reins over the trotters and turned into the by-roads leading to Portsmouth. The wind had dropped and a faint haze on the horizon showed that a fog was waiting to steal up the Saconnet on the turn of the tide; but all about him fields and woods were steeped in golden light.

He drove past grey-shingled farm-houses in orchards, past hay-fields and groves of oak, past villages with white steeples rising sharply into the fading sky; and at last, after stopping to ask the way of some men at work in a field, he turned down a lane between high banks of gold-enrod and brambles. At the end of the lane was the blue glimmer of the river; to the left, standing in front of a clump of oaks and maples, he saw a long tumble-down house with white paint peeling from its clapboards.

On the road-side facing the gateway stood one of the open sheds in which the New Englander shelters his farming implements and visitors "hitch" their "teams." Archer, jumping down, led his pair into the shed, and after tying them to a post turned toward the house. The patch of lawn before it had relapsed into a hay-field; but to the left an overgrown box-garden full of dahlias and rusty rose-bushes encircled a ghostly summer-house of trellis-work that had once been white, surmounted by a wooden Cupid who had lost his bow and arrow but con-tinued to take ineffectual aim.

Archer leaned for a while against the gate. No one was in sight, and not a sound came from the open win-dows of the house: a grizzled Newfoundland dozing be-fore the door seemed as ineffectual a guardian as the arrowless Cupid. It was strange to think that this place of silence and decay was the home of the turbulent Blenkers; yet Archer was sure that he was not mistaken.

For a long time he stood there, content to take in the scene, and gradually falling under its drowsy spell; but at length he roused himself to the sense of the passing time. Should he look his fill and then drive away? He stood irresolute, wishing suddenly to see the inside of the house, so that he might picture the room that Madame Olenska sat in. There was nothing to prevent his walking up to the door and ringing the bell; if, as he supposed, she was away with the rest of the party, he could easily give his name, and ask permission to go into the sitting-room to write a message.

But instead, he crossed the lawn and turned toward the box-garden. As he entered it he caught sight of something bright-coloured in the summer-house, and presently made it out to be a pink parasol. The parasol drew him like a magnet: he was sure it was hers. He went into the summer-house, and sitting down on the rickety seat picked up the silken thing and looked at its carved handle, which was made of some rare wood that gave out an aromatic scent. Archer lifted the handle to his lips.

He heard a rustle of skirts against the box, and sat motionless, leaning on the parasol handle with clasped hands, and letting the rustle come nearer without lifting his eyes. He had always known that this must happen . . .

"Oh, Mr. Archer!" exclaimed a loud young voice; and looking up he saw before him the youngest and largest of the Blenker girls, blonde and blowsy, in bedraggled muslin. A red blotch on one of her cheeks seemed to show that it had recently been pressed against a pillow, and her half-awakened eyes stared at him hospitably but confusedly.

"Gracious—where did you drop from? I must have been sound asleep in the hammock. Everybody else has gone to Newport. Did you ring?" she incoherently enquired.

Archer's confusion was greater than hers. "I—no—that is, I was just going to. I had to come up the island to see about a horse, and I drove over on a chance of finding Mrs. Blenker and your visitors. But the house seemed empty—so I sat down to wait."

Miss Blenker, shaking off the fumes of sleep, looked at him with increasing interest. "The house *is* empty. Mother's not here, or the Marchioness—or anybody but me." Her glance became faintly reproachful. "Didn't you know that Professor and Mrs. Sillerton are giving a garden-party for mother and all of us this afternoon? It was too unlucky that I couldn't go; but I've had a sore throat, and mother was afraid of the drive home this evening. Did you ever know anything so disappointing? Of course," she added gaily, "I shouldn't have minded half as much if I'd known you were coming."

Symptoms of a lumbering coquetry became visible in her, and Archer found the strength to break in: "But Madame Olenska—has she gone to Newport too?"

Miss Blenker looked at him with surprise. "Madame Olenska—didn't you know she'd been called away?"

"Called away?—"

"Oh, my best parasol! I lent it to that goose of a Katie, because it matched her ribbons, and the careless thing must have dropped it here. We Blenkers are all like that . . . real Bohemians!" Recovering the sunshade with a powerful hand she unfurled it and suspended its rosy dome above her head. "Yes, Ellen was called away yesterday: she lets us call her Ellen, you know. A telegram came from Boston: she said she might be gone for two days. I do *love* the way she does her hair, don't you?" Miss Blenker rambled on.

Archer continued to stare through her as though she had been transparent. All he saw was the trumpery parasol that arched its pinkness above her giggling head.

After a moment he ventured: "You don't happen to know why Madame Olenska went to Boston? I hope it was not on account of bad news?"

Miss Blenker took this with a cheerful incredulity. "Oh, I don't believe so. She didn't tell us what was in the telegram. I think she didn't want the Marchioness to know. She's so romantic-looking, isn't she? Doesn't she remind you of Mrs. Scott-Siddons when she reads 'Lady Geraldine's Courtship'? Did you never hear her?"

Archer was dealing hurriedly with crowding thoughts. His whole future seemed suddenly to be unrolled before him; and passing down its endless emptiness he saw the dwindling figure of a man to whom nothing was ever to happen. He glanced about him at the unpruned garden, the tumble-down house, and the oak-grove under which the dusk was gathering. It had seemed so exactly the place in which he ought to have found Madame Olenska; and she was far away, and even the pink sunshade was not hers . . .

He frowned and hesitated. "You don't know, I suppose—I shall be in Boston tomorrow. If I could manage to see her—"

He felt that Miss Blenker was losing interest in him, though her smile persisted. "Oh, of course; how lovely of you! She's staying at the Parker House; it must be horrible there in this weather."

After that Archer was but intermittently aware of the remarks they exchanged. He could only remember stoutly resisting her entreaty that he should await the returning family and have high tea with them before he drove home. At length, with his hostess still at his side, he passed out of range of the wooden Cupid, unfastened his horses and drove off. At the turn of the lane he saw Miss Blenker standing at the gate and waving the pink parasol.

XXIII

THE next morning, when Archer got out of the Fall
River train, he emerged upon a steaming midsummer Boston. The streets near the station were full
of the smell of beer and coffee and decaying fruit and a
shirt-sleeved populace moved through them with the intimate abandon of boarders going down the passage to the
bathroom.

Archer found a cab and drove to the Somerset Club
for breakfast. Even the fashionable quarters had the
air of untidy domesticity to which no excess of heat ever
degrades the European cities. Care-takers in calico
lounged on the door-steps of the wealthy, and the Common looked like a pleasure-ground on the morrow of a
Masonic picnic. If Archer had tried to imagine Ellen
Olenska in improbable scenes he could not have called
up any into which it was more difficult to fit her than this
heat-prostrated and deserted Boston.

He breakfasted with appetite and method, beginning
with a slice of melon, and studying a morning paper
while he waited for his toast and scrambled eggs. A
new sense of energy and activity had possessed him ever
since he had announced to May the night before that he
had business in Boston, and should take the Fall River
boat that night and go on to New York the following
evening. It had always been understood that he would
return to town early in the week, and when he got back
from his expedition to Portsmouth a letter from the

[230]

office, which fate had conspicuously placed on a corner of the hall table, sufficed to justify his sudden change of plan. He was even ashamed of the ease with which the whole thing had been done: it reminded him, for an uncomfortable moment, of Lawrence Lefferts's masterly contrivances for securing his freedom. But this did not long trouble him, for he was not in an analytic mood.

After breakfast he smoked a cigarette and glanced over the Commercial Advertiser. While he was thus engaged two or three men he knew came in, and the usual greetings were exchanged: it was the same world after all, though he had such a queer sense of having slipped through the meshes of time and space.

He looked at his watch, and finding that it was half-past nine got up and went into the writing-room. There he wrote a few lines, and ordered a messenger to take a cab to the Parker House and wait for the answer. He then sat down behind another newspaper and tried to calculate how long it would take a cab to get to the Parker House.

"The lady was out, sir," he suddenly heard a waiter's voice at his elbow; and he stammered: "Out?—" as if it were a word in a strange language.

He got up and went into the hall. It must be a mistake: she could not be out at that hour. He flushed with anger at his own stupidity: why had he not sent the note as soon as he arrived?

He found his hat and stick and went forth into the street. The city had suddenly become as strange and vast and empty as if he were a traveller from distant lands. For a moment he stood on the door-step hesitating; then he decided to go to the Parker House. What if the messenger had been misinformed, and she were still there?

He started to walk across the Common; and on the first bench, under a tree, he saw her sitting. She had a grey silk sunshade over her head—how could he ever have imagined her with a pink one? As he approached he was struck by her listless attitude: she sat there as if she had nothing else to do. He saw her drooping profile, and the knot of hair fastened low in the neck under her dark hat, and the long wrinkled glove on the hand that held the sunshade. He came a step or two nearer, and she turned and looked at him.

"Oh"—she said; and for the first time he noticed a startled look on her face; but in another moment it gave way to a slow smile of wonder and contentment.

"Oh"—she murmured again, on a different note, as he stood looking down at her; and without rising she made a place for him on the bench.

"I'm here on business—just got here," Archer explained; and, without knowing why, he suddenly began to feign astonishment at seeing her. "But what on earth are *you* doing in this wilderness?" He had really no idea what he was saying: he felt as if he were shouting at her across endless distances, and she might vanish again before he could overtake her.

"I? Oh, I'm here on business too," she answered, turning her head toward him so that they were face to face. The words hardly reached him: he was aware only of her voice, and of the startling fact that not an echo of it had remained in his memory. He had not even remembered that it was low-pitched, with a faint roughness on the consonants.

"You do your hair differently," he said, his heart beating as if he had uttered something irrevocable.

"Differently? No—it's only that I do it as best I can when I'm without Nastasia."

"Nastasia; but isn't she with you?"

"No; I'm alone. For two days it was not worth while to bring her."

"You're alone—at the Parker House?"

She looked at him with a flash of her old malice. "Does it strike you as dangerous?"

"No; not dangerous—"

"But unconventional? I see; I suppose it is." She considered a moment. "I hadn't thought of it, because I've just done something so much more unconventional." The faint tinge of irony lingered in her eyes. "I've just refused to take back a sum of money—that belonged to me."

Archer sprang up and moved a step or two away. She had furled her parasol and sat absently drawing patterns on the gravel. Presently he came back and stood before her.

"Some one—has come here to meet you?"

"Yes."

"With this offer?"

She nodded.

"And you refused—because of the conditions?"

"I refused," she said after a moment.

He sat down by her again. "What were the conditions?"

"Oh, they were not onerous: just to sit at the head of his table now and then."

There was another interval of silence. Archer's heart had slammed itself shut in the queer way it had, and he sat vainly groping for a word.

"He wants you back—at any price?"

"Well—a considerable price. At least the sum is considerable for me."

[233]

He paused again, beating about the question he felt he must put.

"It was to meet him here that you came?"

She stared, and then burst into a laugh. "Meet him— my husband? *Here?* At this season he's always at Cowes or Baden."

"He sent some one?"

"Yes."

"With a letter?"

She shook her head. "No; just a message. He never writes. I don't think I've had more than one letter from him." The allusion brought the colour to her cheek, and it reflected itself in Archer's vivid blush.

"Why does he never write?"

"Why should he? What does one have secretaries for?"

The young man's blush deepened. She had pronounced the word as if it had no more significance than any other in her vocabulary. For a moment it was on the tip of his tongue to ask: "Did he send his secretary, then?" But the remembrance of Count Olenski's only letter to his wife was too present to him. He paused again, and then took another plunge.

"And the person?"—

"The emissary? The emissary," Madame Olenska rejoined, still smiling, "might, for all I care, have left already; but he has insisted on waiting till this evening . . . in case . . . on the chance . . ."

"And you came out here to think the chance over?"

"I came out to get a breath of air. The hotel's too stifling. I'm taking the afternoon train back to Portsmouth."

They sat silent, not looking at each other, but straight ahead at the people passing along the path. Finally she turned her eyes again to his face and said: "You're not changed."

He felt like answering: "I was, till I saw you again;" but instead he stood up abruptly and glanced about him at the untidy sweltering park.

"This is horrible. Why shouldn't we go out a little on the bay? There's a breeze, and it will be cooler. We might take the steamboat down to Point Arley." She glanced up at him hesitatingly and he went on: "On a Monday morning there won't be anybody on the boat. My train doesn't leave till evening: I'm going back to New York. Why shouldn't we?" he insisted, looking down at her; and suddenly he broke out: "Haven't we done all we could?"

"Oh"—she murmured again. She stood up and re-opened her sunshade, glancing about her as if to take counsel of the scene, and assure herself of the impossibility of remaining in it. Then her eyes returned to his face. "You mustn't say things like that to me," she said.

"I'll say anything you like; or nothing. I won't open my mouth unless you tell me to. What harm can it do to anybody? All I want is to listen to you," he stammered.

She drew out a little gold-faced watch on an enamelled chain. "Oh, don't calculate," he broke out; "give me the day! I want to get you away from that man. At what time was he coming?"

Her colour rose again. "At eleven."

"Then you must come at once."

"You needn't be afraid—if I don't come."

"Nor you either—if you do. I swear I only want to hear about you, to know what you've been doing. It's a hundred years since we've met—it may be another hundred before we meet again."

She still wavered, her anxious eyes on his face. "Why didn't you come down to the beach to fetch me, the day I was at Granny's?" she asked.

"Because you didn't look round—because you didn't know I was there. I swore I wouldn't unless you looked round." He laughed as the childishness of the confession struck him.

"But I didn't look round on purpose."

"On purpose?"

"I knew you were there; when you drove in I recognised the ponies. So I went down to the beach."

"To get away from me as far as you could?"

She repeated in a low voice: "To get away from you as far as I could."

He laughed out again, this time in boyish satisfaction. "Well, you see it's no use. I may as well tell you," he added, "that the business I came here for was just to find you. But, look here, we must start or we shall miss our boat."

"Our boat?" She frowned perplexedly, and then smiled. "Oh, but I must go back to the hotel first: I must leave a note—"

"As many notes as you please. You can write here." He drew out a note-case and one of the new stylographic pens. "I've even got an envelope—you see how everything's predestined! There—steady the thing on your knee, and I'll get the pen going in a second. They have to be humoured; wait—" He banged the hand that held the pen against the back of the bench. "It's like jerking down the mercury in a thermometer: just a trick. Now try—"

She laughed, and bending over the sheet of paper which he had laid on his note-case, began to write. Archer walked away a few steps, staring with radiant unseeing eyes at the passers-by, who, in their turn, paused to stare at the unwonted sight of a fashionably-dressed lady writing a note on her knee on a bench in the Common.

Madame Olenska slipped the sheet into the envelope, wrote a name on it, and put it into her pocket. Then she too stood up.

They walked back toward Beacon Street, and near the club Archer caught sight of the plush-lined "herdic" which had carried his note to the Parker House, and whose driver was reposing from this effort by bathing his brow at the corner hydrant.

"I told you everything was predestined! Here's a cab for us. You see!" They laughed, astonished at the miracle of picking up a public conveyance at that hour, and in that unlikely spot, in a city where cab-stands were still a "foreign" novelty.

Archer, looking at his watch, saw that there was time to drive to the Parker House before going to the steamboat landing. They rattled through the hot streets and drew up at the door of the hotel.

Archer held out his hand for the letter. "Shall I take it in?" he asked; but Madame Olenska, shaking her head, sprang out and disappeared through the glazed doors. It was barely half-past ten; but what if the emissary, impatient for her reply, and not knowing how else to employ his time, were already seated among the travellers with cooling drinks at their elbows of whom Archer had caught a glimpse as she went in?

He waited, pacing up and down before the herdic. A Sicilian youth with eyes like Nastasia's offered to shine his boots, and an Irish matron to sell him peaches; and every few moments the doors opened to let out hot men with straw hats tilted far back, who glanced at him as they went by. He marvelled that the door should open so often, and that all the people it let out should look so like each other, and so like all the other hot men who, at that hour, through the length and breadth of the land, were passing continuously in and out of the swinging doors of hotels.

And then, suddenly, came a face that he could not relate to the other faces. He caught but a flash of it, for his pacings had carried him to the farthest point of his beat, and it was in turning back to the hotel that he saw, in a group of typical countenances—the lank and weary, the round and surprised, the lantern-jawed and mild—this other face that was so many more things at once, and things so different. It was that of a young man, pale too, and half-extinguished by the heat, or worry, or both, but somehow, quicker, vivider, more conscious; or perhaps seeming so because he was so different. Archer hung a moment on a thin thread of memory, but it snapped and floated off with the disappearing face—apparently that of some foreign business man, looking doubly foreign in such a setting. He vanished in the stream of passers-by, and Archer resumed his patrol.

He did not care to be seen watch in hand within view of the hotel, and his unaided reckoning of the lapse of time led him to conclude that, if Madame Olenska was so long in reappearing, it could only be because she had met the emissary and been waylaid by him. At the thought Archer's apprehension rose to anguish.

"If she doesn't come soon I'll go in and find her," he said.

The doors swung open again and she was at his side. They got into the herdic, and as it drove off he took out his watch and saw that she had been absent just three minutes. In the clatter of loose windows that made talk impossible they bumped over the disjointed cobblestones to the wharf.

Seated side by side on a bench of the half-empty boat they found that they had hardly anything to say to each other, or rather that what they had to say communicated itself best in the blessed silence of their release and their isolation.

As the paddle-wheels began to turn, and wharves and shipping to recede through the veil of heat, it seemed to Archer that everything in the old familiar world of habit was receding also. He longed to ask Madame Olenska if she did not have the same feeling: the feeling that they were starting on some long voyage from which they might never return. But he was afraid to say it, or anything else that might disturb the delicate balance of her trust in him. In reality he had no wish to betray that trust. There had been days and nights when the memory of their kiss had burned and burned on his lips; the day before even, on the drive to Portsmouth, the thought of her had run through him like fire; but now that she was beside him, and they were drifting forth into this unknown world, they seemed to have reached the kind of deeper nearness that a touch may sunder.

As the boat left the harbour and turned seaward a breeze stirred about them and the bay broke up into long oily undulations, then into ripples tipped with spray. The fog of sultriness still hung over the city, but ahead lay a fresh world of ruffled waters, and distant promontories with light-houses in the sun. Madame Olenska, leaning back against the boat-rail, drank in the coolness between parted lips. She had wound a long veil about her hat, but it left her face uncovered, and Archer was struck by the tranquil gaiety of her expression. She seemed to take their adventure as a matter of course, and to be neither in fear of unexpected encounters, nor (what was worse) unduly elated by their possibility.

In the bare dining-room of the inn, which he had hoped they would have to themselves. they found a strident party of innocent-looking young men and women—schoolteachers on a holiday, the landlord told them—and Archer's heart sank at the idea of having to talk through their noise.

"This is hopeless—I'll ask for a private room," he said; and Madame Olenska, without offering any objection, waited while he went in search of it. The room opened on a long wooden verandah, with the sea coming in at the windows. It was bare and cool, with a table covered with a coarse checkered cloth and adorned by a bottle of pickles and a blueberry pie under a cage. No more guileless-looking *cabinet particulier* ever offered its shelter to a clandestine couple: Archer fancied he saw the sense of its reassurance in the faintly amused smile with which Madame Olenska sat down opposite to him. A woman who had run away from her husband—and reputedly with another man—was likely to have mastered the art of taking things for granted; but something in the quality of her composure took the edge from his irony. By being so quiet, so unsurprised and so simple she had managed to brush away the conventions and make him feel that to seek to be alone was the natural thing for two old friends who had so much to say to each other. . . .

XXIV

THEY lunched slowly and meditatively, with mute intervals between rushes of talk; for, the spell once broken, they had much to say, and yet moments when saying became the mere accompaniment to long duologues of silence. Archer kept the talk from his own affairs, not with conscious intention but because he did not want to miss a word of her history; and leaning on the table, her chin resting on her clasped hands, she talked to him of the year and a half since they had met.

She had grown tired of what people called "society"; New York was kind, it was almost oppressively hospitable; she should never forget the way in which it had welcomed her back; but after the first flush of novelty she had found herself, as she phrased it, too "different" to care for the things it cared about—and so she had decided to try Washington, where one was supposed to meet more varieties of people and of opinion. And on the whole she should probably settle down in Washington, and make a home there for poor Medora, who had worn out the patience of all her other relations just at the time when she most needed looking after and protecting from matrimonial perils.

"But Dr. Carver—aren't you afraid of Dr. Carver? I hear he's been staying with you at the Blenkers'."

She smiled. "Oh, the Carver danger is over. Dr. Carver is a very clever man. He wants a rich wife to finance his plans, and Medora is simply a good advertisement as a convert."

"A convert to what?"

"To all sorts of new and crazy social schemes. But, do you know, they interest me more than the blind conformity to tradition—somebody else's tradition—that I see among our own friends. It seems stupid to have discovered America only to make it into a copy of another country." She smiled across the table. "Do you suppose Christopher Columbus would have taken all that trouble just to go to the Opera with the Selfridge Merrys?"

Archer changed colour. "And Beaufort—do you say these things to Beaufort?" he asked abruptly.

"I haven't see him for a long time. But I used to; and he understands."

"Ah, it's what I've always told you; you don't like us. And you like Beaufort because he's so unlike us." He looked about the bare room and out at the bare beach and the row of stark white village houses strung along the shore. "We're damnably dull. We've no character, no colour, no variety.—I wonder," he broke out, "why you don't go back?"

Her eyes darkened, and he expected an indignant rejoinder. But she sat silent, as if thinking over what he had said, and he grew frightened lest she should answer that she wondered too.

At length she said: "I believe it's because of you."

It was impossible to make the confession more dispassionately, or in a tone less encouraging to the vanity of the person addressed. Archer reddened to the temples, but dared not move or speak: it was as if her words had been some rare butterfly that the least motion might drive off on startled wings, but that might gather a flock about it if it were left undisturbed.

"At least," she continued, "it was you who made me understand that under the dullness there are things so fine and sensitive and delicate that even those I most cared for in my other life look cheap in comparison. I don't know how to explain myself"—she drew together her troubled brows—"but it seems as if I'd never before understood with how much that is hard and shabby and base the most exquisite pleasures may be paid."

"Exquisite pleasures—it's something to have had them!" he felt like retorting; but the appeal in her eyes kept him silent.

"I want," she went on, "to be perfectly honest with you —and with myself. For a long time I've hoped this chance would come: that I might tell you how you've helped me, what you've made of me—"

Archer sat staring beneath frowning brows. He interrupted her with a laugh. "And what do you make out that you've made of me?"

She paled a little. "Of you?"

"Yes: for I'm of your making much more than you ever were of mine. I'm the man who married one woman because another one told him to."

Her paleness turned to a fugitive flush. "I thought— you promised—you were not to say such things today."

"Ah—how like a woman! None of you will ever see a bad business through!"

She lowered her voice. "*Is* it a bad business—for May?"

He stood in the window, drumming against the raised sash, and feeling in every fibre the wistful tenderness with which she had spoken her cousin's name.

[243]

"For that's the thing we've always got to think of—haven't we—by your own showing?" she insisted.

"My own showing?" he echoed, his blank eyes still on the sea.

"Or if not," she continued, pursuing her own thought with a painful application, "if it's not worth while to have given up, to have missed things, so that others may be saved from disillusionment and misery—then everything I came home for, everything that made my other life seem by contrast so bare and so poor because no one there took account of them—all these things are a sham or a dream—"

He turned around without moving from his place. "And in that case there's no reason on earth why you shouldn't go back?" he concluded for her.

Her eyes were clinging to him desperately. "Oh, *is* there no reason?"

"Not if you staked your all on the success of my marriage. My marriage," he said savagely, "isn't going to be a sight to keep you here." She made no answer, and he went on: "What's the use? You gave me my first glimpse of a real life, and at the same moment you asked me to go on with a sham one. It's beyond human enduring—that's all."

"Oh, don't say that; when I'm enduring it!" she burst out, her eyes filling.

Her arms had dropped along the table, and she sat with her face abandoned to his gaze as if in the recklessness of a desperate peril. The face exposed her as much as if it had been her whole person, with the soul behind it: Archer stood dumb, overwhelmed by what it suddenly told him.

"You too—oh, all this time, you too?"

For answer, she let the tears on her lids overflow and run slowly downward.

Half the width of the room was still between them, and neither made any show of moving. Archer was conscious of a curious indifference to her bodily presence: he would hardly have been aware of it if one of the hands she had flung out on the table had not drawn his gaze as on the occasion when, in the little Twenty-third Street house, he had kept his eye on it in order not to look at her face. Now his imagination spun about the hand as about the edge of a vortex; but still he made no effort to draw nearer. He had known the love that is fed on caresses and feeds them; but this passion that was closer than his bones was not to be superficially satisfied. His one terror was to do anything which might efface the sound and impression of her words; his one thought, that he should never again feel quite alone.

But after a moment the sense of waste and ruin overcame him. There they were, close together and safe and shut in; yet so chained to their separate destinies that they might as well have been half the world apart.

"What's the use—when you will go back?" he broke out, a great hopeless *How on earth can I keep you?* crying out to her beneath his words.

She sat motionless, with lowered lids. "Oh—I shan't go yet!"

"Not yet? Some time, then? Some time that you already foresee?"

At that she raised her clearest eyes. "I promise you: not as long as you hold out. Not as long as we can look straight at each other like this."

He dropped into his chair. What her answer really said was: "If you lift a finger you'll drive me back:

back to all the abominations you know of, and all the temptations you half guess." He understood it as clearly as if she had uttered the words, and the thought kept him anchored to his side of the table in a kind of moved and sacred submission.

"What a life for you!—" he groaned.

"Oh—as long as it's a part of yours."

"And mine a part of yours?"

She nodded.

"And that's to be all—for either of us?"

"Well; it *is* all, isn't it?"

At that he sprang up, forgetting everything but the sweetness of her face. She rose too, not as if to meet him or to flee from him, but quietly, as though the worst of the task were done and she had only to wait; so quietly that, as he came close, her outstretched hands acted not as a check but as a guide to him. They fell into his, while her arms, extended but not rigid, kept him far enough off to let her surrendered face say the rest.

They may have stood in that way for a long time, or only for a few moments; but it was long enough for her silence to communicate all she had to say, and for him to feel that only one thing mattered. He must do nothing to make this meeting their last; he must leave their future in her care, asking only that she should keep fast hold of it.

"Don't—don't be unhappy," she said, with a break in her voice, as she drew her hands away; and he answered: "You won't go back—you won't go back?" as if it were the one possibility he could not bear.

"I won't go back," she said; and turning away she opened the door and led the way into the public dining-room.

THE AGE OF INNOCENCE

The strident school-teachers were gathering up their possessions preparatory to a straggling flight to the wharf; across the beach lay the white steam-boat at the pier; and over the sunlit waters Boston loomed in a line of haze.

XXV

ONCE more on the boat, and in the presence of others, Archer felt a tranquillity of spirit that surprised as much as it sustained him.

The day, according to any current valuation, had been a rather ridiculous failure; he had not so much as touched Madame Olenska's hand with his lips, or extracted one word from her that gave promise of farther opportunities. Nevertheless, for a man sick with unsatisfied love, and parting for an indefinite period from the object of his passion, he felt himself almost humiliatingly calm and comforted. It was the perfect balance she had held between their loyalty to others and their honesty to themselves that had so stirred and yet tranquillized him; a balance not artfully calculated, as her tears and her falterings showed, but resulting naturally from her unabashed sincerity. It filled him with a tender awe, now the danger was over, and made him thank the fates that no personal vanity, no sense of playing a part before sophisticated witnesses, had tempted him to tempt her. Even after they had clasped hands for good-bye at the Fall River station, and he had turned away alone, the conviction remained with him of having saved out of their meeting much more than he had sacrificed.

He wandered back to the club, and went and sat alone in the deserted library, turning and turning over in his thoughts every separate second of their hours together. It was clear to him, and it grew more clear under closer scrutiny, that if she should finally decide on returning to Europe—returning to her husband—it would not be because her old life tempted her, even on the new terms offered. No: she would go only if she felt herself becoming a temptation to Archer, a temptation to fall away from the standard they had both set up. Her choice would be to stay near him as long as he did not ask her to come nearer; and it depended on himself to keep her just there, safe but secluded.

In the train these thoughts were still with him. They enclosed him in a kind of golden haze, through which the faces about him looked remote and indistinct: he had a feeling that if he spoke to his fellow-travellers they would not understand what he was saying. In this state of abstraction he found himself, the following morning, waking to the reality of a stifling September day in New York. The heat-withered faces in the long train streamed past him, and he continued to stare at them through the same golden blur; but suddenly, as he left the station, one of the faces detached itself, came closer and forced itself upon his consciousness. It was, as he instantly recalled, the face of the young man he had seen, the day before, passing out of the Parker House, and had noted as not conforming to type, as not having an American hotel face.

The same thing struck him now; and again he became aware of a dim stir of former associations. The young man stood looking about him with the dazed air of the foreigner flung upon the harsh mercies of American travel; then he advanced toward Archer, lifted his hat, and said in English: "Surely, Monsieur, we met in London?"

"Ah, to be sure: in London!" Archer grasped his hand with curiosity and sympathy. "So you *did* get here, after all?" he exclaimed, casting a wondering eye on the astute and haggard little countenance of young Carfry's French tutor.

"Oh, I got here—yes," M. Rivière smiled with drawn lips. "But not for long; I return the day after tomorrow." He stood grasping his light valise in one neatly gloved hand, and gazing anxiously, perplexedly, almost appealingly, into Archer's face.

"I wonder, Monsieur, since I've had the good luck to run across you, if I might—"

"I was just going to suggest it: come to luncheon, won't you? Down town, I mean: if you'll look me up in my office I'll take you to a very decent restaurant in that quarter."

M. Rivière was visibly touched and surprised. "You're too kind. But I was only going to ask if you would tell me how to reach some sort of conveyance. There are no porters, and no one here seems to listen—"

"I know: our American stations must surprise you. When you ask for a porter they give you chewing-gum. But if you'll come along I'll extricate you; and you must really lunch with me, you know."

The young man, after a just perceptible hesitation, replied, with profuse thanks, and in a tone that did not carry complete conviction, that he was already engaged; but when they had reached the comparative reassurance of the street he asked if he might call that afternoon.

Archer, at ease in the midsummer leisure of the office, fixed an hour and scribbled his address, which the Frenchman pocketed with reiterated thanks and a wide flourish of his hat. A horse-car received him, and Archer walked away.

Punctually at the hour M. Rivière appeared, shaved, smoothed-out, but still unmistakably drawn and serious.

Archer was alone in his office, and the young man, be-fore accepting the seat he proffered, began abruptly: "I believe I saw you, sir, yesterday in Boston."

The statement was insignificant enough, and Archer was about to frame an assent when his words were checked by something mysterious yet illuminating in his visitor's insistent gaze.

"It is extraordinary, very extraordinary," M. Rivière continued, "that we should have met in the circumstances in which I find myself."

"What circumstances?" Archer asked, wondering a lit-tle crudely if he needed money.

M. Rivière continued to study him with tentative eyes. "I have come, not to look for employment, as I spoke of doing when we last met, but on a special mission—"

"Ah—!" Archer exclaimed. In a flash the two meet-ings had connected themselves in his mind. He paused to take in the situation thus suddenly lighted up for him, and M. Rivière also remained silent, as if aware that what he had said was enough.

"A special mission," Archer at length repeated.

The young Frenchman, opening his palms, raised them slightly, and the two men continued to look at each other across the office-desk till Archer roused himself to say: "Do sit down"; whereupon M. Rivière bowed, took a distant chair, and again waited.

"It was about this mission that you wanted to consult me?" Archer finally asked.

M. Rivière bent his head. "Not in my own behalf: on that score I—I have fully dealt with myself. I should like—if I may—to speak to you about the Countess Olenska."

Archer had known for the last few minutes that the words were coming; but when they came they sent the

[251]

blood rushing to his temples as if he had been caught
by a bent-back branch in a thicket.

"And on whose behalf," he said, "do you wish to do
this?"

M. Rivière met the question sturdily. "Well—I might
say *hers*, if it did not sound like a liberty. Shall I say
instead: on behalf of abstract justice?"

Archer considered him ironically. "In other words:
you are Count Olenski's messenger?"

He saw his blush more darkly reflected in M. Rivière's
sallow countenance. "Not to *you*, Monsieur. If I come
to you, it is on quite other grounds."

"What right have you, in the circumstances, to *be* on
any other ground?" Archer retorted. "If you're an
emissary you're an emissary."

The young man considered. "My mission is over: as
far as the Countess Olenska goes, it has failed."

"I can't help that," Archer rejoined on the same note
of irony.

"No: but you can help—" M. Rivière paused, turned
his hat about in his still carefully gloved hands, looked
into its lining and then back at Archer's face. "You can
help, Monsieur, I am convinced, to make it equally a
failure with her family."

Archer pushed back his chair and stood up. "Well—
and by God I will!" he exclaimed. He stood with his
hands in his pockets, staring down wrathfully at the little
Frenchman, whose face, though he too had risen, was
still an inch or two below the line of Archer's eyes.

M. Rivière paled to his normal hue: paler than that
his complexion could hardly turn.

"Why the devil," Archer explosively continued, "should
you have thought—since I suppose you're appealing to me
on the ground of my relationship to Madame Olenska—

that I should take a view contrary to the rest of her family?"

The change of expression in M. Rivière's face was for a time his only answer. His look passed from timidity to absolute distress: for a young man of his usually resourceful mien it would have been difficult to appear more disarmed and defenceless. "Oh, Monsieur—"

"I can't imagine," Archer continued, "why you should have come to me when there are others so much nearer to the Countess; still less why you thought I should be more accessible to the arguments I suppose you were sent over with."

M. Rivière took this onslaught with a disconcerting humility. "The arguments I want to present to you, Monsieur, are my own and not those I was sent over with."

"Then I see still less reason for listening to them."

M. Rivière again looked into his hat, as if considering whether these last words were not a sufficiently broad hint to put it on and be gone. Then he spoke with sudden decision. "Monsieur—will you tell me one thing? Is it my right to be here that you question? Or do you perhaps believe the whole matter to be already closed?"

His quiet insistence made Archer feel the clumsiness of his own bluster. M. Rivière had succeeded in imposing himself: Archer, reddening slightly, dropped into his chair again, and signed to the young man to be seated.

"I beg your pardon: but why isn't the matter closed?"

M. Rivière gazed back at him with anguish. "You do, then, agree with the rest of the family that, in face of the new proposals I have brought, it is hardly possible for Madame Olenska not to return to her husband?"

"Good God!" Archer exclaimed; and his visitor gave out a low murmur of confirmation.

"Before seeing her, I saw—at Count Olenski's request —Mr. Lovell Mingott, with whom I had several talks before going to Boston. I understand that he represents his mother's view; and that Mrs. Manson Mingott's influence is great throughout her family."

Archer sat silent, with the sense of clinging to the edge of a sliding precipice. The discovery that he had been excluded from a share in these negotiations, and even from the knowledge that they were on foot, caused him a surprise hardly dulled by the acuter wonder of what he was learning. He saw in a flash that if the family had ceased to consult him it was because some deep tribal instinct warned them that he was no longer on their side; and he recalled, with a start of comprehension, a remark of May's during their drive home from Mrs. Manson Mingott's on the day of the Archery Meeting: "Perhaps, after all, Ellen would be happier with her husband."

Even in the tumult of new discoveries Archer remembered his indignant exclamation, and the fact that since then his wife had never named Madame Olenska to him. Her careless allusion had no doubt been the straw held up to see which way the wind blew; the result had been reported to the family, and thereafter Archer had been tacitly omitted from their counsels. He admired the tribal discipline which made May bow to this decision. She would not have done so, he knew, had her conscience protested; but she probably shared the family view that Madame Olenska would be better off as an unhappy wife than as a separated one, and that there was no use in discussing the case with Newland, who had an awkward way of suddenly not seeming to take the most fundamental things for granted.

Archer looked up and met his visitor's anxious gaze.

"Don't you know, Monsieur—is it possible you don't know—that the family begin to doubt if they have the right to advise the Countess to refuse her husband's last proposals?"

"The proposals you brought?"

"The proposals I brought."

It was on Archer's lips to exclaim that whatever he knew or did not know was no concern of M. Rivière's; but something in the humble and yet courageous tenacity of M. Rivière's gaze made him reject this conclusion, and he met the young man's question with another. "What is your object in speaking to me of this?"

He had not to wait a moment for the answer. "To beg you, Monsieur—to beg you with all the force I'm capable of—not to let her go back.—Oh, don't let her!" M. Rivière exclaimed.

Archer looked at him with increasing astonishment. There was no mistaking the sincerity of his distress or the strength of his determination: he had evidently resolved to let everything go by the board but the supreme need of thus putting himself on record. Archer considered.

"May I ask," he said at length, "if this is the line you took with the Countess Olenska?"

M. Rivière reddened, but his eyes did not falter. "No, Monsieur: I accepted my mission in good faith. I really believed—for reasons I need not trouble you with—that it would be better for Madame Olenska to recover her situation, her fortune, the social consideration that her husband's standing gives her."

"So I supposed: you could hardly have accepted such a mission otherwise."

"I should not have accepted it."

"Well, then—?" Archer paused again, and their eyes met in another protracted scrutiny.

"Ah, Monsieur, after I had seen her, after I had listened to her, I knew she was better off here."

"You knew—?"

"Monsieur, I discharged my mission faithfully: I put the Count's arguments, I stated his offers, without adding any comment of my own. The Countess was good enough to listen patiently; she carried her goodness so far as to see me twice; she considered impartially all I had come to say. And it was in the course of these two talks that I changed my mind, that I came to see things differently."

"May I ask what led to this change?"

"Simply seeing the change in *her,*" M. Rivière replied.

"The change in her? Then you knew her before?"

The young man's colour again rose. "I used to see her in her husband's house. I have known Count Olenski for many years. You can imagine that he would not have sent a stranger on such a mission."

Archer's gaze, wandering away to the blank walls of the office, rested on a hanging calendar surmounted by the rugged features of the President of the United States. That such a conversation should be going on anywhere within the millions of square miles subject to his rule seemed as strange as anything that the imagination could invent.

"The change—what sort of a change?"

"Ah, Monsieur, if I could tell you!" M. Rivière paused. "*Tenez*—the discovery, I suppose, of what I'd never thought of before: that she's an American. And that if you're an American of *her* kind—of your kind—things that are accepted in certain other societies, or at least put up with as part of a general convenient give-and-take—become unthinkable, simply unthinkable. If Madame Olenska's relations understood what these things were, their opposition to her returning would no doubt be as unconditional as her own; but they seem to regard her husband's wish to have her back as proof of an irresistible longing for domestic life." M. Rivière paused, and then added: "Whereas it's far from being as simple as that."

Archer looked back to the President of the United States, and then down at his desk and at the papers scattered on it. For a second or two he could not trust himself to speak. During this interval he heard M. Rivière's chair pushed back, and was aware that the young man had risen. When he glanced up again he saw that his visitor was as moved as himself.

"Thank you," Archer said simply.

"There's nothing to thank me for, Monsieur: it is I, rather—" M. Rivière broke off, as if speech for him too were difficult. "I should like, though," he continued in a firmer voice, "to add one thing. You asked me if I was in Count Olenski's employ. I am at this moment: I returned to him, a few months ago, for reasons of private necessity such as may happen to any one who has persons, ill and older persons, dependent on him. But from the moment that I have taken the step of coming here to say these things to you I consider myself discharged, and I shall tell him so on my return, and give him the reasons. That's all, Monsieur."

M. Rivière bowed and drew back a step.

"Thank you," Archer said again, as their hands met.

XXVI

EVERY year on the fifteenth of October Fifth Avenue opened its shutters, unrolled its carpets and hung up its triple layer of window-curtains.

By the first of November this household ritual was over, and society had begun to look about and take stock of itself. By the fifteenth the season was in full blast, Opera and theatres were putting forth their new attractions, dinner-engagements were accumulating, and dates for dances being fixed. And punctually at about this time Mrs. Archer always said that New York was very much changed.

Observing it from the lofty stand-point of a non-participant, she was able, with the help of Mr. Sillerton Jackson and Miss Sophy, to trace each new crack in its surface, and all the strange weeds pushing up between the ordered rows of social vegetables. It had been one of the amusements of Archer's youth to wait for this annual pronouncement of his mother's, and to hear her enumerate the minute signs of disintegration that his careless gaze had overlooked. For New York, to Mrs. Archer's mind, never changed without changing for the worse; and in this view Miss Sophy Jackson heartily concurred.

Mr. Sillerton Jackson, as became a man of the world, suspended his judgment and listened with an amused impartiality to the lamentations of the ladies. But even he never denied that New York had changed; and Newland Archer, on the winter of the second year of his marriage, was himself obliged to admit that if it had not actually changed it was certainly changing.

These points had been raised, as usual, at Mrs. Archer's Thanksgiving dinner. At the date when she was officially enjoined to give thanks for the blessings of the year it was her habit to take a mournful though not embittered stock of her world, and wonder what there was to be thankful for. At any rate, not the state of society; society, if it could be said to exist, was rather a spectacle on which to call down Biblical imprecations—and in fact, every one knew what the Reverend Dr. Ashmore meant when he chose a text from Jeremiah (chap. ii., verse 25) for his Thanksgiving sermon. Dr. Ashmore, the new Rector of St. Matthew's, had been chosen because he was very "advanced": his sermons were considered bold in thought and novel in language. When he fulminated against fashionable society he always spoke of its "trend"; and to Mrs. Archer it was terrifying and yet fascinating to feel herself part of a community that was trending.

"There's no doubt that Dr. Ashmore is right: there *is* a marked trend," she said, as if it were something visible and measurable, like a crack in a house.

"It was odd, though, to preach about it on Thanksgiving," Miss Jackson opined; and her hostess drily rejoined: "Oh, he means us to give thanks for what's left."

Archer had been wont to smile at these annual vaticinations of his mother's; but this year even he was obliged to acknowledge, as he listened to an enumeration of the changes, that the "trend" was visible.

"The extravagance in dress—" Miss Jackson began. "Sillerton took me to the first night of the Opera, and I can only tell you that Jane Merry's dress was the only one I recognised from last year; and even that had had

the front panel changed. Yet I know she got it out from
Worth only two years ago, because my seamstress always
goes in to make over her Paris dresses before she wears
them."

"Ah, Jane Merry is one of *us*," said Mrs. Archer sighing, as if it were not such an enviable thing to be in an
age when ladies were beginning to flaunt abroad their
Paris dresses as soon as they were out of the Custom
House, instead of letting them mellow under lock and
key, in the manner of Mrs. Archer's contemporaries.

"Yes; she's one of the few. In my youth," Miss Jackson rejoined, "it was considered vulgar to dress in the
newest fashions; and Amy Sillerton has always told me
that in Boston the rule was to put away one's Paris
dresses for two years. Old Mrs. Baxter Pennilow, who
did everything handsomely, used to import twelve a year,
two velvet, two satin, two silk, and the other six of
poplin and the finest cashmere. It was a standing order,
and as she was ill for two years before she died they
found forty-eight Worth dresses that had never been
taken out of tissue paper; and when the girls left off
their mourning they were able to wear the first lot at
the Symphony concerts without looking in advance of the
fashion."

"Ah, well, Boston is more conservative than New
York; but I always think it's a safe rule for a lady to
lay aside her French dresses for one season," Mrs.
Archer conceded.

"It was Beaufort who started the new fashion by making his wife clap her new clothes on her back as soon
as they arrived: I must say at times it takes all Regina's
distinction not to look like . . . like . . ." Miss Jackson
glanced around the table, caught Janey's bulging gaze,
and took refuge in an unintelligible murmur.

"Like her rivals," said Mr. Sillerton Jackson, with the air of producing an epigram.

"Oh,—" the ladies murmured; and Mrs. Archer added, partly to distract her daughter's attention from forbidden topics: "Poor Regina! Her Thanksgiving hasn't been a very cheerful one, I'm afraid. Have you heard the rumours about Beaufort's speculations, Sillerton?"

Mr. Jackson nodded carelessly. Every one had heard the rumours in question, and he scorned to confirm a tale that was already common property.

A gloomy silence fell upon the party. No one really liked Beaufort, and it was not wholly unpleasant to think the worst of his private life; but the idea of his having brought financial dishonour on his wife's family was too shocking to be enjoyed even by his enemies. Archer's New York tolerated hypocrisy in private relations; but in business matters it exacted a limpid and impeccable honesty. It was a long time since any well-known banker had failed discreditably; but every one remembered the social extinction visited on the heads of the firm when the last event of the kind had happened. It would be the same with the Beauforts, in spite of his power and her popularity; not all the leagued strength of the Dallas connection would save poor Regina if there were any truth in the reports of her husband's unlawful speculations.

The talk took refuge in less ominous topics; but everything they touched on seemed to confirm Mrs. Archer's sense of an accelerated trend.

"Of course, Newland, I know you let dear May go to Mrs. Struthers's Sunday evenings—" she began; and May interposed gaily: "Oh, you know, everybody goes to Mrs. Struthers's now; and she was invited to Granny's last reception."

It was thus, Archer reflected, that New York managed its transitions: conspiring to ignore them till they were well over, and then, in all good faith, imagining that they had taken place in a preceding age. There was always a traitor in the citadel; and after he (or generally she) had surrendered the keys, what was the use of pretending that it was impregnable? Once people had tasted of Mrs. Struthers's easy Sunday hospitality they were not likely to sit at home remembering that her champagne was transmuted Shoe-Polish.

"I know, dear, I know," Mrs. Archer sighed. "Such things have to be, I suppose, as long as *amusement* is what people go out for; but I've never quite forgiven your cousin Madame Olenska for being the first person to countenance Mrs. Struthers."

A sudden blush rose to young Mrs. Archer's face; it surprised her husband as much as the other guests about the table. "Oh, *Ellen*—" she murmured, much in the same accusing and yet deprecating tone in which her parents might have said: "Oh, *the Blenkers*—."

It was the note which the family had taken to sounding on the mention of the Countess Olenska's name, since she had surprised and inconvenienced them by remaining obdurate to her husband's advances; but on May's lips it gave food for thought, and Archer looked at her with the sense of strangeness that sometimes came over him when she was most in the tone of her environment.

His mother, with less than her usual sensitiveness to atmosphere, still insisted: "I've always thought that people like the Countess Olenska, who have lived in aristocratic societies, ought to help us to keep up our social distinctions, instead of ignoring them."

May's blush remained permanently vivid: it seemed

to have a significance beyond that implied by the recognition of Madame Olenska's social bad faith.

"I've no doubt we all seem alike to foreigners," said Miss Jackson tartly.

"I don't think Ellen cares for society; but nobody knows exactly what she does care for," May continued, as if she had been groping for something noncommittal.

"Ah, well—" Mrs. Archer sighed again.

Everybody knew that the Countess Olenska was no longer in the good graces of her family. Even her devoted champion, old Mrs. Manson Mingott, had been unable to defend her refusal to return to her husband. The Mingotts had not proclaimed their disapproval aloud: their sense of solidarity was too strong. They had simply, as Mrs. Welland said, "let poor Ellen find her own level"—and that, mortifyingly and incomprehensibly, was in the dim depths where the Blenkers prevailed, and "people who wrote" celebrated their untidy rites. It was incredible, but it was a fact, that Ellen, in spite of all her opportunities and her privileges, had become simply "Bohemian." The fact enforced the contention that she had made a fatal mistake in not returning to Count Olenski. After all, a young woman's place was under her husband's roof, especially when she had left it in circumstances that . . . well . . . if one had cared to look into them . . .

"Madame Olenska is a great favourite with the gentlemen," said Miss Sophy, with her air of wishing to put forth something conciliatory when she knew that she was planting a dart.

"Ah, that's the danger that a young woman like Madame Olenska is always exposed to," Mrs. Archer mournfully agreed; and the ladies, on this conclusion, gathered up their trains to seek the carcel globes of the drawing-room, while Archer and Mr. Sillerton Jackson withdrew to the Gothic library.

Once established before the grate, and consoling himself for the inadequacy of the dinner by the perfection of his cigar, Mr. Jackson became portentous and communicable.

"If the Beaufort smash comes," he announced, "there are going to be disclosures."

Archer raised his head quickly: he could never hear the name without the sharp vision of Beaufort's heavy figure, opulently furred and shod, advancing through the snow at Skuytercliff.

"There's bound to be," Mr. Jackson continued, "the nastiest kind of a cleaning up. He hasn't spent all his money on Regina."

"Oh, well—that's discounted, isn't it? My belief is he'll pull out yet," said the young man; wanting to change the subject.

"Perhaps—perhaps. I know he was to see some of the influential people today. Of course," Mr. Jackson reluctantly conceded, "it's to be hoped they can tide him over —this time anyhow. I shouldn't like to think of poor Regina's spending the rest of her life in some shabby foreign watering-place for bankrupts."

Archer said nothing. It seemed to him so natural—however tragic—that money ill-gotten should be cruelly expiated, that his mind, hardly lingering over Mrs. Beaufort's doom, wandered back to closer questions. What was the meaning of May's blush when the Countess Olenska had been mentioned?

Four months had passed since the midsummer day that he and Madame Olenska had spent together; and since then he had not seen her. He knew that she had returned to Washington, to the little house which she and

Medora Manson had taken there: he had written to her once—a few words, asking when they were to meet again —and she had even more briefly replied: "Not yet."

Since then there had been no farther communication between them, and he had built up within himself a kind of sanctuary in which she throned among his secret thoughts and longings. Little by little it became the scene of his real life, of his only rational activities; thither he brought the books he read, the ideas and feelings which nourished him, his judgments and his visions. Outside it, in the scene of his actual life, he moved with a growing sense of unreality and insufficiency, blundering against familiar prejudices and traditional points of view as an absent-minded man goes on bumping into the furniture of his own room. Absent—that was what he was: so absent from everything most densely real and near to those about him that it sometimes startled him to find they still imagined he was there.

He became aware that Mr. Jackson was clearing his throat preparatory to farther revelations.

"I don't know, of course, how far your wife's family are aware of what people say about—well, about Madame Olenska's refusal to accept her husband's latest offer."

Archer was silent, and Mr. Jackson obliquely continued: "It's a pity—it's certainly a pity—that she refused it."

"A pity? In God's name, why?"

Mr. Jackson looked down his leg to the unwrinkled sock that joined it to a glossy pump.

"Well—to put it on the lowest ground—what's she going to live on now?"

"Now—?"

"If Beaufort—"

Archer sprang up, his fist banging down on the black

walnut-edge of the writing-table. The wells of the brass double-inkstand danced in their sockets.

"What the devil do you mean, sir?"

Mr. Jackson, shifting himself slightly in his chair, turned a tranquil gaze on the young man's burning face.

"Well—I have it on pretty good authority—in fact, on old Catherine's herself—that the family reduced Countess Olenska's allowance considerably when she definitely refused to go back to her husband; and as, by this refusal, she also forfeits the money settled on her when she married—which Olenski was ready to make over to her if she returned—why, what the devil do *you* mean, my dear boy, by asking me what *I* mean?" Mr. Jackson good-humouredly retorted.

Archer moved toward the mantelpiece and bent over to knock his ashes into the grate.

"I don't know anything of Madame Olenska's private affairs; but I don't need to, to be certain that what you insinuate—"

"Oh, *I* don't: it's Lefferts, for one," Mr. Jackson interposed.

"Lefferts—who made love to her and got snubbed for it!" Archer broke out contemptuously.

"Ah—*did* he?" snapped the other, as if this were exactly the fact he had been laying a trap for. He still sat sideways from the fire, so that his hard old gaze held Archer's face as if in a spring of steel.

"Well, well: it's a pity she didn't go back before Beaufort's cropper," he repeated. "If she goes *now,* and if he fails, it will only confirm the general impression: which isn't by any means peculiar to Lefferts, by the way."

"Oh, she won't go back now: less than ever!" Archer had no sooner said it than he had once more the feeling that it was exactly what Mr. Jackson had been waiting for.

The old gentleman considered him attentively. "That's your opinion, eh? Well, no doubt you know. But everybody will tell you that the few pennies Medora Manson has left are all in Beaufort's hands; and how the two women are to keep their heads above water unless he does, I can't imagine. Of course, Madame Olenska may still soften old Catherine, who's been the most inexorably opposed to her staying; and old Catherine could make her any allowance she chooses. But we all know that she hates parting with good money; and the rest of the family have no particular interest in keeping Madame Olenska here."

Archer was burning with unavailing wrath: he was exactly in the state when a man is sure to do something stupid, knowing all the while that he is doing it.

He saw that Mr. Jackson had been instantly struck by the fact that Madame Olenska's differences with her grandmother and her other relations were not known to him, and that the old gentleman had drawn his own conclusions as to the reasons for Archer's exclusion from the family councils. This fact warned Archer to go warily; but the insinuations about Beaufort made him reckless. He was mindful, however, if not of his own danger, at least of the fact that Mr. Jackson was under his mother's roof, and consequently his guest. Old New York scrupulously observed the etiquette of hospitality, and no discussion with a guest was ever allowed to degenerate into a disagreement.

"Shall we go up and join my mother?" he suggested curtly, as Mr. Jackson's last cone of ashes dropped into the brass ash-tray at his elbow.

On the drive homeward May remained oddly silent:

through the darkness, he still felt her enveloped in her menacing blush. What its menace meant he could not guess: but he was sufficiently warned by the fact that Madame Olenska's name had evoked it.

They went upstairs, and he turned into the library. She usually followed him; but he heard her passing down the passage to her bedroom.

"May!" he called out impatiently; and she came back, with a slight glance of surprise at his tone.

"This lamp is smoking again; I should think the servants might see that it's kept properly trimmed," he grumbled nervously.

"I'm so sorry: it shan't happen again," she answered, in the firm bright tone she had learned from her mother; and it exasperated Archer to feel that she was already beginning to humour him like a younger Mr. Welland. She bent over to lower the wick, and as the light struck up on her white shoulders and the clear curves of her face he thought: "How young she is! For what endless years this life will have to go on!"

He felt, with a kind of horror, his own strong youth and the bounding blood in his veins. "Look here," he said suddenly, "I may have to go to Washington for a few days—soon; next week perhaps."

Her hand remained on the key of the lamp as she turned to him slowly. The heat from its flame had brought back a glow to her face, but it paled as she looked up.

"On business?" she asked, in a tone which implied that there could be no other conceivable reason, and that she had put the question automatically, as if merely to finish his own sentence.

"On business, naturally. There's a patent case coming up before the Supreme Court—" He gave the name of the inventor, and went on furnishing details with all Lawrence Lefferts's practised glibness, while she listened attentively, saying at intervals: "Yes, I see."

"The change will do you good," she said simply, when he had finished; "and you must be sure to go and see Ellen," she added, looking him straight in the eyes with her cloudless smile, and speaking in the tone she might have employed in urging him not to neglect some irksome family duty.

It was the only word that passed between them on the subject; but in the code in which they had both been trained it meant: "Of course you understand that I know all that people have been saying about Ellen, and heartily sympathise with my family in their effort to get her to return to her husband. I also know that, for some reason you have not chosen to tell me, you have advised her against this course, which all the older men of the family, as well as our grandmother, agree in approving; and that it is owing to your encouragement that Ellen defies us all, and exposes herself to the kind of criticism of which Mr. Sillerton Jackson probably gave you, this evening, the hint that has made you so irritable. . . . Hints have indeed not been wanting; but since you appear unwilling to take them from others, I offer you this one myself, in the only form in which well-bred people of our kind can communicate unpleasant things to each other: by letting you understand that I know you mean to see Ellen when you are in Washington, and are perhaps going there expressly for that purpose; and that, since you are sure to see her, I wish you to do so with my full and explicit approval—and to take the opportunity of letting her know what the course of conduct you have encouraged her in is likely to lead to."

Her hand was still on the key of the lamp when the

last word of this mute message reached him. She turned the wick down, lifted off the globe, and breathed on the sulky flame.

"They smell less if one blows them out," she explained, with her bright housekeeping air. On the threshold she turned and paused for his kiss.

XXVII

WALL STREET, the next day, had more reassuring reports of Beaufort's situation. They were not definite, but they were hopeful. It was generally understood that he could call on powerful influences in case of emergency, and that he had done so with success; and that evening, when Mrs. Beaufort appeared at the Opera wearing her old smile and a new emerald necklace, society drew a breath of relief.

New York was inexorable in its condemnation of business irregularities. So far there had been no exception to its tacit rule that those who broke the law of probity must pay; and every one was aware that even Beaufort and Beaufort's wife would be offered up unflinchingly to this principle. But to be obliged to offer them up would be not only painful but inconvenient. The disappearance of the Beauforts would leave a considerable void in their compact little circle; and those who were too ignorant or too careless to shudder at the moral catastrophe bewailed in advance the loss of the best ball-room in New York.

Archer had definitely made up his mind to go to Washington. He was waiting only for the opening of the law-suit of which he had spoken to May, so that its date might coincide with that of his visit; but on the following Tuesday he learned from Mr. Letterblair that the case might be postponed for several weeks. Nevertheless, he went home that afternoon determined in any event to leave the next evening. The chances were that May, who knew nothing of his professional life, and had never shown any interest in it, would not learn of the postponement, should it take place, nor remember the names of the litigants if they were mentioned before her; and at any rate he could no longer put off seeing Madame Olenska. There were too many things that he must say to her.

On the Wednesday morning, when he reached his office, Mr. Letterblair met him with a troubled face. Beaufort, after all, had not managed to "tide over"; but by setting afloat the rumour that he had done so he had reassured his depositors, and heavy payments had poured into the bank till the previous evening, when disturbing reports again began to predominate. In consequence, a run on the bank had begun, and its doors were likely to close before the day was over. The ugliest things were being said of Beaufort's dastardly manœuvre, and his failure promised to be one of the most discreditable in the history of Wall Street.

The extent of the calamity left Mr. Letterblair white and incapacitated. "I've seen bad things in my time; but nothing as bad as this. Everybody we know will be hit, one way or another. And what will be done about Mrs. Beaufort? What *can* be done about her? I pity Mrs. Manson Mingott as much as anybody: coming at her age, there's no knowing what effect this affair may have on her. She always believed in Beaufort—she made a friend of him! And there's the whole Dallas connection: poor Mrs. Beaufort is related to every one of you. Her only chance would be to leave her husband —yet how can any one tell her so? Her duty is at his side; and luckily she seems always to have been blind to his private weaknesses."

There was a knock, and Mr. Letterblair turned his head sharply. "What is it? I can't be disturbed."

A clerk brought in a letter for Archer and withdrew. Recognising his wife's hand, the young man opened the envelope and read: "Won't you please come up town as early as you can? Granny had a slight stroke last night. In some mysterious way she found out before any one else this awful news about the bank. Uncle Lovell is away shooting, and the idea of the disgrace has made poor Papa so nervous that he has a temperature and can't leave his room. Mamma needs you dreadfully, and I do hope you can get away at once and go straight to Granny's."

Archer handed the note to his senior partner, and a few minutes later was crawling northward in a crowded horse-car, which he exchanged at Fourteenth Street for one of the high staggering omnibuses of the Fifth Avenue line. It was after twelve o'clock when this laborious vehicle dropped him at old Catherine's. The sitting-room window on the ground floor, where she usually throned, was tenanted by the inadequate figure of her daughter, Mrs. Welland, who signed a haggard welcome as she caught sight of Archer; and at the door he was met by May. The hall wore the unnatural appearance peculiar to well-kept houses suddenly invaded by illness: wraps and furs lay in heaps on the chairs, a doctor's bag and overcoat were on the table, and beside them letters and cards had already piled up unheeded.

May looked pale but smiling: Dr. Bencomb, who had just come for the second time, took a more hopeful view, and Mrs. Mingott's dauntless determination to live and get well was already having an effect on her family. May led Archer into the old lady's sitting-room, where the sliding doors opening into the bedroom had been drawn shut, and the heavy yellow damask portières dropped over them; and here Mrs. Welland communicated to him in horrified undertones the details of the catastrophe. It appeared that the evening before something dreadful and mysterious had happened. At about eight o'clock, just after Mrs. Mingott had finished the game of solitaire that she always played after dinner, the door-bell had rung, and a lady so thickly veiled that the servants did not immediately recognise her had asked to be received.

The butler, hearing a familiar voice, had thrown open the sitting-room door, announcing: "Mrs. Julius Beaufort"—and had then closed it again on the two ladies. They must have been together, he thought, about an hour. When Mrs. Mingott's bell rang Mrs. Beaufort had already slipped away unseen, and the old lady, white and vast and terrible, sat alone in her great chair, and signed to the butler to help her into her room. She seemed, at that time, though obviously distressed, in complete control of her body and brain. The mulatto maid put her to bed, brought her a cup of tea as usual, laid everything straight in the room, and went away; but at three in the morning the bell rang again, and the two servants, hastening in at this unwonted summons (for old Catherine usually slept like a baby), had found their mistress sitting up against her pillows with a crooked smile on her face and one little hand hanging limp from its huge arm.

The stroke had clearly been a slight one, for she was able to articulate and to make her wishes known; and soon after the doctor's first visit she had begun to regain control of her facial muscles. But the alarm had been great; and proportionately great was the indignation when it was gathered from Mrs. Mingott's fragmentary phrases that Regina Beaufort had come to ask her—

incredible effrontery!—to back up her husband, see them
through—not to "desert" them, as she called it—in fact
to induce the whole family to cover and condone their
monstrous dishonour.

"I said to her: 'Honour's always been honour, and
honesty honesty, in Manson Mingott's house, and will be
till I'm carried out of it feet first,'" the old woman had
stammered into her daughter's ear, in the thick voice of
the partly paralysed. "And when she said: 'But my
name, Auntie—my name's Regina Dallas,' I said: 'It
was Beaufort when he covered you with jewels, and it's
got to stay Beaufort now that he's covered you with
shame.'"

So much, with tears and gasps of horror, Mrs. Welland
imparted, blanched and demolished by the unwonted
obligation of having at last to fix her eyes on the unpleasant and the discreditable. "If only I could keep it
from your father-in-law: he always says: 'Augusta, for
pity's sake, don't destroy my last illusions'—and how am
I to prevent his knowing these horrors?" the poor lady
wailed.

"After all, Mamma, he won't have *seen* them," her
daughter suggested; and Mrs. Welland sighed: "Ah, no;
thank heaven he's safe in bed. And Dr. Bencomb has
promised to keep him there till poor Mamma is better,
and Regina has been got away somewhere."

Archer had seated himself near the window and was
gazing out blankly at the deserted thoroughfare. It was
evident that he had been summoned rather for the moral
support of the stricken ladies than because of any spe-
cific aid that he could render. Mr. Lovell Mingott had
been telegraphed for, and messages were being despatched
by hand to the members of the family living in New
York; and meanwhile there was nothing to do but to

discuss in hushed tones the consequences of Beaufort's dishonour and of his wife's unjustifiable action.

Mrs. Lovell Mingott, who had been in another room writing notes, presently reappeared, and added her voice to the discussion. In *their* day, the elder ladies agreed, the wife of a man who had done anything disgraceful in business had only one idea: to efface herself, to disappear with him. "There was the case of poor Grandmamma Spicer; your great-grandmother, May. Of course," Mrs. Welland hastened to add, "your great-grandfather's money difficulties were private—losses at cards, or signing a note for somebody—I never quite knew, because Mamma would never speak of it. But she was brought up in the country because her mother had to leave New York after the disgrace, whatever it was: they lived up the Hudson alone, winter and summer, till Mamma was sixteen. It would never have occurred to Grandmamma Spicer to ask the family to 'countenance' her, as I understand Regina calls it; though a private disgrace is nothing compared to the scandal of ruining hundreds of innocent people."

"Yes, it would be more becoming in Regina to hide her own countenance than to talk about other people's," Mrs. Lovell Mingott agreed. "I understand that the emerald necklace she wore at the Opera last Friday had been sent on approval from Ball and Black's in the afternoon. I wonder if they'll ever get it back?"

Archer listened unmoved to the relentless chorus. The idea of absolute financial probity as the first law of a gentleman's code was too deeply ingrained in him for sentimental considerations to weaken it. An adventurer like Lemuel Struthers might build up the millions of his Shoe Polish on any number of shady dealings; but unblemished honesty was the *noblesse oblige* of old finan-

cial New York. Nor did Mrs. Beaufort's fate greatly
move Archer. He felt, no doubt, more sorry for her
than her indignant relatives; but it seemed to him that
the tie between husband and wife, even if breakable in
prosperity, should be indissoluble in misfortune. As
Mr. Letterblair had said, a wife's place was at her husband's side when he was in trouble; but society's place
was not at his side, and Mrs. Beaufort's cool assumption
that it was seemed almost to make her his accomplice.
The mere idea of a woman's appealing to her family to
screen her husband's business dishonour was inadmis-
sible, since it was the one thing that the Family, as an
institution, could not do.

The mulatto maid called Mrs. Lovell Mingott into
the hall, and the latter came back in a moment with a
frowning brow.

"She wants me to telegraph for Ellen Olenska. I had
written to Ellen, of course, and to Medora; but now it
seems that's not enough. I'm to telegraph to her immediately, and to tell her that she's to come alone."

The announcement was received in silence. Mrs. Welland sighed resignedly, and May rose from her seat and
went to gather up some newspapers that had been scattered on the floor.

"I suppose it must be done," Mrs. Lovell Mingott
continued, as if hoping to be contradicted; and May
turned back toward the middle of the room.

"Of course it must be done," she said. "Granny
knows what she wants, and we must carry out all her
wishes. Shall I write the telegram for you, Auntie?
If it goes at once Ellen can probably catch tomorrow
morning's train." She pronounced the syllables of the
name with a peculiar clearness, as if she had tapped on
two silver bells.

"Well, it can't go at once. Jasper and the pantry-boy are both out with notes and telegrams."

May turned to her husband with a smile. "But here's Newland, ready to do anything. Will you take the telegram, Newland? There'll be just time before luncheon."

Archer rose with a murmur of readiness, and she seated herself at old Catherine's rosewood "Bonheur du Jour," and wrote out the message in her large immature hand. When it was written she blotted it neatly and handed it to Archer.

"What a pity," she said, "that you and Ellen will cross each other on the way!—Newland," she added, turning to her mother and aunt, "is obliged to go to Washington about a patent law-suit that is coming up before the Supreme Court. I suppose Uncle Lovell will be back by tomorrow night, and with Granny improving so much it doesn't seem right to ask Newland to give up an important engagement for the firm—does it?"

She paused, as if for an answer, and Mrs. Welland hastily declared: "Oh, of course not, darling. Your Granny would be the last person to wish it." As Archer left the room with the telegram, he heard his mother-in-law add, presumably to Mrs. Lovell Mingott: "But why on earth she should make you telegraph for Ellen Olenska—" and May's clear voice rejoin: "Perhaps it's to urge on her again that after all her duty is with her husband."

The outer door closed on Archer and he walked hastily away toward the telegraph office.

XXVIII

"OL—ol—howjer spell it, anyhow?" asked the tart young lady to whom Archer had pushed his wife's telegram across the brass ledge of the Western Union office.

"Olenska—O-len-ska," he repeated, drawing back the message in order to print out the foreign syllables above May's rambling script.

"It's an unlikely name for a New York telegraph office; at least in this quarter," an unexpected voice observed; and turning around Archer saw Lawrence Lefferts at his elbow, pulling an imperturbable moustache and affecting not to glance at the message.

"Hallo, Newland: thought I'd catch you here. I've just heard of old Mrs. Mingott's stroke; and as I was on my way to the house I saw you turning down this street and nipped after you. I suppose you've come from there?"

Archer nodded, and pushed his telegram under the lattice.

"Very bad, eh?" Lefferts continued. "Wiring to the family, I suppose. I gather it *is* bad, if you're including Countess Olenska."

Archer's lips stiffened; he felt a savage impulse to dash his fist into the long vain handsome face at his side.

"Why?" he questioned.

Lefferts, who was known to shrink from discussion,

raised his eye-brows with an ironic grimace that warned the other of the' watching damsel behind the lattice. Nothing could be worse "form" the look reminded Archer, than any display of temper in a public place.

Archer had never been more indifferent to the requirements of form; but his impulse to do Lawrence Lefferts a physical injury was only momentary. The idea of bandying Ellen Olenska's name with him at such a time, and on whatsoever provocation, was unthinkable. He paid for his telegram, and the two young men went out together into the street. There Archer, having regained his self-control, went on: "Mrs. Mingott is much better: the doctor feels no anxiety whatever"; and Lefferts, with profuse expressions of relief, asked him if he had heard that there were beastly bad rumours again about Beaufort. . . .

That afternoon the announcement of the Beaufort failure was in all the papers. It overshadowed the report of Mrs. Manson Mingott's stroke, and only the few who had heard of the mysterious connection between the two events thought of ascribing old Catherine's illness to anything but the accumulation of flesh and years.

The whole of New York was darkened by the tale of Beaufort's dishonour. There had never, as Mr. Letterblair said, been a worse case in his memory, nor, for that matter, in the memory of the far-off Letterblair who had given his name to the firm. The bank had continued to take in money for a whole day after its failure was inevitable; and as many of its clients belonged to one or another of the ruling clans, Beaufort's duplicity seemed doubly cynical. If Mrs. Beaufort had not taken the tone that such misfortunes (the word was her own) were "the test of friendship," compassion for her might have tempered the general indignation against her husband. As it was—and especially after the object of her nocturnal visit to Mrs. Manson Mingott had become known—her cynicism was held to exceed his; and she had not the excuse—nor her detractors the satisfaction—of pleading that she was "a foreigner." It was some comfort (to those whose securities were not in jeopardy) to be able to remind themselves that Beaufort *was;* but, after all, if a Dallas of South Carolina took his view of the case, and glibly talked of his soon being "on his feet again," the argument lost its edge, and there was nothing to do but to accept this awful evidence of the indissolubility of marriage. Society must manage to get on without the Beauforts, and there was an end of it— except indeed for such hapless victims of the disaster as Medora Manson, the poor old Miss Lannings, and certain other misguided ladies of good family who, if only they had listened to Mr. Henry van der Luyden . . .

"The best thing the Beauforts can do," said Mrs. Archer, summing it up as if she were pronouncing a diagnosis and prescribing a course of treatment, "is to go and live at Regina's little place in North Carolina. Beaufort has always kept a racing stable, and he had better breed trotting horses. I should say he had all the qualities of a successful horse-dealer." Every one agreed with her, but no one condescended to enquire what the Beauforts really meant to do.

The next day Mrs. Manson Mingott was much better: she recovered her voice sufficiently to give orders that no one should mention the Beauforts to her again, and asked —when Dr. Bencomb appeared—what in the world her family meant by making such a fuss about her health.

"If people of my age *will* eat chicken-salad in the evening what are they to expect?" she enquired; and, the doctor having opportunely modified her dietary, the stroke was transformed into an attack of indigestion. But in spite of her firm tone old Catherine did not wholly recover her former attitude toward life. The growing remoteness of old age, though it had not diminished her curiosity about her neighbours, had blunted her never very lively compassion for their troubles; and she seemed to have no difficulty in putting the Beaufort disaster out of her mind. But for the first time she became absorbed in her own symptoms, and began to take a sentimental interest in certain members of her family to whom she had hitherto been contemptuously indifferent.

Mr. Welland, in particular, had the privilege of attracting her notice. Of her sons-in-law he was the one she had most consistently ignored; and all his wife's efforts to represent him as a man of forceful character and marked intellectual ability (if he had only "chosen") had been met with a derisive chuckle. But his eminence as a valetudenarian now made him an object of engrossing interest, and Mrs. Mingott issued an imperial summons to him to come and compare diets as soon as his temperature permitted; for old Catherine was now the first to recognise that one could not be too careful about temperatures.

Twenty-four hours after Madame Olenska's summons a telegram announced that she would arrive from Washington on the evening of the following day. At the Wellands', where the Newland Archers chanced to be lunching, the question as to who should meet her at Jersey City was immediately raised; and the material difficulties amid which the Welland household struggled as if it had been a frontier outpost, lent animation to the debate. It was agreed that Mrs. Welland could not possibly go to Jersey City because she was to accompany her husband to old Catherine's that afternoon, and the brougham could not be spared, since, if Mr. Welland were "upset" by seeing his mother-in-law for the first time after her attack, he might have to be taken home at a moment's notice. The Welland sons would of course be "down town," Mr. Lovell Mingott would be just hurrying back from his shooting, and the Mingott carriage engaged in meeting him; and one could not ask May, at the close of a winter afternoon, to go alone across the ferry to Jersey City, even in her own carriage. Nevertheless, it might appear inhospitable—and contrary to old Catherine's express wishes—if Madame Olenska were allowed to arrive without any of the family being at the station to receive her. It was just like Ellen, Mrs. Welland's tired voice implied, to place the family in such dilemma. "It's always one thing after another," the poor lady grieved, in one of her rare revolts against fate; "the only thing that makes me think Mamma must be less well than Dr. Bencomb will admit is this morbid desire to have Ellen come at once, however inconvenient it is to meet her."

The words had been thoughtless, as the utterances of impatience often are; and Mr. Welland was upon them with a pounce.

"Augusta," he said, turning pale and laying down his fork, "have you any other reason for thinking that Bencomb is less to be relied on than he was? Have you noticed that he has been less conscientious than usual in following up my case or your mother's?"

It was Mrs. Welland's turn to grow pale as the endless consequences of her blunder unrolled themselves before her; but she managed to laugh, and take a second helping of scalloped oysters, before she said, struggling back into her old armour of cheerfulness: "My dear, how could you imagine such a thing? I only meant that, after the decided stand Mamma took about its being Ellen's duty to go back to her husband, it seems strange that she should be seized with this sudden whim to see her, when there are half a dozen other grandchildren that she might have asked for. But we must never forget that Mamma, in spite of her wonderful vitality, is a very old woman."

Mr. Welland's brow remained clouded, and it was evident that his perturbed imagination had fastened at once on this last remark. "Yes: your mother's a very old woman; and for all we know Bencomb may not be as successful with very old people. As you say, my dear, it's always one thing after another; and in another ten or fifteen years I suppose I shall have the pleasing duty of looking about for a new doctor. It's always better to make such a change before it's absolutely necessary." And having arrived at this Spartan decision Mr. Welland firmly took up his fork.

"But all the while," Mrs. Welland began again, as she rose from the luncheon-table, and led the way into the wilderness of purple satin and malachite known as the back drawing-room, "I don't see how Ellen's to be got here tomorrow evening; and I do like to have things settled for at least twenty-four hours ahead."

Archer turned from the fascinated contemplation of a small painting representing two Cardinals carousing, in an octagonal ebony frame set with medallions of onyx.

"Shall I fetch her?" he proposed. "I can easily get away from the office in time to meet the brougham at the ferry, if May will send it there." His heart was beating excitedly as he spoke.

Mrs. Welland heaved a sigh of gratitude, and May,

who had moved away to the window, turned to shed on him a beam of approval. "So you see, Mamma, every-thing *will* be settled twenty-four hours in advance," she said, stooping over to kiss her mother's troubled forehead.

May's brougham awaited her at the door, and she was to drive Archer to Union Square, where he could pick up a Broadway car to carry him to the office. As she set-tled herself in her corner she said: "I didn't want to worry Mamma by raising fresh obstacles; but how can you meet Ellen tomorrow, and bring her back to New York, when you're going to Washington?"

"Oh, I'm not going," Archer answered.

"Not going? Why, what's happened?" Her voice was as clear as a bell, and full of wifely solicitude.

"The case is off—postponed."

"Postponed? How odd! I saw a note this morning from Mr. Letterblair to Mamma saying that he was going to Washington tomorrow for the big patent case that he was to argue before the Supreme Court. You said it was a patent case, didn't you?"

"Well—that's it: the whole office can't go. Letterblair decided to go this morning."

"Then it's *not* postponed?" she continued, with an in-sistence so unlike her that he felt the blood rising to his face, as if he were blushing for her unwonted lapse from all the traditional delicacies.

"No: but my going is," he answered, cursing the un-necessary explanations that he had given when he had announced his intention of going to Washington, and wondering where he had read that clever liars give de-tails, but that the cleverest do not. It did not hurt him half as much to tell May an untruth as to see her trying to pretend that she had not detected him.

"I'm not going till later on: luckily for the convenience of your family," he continued, taking base refuge in sarcasm. As he spoke he felt that she was looking at him, and he turned his eyes to hers in order not to appear to be avoiding them. Their glances met for a second, and perhaps let them into each other's meanings more deeply than either cared to go.

"Yes; it *is* awfully convenient," May brightly agreed, "that you should be able to meet Ellen after all; you saw how much Mamma appreciated your offering to do it."

"Oh, I'm delighted to do it." The carriage stopped, and as he jumped out she leaned to him and laid her hand on his. "Good-bye, dearest," she said, her eyes so blue that he wondered afterward if they had shone on him through tears.

He turned away and hurried across Union Square, repeating to himself, in a sort of inward chant: "It's all of two hours from Jersey City to old Catherine's. It's all of two hours—and it may be more."

XXIX

HIS wife's dark blue brougham (with the wedding varnish still on it) met Archer at the ferry, and conveyed him luxuriously to the Pennsylvania terminus in Jersey City.

It was a sombre snowy afternoon, and the gas-lamps were lit in the big reverberating station. As he paced the platform, waiting for the Washington express, he remembered that there were people who thought there would one day be a tunnel under the Hudson through which the trains of the Pennsylvania railway would run straight into New York. They were of the brotherhood of visionaries who likewise predicted the building of ships that would cross the Atlantic in five days, the invention of a flying machine, lighting by electricity, telephonic communication without wires, and other Arabian Night marvels.

"I don't care which of their visions comes true," Archer mused, "as long as the tunnel isn't built yet." In his senseless school-boy happiness he pictured Madame Olenska's descent from the train, his discovery of her a long way off, among the throngs of meaningless faces, her clinging to his arm as he guided her to the carriage, their slow approach to the wharf among slipping horses, laden carts, vociferating teamsters, and then the startling quiet of the ferry-boat, where they would sit side by side under the snow, in the motionless carriage, while the earth seemed to glide away under them, rolling to the other side of the sun. It was incredible, the number of things he had to say to her, and in what eloquent order they were forming themselves on his lips . . .

The clanging and groaning of the train came nearer, and it staggered slowly into the station like a prey-laden monster into its lair. Archer pushed forward, elbowing through the crowd, and staring blindly into window after window of the high-hung carriages. And then, suddenly, he saw Madame Olenska's pale and surprised face close at hand, and had again the mortified sensation of having forgotten what she looked like.

They reached each other, their hands met, and he drew her arm through his. "This way—I have the carriage," he said.

After that it all happened as he had dreamed. He helped her into the brougham with her bags, and had afterward the vague recollection of having properly re-assured her about her grandmother and given her a summary of the Beaufort situation (he was struck by the softness of her: "Poor Regina!"). Meanwhile the carriage had worked its way out of the coil about the station, and they were crawling down the slippery incline to the wharf, menaced by swaying coal-carts, bewildered horses, dishevelled express-wagons, and an empty hearse—ah, that hearse! She shut her eyes as it passed, and clutched at Archer's hand.

"If only it doesn't mean—poor Granny!"

"Oh, no, no—she's much better—she's all right, really. There—we've passed it!" he exclaimed, as if that made all the difference. Her hand remained in his, and as the carriage lurched across the gang-plank onto the ferry he bent over, unbuttoned her tight brown glove, and kissed her palm as if he had kissed a relic. She disengaged herself with a faint smile, and he said: "You didn't expect me today?"

"Oh, no."

"I meant to go to Washington to see you. I'd made all my arrangements—I very nearly crossed you in the train."

"Oh—" she exclaimed, as if terrified by the narrowness of their escape.

"Do you know—I hardly remembered you?"

"Hardly remembered me?"

"I mean: how shall I explain? I—it's always so. *Each time you happen to me all over again.*"

"Oh, yes: I know! I know!"

"Does it—do I too: to you?" he insisted.

She nodded, looking out of the window.

"Ellen—Ellen—Ellen!"

She made no answer, and he sat in silence, watching her profile grow indistinct against the snow-streaked dusk beyond the window. What had she been doing in all those four long months, he wondered? How little they knew of each other, after all! The precious moments were slipping away, but he had forgotten everything that he had meant to say to her and could only helplessly brood on the mystery of their remoteness and their proximity, which seemed to be symbolised by the fact of their sitting so close to each other, and yet being unable to see each other's faces.

"What a pretty carriage! Is it May's?" she asked, suddenly turning her face from the window.

"Yes."

"It was May who sent you to fetch me, then? How kind of her!"

He made no answer for a moment; then he said explosively: "Your husband's secretary came to see me the day after we met in Boston."

In his brief letter to her he had made no allusion to M. Rivière's visit, and his intention had been to bury the incident in his bosom. But her reminder that they were in his wife's cariage provoked him to an impulse of retaliation. He would see if she liked his reference to Rivière any better than he liked hers to May! As on certain other occasions when he had expected to shake her out of her usual composure, she betrayed no sign of surprise: and at once he concluded: "He writes to her, then."

"M. Rivière went to see you?"

"Yes: didn't you know?"

"No," she answered simply.

"And you're not surprised?"

She hesitated. "Why should I be? He told me in Boston that he knew you; that he'd met you in England I think."

"Ellen—I must ask you one thing."

"Yes."

"I wanted to ask it after I saw him, but I couldn't put it in a letter. It was Rivière who helped you to get away —when you left your husband?"

His heart was beating suffocatingly. Would she meet this question with the same composure?

"Yes: I owe him a great debt," she answered, without the least tremor in her quiet voice.

Her tone was so natural, so almost indifferent, that Archer's turmoil subsided. Once more she had managed, by her sheer simplicity, to make him feel stupidly conventional just when he thought he was flinging convention to the winds.

"I think you're the most honest woman I ever met!" he exclaimed.

"Oh, no—but probably one of the least fussy," she answered, a smile in her voice.

"Call it what you like: you look at things as they are."

"Ah—I've had to. I've had to look at the Gorgon."

"Well—it hasn't blinded you! You've seen that she's just an old bogey like all the others."

"She doesn't blind one; but she dries up one's tears."

The answer checked the pleading on Archer's lips: it seemed to come from depths of experience beyond his reach. The slow advance of the ferry-boat had ceased, and her bows bumped against the piles of the slip with a violence that made the brougham stagger, and flung Archer and Madame Olenska against each other. The young man, trembling, felt the pressure of her shoulder, and passed his arm about her.

"If you're not blind, then, you must see that this can't last."

"What can't?"

"Our being together—and not together."

"No. You ought not to have come today," she said in an altered voice; and suddenly she turned, flung her arms about him and pressed her lips to his. At the same moment the carriage began to move, and a gas-lamp at the head of the slip flashed its light into the window. She drew away, and they sat silent and motionless while the brougham struggled through the congestion of carriages about the ferry-landing. As they gained the street Archer began to speak hurriedly.

"Don't be afraid of me: you needn't squeeze yourself back into your corner like that. A stolen kiss isn't what I want. Look: I'm not even trying to touch the sleeve of your jacket. Don't suppose that I don't understand your reasons for not wanting to let this feeling between us dwindle into an ordinary hole-and-corner love-affair. I couldn't have spoken like this yesterday, because when we've been apart, and I'm looking forward to seeing you, every thought is burnt up in a great flame. But then you come; and you're so much more than I remembered, and what I want of you is so much more than an hour or two every now and then, with wastes of thirsty waiting between, that I can sit perfectly still beside you, like this, with that other vision in my mind, just quietly trusting to it to come true."

For a moment she made no reply; then she asked, hardly above a whisper: "What do you mean by trusting to it to come true?"

"Why—you know it will, don't you?"

"Your vision of you and me together?" She burst into a sudden hard laugh. "You choose your place well to put it to me!"

"Do you mean because we're in my wife's brougham? Shall we get out and walk, then? I don't suppose you mind a little snow?"

She laughed again, more gently. "No; I shan't get out and walk, because my business is to get to Granny's as quickly as I can. And you'll sit beside me, and we'll look, not at visions, but at realities."

"I don't know what you mean by realities. The only reality to me is this."

She met the words with a long silence, during which the carriage rolled down an obscure side-street and then turned into the searching illumination of Fifth Avenue.

"Is it your idea, then, that I should live with you as your mistress—since I can't be your wife?" she asked.

The crudeness of the question startled him: the word was one that women of his class fought shy of, even when their talk flitted closest about the topic. He noticed that Madame Olenska pronounced it as if it had a recognised place in her vocabulary, and he wondered if it had been used familiarly in her presence in the horrible life she had fled from. Her question pulled him up with a jerk, and he floundered.

"I want—I want somehow to get away with you into a world where words like that—categories like that—won't exist. Where we shall be simply two human beings who love each other, who are the whole of life to each other; and nothing else on earth will matter."

She drew a deep sigh that ended in another laugh. "Oh, my dear—where is that country? Have you ever been there?" she asked; and as he remained sullenly dumb she went on: "I know so many who've tried to find it; and, believe me, they all got out by mistake at wayside stations: at places like Boulogne, or Pisa, or Monte Carlo—and it wasn't at all different from the old world they'd left, but only rather smaller and dingier and more promiscuous."

He had never heard her speak in such a tone, and he remembered the phrase she had used a little while before.

"Yes, the Gorgon *has* dried your tears," he said.

"Well, she opened my eyes too; it's a delusion to say that she blinds people. What she does is just the contrary—she fastens their eyelids open, so that they're never again in the blessed darkness. Isn't there a Chinese torture like that? There ought to be. Ah, believe me, it's a miserable little country!"

The carriage had crossed Forty-second Street: May's sturdy brougham-horse was carrying them northward as if he had been a Kentucky trotter. Archer choked with the sense of wasted minutes and vain words.

"Then what, exactly, is your plan for us?" he asked.

"For *us?* But there's no *us* in that sense! We're near each other only if we stay far from each other. Then we can be ourselves. Otherwise we're only Newland Archer, the husband of Ellen Olenska's cousin, and Ellen Olenska, the cousin of Newland Archer's wife, trying to be happy behind the backs of the people who trust them."

"Ah, I'm beyond that," he groaned.

"No, you're not! You've never been beyond. And *I* have," she said, in a strange voice, "and I know what it looks like there."

He sat silent, dazed with inarticulate pain. Then he groped in the darkness of the carriage for the little bell that signalled orders to the coachman. He remembered that May rang twice when she wished to stop. He pressed the bell, and the carriage drew up beside the curbstone.

"Why are we stopping? This is not Granny's," Madame Olenska exclaimed.

"No: I shall get out here," he stammered, opening the door and jumping to the pavement. By the light of a street-lamp he saw her startled face, and the instinctive motion she made to detain him. He closed the door, and leaned for a moment in the window.

"You're right: I ought not to have come today," he said, lowering his voice so that the coachman should not hear. She bent forward, and seemed about to speak; but he had already called out the order to drive on, and the carriage rolled away while he stood on the corner. The snow was over, and a tingling wind had sprung up, that lashed his face as he stood gazing. Suddenly he felt something stiff and cold on his lashes, and perceived that he had been crying, and that the wind had frozen his tears.

He thrust his hands in his pockets, and walked at a sharp pace down Fifth Avenue to his own house.

XXX

THAT evening when Archer came down before dinner he found the drawing-room empty.

He and May were dining alone, all the family engagements having been postponed since Mrs. Manson Mingott's illness; and as May was the more punctual of the
two he was surprised that she had not preceded him. He
knew that she was at home, for while he dressed he had
heard her moving about in her room; and he wondered
what had delayed her.

He had fallen into the way of dwelling on such con-
jectures as a means of tying his thoughts fast to reality.
Sometimes he felt as if he had found the clue to his
father-in-law's absorption in trifles; perhaps even Mr.
Welland, long ago, had had escapes and visions, and had
conjured up all the hosts of domesticity to defend himself against them.

When May appeared he thought she looked tired. She
had put on the low-necked and tightly-laced dinner-dress
which the Mingott ceremonial exacted on the most informal occasions, and had built her fair hair into its usual
accumulated coils; and her face, in contrast, was wan and
almost faded. But she shone on him with her usual tenderness, and her eyes had kept the blue dazzle of the day
before.

"What became of you, dear?" she asked. "I was waiting at Granny's, and Ellen came alone, and said she had

dropped you on the way because you had to rush off on business. There's nothing wrong?"

"Only some letters I'd forgotten, and wanted to get off before dinner."

"Ah—" she said; and a moment afterward: "I'm sorry you didn't come to Granny's—unless the letters were urgent."

"They were," he rejoined, surprised at her insistence. "Besides, I don't see why I should have gone to your grandmother's. I didn't know you were there."

She turned and moved to the looking-glass above the mantel-piece. As she stood there, lifting her long arm to fasten a puff that had slipped from its place in her intricate hair, Archer was struck by something languid and inelastic in her attitude, and wondered if the deadly monotony of their lives had laid its weight on her also. Then he remembered that, as he had left the house that morning, she had called over the stairs that she would meet him at her grandmother's so that they might drive home together. He had called back a cheery "Yes!" and then, absorbed in other visions, had forgotten his promise. Now he was smitten with compunction, yet irritated that so trifling an omission should be stored up against him after nearly two years of marriage. He was weary of living in a perpetual tepid honeymoon, without the temperature of passion yet with all its exactions. If May had spoken out her grievances (he suspected her of many) he might have laughed them away; but she was trained to conceal imaginary wounds under a Spartan smile.

To disguise his own annoyance he asked how her grandmother was, and she answered that Mrs. Mingott was still improving, but had been rather disturbed by the last news about the Beauforts.

"What news?"

"It seems they're going to stay in New York. I believe he's going into an insurance business, or something. They're looking about for a small house."

The preposterousness of the case was beyond discussion, and they went in to dinner. During dinner their talk moved in its usual limited circle; but Archer noticed that his wife made no allusion to Madame Olenska, nor to old Catherine's reception of her. He was thankful for the fact, yet felt it to be vaguely ominous.

They went up to the library for coffee, and Archer lit a cigar and took down a volume of Michelet. He had taken to history in the evenings since May had shown a tendency to ask him to read aloud whenever she saw him with a volume of poetry: not that he disliked the sound of his own voice, but because he could always foresee her comments on what he read. In the days of their engagement she had simply (as he now perceived) echoed what he told her; but since he had ceased to provide her with opinions she had begun to hazard her own, with results destructive to his enjoyment of the works commented on.

Seeing that he had chosen history she fetched her work-basket, drew up an arm-chair to the green-shaded student lamp, and uncovered a cushion she was embroidering for his sofa. She was not a clever needle-woman; her large capable hands were made for riding, rowing and open-air activities; but since other wives embroidered cushions for their husbands she did not wish to omit this last link in her devotion.

She was so placed that Archer, by merely raising his eyes, could see her bent above her work-frame, her ruffled elbow-sleeves slipping back from her firm round arms, the betrothal sapphire shining on her left hand above her broad gold wedding-ring, and the right hand slowly and laboriously stabbing the canvas. As she sat thus, the lamplight full on her clear brow, he said to himself with a secret dismay that he would always know the thoughts behind it, that never, in all the years to come, would she surprise him by an unexpected mood, by a new idea, a weakness, a cruelty or an emotion. She had spent her poetry and romance on their short courting: the function was exhausted because the need was past. Now she was simply ripening into a copy of her mother, and mysteriously, by the very process, trying to turn him into a Mr. Welland. He laid down his book and stood up impatiently; and at once she raised her head.

"What's the matter?"

"The room is stifling: I want a little air."

He had insisted that the library curtains should draw backward and forward on a rod, so that they might be closed in the evening, instead of remaining nailed to a gilt cornice, and immovably looped up over layers of lace, as in the drawing-room; and he pulled them back and pushed up the sash, leaning out into the icy night. The mere fact of not looking at May, seated beside his table, under his lamp, the fact of seeing other houses, roofs, chimneys, of getting the sense of other lives outside his own, other cities beyond New York, and a whole world beyond his world, cleared his brain and made it easier to breathe.

After he had leaned out into the darkness for a few minutes he heard her say: "Newland! Do shut the window. You'll catch your death."

He pulled the sash down and turned back. "Catch my death!" he echoed; and he felt like adding: "But I've caught it already. I *am* dead—I've been dead for months and months."

And suddenly the play of the word flashed up a wild

suggestion. What if it were *she* who was dead! If she were going to die—to die soon—and leave him free! The sensation of standing there, in that warm familiar room, and looking at her, and wishing her dead, was so strange, so fascinating and overmastering, that its enormity did not immediately strike him. He simply felt that chance had given him a new possibility to which his sick soul might cling. Yes, May might die—people did: young people, healthy people like herself: she might die, and set him suddenly free.

She glanced up, and he saw by her widening eyes that there must be something strange in his own.

"Newland! Are you ill?"

He shook his head and turned toward his arm-chair. She bent over her work-frame, and as he passed he laid his hand on her hair. "Poor May!" he said.

"Poor? Why poor?" she echoed with a strained laugh.

"Because I shall never be able to open a window without worrying you," he rejoined, laughing also.

For a moment she was silent; then she said very low, her head bowed over her work: "I shall never worry if you're happy."

"Ah, my dear; and I shall never be happy unless I can open the windows!"

"In *this* weather?" she remonstrated; and with a sigh he buried his head in his book.

Six or seven days passed. Archer heard nothing from Madame Olenska, and became aware that her name would not be mentioned in his presence by any member of the family. He did not try to see her; to do so while she was at old Catherine's guarded bedside would have been almost impossible. In the uncertainty of the situation he let himself drift, conscious, somewhere below the surface of his thoughts, of a resolve which had come to him when he had leaned out from his library window into the icy night. The strength of that resolve made it easy to wait and make no sign.

Then one day May told him that Mrs. Manson Mingott had asked to see him. There was nothing surprising in the request, for the old lady was steadily recovering, and she had always openly declared that she preferred Archer to any of her other grandsons-in-law. May gave the message with evident pleasure: she was proud of old Catherine's appreciation of her husband.

There was a moment's pause, and then Archer felt it incumbent on him to say: "All right. Shall we go together this afternoon?"

His wife's face brightened, but she instantly answered: "Oh, you'd much better go alone. It bores Granny to see the same people too often."

Archer's heart was beating violently when he rang old Mrs. Mingott's bell. He had wanted above all things to go alone, for he felt sure the visit would give him the chance of saying a word in private to the Countess Olenska. He had determined to wait till the chance presented itself naturally; and here it was, and here he was on the doorstep. Behind the door, behind the curtains of the yellow damask room next to the hall, she was surely awaiting him; in another moment he should see her, and be able to speak to her before she led him to the sickroom.

He wanted only to put one question: after that his course would be clear. What he wished to ask was simply the date of her return to Washington; and that question she could hardly refuse to answer.

But in the yellow sitting-room it was the mulatto maid

who waited. Her white teeth shining like a keyboard, she pushed back the sliding doors and ushered him into old Catherine's presence.

The old woman sat in a vast throne-like arm-chair near her bed. Beside her was a mahogany stand bearing a cast bronze lamp with an engraved globe, over which a green paper shade had been balanced. There was not a book or a newspaper in reach, nor any evidence of feminine employment: conversation had always been Mrs. Mingott's sole pursuit, and she would have scorned to feign an interest in fancywork.

Archer saw no trace of the slight distortion left by her stroke. She merely looked paler, with darker shadows in the folds and recesses of her obesity; and, in the fluted mob-cap tied by a starched bow between her first two chins, and the muslin kerchief crossed over her billowing purple dressing-gown, she seemed like some shrewd and kindly ancestress of her own who might have yielded too freely to the pleasures of the table.

She held out one of the little hands that nestled in a hollow of her huge lap like pet animals, and called to the maid: "Don't let in any one else. If my daughters call, say I'm asleep."

The maid disappeared, and the old lady turned to her grandson.

"My dear, am I perfectly hideous?" she asked gaily, launching out one hand in search of the folds of muslin on her inaccessible bosom. "My daughters tell me it doesn't matter at my age—as if hideousness didn't matter all the more the harder it gets to conceal!"

"My dear, you're handsomer than ever!" Archer rejoined in the same tone; and she threw back her head and laughed.

"Ah, but not as handsome as Ellen!" she jerked out,

twinkling at him maliciously; and before he could answer she added: "Was she so awfully handsome the day you drove her up from the ferry?"

He laughed, and she continued: "Was it because you told her so that she had to put you out on the way? In my youth young men didn't desert pretty women unless they were made to!" She gave another chuckle, and interrupted it to say almost querulously: "It's a pity she didn't marry you; I always told her so. It would have spared me all this worry. But who ever thought of sparing their grandmother worry?"

Archer wondered if her illness had blurred her faculties; but suddenly she broke out: "Well, it's settled, anyhow: she's going to stay with me, whatever the rest of the family say! She hadn't been here five minutes before I'd have gone down on my knees to keep her—if only, for the last twenty years, I'd been able to see where the floor was!"

Archer listened in silence, and she went on: "They'd talked me over, as no doubt you know: persuaded me, Lovell, and Letterblair, and Augusta Welland, and all the rest of them, that I must hold out and cut off her allowance, till she was made to see that it was her duty to go back to Olenski. They thought they'd convinced me when the secretary, or whatever he was, came out with the last proposals: handsome proposals I confess they were. After all, marriage is marriage, and money's money—both useful things in their way . . . and I didn't know what to answer—" She broke off and drew a long breath, as if speaking had become an effort. "But the minute I laid eyes on her, I said: 'You sweet bird, you! Shut you up in that cage again? Never!' And now it's settled that she's to stay here and nurse her Granny as long as there's a Granny to nurse. It's not a gay prospect, but she doesn't mind; and of course I've told Letterblair that she's to be given her proper allowance."

The young man heard her with veins aglow; but in his confusion of mind he hardly knew whether her news brought joy or pain. He had so definitely decided on the course he meant to pursue that for the moment he could not readjust his thoughts. But gradually there stole over him the delicious sense of difficulties deferred and opportunities miraculously provided. If Ellen had consented to come and live with her grandmother it must surely be because she had recognised the impossibility of giving him up. This was her answer to his final appeal of the other day: if she would not take the extreme step he had urged, she had at last yielded to half-measures. He sank back into the thought with the involuntary relief of a man who has been ready to risk everything, and suddenly tastes the dangerous sweetness of security.

"She couldn't have gone back—it was impossible!" he exclaimed.

"Ah, my dear, I always knew you were on her side; and that's why I sent for you today, and why I said to your pretty wife, when she proposed to come with you: 'No, my dear, I'm pining to see Newland, and I don't want anybody to share our transports.' For you see, my dear—" she drew her head back as far as its tethering chins permitted, and looked him full in the eyes—"you see, we shall have a fight yet. The family don't want her here, and they'll say it's because I've been ill, because I'm a weak old woman, that she's persuaded me. I'm not well enough yet to fight them one by one, and you've got to do it for me."

"I?" he stammered.

"You. Why not?" she jerked back at him, her round eyes suddenly as sharp as pen-knives. Her hand fluttered from its chair-arm and lit on his with a clutch of little pale nails like bird-claws. "Why not?" she searchingly repeated.

Archer, under the exposure of her gaze, had recovered his self-possession.

"Oh, I don't count—I'm too insignificant."

"Well, you're Letterblair's partner, ain't you? You've got to get at them through Letterblair. Unless you've got a reason," she insisted.

"Oh, my dear, I back you to hold your own against them all without my help; but you shall have it if you need it," he reassured her.

"Then we're safe!" she sighed; and smiling on him with all her ancient cunning she added, as she settled her head among the cushions: "I always knew you'd back us up, because they never quote you when they talk about its being her duty to go home."

He winced a little at her terrifying perspicacity, and longed to ask: "And May—do they quote her?" But he judged it safer to turn the question.

"And Madame Olenska? When am I to see her?" he said.

The old lady chuckled, crumpled her lids, and went through the pantomime of archness. "Not today. One at a time, please. Madame Olenska's gone out."

He flushed with disappointment, and she went on: "She's gone out, my child: gone in my carriage to see Regina Beaufort."

She paused for this announcement to produce its effect. "That's what she's reduced me to already. The day after she got here she put on her best bonnet, and told me, as cool as a cucumber, that she was going to call on

Regina Beaufort. 'I don't know her; who is she?' says I. 'She's your grand-niece, and a most unhappy woman,' she says. 'She's the wife of a scoundrel,' I answered. 'Well,' she says, 'and so am I, and yet all my family want me to go back to him.' Well, that floored me, and I let her go; and finally one day she said it was raining too hard to go out on foot, and she wanted me to lend her my carriage. 'What for?' I asked her; and she said: 'To go and see cousin Regina'—*cousin!* Now, my dear, I looked out of the window, and saw it wasn't raining a drop; but I understood her, and I let her have the carriage . . . After all, Regina's a brave woman, and so is she; and I've always liked courage above everything."

Archer bent down and pressed his lips on the little hand that still lay on his.

"Eh—eh—eh! Whose hand did you think you were kissing, young man—your wife's, I hope?" the old lady snapped out with her mocking cackle; and as he rose to go she called out after him: "Give her her Granny's love; but you'd better not say anything about our talk."

XXXI

ARCHER had been stunned by old Catherine's news. It was only natural that Madame Olenksa should have hastened from Washington in response to her grandmother's summons; but that she should have decided to remain under her roof—especially now that Mrs. Mingott had almost regained her health—was less easy to explain.

Archer was sure that Madame Olenska's decision had not been influenced by the change in her financial situation. He knew the exact figure of the small income which her husband had allowed her at their separation. Without the addition of her grandmother's allowance it was hardly enough to live on, in any sense known to the Mingott vocabulary; and now that Medora Manson, who shared her life, had been ruined, such a pittance would barely keep the two women clothed and fed. Yet Archer was convinced that Madame Olenska had not accepted her grandmother's offer from interested motives.

She had the heedless generosity and the spasmodic extravagance of persons used to large fortunes, and indifferent to money; but she could go without many things which her relations considered indispensable, and Mrs. Lovell Mingott and Mrs. Welland had often been heard to deplore that any one who had enjoyed the cosmopolitan luxuries of Count Olenski's establishments should care so little about "how things were done." Moreover, as Archer knew, several months had passed since her allowance had been cut off; yet in the interval she had made no effort to regain her grandmother's favour. Therefore if she had changed her course it must be for a different reason.

He did not have far to seek for that reason. On the way from the ferry she had told him that he and she must remain apart; but she had said it with her head on his breast. He knew that there was no calculated co-quetry in her words; she was fighting her fate as he had fought his, and clinging desperately to her resolve that they should not break faith with the people who trusted them. But during the ten days which had elapsed since her return to New York she had perhaps guessed from his silence, and from the fact of his making no attempt to see her, that he was meditating a decisive step, a step from which there was no turning back. At the thought, a sudden fear of her own weakness might have seized her, and she might have felt that, after all, it was better to ac-cept the compromise usual in such cases, and follow the line of least resistance.

An hour earlier, when he had rung Mrs. Mingott's bell, Archer had fancied that his path was clear before him. He had meant to have a word alone with Madame Olen-ska, and failing that, to learn from her grandmother on what day, and by which train, she was returning to Wash-ington. In that train he intended to join her, and travel with her to Washington, or as much farther as she was willing to go. His own fancy inclined to Japan. At any rate she would understand at once that, wherever she went, he was going. He meant to leave a note for May that should cut off any other alternative.

He had fancied himself not only nerved for this plunge but eager to take it; yet his first feeling on hearing that the course of events was changed had been one of relief.

Now, however, as he walked home from Mrs. Mingott's, he was conscious of a growing distaste for what lay before him. There was nothing unknown or unfamiliar in the path he was presumably to tread; but when he had trodden it before it was as a free man, who was accountable to no one for his actions, and could lend himself with an amused detachment to the game of precautions and prevarications, concealments and compliances, that the part required. This procedure was called "protecting a woman's honour"; and the best fiction, combined with the after-dinner talk of his elders, had long since initiated him into every detail of its code.

Now he saw the matter in a new light, and his part in it seemed singularly diminished. It was, in fact, that which, with a secret fatuity, he had watched Mrs. Thorley Rushworth play toward a fond and unperceiving husband: a smiling, bantering, humouring, watchful and incessant lie. A lie by day, a lie by night, a lie in every touch and every look; a lie in every caress and every quarrel; a lie in every word and in every silence.

It was easier, and less dastardly on the whole, for a wife to play such a part toward her husband. A woman's standard of truthfulness was tacitly held to be lower: she was the subject creature, and versed in the arts of the enslaved. Then she could always plead moods and nerves, and the right not to be held too strictly to account; and even in the most strait-laced societies the laugh was always against the husband.

But in Archer's little world no one laughed at a wife deceived, and a certain measure of contempt was attached to men who continued their philandering after marriage. In the rotation of crops there was a recognised season for wild oats; but they were not to be sown more than once.

Archer had always shared this view: in his heart he thought Lefferts despicable. But to love Ellen Olenska was not to become a man like Lefferts: for the first time Archer found himself face to face with the dread argument of the individual case. Ellen Olenska was like no other woman, he was like no other man: their situation, therefore, resembled no one else's, and they were answerable to no tribunal but that of their own judgment.

Yes, but in ten minutes more he would be mounting his own doorstep; and there were May, and habit, and honour, and all the old decencies that he and his people had always believed in . . .

At his corner he hesitated, and then walked on down Fifth Avenue.

Ahead of him, in the winter night, loomed a big unlit house. As he drew near he thought how often he had seen it blazing with lights, its steps awninged and carpeted, and carriages waiting in double line to draw up at the curbstone. It was in the conservatory that stretched its dead-black bulk down the side street that he had taken his first kiss from May; it was under the myriad candles of the ball-room that he had seen her appear, tall and silver-shining as a young Diana.

Now the house was as dark as the grave, except for a faint flare of gas in the basement, and a light in one upstairs room where the blind had not been lowered. As Archer reached the corner he saw that the carriage standing at the door was Mrs. Manson Mingott's. What an opportunity for Sillerton Jackson, if he should chance to pass! Archer had been greatly moved by old Catherine's account of Madame Olenska's attitude toward Mrs. Beaufort; it made the righteous reprobation of New York seem like a passing by on the other side. But he knew well enough what construction the clubs and drawing-rooms would put on Ellen Olenska's visits to her cousin.

He paused and looked up at the lighted window. No doubt the two women were sitting together in that room: Beaufort had probably sought consolation elsewhere. There were even rumours that he had left New York with Fanny Ring; but Mrs. Beaufort's attitude made the report seem improbable.

Archer had the nocturnal perspective of Fifth Avenue almost to himself. At that hour most people were indoors, dressing for dinner; and he was secretly glad that Ellen's exit was likely to be unobserved. As the thought passed through his mind the door opened, and she came out. Behind her was a faint light, such as might have been carried down the stairs to show her the way. She turned to say a word to some one; then the door closed, and she came down the steps.

"Ellen," he said in a low voice, as she reached the pavement.

She stopped with a slight start, and just then he saw two young men of fashionable cut approaching. There was a familiar air about their overcoats and the way their smart silk mufflers were folded over their white ties; and he wondered how youths of their quality happened to be dining out so early. Then he remembered that the Reggie Chiverses, whose house was a few doors above, were taking a large party that evening to see Adelaide Neilson in Romeo and Juliet, and guessed that the two were of the number. They passed under a lamp, and he recognised Lawrence Lefferts and a young Chivers.

A mean desire not to have Madame Olenska seen at the Beauforts' door vanished as he felt the penetrating warmth of her hand.

THE AGE OF INNOCENCE

"I shall see you now—we shall be together," he broke out, hardly knowing what he said.

"Ah," she answered, "Granny has told you?"

While he watched her he was aware that Lefferts and Chivers, on reaching the farther side of the street corner, had discreetly struck away across Fifth Avenue. It was the kind of masculine solidarity that he himself often practised; now he sickened at their connivance. Did she really imagine that he and she could live like this? And if not, what else did she imagine?

"Tomorrow I must see you—somewhere where we can be alone," he said, in a voice that sounded almost angry to his own ears.

She wavered, and moved toward the carriage.

"But I shall be at Granny's—for the present that is," she added, as if conscious that her change of plans required some explanation.

"Somewhere where we can be alone," he insisted.

She gave a faint laugh that grated on him.

"In New York? But there are no churches . . . no monuments."

"There's the Art Museum—in the Park," he explained, as she looked puzzled. "At half-past two. I shall be at the door . . ."

She turned away without answering and got quickly into the carriage. As it drove off she leaned forward, and he thought she waved her hand in the obscurity. He stared after her in a turmoil of contradictory feelings. It seemed to him that he had been speaking not to the woman he loved but to another, a woman he was indebted to for pleasures already wearied of: it was hateful to find himself the prisoner of this hackneyed vocabulary.

"She'll come!" he said to himself, almost contemptuously.

Avoiding the popular "Wolfe collection," whose anecdotic canvases filled one of the main galleries of the queer wilderness of cast-iron and encaustic tiles known as the Metropolitan Museum, they had wandered down a passage to the room where the "Cesnola antiquities" mouldered in unvisited loneliness.

They had this melancholy retreat to themselves, and seated on the divan enclosing the central steam-radiator, they were staring silently at the glass cabinets mounted in ebonised wood which contained the recovered fragments of Ilium.

"It's odd," Madame Olenska said, "I never came here before."

"Ah, well—. Some day, I suppose, it will be a great Museum."

"Yes," she assented absently.

She stood up and wandered across the room. Archer, remaining seated, watched the light movements of her figure, so girlish even under its heavy furs, the cleverly planted heron wing in her fur cap, and the way a dark curl lay like a flattened vine spiral on each cheek above the ear. His mind, as always when they first met, was wholly absorbed in the delicious details that made her herself and no other. Presently he rose and approached the case before which she stood. Its glass shelves were crowded with small broken objects—hardly recognisable domestic utensils, ornaments and personal trifles—made of glass, of clay, of discoloured bronze and other time-blurred substances.

"It seems cruel," she said, "that after a while nothing matters . . . any more than these little things, that used to be necessary and important to forgotten people, and now have to be guessed at under a magnifying glass and labelled: 'Use unknown.' "

[312]

"Yes; but meanwhile—"

"Ah, meanwhile—"

As she stood there, in her long sealskin coat, her hands thrust in a small round muff, her veil drawn down like a transparent mask to the tip of her nose, and the bunch of violets he had brought her stirring with her quickly-taken breath, it seemed incredible that this pure harmony of line and colour should ever suffer the stupid law of change.

"Meanwhile everything matters—that concerns you." he said.

She looked at him thoughtfully, and turned back to the divan. He sat down beside her and waited; but suddenly he heard a step echoing far off down the empty rooms, and felt the pressure of the minutes.

"What is it you wanted to tell me?" she asked, as if she had received the same warning.

"What I wanted to tell you?" he rejoined. "Why, that I believe you came to New York because you were afraid."

"Afraid?"

"Of my coming to Washington."

She looked down at her muff, and he saw her hands stir in it uneasily.

"Well—?"

"Well—yes," she said.

"You *were* afraid? You knew—?"

"Yes: I knew . . ."

"Well, then?" he insisted.

"Well, then: this is better, isn't it?" she returned with a long questioning sigh.

"Better—?"

"We shall hurt others less. Isn't it, after all, what you always wanted?"

"To have you here, you mean—in reach and yet out of

[313]

reach? To meet you in this way, on the sly? It's the very reverse of what I want. I told you the other day what I wanted."

She hesitated. "And you still think this—worse?"

"A thousand times!" He paused. "It would be easy to lie to you; but the truth is I think it detestable."

"Oh, so do I!" she cried with a deep breath of relief.

He sprang up impatiently. "Well, then—it's my turn to ask: what is it, in God's name, that you think better?"

She hung her head and continued to clasp and unclasp her hands in her muff. The step drew nearer, and a guardian in a braided cap walked listlessly through the room like a ghost stalking through a necropolis. They fixed their eyes simultaneously on the case opposite them, and when the official figure had vanished down a vista of mummies and sarcophagi Archer spoke again.

"What do you think better?"

Instead of answering she murmured: "I promised Granny to stay with her because it seemed to me that here I should be safer."

"From me?"

She bent her head slightly, without looking at him.

"Safer from loving me?"

Her profile did not stir, but he saw a tear overflow on her lashes and hang in a mesh of her veil.

"Safer from doing irreparable harm. Don't let us be like all the others!" she protested.

"What others? I don't profess to be different from my kind. I'm consumed by the same wants and the same longings."

She glanced at him with a kind of terror, and he saw a faint colour steal into her cheeks.

"Shall I—once come to you; and then go home?" she suddenly hazarded in a low clear voice.

[314]

The blood rushed to the young man's forehead. "Dear est!" he said, without moving. It seemed as if he held his heart in his hands, like a full cup that the least motion might overbrim.

Then her last phrase struck his ear and his face clouded. "Go home? What do you mean by going home?"

"Home to my husband."

"And you expect me to say yes to that?"

She raised her troubled eyes to his. "What else is there? I can't stay here and lie to the people who've been good to me."

"But that's the very reason why I ask you to come away!"

"And destroy their lives, when they've helped me to remake mine?"

Archer sprang to his feet and stood looking down on her in inarticulate despair. It would have been easy to say: "Yes, come; come once." He knew the power she would put in his hands if she consented; there would be no difficulty then in persuading her not to go back to her husband.

But something silenced the word on his lips. A sort of passionate honesty in her made it inconceivable that he should try to draw her into that familiar trap. "If I were to let her come," he said to himself, "I should have to let her go again." And that was not to be imagined.

But he saw the shadow of the lashes on her wet cheek, and wavered.

"After all," he began again, "we have lives of our own. . . . There's no use attempting the impossible. You're so unprejudiced about some things, so used, as you say, to looking at the Gorgon, that I don't know why you're afraid to face our case, and see it as it really is—unless you think the sacrifice is not worth making."

She stood up also, her lips tightening under a rapid frown.

"Call it that, then—I must go," she said, drawing her little watch from her bosom.

She turned away, and he followed and caught her by the wrist. "Well, then: come to me once," he said, his head turning suddenly at the thought of losing her; and for a second or two they looked at each other almost like enemies.

"When?" he insisted. "Tomorrow?"

She hesitated. "The day after."

"Dearest—!" he said again.

She had disengaged her wrist; but for a moment they continued to hold each other's eyes, and he saw that her face, which had grown very pale, was flooded with a deep inner radiance. His heart beat with awe: he felt that he had never before beheld love visible.

"Oh, I shall be late—good-bye. No, don't come any farther than this," she cried, walking hurriedly away down the long room, as if the reflected radiance in his eyes had frightened her. When she reached the door she turned for a moment to wave a quick farewell.

Archer walked home alone. Darkness was falling when he let himself into his house, and he looked about at the familiar objects in the hall as if he viewed them from the other side of the grave.

The parlour-maid, hearing his step, ran up the stairs to light the gas on the upper landing.

"Is Mrs. Archer in?"

"No, sir; Mrs. Archer went out in the carriage after luncheon, and hasn't come back."

With a sense of relief he entered the library and flung himself down in his armchair. The parlour-maid followed, bringing the student lamp and shaking some coals onto the dying fire. When she left he continued to sit motionless, his elbows on his knees, his chin on his clasped hands, his eyes fixed on the red grate.

He sat there without conscious thoughts, without sense of the lapse of time, in a deep and grave amazement that seemed to suspend life rather than quicken it. "This was what had to be, then . . . this was what had to be," he kept repeating to himself, as if he hung in the clutch of doom. What he had dreamed of had been so different that there was a mortal chill in his rapture.

The door opened and May came in.

"I'm dreadfully late—you weren't worried, were you?" she asked, laying her hand on his shoulder with one of her rare caresses.

He looked up astonished. "Is it late?"

"After seven. I believe you've been asleep!" She laughed, and drawing out her hat pins tossed her velvet hat on the sofa. She looked paler than usual, but sparkling with an unwonted animation.

"I went to see Granny, and just as I was going away Ellen came in from a walk; so I stayed and had a long talk with her. It was ages since we'd had a real talk. . . ." She had dropped into her usual armchair, facing his, and was running her fingers through her rumpled hair. He fancied she expected him to speak.

"A really good talk," she went on, smiling with what seemed to Archer an unnatural vividness. "She was so dear—just like the old Ellen. I'm afraid I haven't been fair to her lately. I've sometimes thought—"

Archer stood up and leaned against the mantelpiece, out of the radius of the lamp.

[317]

"Yes, you've thought—?" he echoed as she paused.

"Well, perhaps I haven't judged her fairly. She's so different—at least on the surface. She takes up such odd people—she seems to like to make herself conspicuous. I suppose it's the life she's led in that fast European society; no doubt we seem dreadfully dull to her. But I don't want to judge her unfairly."

She paused again, a little breathless with the unwonted length of her speech, and sat with her lips slightly parted and a deep blush on her cheeks.

Archer, as he looked at her, was reminded of the glow which had suffused her face in the Mission Garden at St. Augustine. He became aware of the same obscure effort in her, the same reaching out toward something beyond the usual range of her vision.

"She hates Ellen," he thought, "and she's trying to overcome the feeling, and to get me to help her to overcome it."

The thought moved him, and for a moment he was on the point of breaking the silence between them, and throwing himself on her mercy.

"You understand, don't you," she went on, "why the family have sometimes been annoyed? We all did what we could for her at first; but she never seemed to understand. And now this idea of going to see Mrs. Beaufort, of going there in Granny's carriage! I'm afraid she's quite alienated the van der Luydens . . ."

"Ah," said Archer with an impatient laugh. The open door had closed between them again.

"It's time to dress; we're dining out, aren't we?" he asked, moving from the fire.

She rose also, but lingered near the hearth. As he walked past her she moved forward impulsively, as though to detain him: their eyes met, and he saw that

[318]

hers were of the same swimming blue as when he had left her to drive to Jersey City.

She flung her arms about his neck and pressed her cheek to his.

"You haven't kissed me today," she said in a whisper; and he felt her tremble in his arms.

XXXII

A T the Court of the Tuileries," said Mr. Sillerton
Jackson with his reminiscent smile, "such things
were pretty openly tolerated."

The scene was the van der Luydens' black walnut dining-room in Madison Avenue, and the time the evening
after Newland Archer's visit to the Museum of Art. Mr.
and Mrs. van der Luyden had come to town for a few
days from Skuytercliff, whither they had precipitately
fled at the announcement of Beaufort's failure. It had
been represented to them that the disarray into which
society had been thrown by this deplorable affair made
their presence in town more necessary than ever. It was
one of the occasions when, as Mrs. Archer put it, they
"owed it to society" to show themselves at the Opera,
and even to open their own doors.

"It will never do, my dear Louisa, to let people like
Mrs. Lemuel Struthers think they can step into Regina's
shoes. It is just at such times that new people push in
and get a footing. It was owing to the epidemic of chick-
en-pox in New York the winter Mrs. Struthers first appeared that the married men slipped away to her house
while their wives were in the nursery. You and dear
Henry, Louisa, must stand in the breach as you always
have."

Mr. and Mrs. van der Luyden could not remain deaf
to such a call, and reluctantly but heroically they had

come to town, unmuffled the house, and sent out invitations for two dinners and an evening reception.

On this particular evening they had invited Sillerton Jackson, Mrs. Archer and Newland and his wife to go with them to the Opera, where Faust was being sung for the first time that winter. Nothing was done without ceremony under the van der Luyden roof, and though there were but four guests the repast had begun at seven punctually, so that the proper sequence of courses might be served without haste before the gentlemen settled down to their cigars.

Archer had not seen his wife since the evening before. He had left early for the office, where he had plunged into an accumulation of unimportant business. In the afternoon one of the senior partners had made an unexpected call on his time; and he had reached home so late that May had preceded him to the van der Luydens', and sent back the carriage.

Now, across the Skuytercliff carnations and the massive plate, she struck him as pale and languid; but her eyes shone, and she talked with exaggerated animation.

The subject which had called forth Mr. Sillerton Jackson's favourite allusion had been brought up (Archer fancied not without intention) by their hostess. The Beaufort failure, or rather the Beaufort attitude since the failure, was still a fruitful theme for the drawing-room moralist; and after it had been thoroughly examined and condemned Mrs. van der Luyden had turned her scrupulous eyes on May Archer.

"Is it possible, dear, that what I hear is true? I was told your grandmother Mingott's carriage was seen standing at Mrs. Beaufort's door." It was noticeable that she no longer called the offending lady by her Christian name.

May's colour rose, and Mrs. Archer put in hastily: "If

it was, I'm convinced it was there without Mrs. Mingott's knowledge."

"Ah, you think—?" Mrs. van der Luyden paused, sighed, and glanced at her husband.

"I'm afraid," Mr. van der Luyden said, "that Madame Olenska's kind heart may have led her into the imprudence of calling on Mrs. Beaufort."

"Or her taste for peculiar people," put in Mrs. Archer in a dry tone, while her eyes dwelt innocently on her son's.

"I'm sorry to think it of Madame Olenska," said Mrs. van der Luyden; and Mrs. Archer murmured: "Ah, my dear—and after you'd had her twice at Skuytercliff!"

It was at this point that Mr. Jackson seized the chance to place his favourite allusion.

"At the Tuileries," he repeated, seeing the eyes of the company expectantly turned on him, "the standard was excessively lax in some respects; and if you'd asked where Morny's money came from—! Or who paid the debts of some of the Court beauties . . ."

"I hope, dear Sillerton," said Mrs. Archer, "you are not suggesting that we should adopt such standards?"

"I never suggest," returned Mr. Jackson imperturbably. "But Madame Olenska's foreign bringing-up may make her less particular—"

"Ah," the two elder ladies sighed.

"Still, to have kept her grandmother's carriage at a defaulter's door!" Mr. van der Luyden protested; and Archer guessed that he was remembering, and resenting, the hampers of carnations he had sent to the little house in Twenty-third Street.

"Of course I've always said that she looks at things quite differently," Mrs. Archer summed up.

A flush rose to May's forehead. She looked across the

table at her husband, and said precipitately: "I'm sure Ellen meant it kindly."

"Imprudent people are often kind," said Mrs. Archer, as if the fact were scarcely an extenuation; and Mrs. van der Luyden murmured: "If only she had consulted some one—"

"Ah, that she never did!" Mrs. Archer rejoined.

At this point Mr. van der Luyden glanced at his wife, who bent her head slightly in the direction of Mrs. Archer; and the glimmering trains of the three ladies swept out of the door while the gentlemen settled down to their cigars. Mr. van der Luyden supplied short ones on Opera nights; but they were so good that they made his guests deplore his inexorable punctuality.

Archer, after the first act, had detached himself from the party and made his way to the back of the club box. From there he watched, over various Chivers, Mingott and Rushworth shoulders, the same scene that he had looked at, two years previously, on the night of his first meeting with Ellen Olenska. He had half-expected her to appear again in old Mrs. Mingott's box, but it remained empty; and he sat motionless, his eyes fastened on it, till suddenly Madame Nilsson's pure soprano broke out into *"M'ama, non m'ama . . ."*

Archer turned to the stage, where, in the familiar setting of giant roses and pen-wiper pansies, the same large blonde victim was succumbing to the same small brown seducer.

From the stage his eyes wandered to the point of the horseshoe where May sat between two older ladies, just as, on that former evening, she had sat between Mrs. Lovell Mingott and her newly-arrived "foreign" cousin. As on that evening, she was all in white; and Archer, who had not noticed what she wore, recognised the blue-white satin and old lace of her wedding dress.

It was the custom, in old New York, for brides to appear in this costly garment during the first year or two of marriage: his mother, he knew, kept hers in tissue paper in the hope that Janey might some day wear it, though poor Janey was reaching the age when pearl grey poplin and no bridesmaids would be thought more "appropriate."

It struck Archer that May, since their return from Europe, had seldom worn her bridal satin, and the surprise of seeing her in it made him compare her appearance with that of the young girl he had watched with such blissful anticipations two years earlier.

Though May's outline was slightly heavier, as her goddess-like build had foretold, her athletic erectness of carriage, and the girlish transparency of her expression, remained unchanged: but for the slight languor that Archer had lately noticed in her she would have been the exact image of the girl playing with the bouquet of lilies-of-the-valley on her betrothal evening. The fact seemed an additional appeal to his pity: such innocence was as moving as the trustful clasp of a child. Then he remembered the passionate generosity latent under that incurious calm. He recalled her glance of understanding when he had urged that their engagement should be announced at the Beaufort ball; he heard the voice in which she had said, in the Mission garden: "I couldn't have my happiness made out of a wrong—a wrong to some one else;" and an uncontrollable longing seized him to tell her the truth, to throw himself on her generosity, and ask for the freedom he had once refused.

Newland Archer was a quiet and self-controlled young man. Conformity to the discipline of a small

THE AGE OF INNOCENCE

society had become almost his second nature. It was
deeply distasteful to him to do anything melodramatic
and conspicuous, anything Mr. van der Luyden would
have deprecated and the club box condemned as bad
form. But he had become suddenly unconscious of the
club box, of Mr. van der Luyden, of all that had so long
enclosed him in the warm shelter of habit. He walked
along the semi-circular passage at the back of the house,
and opened the door of Mrs. van der Luyden's box as
if it had been a gate into the unknown.

"M'ama!" thrilled out the triumphant Marguerite; and
the occupants of the box looked up in surprise at
Archer's entrance. He had already broken one of the
rules of his world, which forbade the entering of a box
during a solo.

Slipping between Mr. van der Luyden and Sillerton
Jackson, he leaned over his wife.

"I've got a beastly headache; don't tell any one, but
come home, won't you?" he whispered.

May gave him a glance of comprehension, and he saw
her whisper to his mother, who nodded sympathetically;
then she murmured an excuse to Mrs. van der Luyden,
and rose from her seat just as Marguerite fell into
Faust's arms. Archer, while he helped her on with her
Opera cloak, noticed the exchange of a significant smile
between the older ladies.

As they drove away May laid her hand shyly on his.
"I'm so sorry you don't feel well. I'm afraid they've
been over-working you again at the office."

"No—it's not that: do you mind if I open the window?" he returned confusedly, letting down the pane
on his side. He sat staring out into the street, feeling
his wife beside him as a silent watchful interrogation,
and keeping his eyes steadily fixed on the passing houses.

[325]

At their door she caught her skirt in the step of the carriage, and fell against him.

"Did you hurt yourself?" he asked, steadying her with his arm.

"No; but my poor dress—see how I've torn it!" she exclaimed. She bent to gather up a mud-stained breadth, and followed him up the steps into the hall. The servants had not expected them so early, and there was only a glimmer of gas on the upper landing.

Archer mounted the stairs, turned up the light, and put a match to the brackets on each side of the library mantelpiece. The curtains were drawn, and the warm friendly aspect of the room smote him like that of a familiar face met during an unavowable errand.

He noticed that his wife was very pale, and asked if he should get her some brandy.

"Oh, no," she exclaimed with a momentary flush, as she took off her cloak. "But hadn't you better go to bed at once?" she added, as he opened a silver box on the table and took out a cigarette.

Archer threw down the cigarette and walked to his usual place by the fire.

"No; my head is not as bad as that." He paused. "And there's something I want to say; something important—that I must tell you at once."

She had dropped into an armchair, and raised her head as he spoke. "Yes, dear?" she rejoined, so gently that he wondered at the lack of wonder with which she received this preamble.

"May—" he began, standing a few feet from her chair, and looking over at her as if the slight distance between them were an unbridgeable abyss. The sound of his voice echoed uncannily through the homelike hush, and

he repeated: "There is something I've got to tell you
. . . about myself . . ."

She sat silent, without a movement or a tremor of her
lashes. She was still extremely pale, but her face had
a curious tranquillity of expression that seemed drawn
from some secret inner source.

Archer checked the conventional phrases of self-accusal
that were crowding to his lips. He was determined to
put the case baldly, without vain recrimination or excuse.

"Madame Olenska—" he said; but at the name his
wife raised her hand as if to silence him. As she did so
the gas-light struck on the gold of her wedding-ring.

"Oh, why should we talk about Ellen tonight?" she
asked, with a slight pout of impatience.

"Because I ought to have spoken before."

Her face remained calm. "Is it really worth while,
dear? I know I've been unfair to her at times—perhaps
we all have. You've understood her, no doubt, better
than we did: you've always been kind to her. But what
does it matter, now it's over?"

Archer looked at her blankly. Could it be possible that
the sense of unreality in which he felt himself imprisoned
had communicated itself to his wife?

"All over—what do you mean?" he asked in an indistinct stammer.

May still looked at him with transparent eyes. "Why
—since she's going back to Europe so soon; since Granny
approves and understands, and has arranged to make her
independent of her husband—"

She broke off, and Archer, grasping the corner of the
mantelpiece in one convulsed hand, and steadying himself against it, made a vain effort to extend the same
control to his reeling thoughts.

"I supposed," he heard his wife's even voice go on,

"that you had been kept at the office this evening about the business arrangements. It was settled this morning, I believe." She lowered her eyes under his unseeing stare, and another fugitive flush passed over her face.

He understood that his own eyes must be unbearable, and turning away, rested his elbows on the mantel-shelf and covered his face. Something drummed and clanged furiously in his ears; he could not tell if it were the blood in his veins, or the tick of the clock on the mantel.

May sat without moving or speaking while the clock slowly measured out five minutes. A lump of coal fell forward in the grate, and hearing her rise to push it back, Archer at length turned and faced her.

"It's impossible," he exclaimed.

"Impossible—?"

"How do you know—what you've just told me?"

"I saw Ellen yesterday—I told you I'd seen her at Granny's."

"It wasn't then that she told you?"

"No; I had a note from her this afternoon.—Do you want to see it?"

He could not find his voice, and she went out of the room, and came back almost immediately.

"I thought you knew," she said simply.

She laid a sheet of paper on the table, and Archer put out his hand and took it up. The letter contained only a few lines.

"May dear, I have at last made Granny understand that my visit to her could be no more than a visit; and she has been as kind and generous as ever. She sees now that if I return to Europe I must live by myself, or rather with poor Aunt Medora, who is coming with me. I am hurrying back to Washington to pack up, and we sail next week. You must be very good to Granny

[328]

when I'm gone—as good as you've always been to me. Ellen.

"If any of my friends wish to urge me to change my mind, please tell them it would be utterly useless."

Archer read the letter over two or three times; then he flung it down and burst out laughing.

The sound of his laugh startled him. It recalled Janey's midnight fright when she had caught him rocking with incomprehensible mirth over May's telegram announcing that the date of their marriage had been advanced.

"Why did she write this?" he asked, checking his laugh with a supreme effort.

May met the question with her unshaken candour. "I suppose because we talked things over yesterday—"

"What things?"

"I told her I was afraid I hadn't been fair to her—hadn't always understood how hard it must have been for her here, alone among so many people who were relations and yet strangers; who felt the right to criticise, and yet didn't always know the circumstances." She paused. "I knew you'd been the one friend she could always count on; and I wanted her to know that you and I were the same—in all our feelings."

She hesitated, as if waiting for him to speak, and then added slowly: "She understood my wishing to tell her this. I think she understands everything."

She went up to Archer, and taking one of his cold hands pressed it quickly against her cheek.

"My head aches too; good-night, dear," she said, and turned to the door, her torn and muddy wedding-dress dragging after her across the room.

XXXIII

I T was, as Mrs. Archer smilingly said to Mrs. Welland, a great event for a young couple to give their
first big dinner.

The Newland Archers, since they had set up their
household, had received a good deal of company in an
informal way. Archer was fond of having three or
four friends to dine, and May welcomed them with the
beaming readiness of which her mother had set her the
example in conjugal affairs. Her husband questioned
whether, if left to herself, she would ever have asked
any one to the house; but he had long given up trying to
disengage her real self from the shape into which tradition and training had moulded her. It was expected that
well-off young couples in New York should do a good
deal of informal entertaining, and a Welland married
to an Archer was doubly pledged to the tradition.

But a big dinner, with a hired *chef* and two borrowed
footmen, with Roman punch, roses from Henderson's,
and *menus* on gilt-edged cards, was a different affair, and
not to be lightly undertaken. As Mrs. Archer remarked,
the Roman punch made all the difference; not in itself
but by its manifold implications—since it signified either
canvas-backs or terrapin, two soups, a hot and a cold
sweet, full *décolletage* with short sleeves, and guests of
a proportionate importance.

It was always an interesting occasion when a young
pair launched their first invitations in the third person,

and their summons was seldom refused even by the seasoned and sought-after. Still, it was admittedly a triumph
that the van der Luydens, at May's request, should have
stayed over in order to be present at her farewell dinner
for the Countess Olen ka.

The two mothers-in-i w sat in May's drawing-room on
the afternoon of the great day, Mrs. Archer writing out
the *menus* on Tiffany's thickest gilt-edged bristol, while
Mrs. Welland superintended the placing of the palms and
standard lamps.

Archer, arriving late from his office, found them still
there. Mrs. Archer had turned her attention to the
name-cards for the table, and Mrs. Welland was considering the effect of bringing forward the large gilt sofa,
so that another "corner" might be created between the
piano and the window.

May, they told him, was in the dining-room inspecting
the mound of Jacqueminot roses and maidenhair in the
centre of the long table, and the placing of the Maillard
bonbons in openwork silver baskets between the candelabra. On the piano stood a large basket of orchids
which Mr. van der Luyden had had sent from Skuytercliff. Everything was, in short, as it should be on the
approach of so considerable an event.

Mrs. Archer ran thoughtfully over the list, checking
off each name with her sharp gold pen.

"Henry van der Luyden—Louisa—the Lovell Mingotts
—the Reggie Chiverses—Lawrence Lefferts and Gertrude—(yes, I suppose May was right to have them)—
the Selfridge Merrys, Sillerton Jackson, Van Newland
and his wife. (How time passes! It seems only yesterday that he was your best man, Newland)—and Countess
Olenska—yes, I think that's all. . . ."

Mrs. Welland surveyed her son-in-law affectionately.

"No one can say, Newland, that you and May are not
giving Ellen a handsome send-off."

"Ah, well," said Mrs. Archer, "I understand May's
wanting her cousin to tell people abroad that we're not
quite barbarians."

"I'm sure Ellen will appreciate it. She was to arrive
this morning, I believe. It will make a most charming
last impression. The evening before sailing is usually so
dreary," Mrs. Welland cheerfully continued.

Archer turned toward the door, and his mother-in-law
called to him: "Do go in and have a peep at the table.
And don't let May tire herself too much." But he affected not to hear, and sprang up the stairs to his library.
The room looked at him like an alien countenance composed into a polite grimace; and he perceived that it had
been ruthlessly "tidied," and prepared, by a judicious
distribution of ash-trays and cedar-wood boxes, for the
gentlemen to smoke in.

"Ah, well," he thought, "it's not for long—" and he
went on to his dressing-room.

Ten days had passed since Madame Olenska's departure from New York. During those ten days Archer
had had no sign from her but that conveyed by the return
of a key wrapped in tissue paper, and sent to his office
in a sealed envelope addressed in her hand. This retort
to his last appeal might have been interpreted as a classic
move in a familiar game; but the young man chose to
give it a different meaning. She was still fighting against
her fate; but she was going to Europe, and she was not
returning to her husband. Nothing, therefore, was to
prevent his following her; and once he had taken the
irrevocable step, and had proved to her that it was irrevocable, he believed she would not send him away.

This confidence in the future had steadied him to play his part in the present. It had kept him from writing to her, or betraying, by any sign or act, his misery and mortification. It seemed to him that in the deadly silent game between them the trumps were still in his hands; and he waited.

There had been, nevertheless, moments sufficiently difficult to pass; as when Mr. Letterblair, the day after Madame Olenska's departure, had sent for him to go over the details of the trust which Mrs. Manson Mingott wished to create for her granddaughter. For a couple of hours Archer had examined the terms of the deed with his senior, all the while obscurely feeling that if he had been consulted it was for some reason other than the obvious one of his cousinship; and that the close of the conference would reveal it.

"Well, the lady can't deny that it's a handsome arrangement," Mr. Letterblair had summed up, after mumbling over a summary of the settlement. "In fact I'm bound to say she's been treated pretty handsomely all round."

"All round?" Archer echoed with a touch of derision. "Do you refer to her husband's proposal to give her back her own money?"

Mr. Letterblair's bushy eyebrows went up a fraction of an inch. "My dear sir, the law's the law; and your wife's cousin was married under the French law. It's to be presumed she knew what that meant."

"Even if she did, what happened subsequently—." But Archer paused. Mr. Letterblair had laid his penhandle against his big corrugated nose, and was looking down it with the expression assumed by virtuous elderly gentlemen when they wish their youngers to understand that virtue is not synonymous with ignorance.

"My dear sir, I've no wish to extenuate the Count's transgressions; but—but on the other side . . . I wouldn't put my hand in the fire . . . well, that there hadn't been tit for tat . . . with the young champion. . . ." Mr. Letterblair unlocked a drawer and pushed a folded paper toward Archer. "This report, the result of discreet enquiries . . ." And then, as Archer made no effort to glance at the paper or to repudiate the suggestion, the lawyer somewhat flatly continued: "I don't say it's conclusive, you observe; far from it. But straws show . . . and on the whole it's eminently satisfactory for all parties that this dignified solution has been reached."

"Oh, eminently," Archer assented, pushing back the paper.

A day or two later, on responding to a summons from Mrs. Manson Mingott, his soul had been more deeply tried.

He had found the old lady depressed and querulous.

"You know she's deserted me?" she began at once; and without waiting for his reply: "Oh, don't ask me why! She gave so many reasons that I've forgotten them all. My private belief is that she couldn't face the boredom. At any rate that's what Augusta and my daughters-in-law think. And I don't know that I altogether blame her. Olenski's a finished scoundrel; but life with him must have been a good deal gayer than it is in Fifth Avenue. Not that the family would admit that: they think Fifth Avenue is Heaven with the rue de la Paix thrown in. And poor Ellen, of course, has no idea of going back to her husband. She held out as firmly as ever against that. So she's to settle down in Paris with that fool Medora. . . . Well, Paris is Paris; and you can keep a carriage there on next to nothing. But she

was as gay as a bird, and I shall miss her." Two tears,
the parched tears of the old, rolled down her puffy cheeks
and vanished in the abysses of her bosom.

"All I ask is," she concluded, "that they shouldn't
bother me any more. I must really be allowed to digest
my gruel. . . ." And she twinkled a little wistfully at
Archer.

It was that evening, on his return home, that May
announced her intention of giving a farewell dinner to
her cousin. Madame Olenska's name had not been pronounced between them since the night of her flight to
Washington; and Archer looked at his wife with surprise.

"A dinner—why?" he interrogated.

Her colour rose. "But you like Ellen—I thought you'd
be pleased."

"It's awfully nice—your putting it in that way. But I
really don't see—"

"I mean to do it, Newland," she said, quietly rising and
going to her desk. "Here are the invitations all written.
Mother helped me—she agrees that we ought to." She
paused, embarrassed and yet smiling, and Archer suddenly saw before him the embodied image of the Family.

"Oh, all right," he said, staring with unseeing eyes at
the list of guests that she had put in his hand.

When he entered the drawing-room before dinner May
was stooping over the fire and trying to coax the logs to
burn in their unaccustomed setting of immaculate tiles.

The tall lamps were all lit, and Mr. van der Luyden's
orchids had been conspicuously disposed in various recep-
tacles of modern porcelain and knobby silver. Mrs.
Newland Archer's drawing-room was generally thought
a great success. A gilt bamboo *jardinière,* in which the
primulas and cinerarias were punctually renewed, blocked

the access to the bay window (where the old-fashioned would have preferred a bronze reduction of the Venus of Milo) ; the sofas and arm-chairs of pale brocade were cleverly grouped about little plush tables densely covered with silver toys, porcelain animals and efflorescent photograph frames; and tall rosy-shaded lamps shot up like tropical flowers among the palms.

"I don't think Ellen has ever seen this room lighted up," said May, rising flushed from her struggle, and sending about her a glance of pardonable pride. The brass tongs which she had propped against the side of the chimney fell with a crash that drowned her husband's answer; and before he could restore them Mr. and Mrs. van der Luyden were announced.

The other guests quickly followed, for it was known that the van der Luydens liked to dine punctually. The room was nearly full, and Archer was engaged in showing to Mrs. Selfridge Merry a small highly-varnished Verbeckhoven "Study of Sheep," which Mr. Welland had given May for Christmas, when he found Madame Olenska at his side.

She was excessively pale, and her pallor made her dark hair seem denser and heavier than ever. Perhaps that, or the fact that she had wound several rows of amber beads about her neck, reminded him suddenly of the little Ellen Mingott he had danced with at children's parties, when Medora Manson had first brought her to New York.

The amber beads were trying to her complexion, or her dress was perhaps unbecoming: her face looked lustreless and almost ugly, and he had never loved it as he did at that minute. Their hands met, and he thought he heard her say: "Yes, we're sailing tomorrow in the Russia—"; then there was an unmeaning noise of open-

[336]

ing doors, and after an interval May's voice: "Newland! Dinner's been announced. Won't you please take Ellen in?"

Madame Olenska put her hand on his arm, and he noticed that the hand was ungloved, and remembered how he had kept his eyes fixed on it the evening that he had sat with her in the little Twenty-third Street drawing-room. All the beauty that had forsaken her face seemed to have taken refuge in the long pale fingers and faintly dimpled knuckles on his sleeve, and he said to himself: "If it were only to see her hand again I should have to follow her—."

It was only at an entertainment ostensibly offered to a "foreign visitor" that Mrs. van der Luyden could suffer the diminution of being placed on her host's left. The fact of Madame Olenska's "foreignness" could hardly have been more adroitly emphasised than by this farewell tribute; and Mrs. van der Luyden accepted her displacement with an affability which left no doubt as to her approval. There were certain things that had to be done, and if done at all, done handsomely and thoroughly; and one of these, in the old New York code, was the tribal rally around a kinswoman about to be eliminated from the tribe. There was nothing on earth that the Wellands and Mingotts would not have done to proclaim their unalterable affection for the Countess Olenska now that her passage for Europe was engaged; and Archer, at the head of his table, sat marvelling at the silent untiring activity with which her popularity had been retrieved, grievances against her silenced, her past countenanced, and her present irradiated by the family approval. Mrs. van der Luyden shone on her with the dim benevolence which was her nearest approach to cordiality, and Mr. van der Luyden, from his seat at May's right, cast down the table glances plainly intended to justify all the carnations he had sent from Skuytercliff.

Archer, who seemed to be assisting at the scene in a state of odd imponderability, as if he floated somewhere between chandelier and ceiling, wondered at nothing so much as his own share in the proceedings. As his glance travelled from one placid well-fed face to another he saw all the harmless-looking people engaged upon May's canvas-backs as a band of dumb conspirators, and himself and the pale woman on his right as the centre of their conspiracy. And then it came over him, in a vast flash made up of many broken gleams, that to all of them he and Madame Olenska were lovers, lovers in the extreme sense peculiar to "foreign" vocabularies. He guessed himself to have been, for months, the centre of countless silently observing eyes and patiently listening ears, he understood that, by means as yet unknown to him, the separation between himself and the partner of his guilt had been achieved, and that now the whole tribe had rallied about his wife on the tacit assumption that nobody knew anything, or had ever imagined anything, and that the occasion of the entertainment was simply May Archer's natural desire to take an affectionate leave of her friend and cousin.

It was the old New York way of taking life "without effusion of blood": the way of people who dreaded scandal more than disease, who placed decency above courage, and who considered that nothing was more ill-bred than "scenes," except the behaviour of those who gave rise to them.

As these thoughts succeeded each other in his mind Archer felt like a prisoner in the centre of an armed camp. He looked about the table, and guessed at the inexorableness of his captors from the tone in which, over the asparagus from Florida, they were dealing with Beaufort and his wife. "It's to show me," he thought, "what would happen to *me*—" and a deathly sense of the superiority of implication and analogy over direct action, and of silence over rash words, closed in on him like the doors of the family vault.

He laughed, and met Mrs. van der Luyden's startled eyes.

"You think it laughable?" she said with a pinched smile. "Of course poor Regina's idea of remaining in New York has its ridiculous side, I suppose;" and Archer muttered: "Of course."

At this point, he became conscious that Madame Olenska's other neighbour had been engaged for some time with the lady on his right. At the same moment he saw that May, serenely enthroned between Mr. van der Luyden and Mr. Selfridge Merry, had cast a quick glance down the table. It was evident that the host and the lady on his right could not sit through the whole meal in silence. He turned to Madame Olenska, and her pale smile met him. "Oh, do let's see it through," it seemed to say.

"Did you find the journey tiring?" he asked in a voice that surprised him by its naturalness; and she answered that, on the contrary, she had seldom travelled with fewer discomforts.

"Except, you know, the dreadful heat in the train," she added; and he remarked that she would not suffer from that particular hardship in the country she was going to.

"I never," he declared with intensity, "was more nearly frozen than once, in April, in the train between Calais and Paris."

She said she did not wonder, but remarked that, after

all, one could always carry an extra rug, and that every form of travel had its hardships; to which he abruptly returned that he thought them all of no account compared with the blessedness of getting away. She changed colour, and he added, his voice suddenly rising in pitch: "I mean to do a lot of travelling myself before long." A tremor crossed her face, and leaning over to Reggie Chivers, he cried out: "I say, Reggie, what do you say to a trip round the world: now, next month, I mean? I'm game if you are—" at which Mrs. Reggie piped up that she could not think of letting Reggie go till after the Martha Washington Ball she was getting up for the Blind Asylum in Easter week; and her husband placidly observed that by that time he would have to be practising for the International Polo match.

But Mr. Selfridge Merry had caught the phrase "round the world," and having once circled the globe in his steam-yacht, he seized the opportunity to send down the table several striking items concerning the shallowness of the Mediterranean ports. Though, after all, he added, it didn't matter; for when you'd seen Athens and Smyrna and Constantinople, what else was there? And Mrs. Merry said she could never be too grateful to Dr. Bencomb for having made them promise not to go to Naples on account of the fever.

"But you must have three weeks to do India properly," her husband conceded, anxious to have it understood that he was no frivolous globe-trotter.

And at this point the ladies went up to the drawing-room.

In the library, in spite of weightier presences, Lawrence Lefferts predominated.

The talk, as usual, had veered around to the Beauforts,

and even Mr. van der Luyden and Mr. Selfridge Merry, installed in the honorary arm-chairs tacitly reserved for them, paused to listen to the younger man's philippic.

Never had Lefferts so abounded in the sentiments that adorn Christian manhood and exalt the sanctity of the home. Indignation lent him a scathing eloquence, and it was clear that if others had followed his example, and acted as he talked, society would never have been weak enough to receive a foreign upstart like Beaufort—no, sir, not even if he'd married a van der Luyden or a Lanning instead of a Dallas. And what chance would there have been, Lefferts wrathfully questioned, of his marrying into such a family as the Dallases, if he had not already wormed his way into certain houses, as people like Mrs. Lemuel Struthers had managed to worm theirs in his wake? If society chose to open its doors to vulgar women the harm was not great, though the gain was doubtful; but once it got in the way of tolerating men of obscure origin and tainted wealth the end was total disintegration—and at no distant date.

"If things go on at this pace," Lefferts thundered, looking like a young prophet dressed by Poole, and who had not yet been stoned, "we shall see our children fighting for invitations to swindlers' houses, and marrying Beaufort's bastards."

"Oh, I say—draw it mild!" Reggie Chivers and young Newland protested, while Mr. Selfridge Merry looked genuinely alarmed, and an expression of pain and disgust settled on Mr. van der Luyden's sensitive face.

"Has he got any?" cried Mr. Sillerton Jackson, pricking up his ears; and while Lefferts tried to turn the question with a laugh, the old gentleman twittered into Archer's ear: "Queer, those fellows who are always wanting to set things right. The people who have the

worst cooks are always telling you they're poisoned when
they dine out. But I hear there are pressing reasons for
our friend Lawrence's diatribe:—type-writer this time,
I understand. . . ."

The talk swept past Archer like some senseless river
running and running because it did not know enough to
stop. He saw, on the faces about him, expressions of
interest, amusement and even mirth. He listened to the
younger men's laughter, and to the praise of the Archer
Madeira, which Mr. van der Luyden and Mr. Merry were
thoughtfully celebrating. Through it all he was dimly
aware of a general attitude of friendliness toward himself, as if the guard of the prisoner he felt himself to be
were trying to soften his captivity; and the perception increased his passionate determination to be free.

In the drawing-room, where they presently joined the
ladies, he met May's triumphant eyes, and read in them
the conviction that everything had "gone off" beautifully.
She rose from Madame Olenska's side, and immediately
Mrs. van der Luyden beckoned the latter to a seat on
the gilt sofa where she throned. Mrs. Selfridge Merry
bore across the room to join them, and it became clear
to Archer that here also a conspiracy of rehabilitation
and obliteration was going on. The silent organisation
which held his little world together was determined to
put itself on record as never for a moment having
questioned the propriety of Madame Olenska's conduct,
or the completeness of Archer's domestic felicity. All
these amiable and inexorable persons were resolutely
engaged in pretending to each other that they had never
heard of, suspected, or even conceived possible, the least
hint to the contrary; and from this tissue of elaborate
mutual dissimulation Archer once more disengaged the
fact that New York believed him to be Madame Olenska's

lover. He caught the glitter of victory in his wife's eyes, and for the first time understood that she shared the belief. The discovery roused a laughter of inner devils that reverberated through all his efforts to discuss the Martha Washington ball with Mrs. Reggie Chivers and little Mrs. Newland; and so the evening swept on, running and running like a senseless river that did not know how to stop.

At length he saw that Madame Olenska had risen and was saying good-bye. He understood that in a moment she would be gone, and tried to remember what he had said to her at dinner; but he could not recall a single word they had exchanged.

She went up to May, the rest of the company making a circle about her as she advanced. The two young women clasped hands; then May bent forward and kissed her cousin.

"Certainly our hostess is much the handsomer of the two," Archer heard Reggie Chivers say in an undertone to young Mrs. Newland; and he remembered Beaufort's coarse sneer at May's ineffectual beauty.

A moment later he was in the hall, putting Madame Olenska's cloak about her shoulders.

Through all his confusion of mind he had held fast to the resolve to say nothing that might startle or disturb her. Convinced that no power could now turn him from his purpose ·he had found strength to let events shape themselves as they would. But as he followed Madame Olenska into the hall he thought with a sudden hunger of being for a moment alone with her at the door of her carriage.

"Is your carriage here?" he asked; and at that moment Mrs. van der Luyden, who was being majestically inserted into her sables, said gently: "We are driving dear Ellen home."

Archer's heart gave a jerk, and Madame Olenska, clasping her cloak and fan with one hand, held out the other to him. "Good-bye," she said.

"Good-bye—but I shall see you soon in Paris," he answered aloud—it seemed to him that he had shouted it.

"Oh," she murmured, "if you and May could come—!"

Mr. van der Luyden advanced to give her his arm, and Archer turned to Mrs. van der Luyden. For a moment, in the billowy darkness inside the big landau, he caught the dim oval of a face, eyes shining steadily—and she was gone.

As he went up the steps he crossed Lawrence Lefferts coming down with his wife. Lefferts caught his host by the sleeve, drawing back to let Gertrude pass.

"I say, old chap: do you mind just letting it be understood that I'm dining with you at the club tomorrow night? Thanks so much, you old brick! Good-night."

"It *did* go off beautifully, didn't it?" May questioned from the threshold of the library.

Archer roused himself with a start. As soon as the last carriage had driven away, he had come up to the library and shut himself in, with the hope that his wife, who still lingered below, would go straight to her room. But there she stood, pale and drawn, yet radiating the factitious energy of one who has passed beyond fatigue.

"May I come and talk it over?" she asked.

"Of course, if you like. But you must be awfully sleepy—"

"No, I'm not sleepy. I should like to sit with you a little."

"Very well," he said, pushing her chair near the fire.

She sat down and he resumed his seat; but neither spoke for a long time. At length Archer began abruptly: "Since you're not tired, and want to talk, there's something I must tell you. I tried to the other night——."

She looked at him quickly. "Yes, dear. Something about yourself?"

"About myself. You say you're not tired: well, I am. Horribly tired . . ."

In an instant she was all tender anxiety. "Oh, I've seen it coming on, Newland! You've been so wickedly overworked——"

"Perhaps it's that. Anyhow, I want to make a break——"

"A break? To give up the law?"

"To go away, at any rate—at once. On a long trip, ever so far off—away from everything——"

He paused, conscious that he had failed in his attempt to speak with the indifference of a man who longs for a change, and is yet too weary to welcome it. Do what he would, the chord of eagerness vibrated. "Away from everything——" he repeated.

"Ever so far? Where, for instance?" she asked.

"Oh, I don't know. India—or Japan."

She stood up, and as he sat with bent head, his chin propped on his hands, he felt her warmly and fragrantly hovering over him.

"As far as that? But I'm afraid you can't, dear . . ." she said in an unsteady voice. "Not unless you'll take me with you." And then, as he was silent, she went on, in tones so clear and evenly-pitched that each separate syllable tapped like a little hammer on his brain: "That is, if the doctors will let me go . . . but I'm afraid they won't. For you see, Newland, I've been sure since this

[345]

morning of something I've been so longing and hoping
for—"

He looked up at her with a sick stare, and she sank
down, all dew and roses, and hid her face against his
knee.

"Oh, my dear," he said, holding her to him while his
cold hand stroked her hair.

There was a long pause, which the inner devils filled
with strident laughter; then May freed herself from his
arms and stood up.

"You didn't guess—?"

"Yes—I; no. That is, of course I hoped—"

They looked at each other for an instant and again
fell silent; then, turning his eyes from hers, he asked
abruptly: "Have you told any one else?"

"Only Mamma and your mother." She paused, and
then added hurriedly, the blood flushing up to her forehead: "That is—and Ellen. You know I told you we'd
had a long talk one afternoon—and how dear she was
to me."

"Ah—" said Archer, his heart stopping.

He felt that his wife was watching him intently. "Did
you *mind* my telling her first, Newland?"

"Mind? Why should I?" He made a last effort
collect himself. "But that was a fortnight ago, wasn
it? I thought you said you weren't sure till today."

Her colour burned deeper, but she held his gaze. "No
I wasn't sure then—but I told her I was. And you see
I was right!" she exclaimed, her blue eyes wet with
victory.

XXXIV

NEWLAND ARCHER sat at the writing-table in his library in East Thirty-ninth Street.

He had just got back from a big official reception for the inauguration of the new galleries at the Metropolitan Museum, and the spectacle of those great spaces crowded with the spoils of the ages, where the throng of fashion circulated through a series of scientifically catalogued treasures, had suddenly pressed on a rusted spring of memory.

"Why, this used to be one of the old Cesnola rooms," he heard some one say; and instantly everything about him vanished, and he was sitting alone on a hard leather divan against a radiator, while a slight figure in a long sealskin cloak moved away down the meagrely-fitted vista of the old Museum.

The vision had roused a host of other associations, and he sat looking with new eyes at the library which, for over thirty years, had been the scene of his solitary musings and of all the family confabulations.

It was the room in which most of the real things of his life had happened. There his wife, nearly twenty-six years ago, had broken to him, with a blushing circumlocution that would have caused the young women of the new generation to smile, the news that she was to have a child; and there their eldest boy, Dallas, too delicate to be taken to church in midwinter, had been christened by their old friend the Bishop of New York,

[347]

the ample magnificent irreplaceable Bishop, so long
the pride and ornament of his diocese. There Dallas
had first staggered across the floor shouting "Dad," while
May and the nurse laughed behind the door; there their
second child, Mary (who was so like her mother), had
announced her engagement to the dullest and most relia-
ble of Reggie Chivers's many sons; and there Archer had
kissed her through her wedding veil before they went
down to the motor which was to carry them to Grace
Church—for in a world where all else had reeled on
its foundations the "Grace Church wedding" remained
an unchanged institution.

It was in the library that he and May had always
discussed the future of the children: the studies of Dallas
and his young brother Bill, Mary's incurable indifference
to "accomplishments," and passion for sport and philan-
thropy, and the vague leanings toward "art" which had
finally landed the restless and curious Dallas in the office
of a rising New York architect.

The young men nowadays were emancipating themselves from the law and business and taking up all sorts of
new things. If they were not absorbed in state politics
or municipal reform, the chances were that they were
going in for Central American archæology, for architecture or landscape—engineering; taking a keen and learned
interest in the pre-revolutionary buildings of their own
country, studying and adapting Georgian types, and protesting at the meaningless use of the word "Colonial."
Nobody nowadays had "Colonial" houses except the
millionaire grocers of the suburbs.

But above all—sometimes Archer put it above all—it
was in that library that the Governor of New York,
coming down from Albany one evening to dine and spend
the night, had turned to his host, and said, banging his

clenched fist on the table and gnashing his eye-glasses:
"Hang the professional politician! You're the kind of
man the country wants, Archer. If the stable's ever to
be cleaned out, men like you have got to lend a hand in
the cleaning."

"Men like you—" how Archer had glowed at the
phrase! How eagerly he had risen up at the call! It
was an echo of Ned Winsett's old appeal to roll his
sleeves up and get down into the muck; but spoken by
a man who set the example of the gesture, and whose
summons to follow him was irresistible.

Archer, as he looked back, was not sure that men like
himself *were* what his country needed, at least in the
active service to which Theodore Roosevelt had pointed;
in fact, there was reason to think it did not, for after a
year in the State Assembly he had not been re-elected,
and had dropped back thankfully into obscure if useful
municipal work, and from that again to the writing of
occasional articles in one of the reforming weeklies that
were trying to shake the country out of its apathy. It
was little enough to look back on; but when he remembered to what the young men of his generation and his
set had looked forward—the narrow groove of money-
making, sport and society to which their vision had been
limited—even his small contribution to the new state of
things seemed to count, as each brick counts in a well-
built wall. He had done little in public life; he would
always be by nature a contemplative and a dilettante;
but he had had high things to contemplate, great things
to delight in; and one great man's friendship to be his
strength and pride.

He had been, in short, what people were beginning to
call "a good citizen." In New York, for many years past,
every new movement, philanthropic, municipal or artistic,

had taken account of his opinion and wanted his name.
People said: "Ask Archer" when there was a question
of starting the first school for crippled children, reorgan-
ising the Museum of Art, founding the Grolier Club,
inaugurating the new Library, or getting up a new society
of chamber music. His days were full, and they were
filled decently. He supposed it was all a man ought to
ask.

Something he knew he had missed: the flower of life.
But he thought of it now as a thing so unattainable and
improbable that to have repined would have been like
despairing because one had not drawn the first prize in
a lottery. There were a hundred million tickets in *his*
lottery, and there was only one prize; the chances had
been too decidedly against him. When he thought of
Ellen Olenska it was abstractly, serenely, as one might
think of some imaginary beloved in a book or a picture:
she had become the composite vision of all that he had
missed. That vision, faint and tenuous as it was, had
kept him from thinking of other women. He had been
what was called a faithful husband; and when May had
suddenly died—carried off by the infectious pneumonia
through which she had nursed their youngest child—he
had honestly mourned her. Their long years together
had shown him that it did not so much matter if marriage
was a dull duty, as long as it kept the dignity of a duty:
lapsing from that, it became a mere battle of ugly appe-
tites. Looking about him, he honoured his own past,
and mourned for it. After all, there was good in the
old ways.

His eyes, making the round of the room—done over by
Dallas with English mezzotints, Chippendale cabinets,
bits of chosen blue-and-white and pleasantly shaded
electric lamps—came back to the old Eastlake writing-

table that he had never been willing to banish, and to his first photograph of May, which still kept its place beside his inkstand.

There she was, tall, round-bosomed and willowy, in her starched muslin and flapping Leghorn, as he had seen her under the orange-trees in the Mission garden. And as he had seen her that day, so she had remained; never quite at the same height, yet never far below it: generous, faithful, unwearied; but so lacking in imagination, so incapable of growth, that the world of her youth had fallen into pieces and rebuilt itself without her ever being conscious of the change. This hard bright blindness had kept her immediate horizon apparently unaltered. Her incapacity to recognise change made her children conceal their views from her as Archer concealed his; there had been, from the first, a joint pretence of sameness, a kind of innocent family hypocrisy, in which father and children had unconsciously collaborated. And she had died thinking the world a good place, full of loving and harmonious households like her own, and resigned to leave it because she was convinced that, whatever happened, Newland would continue to inculcate in Dallas the same principles and prejudices which had shaped his parents' lives, and that Dallas in turn (when Newland followed her) would transmit the sacred trust to little Bill. And of Mary she was sure as of her own self. So, having snatched little Bill from the grave, and given her life in the effort, she went contentedly to her place in the Archer vault in St. Mark's, where Mrs. Archer already lay safe from the terrifying "trend" which her daughter-in-law had never even become aware of.

Opposite May's portrait stood one of her daughter. Mary Chivers was as tall and fair as her mother, but large-waisted, flat-chested and slightly slouching, as the

altered fashion required. Mary Chivers's mighty feats
of athleticism could not have been performed with the
twenty-inch waist that May Archer's azure sash so easily
spanned. And the difference seemed symbolic; the
mother's life had been as closely girt as her figure.
Mary, who was no less conventional, and no more intelligent, yet led a larger life and held more tolerant views.
There was good in the new order too.

The telephone clicked, and Archer, turning from the
photographs, unhooked the transmitter at his elbow.
How far they were from the days when the legs of the
brass-buttoned messenger boy had been New York's
only means of quick communication!

"Chicago wants you."

Ah—it must be a long-distance from Dallas, who had
been sent to Chicago by his firm to talk over the plan of
the Lake-side palace they were to build for a young
millionaire with ideas. The firm always sent Dallas on
such errands.

"Hallo, Dad—Yes: Dallas. I say—how do you feel
about sailing on Wednesday? Mauretania: Yes, next
Wednesday as ever is. Our client wants me to look
at some Italian gardens before we settle anything, and
has asked me to nip over on the next boat. I've got to
be back on the first of June—" the voice broke into
a joyful conscious laugh—"so we must look alive. I say,
Dad, I want your help: do come."

Dallas seemed to be speaking in the room: the voice
was as near by and natural as if he had been lounging
in his favourite arm-chair by the fire. The fact would
not ordinarily have surprised Archer, for long-distance
telephoning had become as much a matter of course as
electric lighting and five-day Atlantic voyages. But the
laugh did startle him; it still seemed wonderful that

across all those miles and miles of country—forest, river, mountain, prairie, roaring cities and busy indifferent millions—Dallas's laugh should be able to say: "Of course, whatever happens, I must get back on the first, because Fanny Beaufort and I are to be married on the fifth."

The voice began again: "Think it over? No, sir: not a minute. You've got to say yes now. Why not, I'd like to know? If you can allege a single reason—No; I knew it. Then it's a go, eh? Because I count on you to ring up the Cunard office first thing tomorrow; and you'd better book a return on a boat from Marseilles. I say, Dad; it'll be our last time together, in this kind of way—. Oh, good! I knew you would."

Chicago rang off, and Archer rose and began to pace up and down the room.

It would be their last time together in this kind of way: the boy was right. They would have lots of other "times" after Dallas's marriage, his father was sure; for the two were born comrades, and Fanny Beaufort, whatever one might think of her, did not seem likely to interfere with their intimacy. On the contrary, from what he had seen of her, he thought she would be naturally included in it. Still, change was change, and differences were differences, and much as he felt himself drawn toward his future daughter-in-law, it was tempting to seize this last chance of being alone with his boy.

There was no reason why he should not seize it, except the profound one that he had lost the habit of travel. May had disliked to move except for valid reasons, such as taking the children to the sea or in the mountains: she could imagine no other motive for leaving the house in Thirty-ninth Street or their comfortable quarters at the Wellands' in Newport. After Dallas had taken his degree she had thought it her duty to travel for six months; and the whole family had made the old-fashioned tour through England, Switzerland and Italy. Their time being limited (no one knew why) they had omitted France. Archer remembered Dallas's wrath at being asked to contemplate Mont Blanc instead of Rheims and Chartres. But Mary and Bill wanted mountain-climbing, and had already yawned their way in Dallas's wake through the English cathedrals; and May, always fair to her children, had insisted on holding the balance evenly between their athletic and artistic proclivities. She had indeed proposed that her husband should go to Paris for a fortnight, and join them on the Italian lakes after they had "done" Switzerland; but Archer had declined. "We'll stick together," he said; and May's face had brightened at his setting such a good example to Dallas.

Since her death, nearly two years before, there had been no reason for his continuing in the same routine. His children had urged him to travel: Mary Chivers had felt sure it would do him good to go abroad and "see the galleries." The very mysteriousness of such a cure made her the more confident of its efficacy. But Archer had found himself held fast by habit, by memories, by a sudden startled shrinking from new things.

Now, as he reviewed his past, he saw into what a deep rut he had sunk. The worst of doing one's duty was that it apparently unfitted one for doing anything else. At least that was the view that the men of his generation had taken. The trenchant divisions between right and wrong, honest and dishonest, respectable and the reverse, had left so little scope for the unforeseen. There are moments when a man's imagination, so easily subdued to what it lives in, suddenly rises above its daily level, and surveys the long windings of destiny. Archer hung there and wondered. . . .

What was left of the little world he had grown up in, and whose standards had bent and bound him? He remembered a sneering prophecy of poor Lawrence Lefferts's, uttered years ago in that very room: "If things go on at this rate, our children will be marrying Beaufort's bastards."

It was just what Archer's eldest son, the pride of his life, was doing; and nobody wondered or reproved. Even the boy's Aunt Janey, who still looked so exactly as she used to in her elderly youth, had taken her mother's emeralds and seed-pearls out of their pink cotton-wool, and carried them with her own twitching hands to the future bride; and Fanny Beaufort, instead of looking disappointed at not receiving a "set" from a Paris jeweller, had exclaimed at their old-fashioned beauty, and declared that when she wore them she should feel like an Isabey miniature.

Fanny Beaufort, who had appeared in New York at eighteen, after the death of her parents, had won its heart much as Madame Olenska had won it thirty years earlier; only instead of being distrustful and afraid of her, society took her joyfully for granted. She was pretty, amusing and accomplished: what more did any one want? Nobody was narrow-minded enough to rake up against her the half-forgotten facts of her father's past and her own origin. Only the older people remembered so obscure an incident in the business life of New York as Beaufort's failure, or the fact that after his wife's death he had been quietly married to the notorious Fanny Ring, and had left the country with his new wife, and a little girl who inherited her beauty. He was subsequently heard of in Constantinople, then in Russia; and a dozen years

later American travellers were handsomely entertained
by him in Buenos Ayres, where he represented a large
insurance agency. He and his wife died there in the
odour of prosperity; and one day their orphaned daughter had appeared in New York in charge of May Archer's
sister-in-law, Mrs. Jack Welland, whose husband had
been appointed the girl's guardian. The fact threw her
into almost cousinly relationship with Newland Archer's
children, and nobody was surprised when Dallas's engagement was announced.

Nothing could more clearly give the measure of the
distance that the world had travelled. People nowadays
were too busy—busy with reforms and "movements,"
with fads and fetishes and frivolities—to bother much
about their neighbours. And of what account was anybody's past, in the huge kaleidoscope where all the social
atoms spun around on the same plane?

Newland Archer, looking out of his hotel window at
the stately gaiety of the Paris streets, felt his heart beating with the confusion and eagerness of youth.

It was long since it had thus plunged and reared under
his widening waistcoat, leaving him, the next minute,
with an empty breast and hot temples. He wondered if
it was thus that his son's conducted itself in the presence
of Miss Fanny Beaufort—and decided that it was not.
"It functions as actively, no doubt, but the rhythm is
different," he reflected, recalling the cool composure with
which the young man had announced his engagement,
and taken for granted that his family would approve.

"The difference is that these young people take it for
granted that they're going to get whatever they want,
and that we almost always took it for granted that we
shouldn't. Only, I wonder—the thing one's so certain

of in advance: can it ever make one's heart beat as
wildly?"

It was the day after their arrival in Paris, and the
spring sunshine held Archer in his open window, above
the wide silvery prospect of the Place Vendôme. One of
the things he had stipulated—almost the only one—when
he had agreed to come abroad with Dallas, was that, in
Paris, he shouldn't be made to go to one of the new-
fangled "palaces."

"Oh, all right—of course," Dallas good-naturedly
agreed. "I'll take you to some jolly old-fashioned place
—the Bristol say—" leaving his father speechless at
hearing that the century-long home of kings and emperors
was now spoken of as an old-fashioned inn, where one
went for its quaint inconveniences and lingering local
colour.

Archer had pictured often enough, in the first impatient
years, the scene of his return to Paris; then the personal
vision had faded, and he had simply tried to see the city
as the setting of Madame Olenska's life. Sitting alone
at night in his library, after the household had gone to
bed, he had evoked the radiant outbreak of spring down
the avenues of horse-chestnuts, the flowers and statues
in the public gardens, the whiff of lilacs from the flower-
carts, the majestic roll of the river under the great
bridges, and the life of art and study and pleasure that
filled each mighty artery to bursting. Now the spectacle
was before him in its glory, and as he looked out on it
he felt shy, old-fashioned, inadequate: a mere grey speck
of a man compared with the ruthless magnificent fellow
he had dreamed of being. . . .

Dallas's hand came down cheerily on his shoulder.
"Hullo, father: this is something like, isn't it?" They
stood for a while looking out in silence, and then the

young man continued: "By the way, I've got a message for you: the Countess Olenska expects us both at half-past five."

He said it lightly, carelessly, as he might have imparted any casual item of information, such as the hour at which their train was to leave for Florence the next evening. Archer looked at him, and thought he saw in his gay young eyes a gleam of his great-grandmother Mingott's malice.

"Oh, didn't I tell you?" Dallas pursued. "Fanny made me swear to do three things while I was in Paris: get her the score of the last Debussy songs, go to the Grand-Guignol and see Madame Olenska. You know she was awfully good to Fanny when Mr. Beaufort sent her over from Buenos Ayres to the Assomption. Fanny hadn't any friends in Paris, and Madame Olenska used to be kind to her and trot her about on holidays. I believe she was a great friend of the first Mrs. Beaufort's. And she's our cousin, of course. So I rang her up this morning, before I went out, and told her you and I were here for two days and wanted to see her."

Archer continued to stare at him. "You told her I was here?"

"Of course—why not?" Dallas's eye brows went up whimsically. Then, getting no answer, he slipped his arm through his father's with a confidential pressure.

"I say, father: what was she like?"

Archer felt his colour rise under his son's unabashed gaze. "Come, own up: you and she were great pals, weren't you? Wasn't she most awfully lovely?"

"Lovely? I don't know. She was different."

"Ah—there you have it! That's what it always comes to, doesn't it? When she comes, *she's different*—and one doesn't know why. It's exactly what I feel about Fanny."

His father drew back a step, releasing his arm. "About Fanny? But, my dear fellow—I should hope so! Only I don't see—"

"Dash it, Dad, don't be prehistoric! Wasn't she—once—your Fanny?"

Dallas belonged body and soul to the new generation. He was the first-born of Newland and May Archer, yet it had never been possible to inculcate in him even the rudiments of reserve. "What's the use of making mysteries? It only makes people want to nose 'em out," he always objected when enjoined to discretion. But Archer, meeting his eyes, saw the filial light under their banter.

"My Fanny—?"

"Well, the woman you'd have chucked everything for: only you didn't," continued his surprising son.

"I didn't," echoed Archer with a kind of solemnity.

"No: you date, you see, dear old boy. But mother said—"

"Your mother?"

"Yes: the day before she died. It was when she sent for me alone—you remember? She said she knew we were safe with you, and always would be, because once, when she asked you to, you'd given up the thing you most wanted."

Archer received this strange communication in silence. His eyes remained unseeingly fixed on the thronged sun-lit square below the window. At length he said in a low voice: "She never asked me."

"No. I forgot. You never did ask each other anything, did you? And you never told each other anything. You just sat and watched each other, and guessed at what was going on underneath. A deaf-and-dumb asylum, in fact! Well, I back your generation for knowing more about each other's private thoughts than we ever have time to find out about our own.—I say, Dad," Dallas broke off, "you're not angry with me? If you are, let's make it up and go and lunch at Henri's. I've got to rush out to Versailles afterward."

Archer did not accompany his son to Versailles. He preferred to spend the afternoon in solitary roamings through Paris. He had to deal all at once with the packed regrets and stifled memories of an inarticulate lifetime.

After a little while he did not regret Dallas's indiscretion. It seemed to take an iron band from his heart to know that, after all, some one had guessed and pitied. . . . And that it should have been his wife moved him indescribably. Dallas, for all his affectionate insight, would not have understood that. To the boy, no doubt, the episode was only a pathetic instance of vain frustration, of wasted forces. But was it really no more? For a long time Archer sat on a bench in the Champs Elysées and wondered, while the stream of life rolled by. . . .

A few streets away, a few hours away, Ellen Olenska waited. She had never gone back to her husband, and when he had died, some years before, she had made no change in her way of living. There was nothing now to keep her and Archer apart—and that afternoon he was to see her.

He got up and walked across the Place de la Concorde and the Tuileries gardens to the Louvre. She had once told him that she often went there, and he had a fancy to spend the intervening time in a place where he could think of her as perhaps having lately been. For an hour or more he wandered from gallery to gallery through the dazzle of afternoon light, and one by one the pictures burst on him in their half-forgotten splendour, filling his soul with the long echoes of beauty. After all, his life had been too starved. . . .

Suddenly, before an effulgent Titian, he found himself saying: "But I'm only fifty-seven—" and then he turned away. For such summer dreams it was too late; but surely not for a quiet harvest of friendship, of comradeship, in the blessed hush of her nearness.

He went back to the hotel, where he and Dallas were to meet; and together they walked again across the Place de la Concorde and over the bridge that leads to the Chamber of Deputies.

Dallas, unconscious of what was going on in his father's mind, was talking excitedly and abundantly of Versailles. He had had but one previous glimpse of it, during a holiday trip in which he had tried to pack all the sights he had been deprived of when he had had to go with the family to Switzerland; and tumultuous enthusiasm and cock-sure criticism tripped each other up on his lips.

As Archer listened, his sense of inadequacy and inexpressiveness increased. The boy was not insensitive, he knew; but he had the facility and self-confidence that came of looking at fate not as a master but as an equal. "That's it: they feel equal to things—they know their way about," he mused, thinking of his son as the spokesman of the new generation which had swept away all the old landmarks, and with them the sign-posts and the danger-signal.

Suddenly Dallas stopped short, grasping his father's arm. "Oh, by Jove," he exclaimed.

They had come out into the great tree-planted space before the Invalides. The dome of Mansart floated ethereally above the budding trees and the long grey front of the building: drawing up into itself all the rays of afternoon light, it hung there like the visible symbol of the race's glory.

Archer knew that Madame Olenska lived in a square near one of the avenues radiating from the Invalides; and he had pictured the quarter as quiet and almost obscure, forgetting the central splendour that lit it up. Now, by some queer process of association, that golden light became for him the pervading illumination in which she lived. For nearly thirty years, her life—of which he knew so strangely little—had been spent in this rich atmosphere that he already felt to be too dense and yet too stimulating for his lungs. He thought of the theatres she must have been to, the pictures she must have looked at, the sober and splendid old houses she must have frequented, the people she must have talked with, the incessant stir of ideas, curiosities, images and associations thrown out by an intensely social race in a setting of immemorial manners; and suddenly he remembered the young Frenchman who had once said to him: "Ah, good conversation—there is nothing like it, is there?"

Archer had not seen M. Rivière, or heard of him, for nearly thirty years; and that fact gave the measure of his ignorance of Madame Olenska's existence. More than half a lifetime divided them, and she had spent the long interval among people he did not know, in a society he but faintly guessed at, in conditions he would never wholly understand. During that time he had been living with his youthful memory of her; but she had doubtless had other and more tangible companionship. Perhaps she too had kept her memory of him as something apart; but if she had, it must have been like a relic in a small dim chapel, where there was not time to pray every day. . . .

They had crossed the Place des Invalides, and were

THE AGE OF INNOCENCE

walking down one of the thoroughfares flanking the building. It was a quiet quarter, after all, in spite of its splendour and its history; and the fact gave one an idea of the riches Paris had to draw on, since such scenes as this were left to the few and the indifferent.

The day was fading into a soft sun-shot haze, pricked here and there by a yellow electric light, and passers were rare in the little square into which they had turned. Dallas stopped again, and looked up.

"It must be here," he said, slipping his arm through his father's with a movement from which Archer's shyness did not shrink; and they stood together looking up at the house.

It was a modern building, without distinctive character, but many-windowed, and pleasantly balconied up its wide cream-coloured front. On one of the upper balconies, which hung well above the rounded tops of the horse-chestnuts in the square, the awnings were still lowered, as though the sun had just left it.

"I wonder which floor—?" Dallas conjectured; and moving toward the *porte-cochère* he put his head into the porter's lodge, and came back to say: "The fifth. It must be the one with the awnings."

Archer remained motionless, gazing at the upper windows as if the end of their pilgrimage had been attained.

"I say, you know, it's nearly six," his son at length reminded him.

The father glanced away at an empty bench under the trees.

"I believe I'll sit there a moment," he said.

"Why—aren't you well?" his son exclaimed.

"Oh, perfectly. But I should like you, please, to go up without me."

Dallas paused before him, visibly bewildered. "But, I say, Dad: do you mean you won't come up at all?"

"I don't know," said Archer slowly.

"If you don't she won't understand."

"Go, my boy; perhaps I shall follow you."

Dallas gave him a long look through the twilight.

"But what on earth shall I say?"

"My dear fellow, don't you always know what to say?" his father rejoined with a smile.

"Very well. I shall say you're old-fashioned, and prefer walking up the five flights because you don't like lifts."

His father smiled again. "Say I'm old-fashioned: that's enough."

Dallas looked at him again, and then, with an incredulous gesture, passed out of sight under the vaulted doorway.

Archer sat down on the bench and continued to gaze at the awninged balcony. He calculated the time it would take his son to be carried up in the lift to the fifth floor, to ring the bell, and be admitted to the hall, and then ushered into the drawing-room. He pictured Dallas entering that room with his quick assured step and his delightful smile, and wondered if the people were right who said that his boy "took after him."

Then he tried to see the persons already in the room —for probably at that sociable hour there would be more than one—and among them a dark lady, pale and dark, who would look up quickly, half rise, and hold out a long thin hand with three rings on it. . . . He thought she would be sitting in a sofa-corner near the fire, with azaleas banked behind her on a table.

"It's more real to me here than if I went up," he suddenly heard himself say; and the fear lest that last shadow of reality should lose its edge kept him rooted to his seat as the minutes succeeded each other.

He sat for a long time on the bench in the thickening dusk, his eyes never turning from the balcony. At length a light shone through the windows, and a moment later a man-servant came out on the balcony, drew up the awnings, and closed the shutters.

At that, as if it had been the signal he waited for, Newland Archer got up slowly and walked back alone to his hotel.

(3)

THE END.

PENGUIN POPULAR CLASSICS

Published or forthcoming

Aesop	Aesop's Fables
Hans Andersen	Fairy Tales
Louisa May Alcott	Good Wives
	Little Women
Eleanor Atkinson	Greyfriars Bobby
Jane Austen	Emma
	Mansfield Park
	Northanger Abbey
	Persuasion
	Pride and Prejudice
	Sense and Sensibility
R. M. Ballantyne	The Coral Island
J. M. Barrie	Peter Pan
Frank L. Baum	The Wonderful Wizard of Oz
Anne Brontë	Agnes Grey
	The Tenant of Wildfell Hall
Charlotte Brontë	Jane Eyre
	The Professor
	Shirley
	Villette
Emily Brontë	Wuthering Heights
John Buchan	Greenmantle
	The Thirty-Nine Steps
Frances Hodgson Burnett	A Little Princess
	Little Lord Fauntleroy
	The Secret Garden
Samuel Butler	The Way of All Flesh
Lewis Carroll	Alice's Adventures in Wonderland
	Through the Looking Glass
Geoffrey Chaucer	The Canterbury Tales
G. K. Chesterton	Father Brown Stories
Erskine Childers	The Riddle of the Sands
John Cleland	Fanny Hill
Wilkie Collins	The Moonstone
	The Woman in White
Sir Arthur Conan Doyle	The Adventures of Sherlock Holmes
	His Last Bow
	The Hound of the Baskervilles

PENGUIN POPULAR CLASSICS

Published or forthcoming

Joseph Conrad	Heart of Darkness
	Lord Jim
	Nostromo
	The Secret Agent
	Victory
James Fenimore Cooper	The Last of the Mohicans
Stephen Crane	The Red Badge of Courage
Daniel Defoe	Moll Flanders
	Robinson Crusoe
Charles Dickens	Bleak House
	The Christmas Books
	David Copperfield
	Great Expectations
	Hard Times
	Little Dorrit
	Martin Chuzzlewit
	Nicholas Nickleby
	The Old Curiosity Shop
	Oliver Twist
	The Pickwick Papers
	A Tale of Two Cities
Fyodor Dostoyevsky	Crime and Punishment
George Eliot	Adam Bede
	Middlemarch
	The Mill on the Floss
	Silas Marner
John Meade Falkner	Moonfleet
Henry Fielding	Tom Jones
F. Scott Fitzgerald	The Diamond as Big as the Ritz
	The Great Gatsby
	Tender is the Night
Gustave Flaubert	Madame Bovary
Elizabeth Gaskell	Cousin Phillis
	Cranford
	Mary Barton
	North and South
Kenneth Grahame	The Wind in the Willows

PENGUIN POPULAR CLASSICS

Published or forthcoming

PENGUIN POPULAR CLASSICS

Published or forthcoming

Charles and Mary Lamb	Tales from Shakespeare
D. H. Lawrence	Lady Chatterley's Lover
	The Rainbow
	Sons and Lovers
	Women in Love
Edward Lear	Book of Nonsense
Gaston Leroux	The Phantom of the Opera
Jack London	White Fang *and* The Call of the Wild
Captain Marryat	The Children of the New Forest
Guy de Maupassant	Selected Short Stories
Herman Melville	Billy Budd, Sailor
	Moby-Dick
John Milton	Paradise Lost
Edith Nesbit	The Railway Children
Edgar Allan Poe	Selected Tales
	Spirits of the Dead
Thomas de Quincey	Confessions of an English Opium Eater
Damon Runyon	Guys and Dolls
Sir Walter Scott	Ivanhoe
	Rob Roy
	Waverley
Saki	The Best of Saki
William Shakespeare	Antony and Cleopatra
	As You Like It
	Hamlet
	Henry V
	Julius Caesar
	King Lear
	Macbeth
	Measure for Measure
	The Merchant of Venice
	A Midsummer Night's Dream
	Much Ado About Nothing
	Othello
	Romeo and Juliet
	The Tempest
	Twelfth Night

PENGUIN POPULAR CLASSICS

Published or forthcoming

Anna Sewell	Black Beauty
Mary Shelley	Frankenstein
Johanna Spyri	Heidi
Robert Louis Stevenson	The Black Arrow
	A Child's Garden of Verses
	Dr Jekyll and Mr Hyde
	Kidnapped
	Treasure Island
Bram Stoker	Dracula
Jonathan Swift	Gulliver's Travels
W. M. Thackeray	Vanity Fair
Leo Tolstoy	War and Peace
Anthony Trollope	Barchester Towers
	Framley Parsonage
	The Small House at Allington
	The Warden
Mark Twain	The Adventures of Huckleberry Finn
	The Adventures of Tom Sawyer
	The Prince and the Pauper
Vatsyayana	The Kama Sutra
Jules Verne	Around the World in Eighty Days
	Journey to the Centre of the Earth
	Twenty Thousand Leagues under the Sea
Voltaire	Candide
Edith Wharton	The Age of Innocence
	Ethan Frome
Oscar Wilde	The Happy Prince and Other Stories
	The Importance of Being Earnest
	Lady Windermere's Fan
	Lord Arthur Savile's Crime
	The Picture of Dorian Gray
	A Woman of No Importance
Virginia Woolf	Mrs Dalloway
	Orlando
	To the Lighthouse

PENGUIN POPULAR POETRY

Published or forthcoming

The Selected Poems *of:*

Matthew Arnold
William Blake
Robert Browning
Robert Burns
Lord Byron
John Donne
Thomas Hardy
John Keats
Rudyard Kipling
Alexander Pope
Alfred Tennyson
William Wordsworth
William Yeats

and collections of:

Seventeenth-Century Poetry
Eighteenth-Century Poetry
Poetry of the Romantics
Victorian Poetry
Twentieth-Century Poetry
Scottish Folk and Fairy Tales